# What people are saying

MW01118808

What a gift it is to see fictional entertainment ~~~~~~~~~ ~~~~~~ humanity!

**– Deepak Chopra**
**Author, *The Ultimate Happiness Prescription***

☙

*RIVETING!* 2012 *The Awakening* unveils a powerful vision of hope. It's been said that in seeking to elevate one's consciousness, the journey IS the goal. What an incredible journey Bill Douglas takes us on in his novel *2012 The Awakening*. Pitting seekers of enlightenment against a system bent on controlling its people by dumbing down their minds, Mr. Douglas's vast knowledge of tai chi, meditation, Native American spiritualism, the Bible, and other spiritual disciplines is revealed in a suspense-filled narrative that will keep you guessing with each turn of the page. With the suspense of a *Da Vinci Code,* the spiritual awareness of *The Secret,* and the fearsome aspect of Orwell's *1984, 2012 The Awakening* will keep you thinking about it long after you've put it down. What a terrific film this book will make!

**– Holmes Osborne, Actor: *The Box; That Thing You Do!; The Quiet American; Crazy in Alabama; Windtalkers; ER; Boston Legal; The X Files***

☙

In his debut novel, *2012 The Awakening,* Bill Douglas tackles the 2012 prophecy with a sobering yet uplifting story that should be required reading for everyone on Wall Street and Capitol Hill.

**– Steve Alten, *New York Times* Best-selling Author of *MEG* and *DOMAIN***

☙

WOW! So moving, I wept. So intriguing, I could not put it down!

Bill Douglas shows astonishing clarity about the nature of consciousness as well as about many important issues of our time. If you care about the future of our planet – this is a MUST READ!

**– Kristopher M. Kriner, Sufi Cherag, Composer/Performer of the world-renowned Sufi chant recording *Bismallah***

The unique value of the type of combined science fiction-social commentary in *2012 The Awakening* lies in its ability to educate about some of the current dark and harsh truths of the way so many people are currently being victimized and manipulated.

As it exposes the problem, the fast-reading novel also provides the hope, finally, of a positive human response capable of overcoming Machiavellian-type controls and divide-and-conquer methods.

Whereas the *Left Behind* series well exemplified the power of the use of fear- and pride-based imagination to effectively manipulate people, constructive visionary Bill Douglas understands that there could be an antidote. Dreaming of it may just be the first step to a real "Awakening"!

**– Coleen Rowley, former FBI Agent-Minneapolis Division Counsel and one of *TIME Magazine's* "Whistleblower" Persons of the Year, 2002**

༘

This intelligent page-turning novel kept me up *all night long!*

*2012 The Awakening* is a cautionary tale about the folly of a modern society seduced by the worship of technology, rather than using technology as a tool to facilitate and empower visions of spiritual compassion. It is a clarion call to heed the prophets' advice to turn within and thereby rediscover our inner wisdom and reemphasize the yin-feminine dimension.

Vanguard scientific research into human consciousness, modern environmental-sociological insights, and intriguing esoteric quotes from ancient prophets are all interwoven to make a convincing case that ancient prophets were not issuing airy platitudes, but a roadmap to navigate the troubled waters of our intensifying over-populated modern world by following the compass of empathy and love.

**– Dr. Effie Chow, Member of the President's White House Commission on Complementary and Alternative Medicine Policy (under Clinton); Founder of the World Congress on Qigong**

༘

Douglas's intensive research is as fascinating as Dan Brown's *Da Vinci Code* . . . layered within a nail-biting narrative – the literary equivalent of a hot fudge sundae with the nutritional value of a healthy, organic meal.

**– Jais Booth, Founder of San Francisco Bay Area's Liminal Art Movement**

With amazing grace and clarity, Bill Douglas offers a glimpse of potential reality mixed with hope for a better future. His prolific tale reveals the answer to humanity's quandary and provides the possibility of awakening to a brighter way of living. Bill Douglas is a true visionary.

**– Jill Dutton, Publisher of** *Evolving: A Guide for Conscious Living,* **Author of** *The Joyous Journey: Living Life on Purpose, with Purpose*

ॐ

Blending fact with fiction, Bill Douglas has created a powerful story that may be more reality than fiction. What if 2012 *is* The Awakening, with women and men finally embracing their feminine aspects? Humanity is transformed and the world heals.

**– Sharon Lockhart, Host of** *Every Woman,* **KKFI Radio**

ॐ

2012 fever seems to be upon us, with many stating that "the end of the world is nigh." What if 2012 was, however, *the beginning* instead of the end? It is this viewpoint that is painted for us in Bill Douglas's *2012 The Awakening.* The story explores the idea of 2012 being a time of a global spiritual awakening.

If the doomsayers regarding 2012 are simply putting their visions of hopelessness into the ether of global consciousness, just as Douglas is doing with his vision of hope, the only question remaining is this, *whose vision will gain traction?* . . . even through its spellbinding narrative of intrigue and murder, *2012 The Awakening* again and again breathes this hope of a humanity yearning for connection.

**– Arif Khan**
**Editor,** *Tomb of Jesus,* **Presenter in Documentary** *Jesus in India*

I LOVED this book! Bill Douglas takes us on a riveting journey through the dichotomy of paradigms across humanity. He addresses the complex dual balances that make up our existence within the large scope of the universe.

*2012 The Awakening* challenges us to take a deeper look at the progress in technology and nature and to examine humanity's impact upon the earth and ourselves and our overuse of the planet's valuable resources. This scientific psychologically analytical fiction kept me turning pages . . .

Bill's utilization of Native American/First Nation substance was careful and thoughtful. His introduction of the Two Spirit character, the Healer, brings a contemporary mythos to light, allowing the ideology of the Two Spirit revitalization amongst Native aboriginal cultures of North America. Bill's representation of the Two Spirit character's identity as being a healer accurately depicts the position of Two Spirit individuals among Aboriginal cultures, as they were regarded as healers, mediators, singers, caregivers, skilled artists, and medicine people. Two Spirit people have guided the way for centuries because of the delicate physical and spiritual balance they embodied. Native American ideology has always encompassed the balance in every aspect of their culture from the food that is consumed to the complex operation of their delicate social structures.

Bill Douglas is successful in merging the esoteric world views and cultural representations into one enthralling narrative that reads fluidly. He reminds us that through the work of many we can congregate as one.

**– Crisosto Apache (Mescalero Apache)**
**Director, Two Spirit Society of Denver**

ଧ

What a great read!

Ravi's extraordinary story is a startling reminder of just how threatening ideas can be. Compassion, harmony, forgiveness and peace . . . these things mark the end of powers that have ruled the world for eons. The next chapter in the saga of human history will be ushered in by the courage of a few brave souls like Ravi, and a "slight turning of consciousness" within the many. It is my hope that we will all awaken to "a world of possibility rather than one of fear and uncertainty."

**– Rev. Nathaniel G. Haaland**

# 2012 The Awakening

ᾼ ✡ ☪ ☦ ॐ ☯ ♒ ♓ Ὠ

## Bill Douglas

Illumination Corporation Publishing
www.IlluminationCorporation.com

**Illumination Corporation Publishing**
**www.IlluminationCorporation.com**

Copyright © 2010 by Bill Douglas

Published by Illumination Corporation Publishing

**www.IlluminationCorporation.com**
**www.FinalDraftSecretarialService.com**

Book design by Illumination Corporation Artistic Designs
with text layout by Final Draft Secretarial Service.

ISBN: 1450548792    EAN13: 9781450548793

For orders, you may search your distribution lists for the ISBN of this novel, or contact Illumination Corporation Publishing at www.IlluminationCorporation.com, or call 1-913-648-2256

First Edition

What you are about to read is fictional,
with the exception of what isn't.

# Introduction

*Our world lost connection with its feminine spirit long ago . . . Her greatest desire — her greatest ambition — was to nurture . . . can you see the power of that? Can you understand how profoundly beautiful that ambition is?*

*The feminine force within us will now wield the power of 52,000 years of masculine technological development, and the balance created by this profound marriage will transform — everything.*

– Ravi Shyamalan, Recipient, Nobel Prize for Economics

*Dr. Richard Klein of Stanford argues that the suite of innovations [during what some call the* Great Leap Forward, *approximately 50,000 years ago] reflects some specific neural change that occurred around that time and, because of the advantage it conferred, spread rapidly through the population.*

– *The New York Times*, Science, July 15, 2003

———————

Today is December 21, 2012. A feminine awakening struggles to embrace our planet.

Does this mean women are taking over in a feminist revolution? No, this isn't about gender or sex, but rather a way of approaching the world around us. It is about nothing less than the very future of the human race.

Chinese mystics created the yin-yang image as a symbol of the ultimate power of balance. The lower *dark wave* reflects the yin-passive, receiving, or feminine aspect of consciousness, while the *light wave* above it represents the dominating yang-masculine approach – exploration, conquest, and exploitation.

For example, solar and wind are yin-passive ways of receiving energy, while the exploration and drilling of oil is a masculine method. Many of those advocating solar or wind energy solutions are men, while Sarah Palin's "drill baby drill" strategy is a more masculine approach to energy solutions.

Our his-story has reflected and celebrated the more masculine achievements of both women and men, cataloguing our human exploration and development designed to control the planet's resources.

Today a new page is turning; a balance is being sought. Why?

Our masculine consciousness served the human race well, enabling our dominance of the planet. This began 52,000 years ago when a monumental shift in human consciousness unleashed the technological age – what Chinese mystics would call the yang-masculine age.

At that time, a cosmic event occurred that may have precipitated such an awakening – one that scientists refer to as the *Great Leap Forward*. Fifty-two millennia ago, the earth, our sun, and the black hole at the center of our Milky Way Galaxy aligned – just as they are doing again today.

With this cosmic alignment, an extraordinary lessening of the magnetic force of our planet is occurring. Scientists have predicted for many years that a lessening of the Earth's magnetic force, a trend they had been tracking, would peak at the end of 2012. Social philosophers have suggested that this may be affecting human consciousness, pointing out that in modern history, revolutions in art, cinema, music, and technology sprang from the West Coast of the United States, where the magnetic force has always been weaker than in other areas of the planet.

Given that human consciousness is *made* of electromagnetic energy, what would happen if the magnetic force of the entire planet dramatically lessened? What impact would this have on the human race? Fifty-two thousand years ago it gave birth to the masculine-technological age, the age of exploration, conquest, and exploitation of resources planet-wide.

Today, Earth's resources have been tapped out – our planet sags under the weight of our population, which is rapidly approaching 10 billion people. There is nothing left to explore, conquer, or exploit.

A massive shift is required in how we view ourselves on the planet, if we do not want to see our children and theirs spiral down into a dismal future of increasingly violent wars over a plundered world of shrinking resources. We must redefine ourselves en masse in order to make the next evolutionary leap forward as a human race.

The feminine awakening, stretching its wings like a chrysalis emerging from its cocoon, is yawning into existence in a tightening world of control. For 52,000 years our civilization has been honing the single-minded focus of expanding control over nature, other nations, and ultimately, the resources of the entire planet. One might say our modern religion is one of technological-physical control.

The feminine receptive approach is a contemplative, nurturing, spiritual one – seeing ourselves not as warriors or conquerors of Earth, but as home-makers – seeking a way to stretch the cupboard's contents to nurture the 10 billion members of our planetary household.

The feminine awakening now struggling to spread its fragile wings within our minds has no armies or armaments; it is a spiritual permeation of the mind. The yin-feminine does not seek control; it seeks balance – a marriage of technology and spirituality. The yang-masculine knows *only* control – and it will slash and burn to maintain it.

This physical mind of control, countered by a spiritual awakening across our planet, is about to unfold a battle unlike anything we have ever seen – beyond what our current minds can even stretch to conceive.

The fuse that will ignite this epic event, the cosmic alignment of our Earth, our sun, and our galaxy's center on December 21, 2012, was predicted hundreds of years ago by ancient Mayan mystics.

They called it *the Opening of the Birth Canal of the Cosmic Mother.*

Let the birthing pains of a new world begin.

*Remember to breathe.*

*"[Mary,] tell us the words of the Savior"* . . . Mary answered, *"what is hidden from you I will proclaim to you"* . . . and Peter said, *"Did he prefer her to us?"* and Levi answered, *"Peter, I see you contending against the woman like the adversaries. If the savior made her worthy, who are you indeed to reject her?"*
  – The Gospel of Mary, 7:6-7, and 9:4, 9:7-8


*. . . markedly feminine also in their image and vision . . . were Jesus and Buddha.*
  – Deepak Chopra


*The Tao is called the Great Mother: empty yet inexhaustible, it gives birth to infinite worlds . . . know the masculine, keep to the feminine.*
  – Lao Tse, *Tao Te Ching*

# Prologue

## The Soldier – December 21, 2012

*A strange phenomenon is occurring throughout the world. People have been filling churches, mosques, and temples to capacity. Not for services, but during other hours to sit silently in contemplation.*
– *New York Journal,* Sunday, December 30, 2012

*Military forces worldwide are seeing "absent without leave" rates skyrocket, while intelligence institutions like the CIA, MI6, and Russia's GRU are witnessing mass resignations.*
– *London Post,* Monday, December 31, 2012

*An apparatus and method for remotely monitoring and altering brain waves . . .*
– United States Patent Office, Patent No. 3,951,134

---

It is the morning of December 21, 2012. The Earth is in great flux.

A trembling young trooper struggles to keep up with his superior, the hard man they call *the Soldier.* The young man can barely place one foot in front of the other – grimacing with the absolute focus it takes for him to complete this simple act as his world explodes all around and within him. No bombs, bullets, or enemies are involved. Yet this brutal conflict is devastating.

Ancient spiritual forces duel, wavelength against wavelength, with a projected technological might, fighting for control of this young man. Mankind's consciousness, as always, is at the epicenter of an ageless clash occurring within this soldier's beleaguered mind as it is cleaved in two by competing energetic forces.

The means by which a wave consisting of magnetic and electrical fields travels from one point to another was described in 1864 by Scottish mathematician James Clerk Maxwell. Italian scientist Guglielmo Marconi later received the Nobel Prize in Physics for demonstrating this power by projecting his telegraphic wireless energy technology across the English Channel.

One must wonder whether, when Marconi looked up into the night sky over a century ago, he could have imagined that his transmission of energy would lead to discoveries in technology and human consciousness that would become a high-tech battleground of the mind.

The battles are on many fronts. *Each of us is on the front lines.*

Twenty-two thousand miles above, beyond Earth's thin life-giving, oxygen-rich troposphere, beyond the protective ozone layer, and beyond the ionosphere where the air is so rarified that free electrons can exist for a time without attaching to nearby positive ions, a geostationary operational satellite receives signals from far below in the Himalayas.

The monitoring Russians and Chinese believe this to be one of the ordinary environmental satellites that stay near the equator, traveling at the speed of the Earth's rotation.

However, this satellite has a different mission. It receives analysis information from Earth, but it also has a powerful transmission capability. As the satellite hurtles through space, neck and neck with the Earth's silent orbit, it is abuzz with activity.

Both its receiving and potent transmission apparatus are focused on the gargantuan Himalayan Mountains, where an epic battle is being waged within the energy matrix that is human consciousness. Mechanistic modern forces of linear control are being challenged by ancient powers of faith and compassion.

Here in the Tibetan highlands, the crisp thin mountain air is pierced by a haunting vibration. Monks behind the thick stone walls of the Dalai Lama's temple of residence are joined in meditation, their voices harmonizing in different octaves to create a chant that vibrates through the very beings of those in the surrounding hamlet. A sound so unusual that the villagers, distracted from their morning chores, turn up their faces almost in unison to stare at the temple that towers above their homes on the higher mountainside, framed against the emerging color of an awakening morning sky.

A few hundred feet below the village, a force of men wearing headgear, oxygen masks, and camouflage military uniforms without insignias or identifying marks make their way up the hard-earthed Tibetan mountainside.

The Soldier grits his teeth, raising both hands to press down on his headgear in an attempt to block out the sound coming from above. The din feels like a jackhammer inside his skull, leaving room for only one thought: *This is unbearable!*

He stares blankly as the trooper beside him suddenly takes off his oxygen mask, smiles warmly, and drops his rifle and backpack. He shrugs, and the straps of the equipment sack slip from his shoulders. The young man turns to go back the way they had just climbed, as if he is on a leisurely walk enjoying the sunrise. One of the competing energetic forces has won the battle for his mind. For him, the war no longer exists.

The Soldier watches as his man ambles away. The trooper stumbles on a rock, and the false step sends him into the craggy ravine cutting into the trail behind them. Without a sound, he disappears from the group's sight, dropping down the face of the cliff in an instantaneous descent far beneath where the human eye can follow.

A timeless moment passes before a nearly imperceptible wince crosses the leader's hard face at the faint clanging of the trooper's helmet on the rocks far below.

He signals the others onward, relentless as always, and single-minded. *Got to . . . end this misery!*

The leader's original force of two hundred men has dwindled to little more than thirty. Some collapsed along the way, after flinging off the headgear that supplied oxygen for their high-altitude trek. Others had fled back down the mountainside, sliding down the craggy ravines, blindly tumbling off sheer cliffs into the endless abyss below.

But as the squad drew nearer to the source of the sound, the men deserting the operation seemed to simply transcend the mission, surrendering to the vibrations, just as this man had.

The sounds from above intensify. The leader can see in his men's faces – the few that remain – that they will not last much longer. *I don't know if I can, either.*

Unable to stand any more of this omni-octave vibration that is ripping him apart, the leader holds up his left hand, and the remaining troops fall in behind him, kneeling down to await his orders. He begins to shout orders against the din, but suddenly lifts his headgear and bends sideways to vomit. Wiping his mouth with the back of his hand, he turns again to the men, instructing them to turn on the audio in their headgear. *Have to block it out – only a few more yards to go.*

As they flip the switches, loud heavy metal music throbs through their headsets, escaping into the air around them in a muffled fury of noise.

The surging waves of chants from the temple still find a way through the blasting music. Another man stands, lets his equipment fall to the ground, and turns.

The leader observes the surreal image of his deserting subordinate. The man moves slowly through the kneeling assembly, patting fellow soldiers on their heads, as one would children.

The deserter stops, looking deeply into the eyes of a soldier to his left, before turning to the man kneeling on his right. The trooper reaches out to tenderly stroke the side of the soldier's face, and at his touch the kneeling man's eyes fill with tears as he gazes up in wonder.

He too stands, slipping out of his backpack and weapon straps, following his comrade as he walks among the others, both men looking into the eyes of the soldiers they pass.

They walk slowly through the huddled congregation, completely at ease – not a care in the world – not in *this* world.

The leader's hellish reality, the jarring cacophony, abates as he watches their prolonged exit. Everything slows and quiets. A magnetic pull to join these men draws at the deepest fiber of his being.

One by one, his troops pull their eyes away from those leaving their squad to watch for their leader's orders. From somewhere far away, yet within the center of his mind, a grating screech re-commands his focus. The leader remembers his role, his place in this world. The pounding vibrations from above again unleash their fury, catapulting him into a nerve-scalding fast forward, back to the mission at hand.

Veins throb in the leader's temples. His cranial muscles struggle to prevent the renewed force of the droning chants from entering his mind. *Like nails being pounded into my head!*

Twisting a dial on his helmet, he increases the volume of his headset speakers. The music screams its primal force, helping him to resist the resonating chants by distorting them with its competing racket – but only for a moment. A war of vibrations battles within the deepest reaches of his mind. *Got to stop this! Almost there . . .*

With hand gestures, the leader instructs the men to take pre-loaded syringes from their backpacks. Using their backpack straps to circle their arms and raise a vein, they inject the solution. Within seconds, antidepressants mixed with a highly refined amphetamine course through their blood-brain barrier, and the leader signals them to continue up the mountain.

Even with the drugs and music, designed to numb their feelings and spur their bodies on, crossing the remaining yards between themselves and the target is excruciating. As the troops finally reach the steps of the temple, the chanting within becomes louder and more resonant, an unnatural storm of vibrating waves invading the air. The entire mountain seems to oscillate.

A few of the men stumble and retch, ripping off their headgear as they heave. One collapses, while the others stand bewildered for a moment, fully exposed to the vibrations echoing from the temple. In an instant, those without headgear drop their weapons and backpacks and turn to wander back down the mountain from where they have come.

The group leader watches his men shrink from his sight for only a moment before urging the few remaining troops up the temple steps toward the source of their agony. The bitter taste of bile rises in the back of his throat, as even his internal organs rebel against this mission. His mind swirls. *Can't think . . . split in two . . . FOCUS!*

This leader is a hard man. An adolescent during the height of Vietnam, Frank Delaney had lied about his age and forged documents to get in without his mother's approval. He'd always been a big kid – body hair at twelve – so it wasn't hard for him to lie his way in. Frank hadn't been able to stand the idea of missing that war when Vietnamization signaled it could end before he'd gotten his hand in it. He *needed* to get into it, and his reasons were deep and legion.

Vietnam provided his baptism into doing what was necessary to get the job done. His education took him to Central America, training Contras in the 1980s, and through years of destabilization and assassination missions in the Middle East. His work after Vietnam was the kind of work you don't read about in the papers, and no Congressional committee is ever informed of – for his orders and his actions were unspeakable. Even now, he is harder than most young men a third his age and always ready for combat.

Those who have fought alongside him have never known him as Frank. Frank died many years ago in the jungles of Laos and Cambodia as a Navy SEAL behind enemy lines. His *nom de guerre* is the Soldier, or just *Soldier*. That was all anyone needed to know about him, as that is all he has been since Vietnam. He has known nothing but violence and war since signing up. His dark journey's twists and turns led to darker and darker realms where only the Soldier survived. The human being that had been young Frank never stood a chance.

The Soldier enters the temple through a massive wooden door that is not locked, then leans weak-kneed against the cool smooth wall, gasping for breath even with his oxygen still flowing. With a pounding heart and dry mouth, he can barely overcome the growing nausea assaulting his guts.

A trickle of blood drips from his left nostril as pressure from the war within his own head builds. Now that they are actually inside the building, the sound – *Christ! How can they make such a sound!?*

His few remaining troops stumble through the temple door behind him. Incense drifts through the passageways which seem to vibrate, illuminated by morning sunlight seeping in through the small windows and a few large candles glowing from recesses in the walls.

From somewhere unseen, a powerful gong rhythmically strikes a cosmic heartbeat, which echoes through the halls and beyond, across the rock and snow of the towering peaks above and the plummeting depths below.

Incapable of any physical combat, the Soldier and his men stagger through the dimly lit hallway toward the inner chamber of the temple. They bounce from side to side as their wobbling knees buckle beneath them. Finally exiting the dark passage into the chamber itself, the men fall backward, leaning against the wall for support. Chanting monks are sitting in front of cold stone walls covered with hanging tapestries in rich, warm colors.

The exhausted soldiers meet no physical resistance or guards, only the intensifying vibration as the monks, eyes closed, mouths open, emanate a sound so huge it seems beyond human capability. The monks appear to be merely vessels as an unseen force more powerful than the concussion of an explosion blasts through their lungs, throats, and mouths.

The leader begins to see the room with double vision, barely making out the monks sitting in a circle on square gray stones facing the room's center. *Can't see!* Lurching forward with only two men still behind him, his mind incapable of thought, his body operates on reflex that enables him to open fire on the shifting, blurring images before him.

The smooth-skulled orange-robed monks fall like human dominoes, collapsing into the heart of the circle, their bodies riddled with bullets. Rivers of blood silently pour from their bodies toward the midpoint of the room's sloping floor. A river of life flows ever toward a center that receives it without judgment or pity. The order of the universe exists, even in the midst of chaos and destruction.

One monk sits upright, eyes closed, seemingly unaware of the surrounding chaos or the gun pointing directly at him, the sole remaining monk.

The young man's voice intensifies as if the spirits of all the other monks who'd just died are being channeled through him. Many octaves, many voices, roar from the small monk in a sound beyond human.

The last two men fling off their helmets, retching as they flounder away from the unendurable sound that seems to explode, not just from the mouth of the man before them, but from within their own bodies.

The Soldier's teeth gnash violently, and one of his molars shatters in his mouth. His arm spasms as he struggles to make his finger squeeze the trigger of his automatic weapon. His eyes pinch shut, his jaw clenches fiercely, and another molar shatters, as his finger finally, barely, reaches the pressure necessary to fire his AK-47. Its recoil vibrates savagely against his shoulder as the business end sprays the room, finding its target.

The monk's open mouth falls silent.

The entire universe is suddenly absolutely soundless, as if the very eye of God almighty has turned his vision toward this singular point of existence. The deafening dissonance of the monk's chant and the angry explosion of the weapon are replaced by a still, deep sense that something beyond redemption has occurred. A precious and holy presence has been removed from existence.

The soft brown eyes of the dying monk open and focus on the armed man standing before him. He smiles warmly at the Soldier as his wounded body collapses to the floor. The Soldier stares, blinking in disbelief at the monk's face, morphing for a fleeting moment into his own father's face, before again becoming that of the young monk. His last words are a whisper of resounding force, which sound like – like Frank's *mother's* voice – pleading a final appeal: *Love, Frankie.*

Trembling, the soldier falls to his knees, nausea overcoming him as he retches bright yellow bile onto the floor, his guts containing nothing else to purge. *What have I done?* With a quavering hand, he pulls a fresh syringe from his pack and quickly injects himself. Flinging the used syringe to clatter across the room, he hauls an international satellite phone from his pack with a grunt and punches a number. With great effort, the Soldier controls his trembling voice to report in: "Freedom One, this is Peace Worker. Mission completed."

The grayish skin of the Soldier's face is sheened in cold sweat, beaded around his gasping mouth as he labors to suck in air. Dropping the phone, he collapses to the ground, struggling to draw oxygen into his lungs.

His own stress-constricted torso is preventing him from breathing. Even the drugs are not suppressing the distress assaulting his cellular structure. The Soldier gasps desperately like a grounded fish, writhing in a new universe alien to all he's known. His mind forms three words he had not thought for decades: *God, help me!*

Just before he passes out, from somewhere both distant and yet somehow within the center of his mind, the Soldier hears the vibration the monks uttered just moments before, as if the very foundation of the universe had been struck like a tuning fork.

*We wish all our viewers a very happy New Year! And now to our top story.*

*Today in the United Nations, China suddenly and without explanation backed off of their earlier challenges to American and UK claims on the Middle Eastern oil fields that China had helped develop before the Western nations' liberation of Iran and Syria . . . Wait, we have breaking news coming in!*

*An update just in on the stunningly brutal terrorist attack on defenseless monks at the Dalai Lama's home residence in Tibet that occurred just a few days ago. The Dalai Lama was overseas at the time, but MNBC's intelligence sources believe he was the target.*

*Early CIA reports indicated this heinous attack was perpetrated by elements of China's Communist government, who'd deplored the recent return of Tibetan independence due to international pressure.*

*However, just this hour the CIA updated that initial report and are now certain it was perpetrated by an Al Qaeda cell, moving clandestinely into Tibet through Muslim populations in the northwestern Chinese province of Xinjiang. The Terror Alert level in the U.S. and UK is raised to red, suggesting that possible follow-up strikes in those countries are considered highly probable. Citizens are advised to be hyper-vigilant of any suspicious behavior.*

*Investigators will determine if the Chinese government collaborated in any way with the terrorists. The U.S. Navy's 7th Fleet is positioned off the coast of China in the China Sea. As a result, the Red Army has gone on high alert. More on this as it develops.*

– MNBC News (Mind-Net Broadcasting Company), January 2, 2013

# 1. The Call

*[Jesus said] . . . when you make male and female into a single one . . . then you will enter the kingdom.*
— Gospel of Thomas, Verse 22

———————

Ravi Shyamalan, with Rachel following her, emerged from the funeral limousine. Both had tears in their eyes. Their mother joined them from the second limousine, where she had been comforted by her late husband's two surviving siblings. Rachel, Ravi, and their mother, all wearing white dresses and cloaks as is customary at Hindu funerals, walked from the entrance of Brooklyn's Greenwood Cemetery toward the gravesite. They clung to each other, weeping as they passed among the looming granite monuments.

Earlier, Ravi's mind had been spinning during her father's funeral service at the chapel, with memories of the past – playing with Rachel at the feet of their smiling father at their home in D.C. – the rare holiday dinners with family back in Pune, India – aunties dressed in colorful saris – the rich aromas of dishes made with loving hands. Oddly, it had been Ravi's father and not her mother who'd often taught her how to make the special dishes for the celebrations. How funny her father, so distinguished in his simple black suit, had appeared among the colorful aunties in the kitchen preparing the Bajji (vegetable fritters) and the Uttapam (rice pancakes).

Ravi's tears began anew as she remembered her father's glow at the simple joy of preparing food with the giggling aunties, who teased him endlessly about his culinary obsessions. He was such a gentle and humble man, even though his work cast him into the often ruthless halls of power around the world.

Father found comfort in the household. He often spoke of the quiet power of the homemaker, and how the true engine of civilization, the quantum field that held the human universe together, was not the conquerors or the philosophers, but those who kept the nests of the human family in order.

He saw through the tinsel of the power structures he himself worked within, to the heart of humanity, the endless lineage of feminine power that was this heart. True power came from a deeper place and was passed down as a quiet force more real and solid than any official declaration could ever be. He saw the struggles of the male structures of government, economy, and society as an almost comical attempt to mimic on a societal scale what already existed so elegantly and humbly within homes all over the world. But men, especially men of power, were clumsy at it.

In his cooking, he sought to tap into this elegance, for in it he saw the nurturing feminine force he'd come to regard with awe. He longed for a day when the male power in the world was balanced with the feminine.

The three women took their place beside the freshly dug grave among the assembling crowd, a mound of fresh earth to their left. Father's casket was before them.

Ravi's mind drifted to evenings during her childhood in their home, where her father was often in the kitchen humming to the melodies wafting through the house and her mother sat on cushions in the living room strumming her latest song on her sitar. Ravi's mother was a musician who later in her life gained international acclaim. Ravi could almost see her mother playing her favorite tune as memories of the melody and the smells of Father's cooking transported her back in time.

Suddenly, Ravi's mind was yanked back to the present by the ringing of her cell phone inside her pocketbook. She fumbled through her purse, trying to retrieve it to turn it off, until Rachel, taking control of a situation that was beyond Ravi in her current state of mind, took the cell phone from her.

Rachel was a solid rock of a human being, able to function at times when Ravi was at a loss to do so. Ravi's mind was one that gravitated to the clouds, while Rachel's was an anchor. She was practical, opinionated, and pragmatic, undaunted by the harsh realities of the world. Already whispering into the cell phone, all-business Rachel walked away from the crowd across the vast lawn laid with tombstones of varying shapes and sizes. She walked deeper into this paradoxical New York City cemetery, crowded with silent graves, yet surrounded by the bustle and towering architecture of the vast city beyond.

Apart from the crowd, Rachel held a not-so-quiet conversation into Ravi's cell phone. Ravi, watching her, was irritated and mystified that Rachel would walk away even as father's service was beginning, but her attention turned to the Hindu priestess reciting the sacred Sanskrit verses that began the ceremony.

In Father's will, he'd requested that a woman priest from his hometown of Pune read the last rites at his funeral. As her father was lowered into his grave, Ravi remembered how proudly her father had spoken to her and Rachel about a time in the 1980s when his hometown had become the center of a storm of controversy. Because of a shortage of priests in the city, an elderly Hindu priest named Shankar Thatte began the controversial Shankar Seva Samiti movement by teaching the holy texts to women, including his own wife, Pushpa.

In India, although women priests were rare, Hinduism had been rich with women scholars who'd been a formidable part of Hindu writing: Ghosha, Lopamudra, Romasha, and Indrani in the Vedic period, and women philosophers like Sulabha, Maitreyi, and Gargi in the Upanishadic period.

When Ravi's father told the story of how his village had become the center of a national scandal that reverberated throughout India, his eyes shone with pride. He rejoiced when women took their place in the spiritual halls of his country. He told stories of feminine power as he smiled and patted Ravi's head, as if he could gently pound that power into her mind with his loving hand. Her father's pride in the role his village played in elevating the feminine had become part of who Ravi was, and it was manifested in all her works as an adult.

Ravi watched the dirt being shoveled onto her father's casket, and the sound of the soil hitting the wood was like a stake being driven through her heart. Each shovelful separated her further from her father. It was just too much. Ravi's heart burst, tears streaming from eyes she thought had no more tears to spill. The words shrieked within her mind. *Oh, no, no, noooo! A world without this gentle man, I cannot imagine. Please God, tell me this is a dream, and let me awaken from it!* Her sobs were so forceful that many in the crowd looked toward her with concern.

Ravi wept until her tears had run their course – dabbing her eyes with a tissue she held wadded in her clenched hand. Then the memory was broken as Rachel returned, silently slipping Ravi's cell phone back into her bag. Ravi saw on Rachel's face a look of excitement that was at odds with where they were and what they were doing. Perplexed and irritated by Rachel's mood, Ravi turned back to the funeral rites.

The priestess' closing chant echoed through the silent cemetery. *Om Asato ma sadgamaya, tamaso ma jyotirgamaya, mrityorma amritam gamaya, Om shanti, shanti, shanti.*

For Rachel, the service had taken forever. In other circumstances, Rachel's fidgeting would have had little effect on Ravi, but now it only added to her aggravation. As the service ended, Rachel grabbed Ravi and rushed her back to the line of limousines, pulling her into their car. Ravi closed her door and turned to Rachel with an angry expression that demanded to know what was going on. Rachel bounced in her seat like a child anticipating a carnival ride.

Ravi spoke sharply. "What? Why are you acting like this?"

Rachel's voice squealed with excitement. "You got it! They gave it to you!"

"What? What the hell are you speaking of?"

"The Nobel Prize! You got it!"

Ravi's emotions roiled. "Rachel, at this moment I am not understanding how you can turn away from the burial of Father. I feel ashamed of you."

As the limo pulled down the lane, Rachel burst into tears. Then she spoke with a trembling voice, "Don't you see? It was *he* who made this happen! Father gave a parting gift to you, to the world. This Nobel Prize is the beginning of all that is possible.

"I loved the man so. This is how I honor him, by honoring his gift. Can you not see that? Through his spirit, he has presented a gift to the world, his most precious gift. That gift is *you,* Ravi." Rachel buried her face in Ravi's shoulder.

Ravi's heart swelled with emotion. Although Rachel was older, in many ways she'd always seemed younger than Ravi. Rachel was bigger and clumsier, both physically and in her speech. Rachel spoke bluntly, but was surprised when people took offense, because though she was loud and brash, Rachel had a true heart and thought others could see through to her inner goodness and sincerity.

Ravi's breaking heart expanded to embrace Rachel. Her tears spilled onto Rachel's head, as she remembered earlier times when life and schoolmates had been very hard on her, and how Rachel had always been there, trying to protect her. She remembered her classmates' teasing each time the nurse had called her out of the room for medication, and how Rachel had stood by her, crying for her hurt. Although Rachel had been unable to defend herself or Ravi against the verbal sparring of the other children, she had tried.

As Ravi grew older and her poise developed with her intellect, it was Rachel who more often became the target of schoolyard torment. Her gangly clumsiness and slower wit made her an easy target. As Ravi remembered how many times she had stood by and watched her older sister endure humiliation, shame burned in her, not only for her childhood cowardice, but today for having doubted Rachel's compassion.

Ravi held her sobbing sister gently, rocking her larger frame, awkwardly folded down into her arms. As Rachel exposed her broken heart, Father seemed to again sit with them, his last words to both of them echoing in Ravi's mind: "Watch over one another, for me."

# 2. The Voice

*Magnetic Excitation of Sensory Resonances . . . influencing the nervous system of a subject by a weak externally applied magnetic field . . . which is the physiological effect involved in "rocking the baby."*
— United States Patent Office, Patent No. 5,935,054

*[Psychic perception] is a very systematic, very controlled method of accessing information . . . independent of time . . . independent of location . . . go anywhere on this earth . . . into any mind.*
— Major General Albert Stubblebine, former PSI TECH Chairman and Commanding Officer of the U.S. Army Intelligence and Security Command (INSCOM)

———————

Ravi stood at the podium in the hallowed halls of the 200-year-old Oxford Union Debating Society. It had been two months since her father's funeral, where Rachel received the news of Ravi's Nobel Prize in Economics, and much had happened since then.

This famous university in England had hosted many of the great leaders of modern history, who had come from all over the world to speak at this very podium. Ravi inhaled the aroma of the polished wood while her hands stroked its smooth surface. She wondered, with a wry smile, how many historic figures she'd studied in school and respected deeply had felt their palms sweat in anticipation on this very wood, just as hers did now. Although recently noted for brilliant innovations in her field, Ravi had not suffered the effects of the limelight endured by many great leaders. That was about to change.

Ravi had traveled the globe with her parents in her younger life, exploring many worlds. On their journeys, they'd soared through lavish halls of vast wealth and descended into the most heart-breaking squalor, making Ravi a complex young woman at a very early age.

Ravi's path had not been easy or without challenge. After she was mis-diagnosed with Attention Deficit Disorder as a child, further testing finally revealed that she was an off-the-charts genius. Only then did her life begin to blossom into many areas of both intellect and inspiration. This, too, expanded Ravi's empathy for the misunderstood.

By 19 years of age, Ravi had attained doctorates in physics and medicine, and bachelor's degrees in philosophy, psychology, divinity, and world history. She had also achieved master's levels in fencing, tai chi, and yoga, besides speaking four languages fluently.

In her work with microfinance, her intellect, beauty, and charm had made Ravi appealing to the powerful elite who ran the world – making it possible for her to connect cutting edge inventors and the techno nouveau-riche with impoverished communities.

Ravi's invitation to the renowned Oxford Union followed on the heels of her Nobel Prize, which had been awarded as a result of her visionary work in expanding microbanking and rural development in impoverished nations. Her work had changed the lives of millions worldwide.

Like a magnet her life had drawn her to this moment, just as surely as the tide washes the surfer to the shore. Ravi had simply ridden the wave of her life to this podium. A lifetime of preparation rode on today's performance.

Ravi was rarely rattled or intimidated, not even by the prestige of Oxford Union, or the audience of professors and media, including C-SPAN of the United States, all sitting before her. However, as she lifted the water glass from the podium to her dry lips, her hand trembled. Her other hand gripped the podium to steady herself as her mind swam. *What is going on?*

Ravi shuddered with an unusual feeling of vulnerability. But something else was also occurring – something that felt vast and larger than her. In this moment of powerlessness, Ravi sensed that this was a feeling common to all of humanity.

This sensation of smallness and inadequacy magnified, pressing onto her heart and soul with such heaviness it drove Ravi to speak spontaneously to voice her feelings aloud, to get the weight off her chest. Going completely off script, she began. "We live . . ."

The sound system squealed shrill feedback, causing Ravi to feel even less sure of herself. Tentatively, she continued, speaking into the microphone in a way that instantly endeared her to the audience, who smiled as she spoke to them, not from her notes, but from her heart.

"We live in a world that has so many people, we feel small and powerless. We often think that what we feel is not important, and that we are unworthy to effect a course in the world that really matters."

Ravi's mind returned to her father and to Rachel's tearful belief that he had moved into the world beyond life to put Ravi at this podium today. She added, "I am learning not to believe in accidents. I feel that we are all exactly where we should be at all times, and that indeed we *do matter,* and perhaps this time in history – when humanity is so vast – is the time when each one of us matters the most, not the least.

"Something is very wrong with our world, and yet at the same time, something is very right about it, and about us." Several women in the audience touched their hands to their hearts as their eyes misted.

As Ravi looked out over the audience, a thought – a sound – came into her mind that pulsed and magnified. Unnerved, she used a yogic breathing technique to calm herself, but the technique had other immediate and overwhelming effects: It increased the volume of the vibration and also clarified the sound. She heard a dozen voices chanting a monotone in varying octaves, in a language she did not understand.

She looked with confusion at the audience, wondering why no one was reacting to the sounds buzzing in her ears. None of the faces in the audience showed any acknowledgment of the building vibration. All eyes were raised expectantly to Ravi as their owners anticipated her presentation. *Doesn't anyone else hear this?*

Rachel hadn't noticed Ravi's departure from their carefully worded speech. She was in the wings, peeking out at the assembled media and capacity audience that her organizing efforts had delivered. She was ecstatic. *Look at this crowd!*

Suddenly Rachel froze. Her sister had gone off script – way off script! Her eyes shot to Ravi, then down to her notes. Rifling quickly through the pages, she scanned for any last-minute changes Ravi may have made to their original presentation. There were none. *What the hell is she doing?*

Seeing motion out of the corner of her eye, Ravi nervously looked off stage to Rachel, who was signaling her furiously from the wings. She tried to return from the detour she'd inexplicably taken from her prepared speech on microbanking's promise, back to the script she and Rachel had written. "I-I-I'm here to share about our work in-in-in microbanking." The chanting grew louder, bouncing off the walls of the great hall as if the voices of ten thousand monks were joined in its utterance. "I-I-I . . ."

The audience grew uncomfortable as Ravi struggled. Many shifted in their seats and looked at each other as Ravi grew increasingly distracted by the intensifying vibration. *Why is this happening?*

Panicked at being unable to speak with her normal confidence, Ravi felt her heart pounding. Suddenly her hand opened, and the prepared statement dropped to the floor. The sheets fell like drifting snow, spreading across the stage.

She took a deep breath and, giving up her resistance, surrendered completely to the vibration. Ravi suddenly felt well-being spread through her body. As she relaxed, she heard her own voice, as if she were a member of the audience listening as the words flowed. "I prepared a statement about my economics work to present to you today, but I am choosing in this moment not to deliver it. I feel a more pressing issue must be discussed. I am going to share my true feelings with you.

"Our world must change paths immediately. Our global problems are not economic ones, but problems of the spirit. No tinkering with the system will have the impact needed, unless we fundamentally change the way we view the world and our place in it.

"As a people, we have been led into a state of fear by many of our religious and governmental institutions and leaders, and it is breaking my heart." Ravi's voice trembled as she squeezed the podium. "This must not stand. It is time to paint a new vision, *a vision of hope for the world.* We were not put here for fear and revenge. We must – *I must* –

allow my real purpose to find its way into this world." A tear spilled from her eye, as her voice quivered and the TV cameras closed in.

Ravi's emotional opening had an immediate effect. The room became electric with anticipation. The audience sat erect, as if a raw societal nerve had been struck. Some touched their chests as if the constricting mentality of the endless war on terror were squeezing their expanding hearts. They seemed moved by, and yet fearful of where the speaker was going. Even Ravi herself was unsure where her words would lead them.

Her encyclopedic knowledge of history, divinity, philosophy, and sociology began to spin through her mind like many pieces of a multi-dimensional puzzle. She saw them falling into place, coalescing into a vision. As her lips articulated her message, she was as intrigued and expectant as the spellbound listeners, who were hanging on her words.

Ravi took another deep breath as her heart pounded with the fear of departing from her carefully prepared statement on this world stage. The chanting sounds rose again. She was being magnetically drawn by some force to dive into the deep end of an ocean of human knowledge.

One word from her tempest of thoughts took root, floating in her mind's eye: *faith*. This word calmed the storm around her, drawing her to dive off the cliff. As she let out her breath in a cleansing sigh, her body relaxed. The chants subsided, as if in deference to the words she now spoke.

"As many of you may know, the word astrology comes from the Greek root *aster* meaning *star,* and *logos* meaning *speech, statement, or reason.* Astrologers have always looked for reason in the stars. Astrology has often been laughed at, but some of our most respected thinkers in history have put great stock in it, and Jesus himself referred to *signs in the stars.*

"Some of the greatest scientific minds were actually astrologers as well. One of the early astronomers and mathematicians, Claudius Ptolemaeus, wrote *Tetrabiblos,* which is considered by many to be a work fundamental to Western astrology. During the Middle Ages and Renaissance, astrology was practiced widely and may have been used in determining astronomical progressions. Johannes Kepler and Galileo Galilei both charted horoscopes for national leaders of their times.

"Kepler, in fact, estimated Jesus' birth was actually in the year 7 BC, because he hypothesized that the Star of Bethlehem, which the Magi Kings called *a sign from God leading them to Bethlehem,* had been the rare conjunction of Saturn and Jupiter. Some astrologers have said Saturn rules Saturday, the Jewish Sabbath, calling it the *planet of the Jews,* and Jupiter is the *planet of kings* – making Kepler's theory of planetary alignment congruent with astrology's recognition that this alignment signaled the time of the *King of the Jews,* or Jesus.

"Our Western concept of astrology is thought to have originated in ancient Sumer, more commonly known as Sumeria, around 4,000 years ago and was refined by Greeks several hundred years later. The West was not the only civilization to develop astrology. India's Vedic system of astrology, known as Jyotisha, meaning *science of light,* dates back about 3,400 years."

Ravi noticed bewildered looks from the crowd. "You might be asking yourself, *Why is this important to us today? Who cares about ancient astrology?* The answer to that question is that our future depends on how we see ourselves in the progression of history, and we need to realize that we are in the midst of a great historical shift. It is time for our self-vision to change.

"This astrological time, our time, is so extremely important, it was predicted long ago by someone most of you know and respect – Jesus. In the Bible's Book of Luke 22:10, Jesus told his disciples just prior to his arrest and crucifixion, *Behold, when ye are entered into the city, there shall a man meet you, bearing a pitcher of water; follow him into the house where he entereth in.* The Aquarian symbol is the water bearer. Jesus was foretelling the times we are living in today.

"We live at a rare nexus in history. It is a time when the Piscean Age ushered in by Jesus is ending and being replaced by the beginning of the Aquarian Age, or the Age of Man. We are now entering the birthing pains of the Aquarian Age, and we actually may have been doing so for some time.

"Jesus told us in Luke 21:25, *And there shall be signs in the sun, and in the moon, and in the stars.* The Piscean Age has long been associated by many with Christ's life. It may surprise you that the original symbol for Christianity was not the crucifix, which came much later, but the fish, which is symbolized in the astronomical constellation of Pisces. The two fishes of the Piscean symbol represent the 2,000-year age we are now completing.

"What makes this time extraordinary is that the coming Aquarian Age marks *the dawn of the age of humankind,* which also completes a cycle of the entire twelve zodiac ages. Pisces, the one we are completing, marks the end of the physical animal ages: Leo, the lion; Cancer, the crab; Gemini, the wolves or twin goats; Taurus, the bull; Aries, the ram; and of course, Pisces, the fish. Aquarius – the water bearer, *the human being* – marks the symbol of humanity. This is significant.

"At this moment, our planet's evolution shifts from creature or physical evolutionary change and development to the evolution of consciousness, and the dawning of a new time that will bring the physical world into endless possibility."

Many in the audience leaned in, hungry for a vision of the possibilities this young woman suggested. The persistent lagging economy had beaten down the spirits of many, which made this hope flowing from Ravi's lips magnetic. She could almost hear their murmurs. *My parents have lost their retirement – what can I do? My son's laid off. Will I be able to help my grandchildren?*

Ravi paused for a moment, taken aback by the intensity of the longing in the faces before her. She saw grievous worry for the future behind their eyes. She felt their fear. Her heart and theirs were becoming one.

The vibration she had heard at the beginning of her talk welled up again in her ears. The words poured forth. "Do not dread your future. Be assured that these difficult and unsure times we are in, are *only a transition.*"

Some in the crowd audibly sighed in relief. She herself was relieved by the words. She continued.

"The creative cycle, or days of creation, are being completed. Humanity has reached its hand across the planet. Every area of the earth has been tamed, every resource has been found and tapped, and the planet sags from the weight of almost 10 billion people and their relentless need for sustenance and energy. We have nothing more to explore or exploit. We have reached the limits of physical exploration as a source of subsistence or inspiration."

A rustling in the audience reflected the disturbance this dire insight evoked. Ravi's earlier assurance had given them solace that these trying times were but a transition. But now that comfort quickly faded to fear that hard times were indeed coming – *we've used up all our resources!*

Ravi did not miss their concern. She looked upon them as a mother would – wishing to soothe her children's fears even as her own heart experienced that same fear. She began to search for words, but the message flowing through her came from a deeper place than intellect. The answers formed as she spoke them. "There is purpose to this. Humanity is being prodded to take flight, the way a maturing hatchling is eventually prodded from the nest – in order to truly behold the power of its wings."

One of the local television news crews had come only for short clips of the beginning of Ravi's speech for their six o'clock feed. But observing the rapt audience, as the breadth of her dialectic expanded to the very fate of humankind, the crew director sensed that he had stumbled upon a piece that would be remembered, and he didn't want to be the one who failed to record it. Motioning to his cameraman, he signaled, *keep recording, keep recording!*

"Fortunately, the Piscean Age has prepared us for this flight – this great shift we will experience together – by ushering in lifting winds of wisdom from avatars and prophets, who opened a whole new universe of potential with their visions. They planted the seeds of preparation for this new time. The first inkling of the Piscean Age began with the life of the Buddha some four hundred years before Christ; then it began in earnest with the age of Christ, or Jesus, followed some five hundred years later by the life of Muhammad. This set a foundation for the majority of the world's population, built upon the cornerstone of treating others with compassion."

Ravi recited some of those texts.

"From the Koran: *Allah created nations and tribes that we might know one another, not that we might despise one another.*

"From the Torah: *. . . never to turn aside the stranger, for it is like turning aside the most high God.*

"From the Bible: *Love thy neighbor as thyself.*

"The Buddha said, *Full of love for all things in the world; practicing virtue in order to benefit others, this man alone is happy.*"

Some faces held a question – one Ravi could almost hear being spoken aloud. *How can these admonitions of compassion – these philosophies – help me and my family?*

"Visionaries have since employed those teachings of compassion in the real world on a massive scale, including most recently, Mahatma Gandhi and Dr. Martin Luther King, Jr. They proved that this wisdom is not beyond us, but is in fact the most practical way to achieve worthy goals – redirecting economies to nurture their people, achieving revolution without wars, improving the lives of millions by shifting our consciousness."

No one stirred. All were now invested in the ride they had embarked upon today, as a ray of sun broke through the clouds to shine brilliantly through the high windows above them. This had become much more than the dry economics speech they'd anticipated. Yet the shift was more profound than a change of subject. The mood in the room had transformed from one of individual professional interest to a sense of collective outcome.

Ravi paused, sensing a few moments were needed for these last words to sink into her listeners' awareness. Scanning the audience in this moment of reflection, she could almost see the wheels of their minds unlocking from old tracks, the cogs and gears of their consciousness pulling away from one another, making space for new possibilities.

The warmth of the sunlight spread through the room as the vibrations – the chanting – rose once again in Ravi's mind.

She pressed on with renewed confidence. "So, the Piscean Age has seen an explosion of both technological understanding and of spiritual enlightenment offered through prophets and visionaries throughout time. However, the very important difference is that while technology expanded pervasively and tangibly into people's lives, the spiritual insights, while well known, have not directly touched the lives of humanity. The resulting reality is that the very survival of humanity falls into question.

"Einstein warned, *It has become appallingly clear that our technology has outstripped our humanity.* His concerns were voiced also by General Omar Bradley after World War II when he said, *We have grasped the mystery of the atom, but rejected the Sermon on the Mount."*

Many in the audience nodded at these admonitions about the direction of human development. Members of the media scribbled furiously in their notepads. Seeing this, Ravi sensed in her audience a growing connection with her message.

It became clear that Ravi's presentation had become a group creation, as if her psyche were dancing with the group mind.

She looked out at their faces, each waiting desperately to hear what their own consciousness already knew. They *needed* to hear it, so that they knew it was real. Ravi herself grew anxious to hear the words her lips were yet to form.

"Today God offers us the opportunity to become what we were destined to be. The Aquarian Age is graduation day. Jesus, Buddha, and the others have tutored us well. We are now cast out of our nest with our lessons learned and facing the test of whether we can live them – and take flight. My friends, the Aquarian Age of mankind is the time when all of humanity will awaken together from the delusion that we are not connected, or we will destroy one another as perpetual enemies, competing for resources that will continue to dwindle."

The silence in the hall added weight to the echo of Ravi's words. "The old belief that evolution is the story of survival of the fittest crushing those weaker, is a half-truth at best, and an abomination at worst. For the elegant evolutionary process God sparked in the world teaches something much more profound.

"When we look back at life's history, we see clearly that it was the acts of cohesion and cooperation that assured survival and dominance in the world. Cells that could adapt to collective living and mutually beneficial relationships with other cells evolved into the higher states of life. History, biology, and the spiritual laws of the universe all point in the same direction. The knowledge of the prophets is woven into the very fabric of creation if our minds can open to hear its subtle wisdom.

"There is much fear mongering today. That is not my purpose here. But since many have clamored that we are in the end times, dividing us in spirit by saying some shall be saved and some shall be damned, this issue must be addressed. *They are correct.*"

Audible gasps moved Ravi to quickly explain. "We are in the end times of the Piscean Age. At the time of Jesus, many thought they were in the end times, and they too were correct, for they were in the end times of the Age of Aries. Yet as we now know, they had extraordinary and wonderful days ahead of them, not an end of history. God offers us this same gift. However, we as a species do have the capability of ending our history, if we cannot awaken to the wisdom vibrating within our hearts, minds, and very souls.

"Too many in positions of religious leadership have turned the hope and good news of our spiritual forefathers into a death cult, gritting their teeth to avoid sin, awaiting the end of the world, and encouraging their flocks to vote for political candidates they think will hasten that end. These same leaders often teach us to put people like Jesus on a pedestal so high we need not aspire to the simple admonitions of compassion and forgiveness that he taught. These teachings will not lead to where Jesus was pointing, for they separate us from God that exists within each of us. They cannot take us to our next step of evolution."

A stocky gray-haired man with a gold cross on his dark lapel suddenly stood, turning his back on Ravi as he loudly cut through the row to the aisle and walked heavily out of the room, muttering, "Blasphemy!" Only a few in the audience tracked his movement as he exited, a large black Bible clasped in his tightening fingers. Most eyes remained fixed on Ravi.

A moment of silence stretched, as Ravi felt a shadow cross her heart that drained the hope from her, a fleeting premonition that was gone as quickly as it had come. It was as if something in that moment had sucked all the oxygen from the room. And then, as if a great dam had broken open to release a sea of hope, clean sweet sustenance once again filled her lungs and spirit.

Ravi spoke. "What Jesus and Buddha discovered and revealed was not found in books or buildings, but in their heart of hearts. In the absolute silence of their being, they resonated with the vibration of light, a vibration to which we all have access. Today I implore you to look within. I ask you, can you not feel that vibration echoing within you, reminding us that we are all woven of the same cloth? Can you not feel that we are all a part of a family, *together* – not alone and despairing, but part of each other and becoming whole?"

Ravi leaned heavily into the podium, her voice trembling with urgency, pleading not just for her words to be heard and understood, but for the feelings driving them to be felt – shared. Her expression washed through the room as a surging force. "Like Joan of Arc, I feel God's words pounding within my mind with the force of a tidal wave. I cannot *not speak* the words, or I will be torn apart. All of you, *all of us,* are feeling the very fibers of our consciousness being stretched. I feel in my very being that now is the time in our extraordinary history when we must become the visions we have been given. It is time for us to know what we can be. Jesus told us *these and greater things shall you do.* We can no longer pretend that we and all our world's children are not the children of God, and that all of the world's life is not the precious garden of God, placed in our hands for a reason.

"It is time to awaken! We must not fear, for we are entering a time of great hope. It is time to lose our fear. The promise of these times is directed by the hand of God. God no longer seeks our obedience, but rather our realization of our co-creative power with him. Humanity has reached adulthood. *Breathe in* the realization that we are indeed created in God's image. Endowed with the power to destroy worlds, *we wield the power of gods.*

"It is time for humanity to grow up and become what we are destined to be, promised by Jesus himself. The awakening is occurring. We all feel it. Look within, welcome your becoming. It is stretching you and straining you.

"Embrace . . ." Ravi's voice trailed off.

Suddenly Ravi's world swirled, and the wave of inspiration that had swept her and the audience along in it was gone. The clear words she'd spoken and the visions she'd painted grew distant and unfathomable. Her face flushed with confusion and embarrassment as her mind swam in vertigo. Her heart pounded in her chest, as a fading pixilated world lost both color and light.

Ravi swooned, as if this communication had taken everything she had in her. Stumbling backward away from the podium, her eyes fluttered, and she went limp. The master of ceremonies, standing behind her, reached up just in time to catch her as she nearly fell into his arms. The Oxford audience sat stunned and silent.

A single camera clicked. The sound echoed like a shot fired through the silent hall. Members of the media, as if awakening from a trance, roared back to life, rushing the podium, extending microphones up to young Ravi, and firing questions as fast as the popping of the flashbulbs and the clicking and whirring of the cameras that surrounded her.

# 3. Puzzles

Rachel scurried around the dais, scooping up the pages of the speech Ravi had not given, along with their other belongings, before she hurried to join her sister as she left the stage area. As they pushed the door open, members of the media followed them all the way out to their waiting car. Flashbulbs flashed and microphones were thrust into Ravi's face. Rachel firmly brushed them aside. "I'm sorry, Ravi is late for another meeting. We can't talk now."

The driver opened the limo door, and Rachel threw the documents across the seat and climbed in, sitting on the scattered papers and pulling Ravi in behind her. She turned to the driver. "Hurry, let's go!"

Settling into the backseat, Rachel patted the driver on the shoulder and said, "Jerry, would you give me a cigarette?" He turned around to look at her, shocked at her request. He'd never seen her smoke before.

"Come on Jerry, I know you smoke. I see you hiding around the corner sometimes. Give me one, please." Rachel tapped the back of his seat impatiently.

Rachel held the lighter and cigarette. Getting it lit, she took a deep drag and watched the smoke curl into the air before turning her attention back to Ravi. "Ravi, what the hell just happened in there?"

Ravi reached over to take the cigarette out of Rachel's mouth and took a drag herself. She gave a slight cough, and her eyes watered as she answered, "I am not sure, exactly." Ravi's hand trembled as she gave the cigarette back. She cringed as she thought of her off-topic performance, given in front of the world on her most auspicious day.

Such an outburst was completely unlike her, for once Ravi's gifts had been discovered as a child, she had mapped out her entire life. She'd clearly seen steps and formulae to get from point A to point B, and had methodically cultivated the skills necessary to get there.

But now what had she done? Who was *she* to talk of such things, things of such vast import? Her areas of expertise had been so wide, Ravi had rarely experienced stepping beyond her credentials. But now she felt like a child, unsure of herself. The calm certainty that had flowed through her on the stage, making her appear so powerful and penetrating, were long gone. Ravi was a frightened young woman who felt like she'd just poked a dragon.

The driver looked in the rearview mirror, bewildered at their behavior, as Ravi and Rachel passed the cigarette back and forth. With a lopsided grin, he inquired, "You ladies want a drink, too?"

Rachel fought a smile and ignored him as she focused on her sister. She saw Ravi's distress, but she wanted answers. She'd put many long hours into this presentation and arranging upcoming speaking engagements, and now . . . "What do you mean? Did you just make all that up?"

Ravi thought over what had just happened. "No, it wasn't that. These were all things I had learned over the years – all these disparate facts jelled in new ways – a larger picture formed. I . . ." Her eyes were distant as she tried to piece it all together so she could explain it in a way that wouldn't leave her looking as insane and inept as she felt.

Rachel grew exasperated. "So you *winged* it. The most important speech you would ever give, at the Oxford Debate Club, *and you WINGED it?"* Her voice rose as she glared accusingly.

Ravi looked away, searching for words. Her heart pounded with embarrassment and regret, yet beneath that, an excitement built within her as she spoke. "It's hard to explain. I felt a vibration in my mind. Then thoughts began to come from the deepest corners of my memory and flow together from all different directions, like puzzle pieces coming together to form a picture I could only see as its description came out of my mouth."

Ravi stared out the window, the enormity of what she'd just done pressing down on her, as Rachel's fears became her own. She gnawed on her fingernails, something she hadn't done since she was a schoolgirl. Back then she had often wondered aloud about things that others thought odd. She had been alienated and alone, misunderstood not only by classmates but by teachers and those in authority, sometimes causing even Mother and Father to look at her strangely.

Rachel was looking at Ravi with that same concerned look now, as if trying to determine what was wrong with her. When she pulled her hand away from her mouth, it looked like an alien thing. Ravi, unsure of herself, asked in a fragile voice, "Did you like it?"

She again chewed on her nails as she waited for Rachel's answer. It hurt Rachel's heart to see her confident little sister reduced to a vulnerability she had not seen since they were children, when Ravi had been so lost and alone. Rachel was normally outspoken and honest to the point of bluntness, but now she answered carefully – sensing that much rode on her answer. Rachel nervously tapped on the driver's shoulder with her two first fingers, signaling for another cigarette, before she spoke. "Yes, actually, I think *I did* like it."

*I think,* Rachel repeated silently, as she braced for the likely cancellation of the ten months of speaking engagements she'd worked so hard to organize for Ravi. After the welcome tempest of her Nobel Prize hit only weeks before, there had been a flurry of requests. Now all that hard work may have been for naught, as the world watched her bizarre performance today at Oxford.

A small current of the charge Ravi had felt onstage rippled through her as she heard Rachel's response. That strange multi-octave monotone sound she'd heard when she dropped her prepared speech again vibrated within her.

But as the day wore on, that glow faded and the self-doubt resumed. That night, Ravi's sleep was uncharacteristically fitful. Vast images – larger than could be expressed with words – flashed across her mindscape. Oceans of possibility slammed together, then pulled away, leaving desert, desolation. Her muscles tightened and gripped, trying to control the events in her dreams. And then Ravi surrendered.

The moment she agreed to accept her part in what was happening, a towering wave swept her up. Cool clean wind rushed through her hair, as she peered down at the skyscraper of crystal blue water she rode like Poseidon. The force of this power was staggering, but she knew, as all surfers do, that she did not control the wave. She only agreed to partner with it, knowing that a force this immense could never be held. Such a delusion would send her reeling down, down, down the face of this cliff of water.

Ravi drifted back into the unconscious realms of sleep with one critical realization echoing in her mind: *Trying to control such power is sheer folly. Only humility empowers the surfer.*

Even as that warning echoed in Ravi's mind, beyond the wall of water she rode, she saw a land parched and needy. Millions stood awaiting the cool flowing reality she rode toward their thirsting tongues and fevered minds. Their yearning eyes haunted her . . .

Suddenly, Ravi was washed away from her vision by the screaming of her heart. "I AM NOT WORTHY TO DO THIS!" Every atom of her being felt unworthy, unacceptable, incapable of being or doing anything truly profound. She remembered everything she'd ever done that was shameful, petty, and meaningless.

And, yet, from a quiet place somewhere deep within, she heard a voice: "If not you, *who?* If not now, *when?*"

# 4. Hell

*"You will soon learn that* control *is God."*

———————

A smile crossed his face as he awakened, for in his dreamscape, angelic voices had been singing to him, and his mother, long departed, had been stroking his hair as she had when he was a small boy. He felt no pain.

Then he became aware of his reality. He felt the restraints on his wrists and ankles and looked down to see the soiled hospital gown he wore. Memory flooded back.

A tall, neatly dressed man quietly entered the room, and his memory of this perfectly groomed man caused him to cringe and shrink against the table beneath him.

The tall man spoke evenly. "Yes, Scott, you are remembering where you are. Did you enjoy your deep sleep? You are in the Sleep Room, remember?" He raised a syringe, drawing a clear liquid into the plunger. "You may feel a little prick."

The restrained man cried, "No, not again! Please, God!"

The tall man inserted the needle into his arm. "I'm afraid you'll find that whatever God you are praying to, has no power here. One would assume that this means that your God does not exist, while my God does. You will learn the truth: Control is God."

The tall man picked up a curved metal instrument, stretching it open as one would ear muffs, before he placed it on the subject's head so that pads rested on the young man's temples. "The LSD should take effect quickly. Now, let's pick up where we left off, shall we? Do you remember at what level we last set our shock therapy?"

Later, the subject, although not completely comatose, lay exhausted, his eyes vacantly staring at a television screen above him. Foamy drool spilled from the corner of his slack mouth. The tall man clicked on a DVD player, and on the screen appeared a man opening a black umbrella. The image was followed by an audio track that repeated the same phrases again and again through speakers on either side of the prostrate man's head. "This is the signal," then a short clip of the song, *I'm Singin' in the Rain,* and then again, "This is the signal." Then the song repeated, and on and on. The tall man closed the door gently behind him as he left the room.

Finished with the "re-patterning therapy," the tall man walked down the hall to his office in one of Canada's finest hospitals, Taloncrag Memorial Psychiatric Institute. Located in Montreal, the hospital, like a good neighbor to the North, had kindly provided a section of their facility to the Central Intelligence Agency of the United States for experimentation, often using their own Canadian citizens as subjects.

# 5. Stone Giants

*We are in a battle for the control of men's minds.*
– Allen Dulles, CIA Director (1953-1961) [Initiated MK-ULTRA, mind control project]


*. . . a top secret CIA memo expressed the need to explore "scientific methods for controlling the minds of individuals" . . . test subjects underwent hypnosis, electro-shock, and drug-induced hallucinations, without their knowledge and without their consent . . . thousands and thousands and thousands of people subjected to really damaging unethical experimentation . . .*
– Excerpts from the documentary, *Mind Control: America's Secret War,* The History Channel, July 4, 2006

---

Ian had settled into the luxurious first class seat and was tipping his glass – his third one – to drain the last drops of brandy from it. The United States Navy was paying for it, and God knew they could afford it. Their budget had bloated in recent years as the war on terror had been hammered into the national psyche. He gazed out the window as the plane approached Montréal-Trudeau Airport. Under the soft orange glow of Montreal's street lamps lay a soft white blanket of snow, making the city look soft, inviting, and clean. He hoped this was a sign of good things to come, perhaps a duty he could live with.

It was odd that his orders had been to enter Canada in civilian garb, with his normal U.S. passport instead of his Naval ID. But hey, the Intelligence brass loved this cloak and dagger crap, so what the hell. He was flying first class and they'd given him a credit card. Might as well relax and enjoy the ride. Ian sucked in his gut as the pretty Canadian-Chinese stewardess reached down over his six-foot frame with a smile to ease his seat into the upright landing position.

Had the stewardess seen the normal Ian, there likely would have been no smile. Ian's sharply tailored suit, his freshly shaved face, and his high and tight cut provided a dashing look that did not reflect either his normal attire or, for that matter, his normal state of mind. Ian had pulled himself together for this assignment. The three brandies he'd just drained constituted an act of temperance on his part. His normal graying blond stubble of several days' duration had ended up on the bathroom floor just this morning as part of his temporary disguise of respectability.

That the attendant had not recoiled from him was proof that his disguise was working.

Commander Ian McDonald had most recently served as a senior department officer on the U.S.S. Corpus Christi, a Los Angeles-class submarine capable of launching 25 nuclear-tipped Tomahawk Cruise Missiles, making that single vessel one of the most powerful superpowers in the world.

Years before, Ian had been one of the Navy's youngest commanding officers, serving on a destroyer that had deployed in the second Iraq war, and later in the Iranian and Syrian conflicts. One day while in home port with his family, he woke up with the flu and had stayed home sick, channel surfing the television out of boredom. His hand froze on the channel selector as he fixed on a program that shook him deeply. Al Jazeera television's U.S. station used one whole day – a 24-hour period – to air the footage of the devastation that U.S. missiles and shells had unleashed on cities in Iran and Syria. The heavy DD(X) class destroyer under Ian's command at the time had led that attack force.

Ian's life began to change. He found it difficult to look at his children without seeing the dismembered Sunni and Shiite children that he had seen in the documentary. He lost his ambition – his direction. He never told anyone how he felt. Who could he tell? His work and social networks were not the kind in which one could discuss such things.

Ian's performance declined, but because of his stellar war record, he'd been thrown a bone by sympathetic superiors. He was offered another duty – not in command of a destroyer, but as a serving officer under another's command. But when he was assigned to the U.S.S. Corpus Christi, his altar-boy Latin tripped a wire in his mind. The thought of perhaps one day unleashing a nuclear strike on a country from *the Body of Christ* proved too much for him. His performance slumped, his drinking intensified, and his marriage disintegrated.

Ian's wife viewed Ian with increasing disdain. He was no longer the in-control man she'd married, and his emotional moods became intolerable. Her feelings rubbed off on his kids. They too grew to dislike him, and his life fell apart. An uneventful divorce had been part of the landslide. He'd hired no lawyer, and agreed to whatever his wife and her greedy lawyer demanded.

Ian eventually went AWOL from the *Corpus Christi* during a drinking binge. Because of that and other stains on his record, he had been demoted again to his current status of Lieutenant and transferred out of combat roles into the haven for misfits known as Covert Naval Intelligence.

He was being sent on this strange first-class mission in – of all places – Montreal, to work with physicians on experiments about human consciousness. Maybe he had been chosen to help them understand how combat fatigue affected personnel in the field, since he had no special medical expertise but had experienced combat situations.

Ian McDonald was about to learn that he had been selected for entirely different reasons.

A limousine driver met him at the airport and shuttled him off through the quaint streets of Montreal. Relaxing in the warmth of the car, he cracked the electric window a bit to allow in some of the crisp night air while he lit a cigarette. The castle of the City Hall, Place Jacques Cartier, towered above the other buildings of the city as they passed.

A horse-drawn carriage clomped by, steam billowing from the horse's flaring nostrils. The faux gas-powered street lamps were reminiscent of times long past. Stopped at a signal light, Ian watched the carriage as the horse plodded down the street, its hooves cracking on the chill brick street. Vapors rose up from manhole covers beneath, like spirits rising from the earth. Mesmerized by this otherworldly image, Ian leaned toward his open window listening to – a whispered warning? *Or maybe it was just the wind.*

Ian shook himself from his reverie, issuing a humorless laugh as he took a nervous drag from his cigarette before flinging it out the window. *A bit too soon in our drinking career for delirium tremens, isn't it?* With each street they passed, Ian's apprehension grew as his enthusiasm for his new assignment diminished.

Montreal's French and English architecture, covered in a new snowfall, wasn't as lovely on the ground as it had been from the air. The stream of traffic and grinding snowplows made the city a bit grittier, and a bit too real, as his car wound through northern downtown and up MacTavish Street toward Mount Lord's southern slope, an area known as the Cloven Mile. Of Mount Lord's three peaks, the Montagne d'Obscurité (Mountain of Darkness) is the tallest at 280 meters, shouldered by Montagne Antique (Ancient Mountain), and Montagne Attentive (Watchful Mountain). At these heights, the peaks could be called tall hills, but the locals referred to them as mountains. They exuded a force beyond their size.

The driver eased to the curb outside the psychiatric institute, Taloncrag Memorial, where Ian had been assigned. The gothic revival structure had a medieval look, like the city around it. The institute was located in an old mansion named Taloncrag. The original owner, a wealthy financier who many said had acquired his fortune through slavery and gun running, had donated his estate to the Royal Kings Hospital in the late 1800s.

The building, surrounded by the street lamp-dotted Mount Lord, appeared to be watched by the summits. Overseers, powerful in their darkness, they looked down solemnly upon it, protecting this place from the light of the world. Ian shivered, though the car was warm.

The driver rounded the car and opened his passenger's door. Ian walked up the shadowed stone pathway toward the building's entrance. A large dark wooden door opened, apparently of its own accord.

A chill of wind swept around him as the heavy door closed behind Ian, leaving him standing in a wood-paneled lobby. As his eyes adjusted to the room, he became aware of a small man wearing a white hospital-type smock standing nearby, silently watching him. Spectacles perched on the man's nose glinted in the sparse light from the street lamps that filtered through a small window above the door. The man spoke. "Mr. McDonald, please follow me for your briefing."

Leading him up a spiral staircase, the man opened a door to a dark vestibule that was cross-gabled in three directions. Ian could not see in the subdued light what the two areas to his left and right might be used for. The short gabled hall directly forward off the main room was obviously an office, containing two side chairs and a desk under a small arched window. Ian was led to one of the chairs by the quiet spectacled man.

The walls of the office were very dark wood, making the room seem cloistered and shut away from the world. It was illuminated only by a small lamp between the chairs and the meager light from the street that could find its way through the bare tree branches softly scraping the outside of the window.

The rich smell of pipe tobacco hung in the air. The man indicated that Ian should sit in one of the chairs and offered him a cup of coffee. He handed it to Ian and silently left the room.

Fidgeting in his luxurious leather chair, Ian took a sip from the bone china cup and lowered it onto the delicate matching saucer. The elegant china, the perfect order of the room. Nothing was out of place.

The cup and saucer rattled as his hand trembled. The thin veneer of order and precision hid a seething madness beneath the surface.

# 6. The New Enemy

*Wars are seldom caused by spontaneous hatreds between people . . . They must be urged to the slaughter by politicians who know how to alarm them.*
– H.L. Mencken

*". . . monks showed a dramatic increase in high frequency brain activity [gamma waves] . . . a sort that has never been reported before in the neuroscience literature," says Professor Davidson [neuroscientist at the University of Wisconsin] ". . . a sprawling circuit that switches on at the sight of suffering . . . as if the monks' brains were itching to go to the aid of those in distress."*
– *The Wall Street Journal,* Friday, November 5, 2004

---

A door opened in the wall to the right of the desk, and, ducking ever so slightly to clear the doorway, a tall lanky man with meticulously styled and combed gray hair entered the room. Extending a hand to Ian, the man said with a slight British accent, "My God-given name is Malcolm; however, you may refer to me simply as the Professor if you like. And you are Lieutenant McDonald, I presume?"

Ian began to rise to shake Malcolm's extended hand, but the Professor signaled him to stay seated as he released his hand. He took his own seat behind the desk. The street lamps through the window behind him cast a corona of light around the Professor, making his face difficult to read. He sat silently for a moment, studying Ian, who sat with increasing discomfort before him. Ian began to feel like a bug beneath a microscope.

The Professor stared at Ian as if he were an object, rather than a fellow human, but suddenly seemed to awaken to the awkwardness of the lengthy silence. He took his pipe from the large ruby glass ashtray and struck a match on the underside of his desk. This broke the uncomfortable silence, but it appeared to be an orchestrated effort rather than a natural act of wanting a smoke. Ian's discomfort with the

Professor grew, even as the rich sweet aroma of tobacco, normally a comforting smell, filled the room.

The Professor, silent and thoughtful, looked away to watch the lazy waves of pipe smoke drift across the room. Suddenly the Professor spoke. "Lieutenant, do you know why you are here?"

Ian replied, "I believe it is to participate in studies involving combat fatigue and perhaps delayed stress syndrome."

Professor gazed intently at Ian. "Although it is true your nation now has several million citizens suffering from post traumatic stress disorder from your last decade of combat in the Gulf region and Middle East actions and occupations, today we have a more pressing need. Our research deals with a new enemy, a new threat."

"A *new* enemy?" Ian responded, stunned.

"Indeed. We have been working on behavior modification techniques since the Cold War, and even before. Are you familiar with this?"

Ian said, "You mean, mind control?"

"Yes, quite astute. That is exactly what I mean." The Professor pointed his pipe toward Ian as if he were his star pupil, before continuing. "I should expect no less from you, since U.S. Naval Intelligence has been studying mind control technology since at least the 1990s."

Ian admitted, "Well, I had read about this in history books, but I mean, this stuff is just science fiction, right?"

Professor raised his thick, perfectly trimmed eyebrows. "Quite the contrary, Lieutenant. *This stuff,* as you call it, is a very real part of our arsenal and has been for some time. Are you aware that there are dozens of United States official patents on mind control technologies?"

The Professor handed Ian a dossier. Ian flipped it open to the title page, *Patents of Mind Control and Behavior Modification Technology,* and then quickly shuffled through the remaining pages, both amazed and distressed by what he saw.

Patents of Mind Control
and Behavior Modification Technology
United States Patent Office

U.S. Patent 4,717,343 - Method of Changing a Person's
Behavior

A method of conditioning a person's unconscious
mind in order to effect a desired change in the
person's behavior which does not require the services
of a trained therapist. Instead the person to be
treated views a program of video pictures appearing
on a screen.

U.S. Patent 5,270,800 - Subliminal Message Generator

A combined subliminal and supraliminal message
generator for use with a television receiver permits
complete control of subliminal messages and their
manner of presentation.

U.S. Patent 5,123,899 - Method and System for
Altering Consciousness

A system for altering the states of human
consciousness involves the simultaneous application
of multiple stimuli, preferable sounds, having
differing frequencies and wave forms.

U.S. Patent 4,877,027 - Hearing System

Sound is induced in the head of a person by radiating
the head with microwaves in the range of 100 megahertz to
10,000 megahertz that are modulated with a particular
waveform . . . The bursts are frequency modulated by the
audio input to create the sensation of hearing in the
person whose head is irradiated.

U.S. Patent 5,159,703 – Silent Subliminal Presentation System

A silent communications system in which non-aural carriers, in the very low or very high audio frequency range or in the adjacent ultrasonic frequency spectrum, are amplitude or frequency modulated with the desired intelligence and propagated acoustically or vibrationally, for inducement into the brain, typically through the use of loudspeakers, earphones or piezoelectric transducers.

Ian's eyes widened as he stared at the pages. *Why haven't I read about this in the newspapers? Or seen it on CNN?*

The Professor, amused by Ian's reaction, chuckled. "You seem *shocked*, Lieutenant. You attended Annapolis, correct?"

Ian nodded slowly.

"Well then, you surely are aware that the Gulf of Tonkin incident, in which Americans and the world were told that your Navy had been attacked by the North Vietnamese, was largely a fraud and a fabrication that in effect stimulated Americans' minds into supporting a widening of that war. Are you *not* aware of that?"

Ian stammered, "Yes, of course, but . . ."

Professor leaned in toward Ian, cutting him off. "You still are yet to hear about that in your mainstream media, aren't you? Is this not a form of mind control? I am continually amused how Americans can hold two facts in their minds, and so naively never put the two together, so long as their CNN or FOX News never tells them to. I'm not complaining, of course, as it makes my job so much easier."

Ian, agitated, felt his face flush.

The Professor back-stepped in his assault. "Please don't take offense, Lieutenant, nothing personal. Brits don't put two and two together very well, either. Although it is a bit harder for us to control information and opinions across the pond because those pesky French and Spaniards, and so on and so on, provide different opinions in their media occasionally." Making lazy circles in the air as he spoke, the Professor dismissed the concerns of whole nations.

*We control media in other nations – in ALLIED countries?* Ian placed his coffee cup in its saucer, raising his hand and leaning forward to interrupt.

The Professor's unhesitating continuation of his lecture left Ian with an awkwardly elevated hand and the realization the man had no intention of interrupting his orientation with answers to uninvited questions. "But in America our job is much easier, because citizens are U.S.-centric. Only twenty percent of Americans have passports, and fewer than half of them actually use them, whereas over seventy percent of UK residents have passports. Americans aren't exposed to different ways of looking at issues. It is not unlike herding cattle through a chute – much easier than herding cattle in an open prairie of information."

Ian shifted in his chair and lit another cigarette. "You make this sound as if Gulf of Tonkin incidents happen all the time."

"Our palette is actually much more extensive than that. We are artists in the science of herding mentalities to desired outcomes. You're an educated man, Lieutenant. When Washington trots out tired phrases like *Islamo-Fascism,* and then FOX, CBS, NBC, CNN, and all the others repeat it several times in a news cycle, wouldn't that be a form of the same type of terror-based herding of the flock?

"But to the point. Yes, Gulf of Tonkin, or false-flag . . ."

Without thinking, Ian interrupted. "False-flag?"

Frowning, the Professor sighed in annoyance, but explained. "Governments have used false-flag operations throughout history to deceive their populations into believing they were under attack in order to provoke them into supporting necessary wars of conquest."

Incredulous, Ian blurted, "The *U.S.* government?"

The Professor rolled his eyes. "Yes, Ian. The U.S. government. I'm not at liberty to discuss them all, but one declassified program was Operation Northwoods. Are you familiar with it?"

Ian shook his head.

"Back in 2001, some forty years after the fact, ABC News reported on the military plan – code named Operation Northwoods – which was designed to fool the American public and the world into allowing a U.S. takeover of Cuba. It had the written approval of the entire U.S. Joint Chiefs of Staff and was presented to President Kennedy's defense secretary, Robert McNamara, in March of 1962 by an Eisenhower appointee, Army General Lyman Lemnitzer. But it was rejected by the civilian leadership, and as I mentioned, the plan remained secret for over forty years afterward.

"The plans included the possible assassination of Cuban émigrés, sinking boats of Cuban refugees on the high seas, exploding commercial jets, blowing up a U.S. ship, and even orchestrating violent terrorism in U.S. cities. The U.S. military's top brass wrote at the time, 'We could blow up a U.S. ship in Guantanamo Bay and blame Cuba,' and, 'casualty lists in U.S. newspapers would cause a helpful wave of national indignation.'"

Ian's mind reeled in rewind – all the rationale that had led him into combat so many years ago suddenly became suspect. Inside he flailed in vertigo. Outside he struggled to remain steady. *This is a job interview. I can't screw this one up.*

The Professor continued, "Kennedy's rejection of the plans exposed him as the weakling that he was. He was assassinated a few months later. Kennedy's normal security protection had been inexplicably reduced for his fateful trip to Dallas."

A nostalgic smile flitted across the Professor's face as he thought of the days when a President's security could be manip . . . He brought himself back to the present and continued, "But, as I said, our palette is much larger, our strokes are broader, and they are often much more subtle. The science of behavioral control has developed, and our ability to manufacture consent is more mature now, usually."

The Professor sighed, tiring of the lesson. "Lieutenant, the people are incapable of acting in their own best interest. We are helpers – school monitors if you will – in the hallways of human consciousness."

Ian was uneasy and uncomfortable. "Why are you telling me all of this? Where is this leading?"

"Lieutenant, the fruits of all our many years of carefully cultivating a garden of media plants in domestic and international newspapers, television, and radio news and talk shows – who can steer the minds of millions here and abroad with repetition of a carefully chosen phrase – all of that is in danger of becoming powerless before our eyes. We have built a stone giant of infrastructure, block by block over many decades, that can precisely manage economies, elections, and foreign policies of many nations. It has been a long struggle, and now when it is working so well, we are finding that our stone giant is beginning to be vibrated to pieces."

Ian's guts were churning as he tried to keep his voice steady. "What do you mean?"

The Professor put down his pipe, and with fingertips touching and elbows on his desk, said, "Something is affecting the consciousness of humanity. Our network of media plants that sways public opinion is no longer having its normal effect."

"At first we thought it was due to the internet's information stampede. But that stampede was surgically hobbled when we ended net neutrality, allowing the highest bidder to control where each internet search leads. The net of information was tightened further by the merger of all the major search engines into one, creating the internet megacorp you know as *Mind-Net*.

"This means, in point of fact, that Mind-Net now owns the rights to any words that might stir controversy or cause anyone to challenge the accepted mindset. When corporate media, their viewers, listeners, readers, or anyone else seeks information on key words like "war," "distortions," "impeachment," or "protest," for example, the owning corporation, which now is *only* Mind-Net Corporation, decides what you'll see when you Mind-Net that word.

"Yet, in spite of Mind-Net, our ability to herd human consciousness toward manufactured consent for unpopular policies continues to erode. So we looked deeper into the human mind for answers and discovered the problem was far beyond simply a media control problem.

"We have been studying the subtle energies of the mind for many years, often successfully manipulating them through direct application of microwaves – from great distances when necessary – to affect specific individuals. These too are working less effectively. We are noting changes in the brainwaves of our targe – um, *subjects*. A growing number of people – though not yet most – seem impervious to our technology."

Ian nearly laughed at the mention of microwave brain interference. Images of the tin-foil-hat people long lampooned on comedy programs came to mind. But the Professor was deadly serious.

"Because of this difficulty, our funding has been increased, and we are expanding our workforce. Your presence here is part of that expansion. Your previous high level command and ability to function under combat stress made you a match for our needs. Even your screw-ups and demotion are a plus, as they make you invisible. You know how to keep secrets. You are here to help us as we attempt to discover the source of this blocking technology. We'll train you here for what needs to be done."

The Professor leaned forward, pressing his knuckles into the desk and staring intently at Ian. "Lieutenant, it has never been easy to get human beings to go to war. It takes a great deal of work to create sufficient anxiety in them to actually kill other human beings. We will not be the ones to allow the infrastructure that has enabled the necessary wars of our time – to protect our way of life and the oil that powers it – to be destroyed. *Not on our watch!*

# 7. The Eye Opens

*The Latin root of the word "government" is gubermare (to direct, steer, control) and mente (mind) – mind control.*

*. . . approximately 4,000 participants in the . . . Meditation . . . programs . . . assembled in Washington, D.C., from June 7 to July 30, 1993 . . . as a result of the group's effect of increasing coherence and reducing stress in the collective consciousness of the District . . . Homicides, Rapes, and Assaults dropped significantly . . .*
  *— Social Indicators Research,* Vol. 47, No. 2, June 1999

*. . . [Buddhist Monks] showed a dramatic increase in high frequency brain activity called gamma waves during compassion meditation . . . gamma waves underlie higher mental activity such as consciousness . . . monks showed extremely large increases . . . never reported before in the neuroscience literature.*
  *— The Wall Street Journal,* Friday, November 5, 2004

---

Mark Ratlig lit another cigarette off the end of the one he'd just smoked. He winced at the migraine pain shooting like a needle through his left eye as he gulped his coffee. The coffee was the only thing that kept the pain at bay. Over the last two weeks, his headaches had returned in full force. He'd had them occasionally years ago, but now they were a way of life.

Glowing green radar-like screens surrounded his messy desk. A desk lamp illuminated the stacks of paper that he examined line by line. He was alone in the facility, which had a small overworked staff that had grown even smaller over the last few months. There had been two suicides and one nervous breakdown. Other staffers had simply disappeared, gone AWOL. The days had gotten long and then longer, and eventually melted into the nights. Mark often slept in the office, too tired to go home.

The center was deadly silent, as Mark was the last one in this section tonight. Everyone else was sleeping somewhere far away from the adrenaline-filled world that enveloped Mark, a pasty overworked creature who never saw daylight.

BRRING! BRRING! BRRING! The phone light flashed as its alarm split the night, and Mark nearly leapt out of his skin.

"Yeah! What is it?" Mark growled into the phone.

"The new man, McDonald, is here to be briefed. Should I buzz him up?"

"Might as well, I ain't goin' nowhere."

Moments later, Ian McDonald appeared outside the door of the dark office. Mark reached under his desk and buzzed him in, motioning him to enter, as he buried his face back in the pages of computer data. Ian entered, and without looking up, Mark growled sarcastically, "Lieutenant McDonald, I presume?"

"Yeah, that's me." Ian offered a handshake, then, realizing it wasn't going to happen, self-consciously drew his hand back.

"The Professor instructed me to bring you up to date on our little project here, so you'd have an overview of the operation. You notice the satellite dishes outside?"

Ian looked beyond the windows reflecting the eerie green radar screens toward the red lights bordering the large dishes that he'd passed on his way into the compound. "Yeah, you're a receiving station, I gather."

Mark, still engrossed in the data sheets, corrected him. "We're an *analysis* center. Our mission is top secret. Our data is human intelligence gathered by the satellite grid and the space shuttles."

Ian was perplexed. "I thought human intelligence was gathered on the ground, not by satellites."

Mark finally looked up, lit a cigarette, and watched his exhaled smoke curl through the dim green light of the room. "I don't mean the intelligence is gathered by humans. I mean that our data is *of human origin.*" Mark winced as a new needle of pain seared through his eye, forcing him to gulp more coffee, before extending his cup in Ian's direction. "Want a cup? This'll take a while to explain."

After both men had fresh coffee, Mark resumed. "Have you ever heard of neuroplasticity?" Ian shook his head silently, and Mark continued. "It's a recent discovery. Neuroplasticity refers to the brain's ability to change its structure and function, in particular by expanding or strengthening circuits that are used, and by shrinking or weakening those that are rarely engaged. In the past it's been seen as the result of physical habit, like pianists who play a lot of arpeggios. Their middle finger and index finger hit keys simultaneously over and over again, until the brain regions that control those two fingers eventually fuse together.

"We know from autopsies on dead crack addicts that repetitive action centers of the brain become overdeveloped. The point is that people's brains can be *physically* rewired to function in certain ways.

"Since World War II, the United States has focused heavily on mind control. Some Nazi war criminals who had conducted experiments at Auschwitz and other camps were never punished because our government wanted the information they had collected through their experiments on Jews, Gypsies, and homosexuals. Much modern advertising and political propaganda is based on what we learned from those experiments.

"Today we have war in a world that wants peace, and overconsumption in a society that wants ecologically sound policy. If people got their wish for global peace and a sound low-consumption economy, the entire world economy and power balance would shift. The result would be anarchy and chaos."

Mark sucked down another jolt of coffee as the needle pulsed through his eye with dull ferocity.

Ian's brow furrowed as he tried to understand. "Let me get this straight. People want peace and sound ecology, but they keep demanding more consumables and supporting wars. I don't get it."

"Lieutenant, Lieutenant, Lieutenant. Don't they teach you guys *anything* over in Naval Intelligence?" Mark sighed and spoke as if he were explaining this to a second grader. "Intelligence's job isn't to gather information."

Ratlig paused, rethinking what he'd just said, before flipping his hand in grudging concession. "Well, maybe it is, some. But our main job is to *sell* people on the information we want them to believe – using repetitive messages, often subliminal, via media on all levels, but especially through television.

"Through rapid-fire shorthand blasts of information that increasingly shorten the attention span and lessen broad swath cohesive thought, people can be sold plastic crap 'til the cows come home, or formula music, or huge cars they don't need – *or even wars.*"

Ian raised his cup. "Whoa, cowboy – *broad swath cohesive thought?* Dumb that down a bit."

Ratlig sighed dramatically. He, too, hated to be interrupted. "Higher consciousness – complex thought – involves seeing concepts in many ways, from many angles. It's the opposite of tunnel vision. Your brain uses many parts to image in the concept, rather than just seeing it from one perspective."

Ratlig paused, wondering if Ian was too dim to assimilate the information. *Watch much TV, Ian?*

Ian persisted. "And you say that by limiting this ability, people are sold wars they don't really want? How?"

Ratlig launched in again. "It's really not that complicated. They become unable to entertain facts that may contradict the mainstream media. Their developed neuroplastic tunnel-vision requires that they be bombarded with a fact in order to incorporate it into their view of reality."

Mark lit a cigarette and continued, smoke trailing out of his mouth. "Remember back in 2002, before the Iraq war that started the dominoes tumbling through Iran, Syria, and Lebanon? The White House told the American public that they knew there were weapons of mass destruction because Hussein Kamel, Saddam Hussein's son-in-law who'd been in charge of the Iraqi weapons programs, said they had them when he defected to Jordan. He was right, they did."

Ian nodded. This had been common knowledge to anyone old enough to read a paper at the time.

"But the son-in-law also testified that all the WMD had been destroyed by Saddam after the first Gulf War before the inspections began, so they would not be found. Saddam also ordered that records be destroyed to hide evidence they'd ever had them, which is why the later inspectors before the second Iraq War couldn't find the records. It didn't mean there were weapons. It meant the records AND the weapons had been destroyed. The White House knew this, the Pentagon knew this, the CIA knew this, and the corporate media knew this."

Ian raised his hand in protest. Incredulous, he was having trouble getting any words out. Ratlig watched impatiently, until Ian was finally able to speak.

"Wait – what are you saying? Are you saying that Kamel's testimony that they had destroyed the WMD was suppressed by the interrogators in Jordan?"

"No, everyone who mattered in government and media knew about it. In fact, the son-in-law's testimony was public record, but few Americans could comprehend that the rationale for the war was disproved by it, because no one told them about it over and over and over again."

Ian pressed, "But if it was public record, people could learn about it and tell others."

"Exactamundo! But the kicker is, even if they did, no one would believe them because they hadn't been told by CNN or by FOX News, time and time and time again. That's because of neuroplasticity. The public's mind, through thousands of hours of TV watching, has been reduced to an extremely short attention span. They have to hear things over and over again before it clicks. Because of neuroplasticity, people also have come to believe anything true and important can only come from corporate media. If they don't report it – *it ain't true.*"

Ian stared blankly at Ratlig as the meaning of his words struck him. Ratlig charged on. "It's not just selling them the wars. It goes deeper. We can prevent the economic changes that could make the wars unnecessary."

Ian wasn't breathing. His mind scrambled over terrain he wanted to leave behind him: his combat role – the Sunni and Shiite children from the documentary. Ian forced air into his tightening chest as the flood of words kept coming.

"Do you know the entire United States could have been driving electric cars long before the year 2000?"

Ratlig answered the question before it could be asked. "Yes, this was public record, too. The fact that all of the electrical needs of the U.S. and the power to drive 95% of their cars could have been supplied solely by clean, cheap solar and wind power long before now – *all public record.*

"No wars in the Middle East and Gulf Region were ever necessary to protect oil. They were necessary to protect centralized energy dependence. Free energy equals chaos and a threat to control.

"ALL of this – the bogus war rationale, the existence of technology to end dependence on foreign oil – all was readily accessible via the public record. But people had been trained like Pavlov's dogs to only react when the sanctioned media told them 'truths' – again, and again, and again." Ratlig mimed quotations marks with his fingers when, with a smirk, he said, "truths." He continued, "Until now."

Ian sat up straighter. "What do you mean, *until now?*"

Mark continued, "The neuroplasticity – changing society's physical brain function by decades of mind conditioning – is breaking down. Twenty years ago we learned two things that caught our attention. We found that monks' brains changed as a result of meditation, which produced high level gamma wave emissions."

Ian, "I don't follow you."

Mark sighed again, exasperated but resigned. "Gamma waves have a cohesive effect on thinking, and in these studies they had a 'compassion' effect on the meditating monks. The parts of their brains that empathized with the suffering of others developed and became fused with the 'action' parts of their brains. In other words, they not only could not stand to see others suffer, they had to act on it."

"So, a few monks on a mountainside changed their brains. What's the big deal?"

Mark winced at a fresh stab of pain behind his eye and stood to pour another fix of caffeine, extending the pot to fill Ian's cup. "It's not just the monks. Mind/body and meditation techniques have spread across the planet. Corporate executives and government ministers are meditating, for Christ's sake!

"Compassion is the enemy of war. For war to be acceptable, we have to dehumanize the other people. They have to become *Japs,* or *Gooks,* or *Spics, Ragheads, Sandniggers,* or at the very least, *Islamo-Fascists.* Otherwise, people will never allow them to be bombed into the Stone Age with their approval and tax dollars."

"But still, out of over 300 million people in the U.S., there can't be that many people meditating."

Mark leaned forward in his chair, causing the green glow to reflect eerily on his face. "In 1993, a disturbing thing came to light. A study in Washington, D.C. found that when meditators gathered, it changed the brains of *the people in the city around them.* The effect was powerful enough to override the propaganda fed to them for years. The HRA crime rates dropped dramatically, and when the number of participating meditators increased, there was a corresponding drop in the HRA rates."

"HRA? What's that?"

"Homicides, rapes, and assaults. After a decade of corporate-sponsored rap music dedicated to drumming the god of bling and use and abuse of other people, and corporate television pounding minds with images of black people in handcuffs – a bunch of friggin' nit-wit hippy meditators broke the spell. The HRA rates dropped almost 25 percent. We nearly crapped a brick, and this project became one of the first large-scale covert operations created to gather intelligence on the escalating gamma wave threat."

"So, what exactly is it that you do here besides watch radar screens and drink coffee?" Ian leaned back in his chair, assessing Ratlig and his mission.

Mark shot Ian a look, but moved on. The Professor wanted McDonald to get this. "At first we were tracking the spread of gamma wave intensity among groups of people using advanced instruments kinda like Geiger counters."

"Geiger counters?"

"Yeah, like the Ghost Busters. That wasn't BS. Paranormal investigators learned a long time ago that Geiger counters could detect gamma waves, which can occur when higher intelligence is present and at that vibratory level – even if it is disembodied consciousness."

"Disembodied? You don't mean – like *spirits?*"

Ratlig gave a shrug.

Ian's mind went back to the spectral image he'd sensed whispering a warning when his limo driver had driven him through Montreal's chilly streets to deliver him to Taloncrag.

Ratlig moved back on point. "On the physical level, which is our issue of concern, gamma waves are brainwave patterns associated with consciousness and perception. They're produced when masses of neurons – a sign of cohesive thought – emit electrical signals at the rate of 40 times per second. That's also called 40 hertz. However, they can even be upwards of 70 Hz.

"Let me back up for you. This is important. Brainwave frequency is measured in cycles per second. Different brainwave activity indicates different levels of consciousness. The lowest frequency is exhibited by delta waves that occur during sleep, below 4 Hz. Between 8 to 13 Hz indicates alpha waves, which are associated with relaxed, quiet times. Beta waves – 15 to 40 Hz – occur during normal daily tasks that require active thinking. Gamma waves – higher than 40 Hz – are involved in higher mental acuity and play an important role in nerve cell communication and integration. Remember the broad swath thinking? That's gamma wave brain activity."

Mark slugged down a mouthful of coffee and continued. "A Geiger counter measures alpha, beta, and gamma wave radiation. It was the gamma wave radiation that paranormal investigators were using as a measure to detect the consciousness of disembodied spirits."

Ian smiled at the thought of this no-nonsense U.S. intelligence officer's serious reference to otherworldly research.

Ignoring him, Mark continued. "Expanding on that paranormal research, we found that thin shields used over Geiger counter wands could block certain kinds of radiation so we could focus on other kinds. For example, paper and aluminum shields block alpha and beta waves, so we can tune in on gamma waves. In normal Geiger counters, a thin mica shield is used, but our bright boys have evolved the technology so we can track high levels of gamma waves in population centers or in small towns worldwide. Right now our lab boys are refining the technology to track individuals of interest."

Mark took another swallow of what had become barely lukewarm coffee, grimacing as his stomach revolted and sent a jolt of acid into his esophagus. He lit yet another cigarette. "What is disturbing the powers that be – the guys who give us our paychecks – is that this resistance to traditional mind control techniques is spreading at an accelerated rate."

Mark waved his hand across the stacks of data readouts and glowing green screens. "We're tracking the gamma wave increases with our instrumentation."

"So what's the game plan?"

"We have to find a test subject who has proven to be impervious to cultural propaganda and to our more radical individually focused tools that control behavior. In recent months we found that this effect – whatever it is – is even making people resistant to direct mind control weapons we've developed using microwaves and other technologies. That's why you're here."

Ian frowned. The Professor had alluded to this. He squirmed. He could not find a comfortable position in his chair. "Microwaves?"

"Yes, microwave technology has been used for years to disrupt thinking. It can make a presidential candidate stumble on his or her words and look like an idiot at a key moment in front of the nation. It can irritate the minds of activists who challenge the system."

Ian looked skeptical, "Surely, this hasn't . . ."

Mark cut him off. "Sure it has. Look back in history, and you'll find that highly articulate candidates have suddenly become inept speakers at key national debates at key moments in campaigns. And it is always the candidate who would reduce the military-industrial complex.

"But, of course, media stories help spin things. They can forgive a truly idiot candidate for lunatic remarks off the cuff, and they can thoroughly destroy another candidate by isolating his scream at a loud campaign rally, conveniently cutting the crowd noise to make him appear to be out of his mind.

"The media's focus on horse-race banter instead of substance helps, too. The inane discussions of, 'he's poised,' 'he's presidential,' 'he's irritating,' 'he's witty,' take up time that could be used to discuss actual positions on issues. This isn't a pure science, but a multi-dimensional art – the art of shaping consciousness.

"Anyway . . . " Mark swept his hand, as if clearing the air to move on. "There is one particular person who has risen to a level of prominence. Even among media heavyweights she has become something of a darling. Our main problem with her is that even the direct application of microwaves is not disrupting her speech or performance. This is disturbing. But as so often happens in life, crisis can become opportunity. She offers us the opportunity to find out why her mind is different and to help us develop ways to remove this problem in others."

Anticipating a question Ian hadn't even thought of, Mark continued, "Oh, we could *remove* her, and we may still do it. We've located other gamma wave disturbances across the globe, and we've simply dispatched elite forces to eliminate them, most recently a particularly troublesome bunch in the mountains of Tibet. But these eliminations are dangerous and costly, and they are not stopping the spread of the problem."

Mark waved his hand across his stacks of data sheets. "The boys upstairs are getting anxious. The gamma wave phenomenon is spreading too quickly. They need an antidote *tout suite!* We need to have a guinea pig – a quintessential guinea pig – and soon!"

Mark drew deeply on yet another cigarette and watched the exhaled smoke drift through the green light. With a concluding sweep of his hand, he dismissed all responsibility as he sighed, "But that's the Professor's department, and yours, too, I suppose."

# 8. The Volume Increases

*Where there is no vision, the people perish . . .*
— Proverbs, 29:18

*Believe me, it is not the technology guys that are holding this back [enacting cost effective compassionate global solutions to world poverty] . . .*
— Dean Kamen, American Inventor and Entrepreneur, Sundance Channel, Iconoclast Series, 2006

*Reports from Rangoon suggest soldiers are mutinying . . . have turned their weapons against other government troops . . . and are defending the protesters.*
— *The First Post,* NewsDeskSpecial.co.uk, September 2007

———————

Rachel handed Ravi a package sent by their mother as they were driven across Washington, D.C. toward the National Press Club, and then went back to checking her email. Her fears of mass cancellations of Ravi's speaking engagements had not come to pass; on the contrary, her email box was jammed with urgent requests for Ravi to speak at upcoming events. It was true some staunchly traditional institutions had decided to pass on Ravi after the Oxford incident, but many other offers took their place.

Rachel had the difficult job of deciding which ones to take. Stephen Colbert's people wanted her badly, as did Jon Stewart and the Sunday morning news programs. Even Saturday Night Live had emailed her, referring to Ravi as *a phenomenon.* A Toyota Prius hybrid car drove by, sporting a bright bumper sticker on the back window reading, "Ravi for President!"

Ravi opened her mother's package, finding a copy of the current TIME Magazine, with her own glowing face on the cover. "Woman of the Year" was printed beneath it. Paper-clipped to the cover's upper left-hand corner was a note penned in her mother's handwriting. *I am so very proud of you — and so is your father. I* know *he is.*

Ravi smiled. Her mother was probably showing the magazine to everyone, from strangers at the supermarket to her musician friends, and everyone in between. She didn't begrudge her mother this. She had been ill and despondent since Ravi's father died, and she was glad that her mother was excited about something.

She placed the magazine in her briefcase, preferring not to spend time on such flattery, but rather on being fully in the moment at hand. She was walking a tightrope. Ravi didn't want to be seduced by her rapid ascendance to fame or distracted by the need to be popular. So much had happened so fast, she barely understood what was happening to her – it was frightening and yet exciting.

It was important not to seek approval from those who heard her. This was the problem most celebrities had with public life: There was a danger of needing the public life to continue, for the excitement of notoriety – the big house – the money – but ultimately for the approval that these things represented.

She had to speak for truth, not for popularity.

The media attention had not all been good. Talk radio and certain television cable news pundits had begun rumblings of discord about Ravi's *channeled visions,* as they called them with a sneer. Even the phrase *false prophet* had been bandied about.

For her to hold onto the good would entail holding onto the bad as well, and there was no room for flow if she indulged in grasping for either.

Ravi's recent years of tai chi study and earlier years of yoga training taught her that to hold onto anything impedes both the body's ability to open to energy and oxygen and the mind's ability to open to new information and possibilities. To harbor pride in her heart would impede the full breadth of what needed to be expressed through her.

This was equally true of self-doubt or fear or any other emotion. Emotions were meant to flow through us as we experience them, and it was unhealthy to cling to them. She had tried to express this theory of flow in her microbanking work, suggesting that money was liquid energy, that it should be held lightly and allowed to flow to where it was most needed in order to do the most good. It was remarkable that the microbanks that regularly made loans to impoverished people in the developing world had a higher payback rate than banks in wealthy nations that loaned only to upper middle income and wealthy people.

Ravi watched out the window of her limousine as they passed monuments to liberty and freedom. Her mother and father had both been great fans of the American democratic experiment and had made their home here for many years before Ravi was born as a U.S. citizen. They saw America as a shining light of hope for all who yearned for freedom and justice worldwide, and they were devastated when the American public had been so easily misled into unleashing one preemptive war after another against the oil-rich nations of the Gulf region and the Middle East.

The ivory Washington Monument stood tall, pointing to the blue heavens above. The shimmering reflecting pool connected Washington's early vision to the symbol of freedom, the Lincoln Memorial. Ravi's eye was caught by the statue that stood above the silent Vietnam Memorial that warned of the horrors a government was capable of inflicting on its own people and those a world away.

The hope and pain represented by the Mall's elegantly intertwined monuments pulled at her heart. She wanted so much for her country and the world. Great hope and great despair were only a breath away from one another, just as these monuments stood side by side. A small turning of human consciousness would determine so much for so many.

Ravi watched the growing army of homeless people wandering through D.C., between the monuments of compassion, courage, and power. A *grapes of wrath* population had expanded, wearing the ragtag uniform of growing poverty, as over the years of the endless war on terror, America's economic might tilted more and more heavily toward the side of military spending. Ravi's thoughts flowed with the passing scenes, until suddenly she was rocked into Rachel as the driver pulled sharply over to the curb. Ravi and Rachel watched as several uniformed men in battle gear approached their car. Rachel lowered her window.

The officer who appeared to be in charge looked at Ravi and then at Rachel. "Good morning. May I see your papers or other form of ID?"

Ravi nervously rifled through her pocketbook for her ID, but Rachel's big-sister scrappiness kicked in as she watched Ravi's nervousness. Rachel, with her degree in constitutional law from Roosevelt University in Chicago, had a few pertinent questions, and she fired them in staccato manner at the officer. "Why did you stop us? Are you an Army unit?"

His pale blue eyes looked over his dark sunglasses, as he replied, "Yes, ma'am, we are Army, and this is a new security checkpoint. We stopped you for a routine check."

"Sir, are you aware that the Posse Comitatus Act of 1878 prohibits the use of U.S. military as a domestic police force, except under special circumstances or by an act of Congress? I haven't heard of a change in the Constitution or of an act authorizing this!"

The soldier bristled at the affront to his authority, but remained business-like, replying coolly, "Perhaps you are unaware of the National Security and Homeland Security Presidential Directives NSPD51 and HSPD20, and House Resolution 5122 of 2007." He paused and then added, "If you were aware of it, you'd know that it enables domestic law enforcement by the U.S. military whenever the President declares a national crisis. Currently the nation's Homeland Security level is on Red Alert, due to a terrorist act in Tibet and possible homeland strikes."

Rachel's voice rose. "The Presidency cannot declare that they have sole power over the nation. It's unconstitutional!"

A flash of anger shone in the officer's eyes before he slid his dark sunglasses up his nose, covering them. He drew himself up. "Ma'am, the Presidency has had that power since 2007, and it does today." Lifting his sunglasses off his eyes for a moment, he peered down at the colorful traditional saris the women were wearing, then dropped his glasses and spoke through their dark anonymity, "I wouldn't expect you to know all the laws of the United States, ma'am. Just hand me your papers."

Two soldiers behind the officer moved forward as if to back up his authority. He held up a hand to keep them behind him.

Rachel nearly yelled, "What? Why would I not know the laws of *my own country?*"

Ravi had found her driver's license and offered it to the officer, while speaking under her breath to Rachel. "Rachel, please, the man is only doing his job."

Rachel wouldn't be suppressed, as she began to rant at Ravi. "Oh yes, that is what the Nazis said, isn't it? Only doing our job." Then she turned again to confront the officer. "And let me ask you, why is it that you did not ask our Caucasian driver, for his papers, but only asked my little sister and me? *We are Americans, dammit!*" Rachel's voice broke in a moment of emotion as she was forced to defend her citizenship in her own homeland, something she'd had to do too many times, especially since the war on terror began.

Ravi's eyes widened with worry and embarrassment as the officer once more scanned their saris and dismissed Rachel's claim of American citizenship with two sarcastic syllables. "Uh huh." Ravi's mediating efforts dissolved as she felt a flash of anger.

At that critical moment, the humor that had served Father so well as a diplomat emerged through Rachel, as she spoke with a deliberate imitation of a southern drawl, "If we all had ta give up our heritage to be Americans, then we'd both be speakin' Cherokee, huh, sheriff?"

The officer leaned down to their window to look directly into Rachel's eyes as his hand touched his side-arm. Then the corner of his lips formed a small smile, belying the hardness of his sunglassed eyes, as he replied, "Okay, hon, I guess ya got me there." At that moment, a disturbance broke out in the street.

Across the intersection, a man on a bicycle wearing a Washington Redskins cap had been asked for his papers, and he had none with him. When the trooper pulled out handcuffs, the startled man became unstable, falling off his bike. As he struggled to his feet, he pleaded, "Wait, I have them at home. I just went out to get milk for my kids' cereal. They're in the apartment waiting for me. You can't take me in!"

Another soldier stepped up from behind, pushing him forward. The man and his bike knocked into the first soldier, and a small group of converging onlookers surged forward to see what was happening.

The first soldier stumbled back, grabbing his baton automatically. He brought it out, up, and down on the man's head and shoulders with a sharp crack. The man slid to the ground, his bike falling on top of him.

Angry shouts rose from some in the gathering crowd of morning commuters, and a couple of soda cans came flying toward the soldiers. The other troops turned to face the crowd with batons lifted.

An elderly black woman looked earnestly into the face of a young soldier, as if scolding her own grandson, "Baby, that man did nothin' wrong. You know better than to treat people like that!"

Another soda can hit the baton-wielding soldier on the back as he stood over the sprawled man, commanding, "Stay on the ground. Do not move!"

The man began to rise, pleading, "Man, my kids are at home alone. This is friggin' nuts!" With his movement, everything came unraveled.

The club came smashing down again. "I told you to stay DOWN!" The man cowered back and away from the trooper. "Down! Stay down! Hands behind your back, NOW!"

The man's surging adrenaline sent him into a flight response. He scrambled back and away from the soldier's club as it came down on him again and again.

Another club-wielding soldier approached from behind the crab-crawling man to block his escape.

Rachel and Ravi watched from their car. The officer who'd challenged them turned and began to move toward the disturbance. Another trooper stepped between the prostrate man and the soldier who stood above him. The second trooper grabbed the other's baton as he raised it, and said, "That's enough."

The bicyclist held his wrist, damaged by the blows, which was bent at an odd angle and hanging loosely. He looked at his misshapen arm with horror and pain.

The soldiers, confused, did not know what to do. The young soldiers were not trained as police officers; they were Army troops trained to deal with foreign enemies, now shouldered with this new duty, "enhanced homeland security."

Some took sides with their comrade who had administered the beating, some with the one who'd stopped it. Soldiers began squaring off against other soldiers, and batons were raised. Then one crashed down, and a sea of green fatigues swarmed in on one another.

The officer approaching from Ravi's car yelled at the top of his lungs, trying to bring order. The crowd drew closer and cheered for the soldiers who were trying to stop the beating.

A trooper stepped toward the limo, instructing Ravi's driver, "Move along, nothin' to see here." The driver stepped on the gas, accelerating away from the melee. As they left the commotion behind them, Ravi and Rachel twisted in their seats to look through the back window. From this vantage point, they saw fast-moving television and radio crews moving in to cover the riot.

The reporters had originally gathered for a press conference at the checkpoint for a story on the recent implementation of the Homeland Security Act. They now moved quickly out of the press zone to film the scene with boom mikes extended out over the ruckus.

Rachel turned back to her laptop as Ravi watched the scene behind them shrink into the distance. While they drove toward Ravi's speaking engagement, the driver switched on the radio. A newscast was in progress. Both sisters looked up. "This is a FAX National Radio News Special Report. Just in, in metro D.C. only moments ago, an unruly citizen provoked soldiers at a Homeland Security checkpoint. Force was required to quell the disturbance, and several soldiers were injured. The suspect is reportedly in custody and is being hospitalized with possible bone fractures. The charges against him are yet to be determined. Now, let's turn to economic news . . ."

The driver turned off the radio with a smirk. "So much for the fourth estate." Ravi and Rachel exchanged nervous glances, rattled by the distorted reporting on what they had witnessed only moments before.

The limo stopped outside the National Press Club. Established in 1908, the Press Club was a celebrated landmark that embodied the very spirit of the country's freedom of the press. Ravi and Rachel were met at the car by an entourage that escorted them inside to the elevator, where they quickly ascended to the famed thirteenth floor. Here renowned speakers had enlivened the many meeting rooms with their presence for over a century. Passing by the Murrow Room, named after Edward R. Murrow, a journalist who put everything on the line to kindle the nation's rejection of political witch hunts in the 1950s, they moved on to their destination. Because of Ravi's sudden ascendance to the status of an unofficial national leader, her speech today was to be given in the vast Ballroom.

After her introduction, Ravi stood before the collection of microphones and representatives of international media seated before her with pads and pens in hand. Her heart began to beat faster. Suddenly Ravi felt a sense of confusion and disorientation, as if something, *someone,* were reaching into her brain. Her pulse quickened even more, and she felt her chest tighten as her cranial muscles gripped her skull. The crowd had begun to fidget and whisper to one another.

Ravi took a deep qigong cleansing breath, and immediately a cool lightness spread through her. Her muscles relaxed into the mode of *letting go,* which had allowed the unprepared words to flow through her at Oxford and at other engagements since. In the quiet space, the oscillation of sound she'd come to know began its multi-octave drone, vibrating her being with a knowing that couldn't be practiced or scripted.

Ravi began, "The physical world you see is a mere reflection of your consciousness. We are in effect, *dreaming our world.* In the past it took centuries or even millennia to bring complex visions and dreams into physical reality. However, the line of time has shortened. Today we are experiencing a quickening.

"Before humanity's existence, evolutionary change occurred at the speed of biological change, a slow, glacial pace of subtle quiet changes. However, once human beings came on the scene, the speed of change increased dramatically, and vast changes were made across the planet, often in the lifetime of one single generation. The printed word further accelerated change, and then radio and television shifted change up into fourth and fifth gear.

"However, the advent of the internet moved change into light-speed, as dreams and visions began to root in our global reality within nano-seconds of their creation in the human mind. Intellectual tidal waves that could both create and prevent wars shot across the webbed landscape of consciousness that we all know as the internet. Whole economies could be shifted as knowledge of an innovative idea could be creatively shared with the world through wired and wireless information networks spanning the globe and connecting all of humanity.

"Bill Joy, Chief Scientist for Sun Microsystems, a company whose technology provided the very backbone of the original internet, explained years ago that the speed of technological change is now doubling every few months.

"But again, this physical internet connection of humanity is a mirror reflecting to us what is occurring *within our consciousness.* Humanity is being pressed to change the way we think. We are becoming collectively conscious, aware of our interdependence – opening to the collective unconscious that Carl Jung wrote of a century ago. Our planet's physical evolution, intensified by humanity's social and technological progression, has led to a time in history where the next stage of the evolution of life will be on the level of consciousness. The next leap of development for our world will not be physical, for we have explored and exploited our entire planet to the breaking point. The only frontier left is *within.*

"The Roman Emperor Marcus Aurelius once said, *The world you see is the one created with your own thoughts.* His life embodied this. He ended the barbaric gladiator games in Rome and worked to stop the persecution of Christians, both revolutionary changes for his time. Today we have the power through technology to do far greater things – or far more terrible things."

Ravi pressed forward on the podium, her hands gripping the sides as she leaned toward the audience.

Penetrated by Ravi's dark eyes, the people present and the TV audience were captivated. Even the wait staff serving the tables stopped to listen to her. Her voice became deeper, more resonant, and powerful.

"We are now wielding the power of gods! We must begin to act with the wisdom of God, for the world we dream is becoming reality at a staggering pace. We cannot stumble blindly into our future as past generations have. The margin for error is shrinking. Our hope should be limitless, but not careless. It is time for each of our decisions and actions to become conscious ones. The products we use, the entertainment we support, the governments we elect – all must ride on one question, *what nurtures the interconnected web of life?*

"We are a collective consciousness. Our thoughts can contaminate the river of life or they can purify it. Our thoughts matter. We are seeing and will see more and more clearly that the physical world is the reflection of our minds, and not the other way around. Please cherish our world with me, for it is precious – as are you."

Ravi's demeanor became more intense. With each word, she leaned further into the podium, the cameras, and America's living rooms. "It is critical to consider those who are fervently pointing to what is being called *the end times*. They point to wars and conflict, or to the declining environmental state of our planet, as indicative of the end times and God's coming wrath.

"This is misleading and dangerous, and must be dismissed, for the intensification of life we feel is due to the growth of the human population. Humanity has grown exponentially in recent years. When the first modern humans appeared on earth around 160,000 BC, the human population grew relatively slowly.

"However, since World War II's population of two billion, we have grown as a species to nearly 10 billion in 2013. After taking 162,000 years to get to two billion, *we will have nearly quintupled our numbers in only 68 years*. This has sent shockwaves through our collective consciousness and the planet.

"But the pressures of the world's burgeoning population, the need for more resources on a finite planet, the strains gathering like a storm, and the environmental shifts spreading across our world are all as it should be. This time and these challenges are here now so that humanity will have no other choice but to learn the wisdom written into the very fabric of the universe. We can no longer run from each other. We must learn how to care for one another, because the earth is so small that when chaos and disruption occur socially or environmentally anywhere, it affects all people everywhere.

"God will not elevator-lift anyone out of this, as some ministers are promising their flocks. We will make of *this earth* a heaven or a hell. For these challenges are not God's wrath, they are part of our evolution. Now that we've stretched the physical limits of our world, we have no other aspect of reality to stretch than that of humanity's consciousness. The great remaining frontier to be explored is the many dimensions of human awareness. These are the realms of spirituality."

Ravi's arms extended wide, her palms turned up with a question. "What stands in our way of graduating the test of these times?"

She looked into the eyes of the audience, awaiting an answer that none seemed to have. Ravi answered for them. "Nothing. There is nothing in our way. All that is required of us is – *a change of consciousness.* Resources are plentiful if used well, and wisdom is everywhere when we seek it. For example, I saw an image on a box of herbal tea once . . ."

Some in the crowd smiled at the idea of finding great wisdom on a box of tea.

"The tea box had two images, one of hell and one of heaven. In the first image, people sat around a pot of stewing food, starving and emaciated." An ornery smile crossed Ravi's face.

Many seemed perplexed at her amusement at this dreadful image. Ravi quickly explained with her slight Indian-British clip, "I know, that is not a funny image. But the reason for their misery *is* sadly comical. You see, the problem was not that they had no food; it was only that their chopsticks were too long to get food into their own mouths."

Ravi's face became serious. "In the image of heaven the same group sat around the stew pot, this time full and happy *because they had learned to reach across the pot and feed one another."* Many nodded approval, as this simple solution to the strains of the modern world resonated deeply within them.

"Those who preach the desolation of the precious garden God has given us are stale cadavers blocking the way of a new world of vision. God has given us all we need, a world – a school – where we can – indeed, where we are *required* – to practice our evolution of consciousness. Through this long process we have stretched earth's physical limits by expanding our population and our technological constructs. God has positioned us well.

"Now all we need to do is decide whether our profound technological powers will be used to control and destroy in order to sustain a few, or whether we will turn this awesome might toward caring for each individual and the garden God has given us. Everything rides on *a slight turning of the human consciousness,* for as the tea box illustrated, what we need has always been here. It is only our approach that must change, ever so slightly."

The crowd sighed as great tension released, even as tears of relief misted in some eyes. They had been waiting for someone to simply point to what now seemed so obvious: *a world of possibility rather than one of fear and uncertainty.*

"To change the world, we must change our consciousness. How do we shift human consciousness toward compassion on a global scale? To save the world, we must save ourselves. If we as individuals are rigid, our world cannot change. If we can become fluid, our world can transform."

Ravi could see that some were confused. She pondered. *How can I link global and personal consciousness so that they'll understand?*

"Think of it this way: In the evolutionary scheme of life, the critical mass required to elevate consciousness to the human level was 10 billion neurons – the number of neurons in the human brain. Today humanity will soon reach a population of 10 billion. We are rapidly approaching critical mass – we are becoming a *global brain.*

"But how do we change this global mind? Again, we do so by changing our individual central nervous systems. The loosening of the human central nervous system will make everything possible.

"Tomorrow I am inviting one print journalist, one photographer, and one television crew to meet with me. I want to discuss how we can affect the collective consciousness of our society to create a more humane world."

# 9. Tumbling Walls

*Method of Changing a Person's Behavior — A method of conditioning a person's unconscious mind . . . video pictures appearing on a screen . . .*
— United States Patent Office, Patent No. 4,717,343


*We must electrically control the brain. Some day armies and generals will be controlled by electric stimulation of the brain.*
— Dr. Jose Delgado, Director of Neuropsychiatry, Yale University Medical School, Congressional Record No. 26, Vol. 118, February 24, 1974 (MK-ULTRA experimenter who demonstrated a radio-controlled bull on CNN in 1985)


*The director of national intelligence affirmed rather bluntly today that the U.S. intelligence community has authority to target American citizens for assassination.*
— ABC News, Feb. 3, 2010


*Tina Foster, of the US-based International Justice Network, told The Times: "I am in shock that they would do this. It is shocking that our Government would go to these extremes, even depriving someone of their life without a legal process."*
— TimesOnline, UK, April 7, 2010

———————

A light rain begins to fall, giving D.C. a mournful, contemplative look as meteorological tears drip from the sky. Outside the National Press Club, on the corner of F Street and 14th, just blocks from the White House, a man stands — *waiting.*

Unsure why he's standing here, he simply knows to stand and wait. *For what,* he's not sure.

Three hours before, he had awakened, fully clothed, in one of the many vacant and condemned buildings in Columbia Heights, not knowing where he was or how he'd gotten there. He'd lain there watching a rat the size of a small cat rummaging around the filthy kitchen cabinets. By the looks of them, the cabinets had not held any food for a long, *long* while. When a cockroach climbed up his sleeve, he got up.

Leaving the rat-infested tenement, he had no idea where to go. He had simply put one foot in front of the other, wandering down through Malcolm X Park, barely noticing the statues he passed – James Buchanan, Joan of Arc, and Dante.

His walk had led him to a bus stop. A bus had pulled up and ground to a halt, the door hissing open before him. He had stepped on, his heart accelerating as he'd reached into his pocket, hoping he had enough money for bus fare. He did. In fact, the bus fare was exactly what he'd had, not a penny more or less.

At certain moments, his hand had reached up, grabbing the cord to signal his stop, and he'd gotten off. When other buses had pulled up, he either stepped onto them or not, offering his transfer pass to the driver. His travels eventually had led him down 13th Street to Vermont Ave. NW, then back east through the shadow of the valley of government lobbying known as K Street. Finally, the last bus had stopped, the door had opened, and now here he was standing at F Street and 14th – *waiting*.

Above his head, the sign reads, "The National Press Club." He sees only the blur of passing pedestrians and busy traffic. He sees no individuals, but a sea of human activity flashing across his vision.

Waiting brings back a memory. He remembers sitting in a waiting room in a place that was white and shiny. There were people in white coats, and an older man talking to one of them while he waited. *"Scott,"* the older man had said, looking directly at him. *Was my name Scott?*

There was something familiar about the older man. He wanted him to hold him, to love him, not like a lover, but like – a word just on the tip of his mind flitted around him like a butterfly. *Like a father.*

Another memory arose. There were sparkling crystal goblets and glittering candelabras, elegant parties where he was to be seen and not heard. There had been a dinner at the White House where his father had barely acknowledged his presence and did not introduce him to any of the important people.

Scott's father had been a power broker who traveled in wealthy circles. His business contacts and lofty social position placed him in the right place at the right time.

However, Scott had found himself in exactly the wrong place at the wrong time since the very beginning. His delivery had been difficult, and his mother had died four years later, never having fully recovered from childbirth. His father had never forgiven him.

Going through his teenage years at the height of his father's ascension to power guaranteed that he would become a troubled young man. His father was so crushingly successful he knew he'd never measure up, and Father did not hide his disappointment. Even in the best of times, Scott had never been more than an inconvenience.

The normal strain of adolescent change, coupled with his own self-worth issues, had been too much for him. His angry and sometimes cruel behavior toward weaker students had become intolerable to the administrators at his prestigious school. He had been forced to seek treatment.

It was at this time that Scott's father needed money *badly,* and not just a little. A series of bad investments was beginning to bring down his house of power and prestige. He'd squandered a massive fortune and had accumulated serious debts. If funds could not be acquired quickly, he would have to borrow from his lesser – but richer – associates and endure the embarrassment of groveling to people he'd spent many years denigrating and humiliating. He'd be a laughingstock among his peers.

Scott has a faint memory of hearing the maids at their palatial home whispering about some very expensive scandals involving very young women and their very angry and money-hungry parents.

Scott's father knew the CIA was involved in human experimentation, dedicating a substantial percentage of their overall funding to it. Staggering amounts of money were changing hands in a frenzy to create, expand, and maintain this program, called MK-ULTRA. His father had overheard enough conversations at the club to know what he needed to know.

There was little downside. The experiments were being done at a highly respected mental hospital. Scott needed treatment – everyone knew that. This hospital would be as good as any to anyone not in the know. But Scott's father knew. A few well placed phone calls assured him that Scott's services as a subject in the experiments at the hospital would procure a handsome reward, even by his standards. *Mind control* might actually do Scott some good, as he was increasingly out of control.

Standing on 14th Street, Scott feels little. He is an observer, not a participant in these memories. The images flow almost without any connection to him, as if he is seeing a film about someone else's life. Then his hands tighten into fists as his mind returns to the white room that now is clearly a hospital. Scott's heart beats faster, as memories leap out at him from the halls of the institution.

He was sitting in the waiting room where his father was discussing his imminent admission with a tall, striking man with a British accent. Scott knew his future in this shiny white place even as his father was checking him in. His heart pounded furiously as the tall doctor looked appraisingly at him and his own father signed away his life on a clipboard form. Scott opened his mouth to scream, "Father! Daddy! PLEASE, NO!"

The memory was too much. The hospital – Father – the pain. The images disappeared as suddenly as a TV screen goes black when the plug is pulled.

Suddenly he is back on the street, still waiting for *something*, something he isn't supposed to know yet. This channel is forbidden until it is time to watch it. His mind had changed momentarily to that other channel that showed the past, as a defective television might lose its main signal, but now he is back on the channel he'd been watching all along.

He once again had become *the waiting man*.

A clamor drew his attention as a crowd of what appeared to be reporters rushed out of a side door and around toward the front of the building. The front door opened, and a young Indian woman in a colorful sari stepped out. The waiting man's hand instinctively reached toward his waist, and his fingers found something rigid tucked into his waistband beneath his shirt. His fingers wrapped around it. It fit well in his hand, one finger encircling the trigger.

He wasn't sure how – but he *knew* that this was the trigger of a Charter Arms .38 revolver containing hollow-point bullets,

A tall, well dressed man with an umbrella was also waiting farther down the street. Many were concerned about the effect this woman was having on the public. Ravi's ramblings had grown too loud, too fast. Rapid action was required. The hope of having a guinea pig had to be released in favor of a more expedient solution. Fortunately, they'd spent years creating tools to handle such solutions.

The tall man approached the waiting man standing in front of the building, whose hand still lingered on the weapon concealed beneath his untucked shirt. The tall man was perhaps a bit irritated at the commotion on the sidewalk as he walked around the crowd. The tall man popped open his black umbrella as he passed the waiting man, shielding himself from the press. He turned toward the armed man and began to sing softly under his breath words from the song, *Singin' in the Rain.* And then quickly he was gone.

The waiting man's fingers closed on the weapon. He began to move forward, pressing through the crowd – toward the woman.

Ravi and Rachel pushed through the throng toward their waiting vehicle, which was only a few feet from them, but might as well have been miles at the pace they were going. All the attending media wanted to be the first one with *the line,* the magical line that all the other broadcasts would pick up in the coming news cycle.

Suddenly, Ravi was stopped in her tracks by a feeling of absolute terror. She felt her heart grip in her chest. Stumbling, she nearly fell as she tried to catch her breath. Her left hand flailed at the air for support – support that wasn't there because Rachel had already moved on toward the waiting car.

Disoriented, Ravi was swept up in a tide of hopelessness, a feeling of being utterly abandoned by life and by everyone in the world. An image flashed before her of doctors and white rooms, fear and desolation, pain, and impersonal cold-minded cruelty that filled the world completely.

In the next instant, the fear was replaced by the vibration Ravi had first felt at the Oxford Club, the multi-octave chant. She drew her awareness into her body and focused on a yogic breathing technique. Deep full breaths lifted her from within, and great releasing exhales cleansed her as if each atom within her were radiating soothing energy. The vibration increased to a deafening crescendo. Ravi was stunned by its volume, even as the crowd remained oblivious to the sound accompanying the shifting tides within her.

A television newswoman was the first to scream as the man raised a handgun, aiming directly into Ravi's face. The crowd peeled away like the parting Red Sea, forming a V with Ravi at the tip, as the armed man walked purposefully toward her. Ravi was hopelessly stuck in front of the thick crowd, who could back up no farther; any retreat was blocked by the building. The crowd grew silent. The only sound was Ravi's deep breathing.

For Ravi, the pulsing vibration had become all encompassing, though the others seemed unable to hear or feel it. Except for the young man holding the weapon. *He hears it too!* Ravi watched his hands fly upward to cover both of his ears – with such force that his gunsight scraped his head just above his right ear. Blood trickled down the side of his face. Ravi watched his confused eyes flinch at the sounds that no one but she, and apparently now this man, could hear.

The same confusion suddenly filled Ravi's mind. She lost her sense of self; her eyes could no longer see the crowd or the man with the gun. She fell into a world of turmoil – *his world.* White rooms – cold white-coated people wielding even colder instruments stood over her.

Then everything came back into focus: the crowd cowering against the wall of the building, the young man with the gun before her. The faces and the city swirled around her. She could not remember who she was. *How did I get here?*

The gunman suddenly turned away from Ravi, looking up at the surrounding buildings as if seeing them for the first time. The crowd gasped as his weapon swept the area around him, including all of them as potential targets.

The man barely noticed their reaction, as the hammering tremor within him rattled apart a complex construction of hallways – a confusing mental maze of white tile and chrome. He cowered as though the buildings around him were tumbling down. He bobbed and ducked to avoid debris from the crumbling walls.

The crowd dodged and weaved each time he did, to avoid being in the line of fire of his wildly waving pistol. What was going on in this man's head?

The increasing vibration unglued the walls of Scott's mind – walls that had been carefully constructed through years of invasive manipulation.

Scott's upheaval escalated. His memories of the tall doctor – the needles, shocks, and despair – it was beyond suffering. *The doctor was just here, singing to me! Why?* Suddenly, he saw exactly where he was, here in the present. Buildings stood all around him. *Who are all these people? Why am I holding this gun?* The world swirled. He felt nausea and vertigo. *How did I get here?*

The oscillating sound – now clearly the resonance of many voices chanting – grew inside Scott's head. As he looked into Ravi's eyes, she saw his demeanor change, as if gossamer veils were lifting off his face, revealing a long lost lucidity. His cold menace melted into a countenance of vast sorrow. He began rubbing his ears. He dropped his weapon to the sidewalk so he could put both hands over his ears to block out the noise.

A security guard leapt at the man, simultaneously kicking the weapon away. One of the reporters picked up the gun, holding it with his fingertips as if it were contaminated. Other journalists helped the guard subdue the man. A police car arrived, siren screaming and lights flashing.

In the confusion, Rachel pulled Ravi into their waiting car and ordered their driver to get moving. He needed no prompting. He stomped on the gas even before Rachel's door closed fully, the car's acceleration slamming the heavy limo door shut.

Rachel nervously watched the scene behind them, her eyes darting all around for more danger, before she turned back to Ravi, eyes aflame. "Ravi, this is crazy! You can't be thinking of continuing this *crusade,* or whatever you think it is! These creeps will turn up out of the woodwork. Have you thought maybe the world's not ready for what you're saying? You know I was on board for your economics work, but what you're doing and saying now . . . " Her voice trailed off.

Ravi took long, slow breaths to calm herself. The deafening chant she had been hearing had diminished. "I-I-I haven't thought of that."

She looked beyond Rachel, searching for words to explain. "What I've been doing hasn't been a conscious decision, not the kind we normally make. But I feel that I'm somehow moving more consciously than I ever have before, as if a kind of super-consciousness were coming through, and it has some purpose larger than I can conceive. I believe if I try to reduce it to a logical explanation, it will disappear – like trying to grab onto water in a flowing river."

Rachel raised her hand in protest, "But, Ravi, think about . . ."

Ravi interrupted, "What I *do* know is that I am not the only one being pushed to act. That man back there with the gun – he experienced it too, but with him there were two forces. I could feel it happening to him – I felt it myself. I can't explain it. It was some kind of connection between us that stopped him, and saved me."

As confused as she was, Ravi's years of mind/body training had prepared her for what was happening. Her heightened awareness of subtle internal perceptions and powerful stress management techniques enabled her to stay centered in her breath and internal awareness, even at a time of crisis.

This ability opened her mind to broadened consciousness, allowing new inspiration to come through, even as the world around her grew increasingly intense and foreboding.

As Ravi thought about the trauma with the shooter, she did so with a calm focus on the bigger meaning of what had happened. Ravi was learning that all events had purpose. She was sensing the universe as a web where all things, all people, and all events were connected.

As she watched the city roll by, she mused upon the larger issue of how this event influenced her next step in unveiling humanity's potential. Her mind hummed, as a message formed – the near act of criminal violence – the young man's transformation from mindlessness, to sorrow, to clarity – her promise to the media.

*How can I explain to them* . . . not just how individual consciousness can more rapidly evolve, but how *all of human consciousness can evolve as a collective entity?*

Suddenly it came to her: *Folsom Prison.*

# 10. The Center of the Universe ~ Folsom Prison

*Profits oil the machinery, keep it humming and speed its growth.*
— Judith Greene, Essay, *Prison Profiteers: Who Makes Money from Mass Incarceration?*

*"[Mary] Tell us the words of the Savior . . . which you know, but we do not . . . " Mary answered, "What is hidden from you I will proclaim to you."*
— The Gospel of Mary, 7:6-7, and 9:4, 9:7-8

*Woman's world is her husband, her family, her children and her home. We do not find it right when she presses into the world of men.*
— Adolf Hitler, quoted in *The New Feminism*, Lucy Komisar

---

A stretch limousine, followed by a news van, pulled up in front of the high granite walls and steel mesh gates of the California Maximum Security Prison at Folsom in Northern California. Ravi stepped out, her colorful flowing sari in bright contrast to the solemn gray walls and guard towers high above. Rachel had declined to attend today's press conference, claiming that the near assassination in Washington had fried her nerves. Ravi, undaunted, was eager for today's event. She put her hands into the small of her back and arched her spine, looking up at a perfect blue sky.

A black woman reporter from TIME Magazine and an Asian woman reporter from The Washington Post followed Ravi out of the limo they'd shared from the airport. The television crew emerged from their van, including a woman from CNN with smartly bobbed blond hair, her cameraman, and a sound tech.

Ravi led them from the parking area up toward the towering prison walls. The group crested a hill; then Ravi turned off the main path to enter a small open-air hut. A female guard stood impassively behind the desk inside it. The entourage crowded in around Ravi as she shook hands with the guard.

Surveying the group, the guard was brusque. "My job is to prepare you for the world within the walls of the maximum security penal institution that is Folsom State Prison. All belts must come off and be checked here with us before you enter." Looking down at the cameraman's and sound technician's blue jeans, she added, "No blue jeans allowed in the prison. You'll have to take those off and put these on. There's a bathroom over there." Ignoring their groans of protest, she held out two pairs of surgical scrub pants.

The two men took the pants and headed to the bathroom to change, until the guard, without looking up from her clipboard, added, "Wait. Before you go, one last thing. All of you must sign a release form that states if you are taken hostage, the warden will not negotiate for your release."

The room fell silent. Where they were, and where they were about to go, began to sink in for real. Confronted with the 17-foot-high solid granite walls of the prison just beyond the hut, they looked into each other's eyes and saw their own growing trepidation reflected back to them. Adam's apples lurched as throats constricted, and sweaty palms were wiped on shirts and pants.

. . . .

The guard pressed a large red button, producing a bone-jarring buzz. A mechanical-sounding voice rasped from the speaker above the door: "Clear the door!"

A heavy metal lock clicked and slammed within the door, and its bulk swung open for them. They entered a chamber, and the heavy door clanged closed behind them, as the locks reversed their movements. The sounds seemed much louder from the inside.

Each member of the group placed their equipment on an inspection table and lifted their arms as instructed by a guard with a metal detecting wand.

Another guard beyond the holding chamber unlocked the next interior door, allowing them to exit the entrance chamber into the prison proper. Again they were scanned with metal detectors, the camera and sound equipment were inspected, and then a burly guard motioned for Ravi to follow him. The group followed like school children trying to stay close to their teacher.

They proceeded down the main hall of the prison dormitory. Windows high above allowed a trickle of light to spill down into the otherwise dark hall. The technical crewmen behind Ravi hustled with their heavy equipment. The women reporters, compelled by their training to observe, stared into the constricting dark cells only a few feet to their left as they passed. Tiny cells each housed two prisoners, who had barely enough room to stand when out of their bunks. The claustrophobic weight of this alien world pressed the group onward.

Some prisoners stood in shower lines, holding clean folded prison garments, soap, and shampoo as they waited. As Ravi walked down the hall, a few smatterings of applause came from those who recognized her, along with cat calls and wolf whistles emanating from the dark prison cells. The media entourage followed even more closely behind Ravi and their escort as they descended deeper into the bowels of the prison. More doors unlocked before them and then slammed locked behind them. It was like entering the colossal jaws of a concrete and steel Venus Fly Trap, always opening to the victim, but with no intention of ever letting them out.

Ravi walked out into the prison yard, navigating the group through the labyrinth of razor wire fences. The yard was a large dirt lot nestled within the shadows of the looming prison dormitories, but it wasn't completely open, as sections of it were separated from each other by a maze of chain link fences topped with barbed wire.

Ravi remained unfazed, turning to face the reporters while the guard waited patiently. She appeared so at home and relaxed, she might have been giving a tour of her garden – a garden framed by the dangerous gleam of concertina razor wire. The cameraman hoisted his camera to his shoulder to focus on her, as the sound tech held the boom mic with the large fuzzy end over Ravi's head just out of camera range. He watched for cues from the cameraman, who raised his camera to frame Ravi's soft feminine image against the hard gray armed guard towers behind.

She began. "Dear friends, yesterday at the National Press Club, I spoke about the stresses that humanity faces, resulting from an expanding population sharing finite global resources – but also about the technological revolutions that make a whole new abundant way of life possible for us all. You may remember I concluded with the problem, and that problem was the struggle of human consciousness to make the changes required to enact a mutually uplifting technological revolution of abundance, rather than one that spirals downward in conflicts over resource-sharing, favoring tools of fear and control. Today, we will explore what holds us back and how humans can accelerate their ability to evolve consciousness, not just individually, but as a whole.

"I repeat what I said yesterday: The loosening of the human central nervous system will make everything possible.

"I want you to imagine for a moment that here within these high walls and barbed wire of Folsom Prison, we are standing in the center of the universe. The seeds of our world's great hope can blossom in the most unexpected places, and this is one of them. Yet, this place obviously also represents despair, an imbalance in our world.

"Our world is in the process of finding answers to our problems. We are deciding between feminine healing choices and masculine controlling ones. For example, over the last three decades our attempts to solve the problem of criminality have focused on tough prison expansion solutions. This hard approach trumped the more feminine concepts of reform and healing to solve crime problems.

"Today we taxpayers spend $55 billion per year nationally for prison costs alone, not counting court, police, and other related costs – four times more than we did three decades ago. Has this made our nation four times safer, as politicians promised? Obviously not.

"Here we see the quintessential hardened symbol of our world's imbalance, weighted toward masculine or control energy. Chinese mystics would have called it yang energy. Yesterday I spoke of a compassionate, mutually supportive global vision, which is a feminine or yin vision. Today you will see Folsom as a point where the endless futility of masculine dominance intersects with the unveiling hope of healing compassion like the overlapping waves of the yin-yang symbol.

"The world's imbalance toward the masculine we see here," Ravi extended her arms, causing the cameraman to wide-angle his shot to include the gray prison walls around her, "is an ancient story. Jesus saw the need for compassion, for balance, in his time, and his compassion extended to those suffering among us, including those in prison. In fact, Jesus said that how we treat those within these walls is *exactly* how we are treating him, exhibiting with these words a very feminine act of empathy, like a mother who feels for her child as she does for herself.

"The fact that Jesus extolled the nurturing power of humanity may explain why, in the long-lost *Gospel of Mary,* he passed the mantle of the church to Mary, a feminine force. However, our world lost connection with its feminine spirit long ago, when the Gospel of Mary was effectively censored from the Bible, excluded from that holy book just as our feminine energy has been repressed in the world. This denial of feminine power has caused a rent in the soul of mankind for centuries, in both men and women alike.

"The feminine was further denigrated when Mary was slandered as a prostitute, resulting in a further dissolution of feminine energy, which led eventually to millions of outspoken women being murdered in the name of precious Christ throughout Europe by his very church, and even here in what would become the United States during the witch trials. This renunciation of the feminine has hardened the heart of mankind."

Ravi stopped short as a shadow crossed her mind. Her demeanor became more intense as she finished these last words. Her jaw tightened, and her spine stiffened – her instinctual body preparing for – *a knife in her own back.*

Ravi felt a cold chill even as she stood in the sun. The walls drew in, becoming even more colorless. She flashed on the ominous sense of premonition she had experienced when the stocky man gripping his Bible had stormed out during her first message at Oxford, fuming *Blasphemy!* under his breath.

Ravi's far-away eyes revealed the dread stealing her awareness. The Post reporter noticed Ravi's troubled shift and scribbled a note in her pad: *The hardening of humanity that had fallen on the backs of persecuted women, seemed to weigh upon her at this moment.* The sound of pen scratching on paper filled the dead air. The silence expanded. The media members exchanged glances.

Ravi shivered visibly before steadying herself, pulling herself with an act of will back to the moment.

She spoke to the reporters with renewed purpose. "Today we stand at the vortex of a hardened heart, the maximum security prison at Folsom. I chose to deliver my message here for two reasons. First, because this prison reflects a larger trend of hardness in our nation that we should all be aware of. Today the United States imprisons more of our people than any other nation, with more than 2.3 million behind bars, well ahead of China's 1.5 million and Russia's 890,000.

"However, I also chose Folsom for a hopeful reason. For here in the midst of hardened hearts, a miracle is occurring and has been for some time. Here the feminine balance of compassion and caring has permeated the hearts of men who have seen violence, both committed upon them and committed by them. Here in this hardened heart of society, if we can find hope for them, we can find hope for all of humanity."

Many miles away, the eyes of those wielding power had already begun to narrow on their television screens as Ravi's clear voice carried powerful words – threatening words. Her message of hope was stepping on toes. A webbed matrix experienced a disturbance in the field of their control – and a message of alarm quickly spread. The matrix included both those whose power is dependent on getting elected and re-elected, and those who amass great fortunes by propagating a climate of fear and division. They saw no hope or possibility in Ravi's vision of compassion – only a threat to a very lucrative status quo.

For them, the nationwide privatization of penal systems had been the equivalent of a modern gold rush. Among the prospectors were prison corporations, businesses involved in the construction and maintenance of the prisons, and politicians who supported penal privatization. The fever for profits had trickled down to the judicial system and law enforcement, where kickbacks found their way into the wallets of judges who packed the prisons with their harsh sentences, and officers whose skyrocketing arrest rates herded this tragic human stampede into their courts.

A Congressional committee member had once challenged a prison corporation executive, demanding to know if indeed they projected future profits based on the current illiteracy rates of school children. When he admitted that they had, she further demanded that he divulge the fact that his corporation had actively lobbied against education funding, so as to shore up future prison profits.

In the next election, the congresswoman's campaign was overwhelmed by a massive influx of funds donated to her opponent, a free market candidate, who demanded expansion of prison privatization and harsher sentences for all types of offenders.

As Ravi's message of finding hope for humanity was carried to millions via television screens worldwide, a confederacy pulled together. Phones were lifted and connections were made. An emergency meeting was organized, which would soon call upon forces that had been very dependable in the past. They, in turn, would stimulate many more calls.

In the warm California sun shining down upon her, Ravi again felt a cold chill run up her spine.

Ravi's words envisioning inexpensive solutions to societal problems, although hopeful and seemingly non-controversial to the undiscerning viewer, augured the possibility of hundreds of billions of dollars of lost future profits. And Ravi wasn't finished. Before she was done today, she would paint a vision that could cost industries trillions of dollars in annual profits.

Words like these had not gone unnoticed two thousand years ago in the Biblical times Ravi had just referred to — *and they were not going unnoticed today.*

A large shadow passed over Ravi before settling on the ground behind her. The television techs' and reporters' eyes went upward, staring behind Ravi as more than one mouth gaped open.

When Ravi turned around, her colorful sari flowing in the sun of the prison yard, she smiled up at the source of the very large and foreboding shadow. The man towered over her as she spoke. "I want to introduce you to a kindred heart, Tim Franklin. Tim is serving a life sentence for wrongs he has done. But today I honor him for the right he is sharing with his fellow inmates, and, through the select journalists invited to be with us today, with the world.

"So, without further ado, may I present Prisoner #125873, my friend, Tim Franklin."

Franklin, a muscular Caucasian man, stood next to Ravi in his prison fatigues. The big man had an air of calmness and clarity, despite the prison yard, the barbed wire, and the towers that loomed above them. In a deep voice, he began. "I want to welcome you all to Folsom Prison, but more particularly, to our tai chi community. We practice here three times a week in the prison chapel."

Tim swung open the wooden door of the chapel that stood just off the prison yard, and the group entered its dark confines. Three dozen prisoners sat watching seven other prisoners who moved through the gentle contemplative postures of tai chi, all breathing in unison. The trepidation and fear of the infamous Folsom Prison that the reporters and their support staff had experienced faded. They could have been in a church or park anywhere in the world, watching ordinary people flowing through the peaceful movements before them. A softness permeated the air.

Big Tim led the group deeper into the chapel, as he spoke quietly to Ravi's media entourage. "Here in Folsom, like in most prisons, inmates are divided racially and tend to stay with their own kind. This is a survival mechanism, because to be alone with no allies can mean constant abuse and sometimes even death. So whites entering prison often gravitate to the Aryan Nations, while blacks go to the brotherhood of the various versions of Crips or Bloods, and Latinos to the Norteño – Northern California gangs – or Sureño – Southern gangs – or the Mexican Mafia. There are also Native American gangs."

As he spoke, the media members looked around at the Latino, black, Indian, and white inmates who sat with each other, watching other prisoners of various races doing tai chi together. Tim continued, "But here in our tai chi and meditation group, we have never had racial problems. Here we have created a sanctuary of acceptance. When one practices these techniques, there is a serenity and peace that flows through the body and mind. All of us here know what that feels like."

Turning to the seated inmates, he spoke a little more loudly, "Am I right, my brothers?"

"Thas' right! You know thas' right!" the men responded. One young black man sitting near Tim reached out to slap his hand before grasping it in a thumb-lock handshake.

Ravi smiled at the scene. "Tim has kept statistics of incident rates here at Folsom since this tai chi program began."

The CNN reporter asked, "I'm sorry, incident rates?"

"Yes, that refers to infractions committed by inmates who break the rules, anything from fights to disobedience."

Big Tim stepped in with enthusiasm, "Yes, when we began the tai chi meditation program at Folsom we began to see incident rates dropping among the participating prisoners."

Ravi exclaimed, "But what is so very exciting is that the incident rates throughout the entire prison have fallen since the beginning of the tai chi program. The entire community has been influenced by the calming and healing of a few."

The media people smiled, exchanging glances, as they watched little Ravi almost elbowing big Tim aside in her enthusiasm to tell the story. Tim and Ravi were like two children, both excited to tell their version of things that had happened at school that day.

The CNN reporter pointed a microphone at Ravi. "How do you explain that?"

Ravi had become so effervescent that even big Tim, who'd lost the battle for the mic, had to smile. "I have two explanations, one physical," she said, continuing with a coy smile, "And one *metaphysical.*"

The CNN reporter looked perplexed, as Ravi rushed to explain. "Let's begin with the physical reason for this effect that changes a community when one person changes his or her consciousness. Have you ever heard of the *kick-the-cat theory?*"

Now the whole crew looked puzzled, as they followed Tim and Ravi back out into the bright sunlit prison yard, leaving the peace of the tai chi meditation group behind them in the chapel.

Ravi looked into the camera, thoroughly enjoying the process of explaining how the miracle within these walls actually worked. Prisoners in the adjoining sections of the yard drew close to the fence behind her. With fingers hooked onto its cross-hatches, they, too, listened intently. "Here's an example of the *kick-the-cat theory.* A CEO of a company gets a speeding ticket on the way to work. Arriving at work, he snaps at the executive secretary in charge of the secretarial pool, who then snaps at the other secretaries, who all then in turn snap at the executives and their co-workers. The mood of the company shifts as this grumpiness is passed on to everyone they encounter – the sales people, the branch office employees, and vendors who call on the phone during the work day.

"On the way home, they flip off other drivers who cut them off or otherwise annoy them." Several prisoners listening nearby burst into laughter at the image of thousands of people flipping off the rest of humanity who "otherwise annoy them." More prisoners drew closer to hear what was so funny.

"Finally, when they all arrive home, fifty thousand people or so yell at their spouses, who yell at their kids, who go upstairs and kick fifty thousand cats. That is the *kick-the-cat theory,"* Ravi concluded with a giggle, beaming even more brightly.

She looked around at the gathered crowd and took a theatrical bow for them. The prisoners played along, applauding loudly. The television image jiggled as the TV cameraman chuckled at the response from the big tattooed prisoners.

Ravi and the others refocused as the CNN reporter inquired, "But what does that have to do with Folsom?"

"Well, if that happens in the real world, which I believe it does all the time," Ravi explained, "in here, where people are enclosed tightly, that theory is even more immediate." Ravi's playfulness faded, and a serious look crossed her face as she spoke to the thousands or perhaps millions of people watching her on their TV sets.

"This can be reversed. We can, by altering our state of mind, create a phenomenon that alters all the millions of crossing rivulets of mood and actions in our world. We can – each one of us – alter the flow of aggression and frustration with one act, one word, when we allow the personal challenges to be exhaled and evaporated out of our psyches. This is what technologies of the mind and body – like tai chi, yoga, and other transcendental techniques – have to offer our world. This effect can change the course of not only communities like Folsom or cities and towns, but on an even larger scale – of nations, and even world society."

As the media and crowd grew silent, absorbing the enormity of what Ravi had just laid out for them, Ravi remembered the second part of the question, why mind/body tools like tai chi had a community effect *beyond* the practitioners.

"I mentioned at the beginning there is a second reason this occurs, a *metaphysical* reason, that changing our consciousness affects the community around us, as it has here in Folsom. Being of Indian descent, I was exposed to yoga at an early age, and I believe it is a powerful tool. However, later I studied tai chi and meditation, as well. All of these can reverse the kick-the-cat phenomenon."

Ravi looked into each reporter's eyes, so they would know this was important to note. "However, this effect is not just because of the physical calming it creates in the individual practicing it or those they encounter. As I said yesterday, the loosening of the human central nervous system will make everything possible."

Ravi paused, before adding with great emphasis, "We're talking about nothing short of a quantum leap forward for the entire human race."

The print reporters' hands hovered over their pads, as they lifted their heads, waiting to hear what Ravi would say next.

"A few years ago, research in Washington, D.C., in conjunction with the Police Department's crime statistics office, revealed that a group of people trained in acquiring higher states of consciousness using meditation techniques, actually lowered the crime rate *for the entire city.* A small percentage of people bringing in a higher awareness helped to evolve society as a whole. Their rise in consciousness actually permeated the minds of others with a good influence, which affected much of the city's actions."

The reporters stared at Ravi, for she was unveiling amazing possibilities. As each remembered why they were here, their hands took off again on their pads.

Ravi continued. "Folsom Prison has shown us it can work. Today I am pleading with leaders here and worldwide to make yoga, qigong, tai chi, meditation, and other proven, time-tested mind/body technologies that are the gift of the East, part of public education from kindergarten through high school. There is no reason that every child should not graduate high school a master of each of these practices.

"As I said before, today the United States imprisons more of its people than any nation on earth, per capita, at a total annual cost of not just the $55 billion for prisons, but hundreds of billions of dollars annually, when law enforcement, courts, and labor loss is added to the calculation. It costs approximately twice as much to imprison a young man as it would to send him to Harvard. What could society save by providing life-tools that may not only keep people out of the expensive court system, but also mitigate the greatest threat to ALL modern humans – *unmanaged stress?*

Ravi headed off the questions she knew would come next – *How is stress our greatest threat? What about terrorism?*

"According to a twenty-year study by Kaiser Permanente, upwards of 75% of all illnesses that send patients to their doctors are caused by stress. Not just *aggravated* by it, but *caused* by it. Stress is the number one killer of Americans. Not terrorists. *Stress.*

"Just think about it. If we taught our people these stress releasing techniques, we could save trillions of dollars in annual health costs worldwide, year after year, in addition to the saved police, court, and penal costs I just mentioned. How much do we spend to fight terrorism? As agonizing as their loss is, think about how many Americans are killed in even the worst terrorist attacks. MILLIONS are killed by stress each year — and teaching our people these techniques to keep them safe would cost a tiny fraction of what we spend on the war on terror."

Ravi's words came in a torrent, and the reporters rushed to get all of it down. The woman was painting a world-altering image, and they struggled to record each bold stroke.

Ravi unfolded her next thought with great care. Clarity was extremely important on this point. "The critical gift these Eastern disciplines offer is to help humanity bring back the balance of *feminine energy* into our world. Opening to receive the power of personal and social healing that God has given us all is a feminine quality our world sorely needs. Both men and women need the balance of yin — feminine — and yang — male — energy, for maximum health and performance. The way we do business and the way we conduct national and international policy begins in the hearts and minds of individual people. If we are out of balance in here," Ravi pointed to her heart and her head, "then we are out of balance, *out here.*" Her hands expanded outward to indicate the outside world.

"We have used our male energy well. The industrial and technological expansions of this century are proud achievements. But half of our people live on less than two dollars a day. Over two million children will die needlessly because of extreme poverty this year. Two million more will die next year, and the next, and the next. When our world grows richer and richer, but so many are left out, we are out of balance. It portends growing suffering and conflict on a global scale."

Ravi's eyes burned with a soft magnetism, drawing them all in. She spread her arms open, continuing, "This power of the feminine unleashed here in Folsom, which is lessening suffering and conflict, is no less a power than these walls and barbed wire, or the global development that humanity's male yang energy has achieved. Although more subtle, this power is no less effective than the splitting of the atom, and, indeed, in a world that has unleashed such male power, we may need these subtle, feminine tools of compassion now more than ever to enable us to usher in a world of technology we can all not only survive, but *love living in.*"

Ravi's hands folded over her heart as she finished these last words, imploring those watching to feel the great promise swelling in her own breast. Ravi concluded with one last image to drive this wondrous possibility home.

"In the Gospel of Thomas, verse 22, Jesus said, *when you make male and female into a single one, then you will enter the kingdom.* The East has provided powerful tools of the mind and body that can help bring our world into such balance – opening the gates Jesus himself promised would lead to the very kingdom of God."

The camera closed in on Ravi's dark eyes, as the reporters scribbled furiously on their pads.

# 11. So Many Paths for the Psychopath

The Professor had been called away from his clandestine work at the psychiatric hospital in Montreal by an emergency that required his other talents.

His private jet was about to land at Reagan National Airport in Arlington County, Virginia, just across the Potomac River from downtown Washington, D.C. He could see the phallic Washington Monument, so stark in that blue-white brilliance cast by the night lights of D.C. on all its monuments. The darkness of the Arlington National Cemetery lay just across the river, in solemn contrast to the celebrated erections of tribute. The Professor turned away from the cemetery's contemplative silence in favor of the glory across the water.

The city's shrines to power were, as always, magnificent to behold as his jet circled around for landing, disappearing from sight at the last moments of his plane's descent. The engines whistled and hissed as his jet taxied toward the hangar. The blue and green runway lights glowed in the crisp night air in a welcoming embrace.

Although he had great aptitude for and loved his work in Canada at the psychiatric hospital, he'd become quite fond of these excursions as well. They came easy for him because he'd had the good fortune of being brought up in an upright ultraconservative Christian home, introduced to all the movers and shakers of the powerful churches, and had even been ordained, obediently following in Father's giant footsteps.

Father had made sure he rose within the ranks in all the right circles of Christian hierarchy. He'd become Father's heir apparent as the powerful nexus, the hub connecting the many spokes of the rapidly mobilizing political fundamentalist movement. He now embodied the culmination of his father's lifelong ambition, completing his crusade to create a direct line from the highest echelons of power into the lowly pulpits throughout fundamentalist Christendom.

Father, as a devoted apostle of the church, had the respect of all those who counted. But behind the walls of their fine Tudor home, another man had existed beneath the cloth of his religion – another man entirely.

The Professor was escorted to the limousine waiting just a few steps from where his feet touched the tarmac to shuttle him to the Four Seasons. His hotel was just blocks away from the White House on Pennsylvania Avenue. As they headed up 395 to Constitution Avenue NW, the Capitol building was exquisitely lit with bright white lights.

His pulse quickened with each passing mile. Tomorrow he was to speak at an emergency meeting of the country's evangelical church leaders on national television via C-SPAN, Christian stations, and whatever other media might attend, but tonight was his own. He liked to be relaxed for his occasional public appearances before the faithful, and arrangements had been made.

The limousine stopped at the main entrance of the hotel. The chauffeur opened the car door as the hotel doorman ushered him past the sparkling glass gateway to the hotel. He was barely contaminated by the world, hopping from jet to limo to hotel, as doors opened for him. They always had. The faces of those holding them open were unmemorable.

The rich dark wood of the lobby excited his desire for things to come. The concierge inserted a golden key-card into the panel in the elevator, enabling their ascent to the penthouse. The elevator moved swiftly upward as the Professor and the hotel employee stood in silence. As the elevator door opened onto the penthouse suite, the concierge stepped out of the elevator and swept his arm, presenting the room to the Professor. He stacked the luggage in the corner next to the window where a table was topped with a display of tall white lilies in a brilliant red vase – a nicety ordered by the Professor. The Professor tipped the man generously and quickly, to be rid of him.

Then, finally, he opened the door to the master bedroom to see if his other instructions had been followed. There, thank God, he found that they had been. A young effeminate black man, dressed only in the skin he had been born with, lay spread-eagled on the king-size bed on a white lambskin bedspread, the stem of a red rose clenched between his gleaming white teeth. The young man, a child really, looked nervously from the Professor to the black leather whip lying next to him.

The fear in the boy's eyes sent a thrill up the Professor's spine. Indeed, the Professor thought, he would be *very* relaxed for his speech tomorrow.

# 12. False Prophets

*Watch out for false prophets. They come to you in sheep's clothing, but inwardly they are ferocious wolves. By their fruit you will recognize them.*
— Matthew, 7:15-20

*[The President] met privately with* Focus on the Family *Founder and Chairman James Dobson and approximately a dozen Christian right leaders last week to rally support for his policies on Iraq, Iran and the so-called "war on terror."*
— *Raw Story,* May 14, 2007

*Propaganda to the home front must create an optimum anxiety level.*
— Joseph Goebbels, Nazi propagandist

―――――――

The Professor waited for his cue to enter the room. Dramatic timing was so important in the herding of men's souls. He waited, basking in the sounds of his own glowing biography being read, to assure the audience appropriately of his unassailable credentials for leading them and their flocks. Through those gathered here today, he had turned the minds of thousands of Christians across the nation and the world with speeches just like the one he was about to deliver.

Just beyond the stage door of the convention hall where the Professor waited, the minister's voice rose and fell in perfect rhythm to swell the hearts of the audience with anticipation, for the *greatness* about to speak to them. As the minister finished, he signaled the group with his own applause to begin the thunderous ovation. On cue, the entire room joined in, none wanting to appear outside of the flock or any less faithful than the others around him.

The Professor strode to the podium, accepting the adoration in faces he would not remember. There was no reason he should. Clearing his throat before he lifted his chilled water glass to his lips, he reviewed his message in his mind. He'd delivered so many of these, it took only slight alterations to fit the needs of the day. The standard messages of fear and doom came so easily after years of practice at key moments when society had required prodding by one ordained as the voice of God.

He began. "Gentlemen and ladies, God be with you all. I am here today to reveal a false prophet in our midst. A woman, a temptress, and a sower of the seeds of the dark forces is spreading the Satanic rituals of the Eastern pagan religions on the soil of our hallowed land. The liberal media loves her. TIME Magazine made her *woman* of the year," the Professor sneered.

An appropriate smattering of pre-arranged moans and boos erupted and quickly spread through the crowd.

The Professor continued. "There is a war going on for the mind of man. We know that we, as Christians, are *not of this earth*. However, for years *they* have infiltrated our schools with gibberish about our children being related to animals – beasts – and trying to make them worship the Pagan god, "mother" earth. They seek to distract us from seeking God's redemption and from preparing for the end times we know are destined for this sinful planet.

"There is work to do. We cannot stand by and allow their continued attacks on the minds of our young, exposing them to the perverse literature and discussions meant to twist their minds into accepting the abomination of homosexuality."

Claps, cheers, and boos of agreement.

"Now, my dear compatriots in the army of our Lord, they have gone too far. This *foreign woman,* this Ravi, whatever her name is . . . " The booing intensified as his voice rose and his fist pounded the pulpit. "wants to spread a heathen form of mind control throughout our nation and the world's education system.

"She – *this woman* – is advocating systems of mind control brought in from foreign lands, things like tai chi and yoga and other meditations. What is worse, my friends, is that she is selling people on the need to 'feminize' our culture, away from the Father in heaven. She is trying to weave the sin and abomination of homosexuality, in the form of bi-sexuality, right into the hearts and minds of our innocent young!"

A large screen behind the Professor showed the CNN broadcast from Folsom Prison. Ravi was speaking directly into the camera, as boos and hisses filled the room. "The critical gift these Eastern disciplines offer is to help humanity bring back the balance of *feminine energy* into our world . . . both men and women need the balance of yin – feminine – as well as yang – male – energy . . . if we are out of balance in here," Ravi pointed to her heart and head, "then we are out of balance, *out here.*"

As the wave of intense booing receded, the Professor resumed. "Do not be misled by medical journals that point out that these 'exercises' provide health and well-being, my friends. For these tools are designed to *empty* the mind of man. And when we open the mind of man with such devious technologies, we create a space, and I ask you, *who* takes advantage of such space in men's minds? Is it not the same dark being who has struggled for millennia to enter our hearts and minds the moment we drop our sword and shield? Who am I talking about?" The Professor's voice rose to a shrill crescendo with his questions, building a pulse-pounding rhythm that filled the room.

The flock stood, stomping and hissing, "Satan! Satan! Satan!"

The Professor smiled a serene smile, gesturing with his hands for all to calm themselves and sit. He was skillful at this, raising the flock to a vicious mob mentality, and then in the midst of the virulent fury he'd created, appearing as the calm ear and voice of the compassionate God he represented.

"Fear not, my friends, God will not let this stand. But we must each do our part. We must all go home to attend our flocks. Protests must be staged at school board and city council meetings, letters must be written to our representatives in this glorious democracy, and the liberal immoral media must be cowed in the face of our righteous army of God!"

Again his voice, with a subtle tremble, rose and fell, building toward a crescendo, as the crowd stood in thunderous applause and absolute approval and agreement.

Now, when the crowd had been aroused to a state of angst and anger that could smash diamonds, the Professor concluded, "God be with you. God speed. Take your faith with you into the streets and corridors of power."

The deafening applause followed the Professor out the door and down the hallway toward his waiting limousine, his hotel room, and his parting opportunity for well deserved *recreation* before returning to the grindstone at the psychiatric hospital.

# 13. The Stakes are Raised

*The Lord . . . repaid; did justice; through His minister, the state . . . that consensus has been upset, I think, by the emergence of democracy . . .*
– Anthony Scalia, Supreme Court Justice, January 25, 2002

*The truth is, there is no Islamic army or terrorist group called Al Qaeda. And any informed intelligence officer knows this. But there is a propaganda campaign to make the public believe in the presence of an identified entity representing the "devil" only in order to drive the "TV watcher" to accept a unified international leadership for a war against terrorism.*
– Major Pierre-Henri Bunel, Former Agent for French Military Intelligence, *Al Qaeda-The Database,* November 20, 2005

―――――――――

As the limo glided through the gleaming monuments of D.C. on the way back to the hotel, the Professor's cell phone rang. He was reluctant to answer it, knowing what delights awaited him back in his hotel room. Yet, it had to be important, for his number was highly classified. He punched the button, and as a voice spoke, the Professor nodded obediently, and finally said, "Yes, of course. I'm on my way."

Disgruntled, he barked the new destination to the driver, and within minutes the limo pulled into an underground structure, where only the guard booth and the gate-controlled entrance to its parking area were visible from the street. The Professor lowered his window, and the guard waved them through.

The car wound through a smooth gray passageway, wide enough for only one car, and with a ceiling too low for a truck or even a van to get through. Fluorescent lights lined the tunnel. Eventually the claustrophobic path opened into a small parking area. The narrow passageway ended in a single door in the center of the far wall.

The Professor exited the car alone. He approached the doorway and pressed a black button on an electronic device. A monotone voice demanded his name and agency rank.

Apparently his answer was satisfactory, for he was buzzed in. The doorway opened into another narrow passageway that declined further into the earth, constricting ever more as it did so. This hallway too was bordered above and below by ongoing lengths of recessed fluorescent lighting. As he proceeded, the ceiling and walls almost imperceptibly continued to draw in, until the chamber was just barely tall enough to permit the Professor to stand upright. Its restrictive width was obviously designed to permit only one man to advance at a time.

The hallway made a ninety-degree turn to the right and narrowed sharply before abruptly ending at a closed door. The door, unremarkable except for the high-tech camera in the upper right corner, filled the end of the tight hall. With a loud mechanical whirring sound, the eye of the camera spun to focus and then fix upon the Professor. He had an eerie feeling that this bug-eyed machine was actually staring at him.

The door opened. Beyond the cold gray concrete of the hallway lay the richly carpeted floor of the underground office of the Vice President of the United States. The Professor stepped forward into the luxuriously appointed antechamber.

The Vice President, not one for social niceties, spoke gruffly from behind his desk, and immediately the staff left them alone. Surrounded by the rich wood of paneled walls and bookshelves, the fireplace's crackling flames gave the false impression that there might be any real warmth generated in this room.

The Professor's elegance dimmed in some intangible way when in the presence of the Vice President. Growing up in his father's world, few human beings had challenged the Professor. He'd learned well the pleasure of putting people in their place. Both his father and mother had been masters at applying the thinly veiled scalpel to the social jugular vein, delicately and genteelly eviscerating those beneath their station. But there were certain people to whom one must pay obeisance.

The Professor had served the Vice President in many capacities as the man had risen through Congress, the Senate, multiple Cabinet positions, and finally here, where he could run the show in a meaningful way.

The Professor's many skills had played no small part in the VP's rise to power. It had not been the Professor who'd terminated the President's first running mate, but one of his "patients." Early on, when the newly elected President had balked at some of the measures necessary for civil control and civilian detention, it had become necessary to place a reliable man near the top of the executive branch.

Following the original VP's assassination, a few well-placed news stories, coupled with strong "advice" to the President from several key Senators, resulted in the man sitting before the Professor being placed in power as the new Vice President of the United States. He would never have been the President's choice, had the screws not been turned with pin-point precision and kidney-punch politics.

Flames in the fireplace cast a glow on the VP's face. He placed his elbows on his desk with hands folded beneath his chin. "We may need your man, the one you call Soldier, again."

The Professor smiled. "Yes, of course. Although at this moment he's in Canada, poised to deal with *the woman* of whom I spoke."

The Vice President waved away this detail. "Whatever. This is more important. Your report detailed the population's growing immunity to fear manipulation. This is a concern we feel we must deal with. Global oil supplies are dwindling, and China and India are demanding more energy. If we resort to alternative energy solutions, the genie of free decentralized energy will quickly be out of the bottle, and we'll lose the power we maintain through energy dominance.

"More wars are on the horizon if we are to maintain control of the world's oil, in Venezuela as well as in the Middle East. If social fear cannot be maintained, wars on this scale will not be possible."

The Vice President shifted in his chair, as if the burr of the shift in social consciousness were digging right into his ample derrière. "You say there is a change in brainwave production on a massive scale?"

"Yes. We've observed this for years, and our analysis shows an increase in a specific type of consciousness that has gone off the charts in certain individuals, while also increasing in much of society. Our focus is on a type of increased gamma wave brain activity that produces what is referred to as *broad swath* thinking. Many parts of the brain are stimulated so that the subject, rather than having tunnel vision, which is best for fear-based propaganda purposes, sees a subject or issue from many angles with feedback from many parts of the brain. This diffuses the impact of fear, making subjects more difficult to manipulate."

The VP had leaned forward, eyes narrowed in concentration. His two forefingers formed a steeple that pressed into his nose as he listened. At this news, he sank back into his red leather chair and sighed deeply. "How long before we lose control of a majority of the U.S. population?"

"Our national mapping corresponds with the global mapping. If current trends continue, we could see an almost wholesale shift in consciousness within the next year or so."

The Vice President swiveled his chair toward the fireplace, the yellow flames reflecting in his glasses. His steeple-pointed fingers tapped lightly on the sides of his nostrils. As he stared into the fire, the wheels of his mind turned furiously behind his calm exterior. Without looking at the Professor, he asked, "When did this start?"

The Professor's hand ascended a slope across the air, describing the rising levels. "There have been steady increases in gamma wave activity since we began analysis about twenty years ago. There has been a corresponding increase in Eastern meditative practices over those years. Research indicates a correlation.

"We weren't too concerned by the constant rise because the increase was relatively insignificant, even as it rose steadily, until September 11, 2001. What put it on our radar was that on 9/11, after the attacks and the media show of the towers burning and collapsing for hours and days on end, we noted a massive disruption in gamma wave thinking.

"The fear generated by this event was so all encompassing that the global consciousness dropped to almost pre-increase levels, as far as gamma wave emissions. Years of gamma wave increases and the cohesive thought it produced were completely reversed *in one day*. The public was completely susceptible to media manipulation." As he detailed this cataclysmic reversal, the VP turned back to face him directly.

The Professor savored having control of the VP, as he hung on every word. Like a stripper, he unveiled his data in his own good time, relishing the raw power of information. The VP waited in anticipation. The Professor continued. "The lowered gamma consciousness in society lasted about a year after 9/11.

"Supportive media, of course, helped narrow the breadth of discussion, and thereby thought. In the months leading up to the Iraq invasion, major news networks hosted over ninety percent pro-war talking heads, with only four percent skeptical or opposed to the Iraq invasion.

"However, when the imminent attack on Iraq built up in early 2003, we saw a backlash. A profound shift occurred. All the gains we'd made somehow disappeared, and this gradual shift we'd associated with Eastern mind/body meditation techniques made a quantum leap, seeming to infect people all over the planet.

"A visceral desire to avoid war seemed to be at the heart of this worldwide consciousness shift, reversing our gains from 9/11. The pressure of the coming war triggered a return of patterns that had been created over the twenty or so years of expanding gamma wave thinking. As the global allergic reaction to the war spread, a few people around the world went off the charts, as if they were lifted up by a rising tide. What we are seeing now, in the form of people like the Tibetans and this woman, is that effect on steroids."

The Vice President mulled over this information, methodically processing potential plans of action.

Pouring himself a cup of coffee from the serving tray next to his chair, the Professor waited. As he sipped his drink, he scanned the shelves and walls that held photos of world leaders, both business and political, as well as major media celebrities smiling arm-in-arm with the VP. The web of linear power and hierarchical control in the world could likely have been charted using the photos displayed in this room.

Finally the VP came to a decision. "Yes, we'd suspected as much, according to external social data we had collected. There is some unease about whether your experiments will bear fruit in time to stop this new upsurge. Which is why it appears we may well have need of your man for another mission. We have a team in position to work with him if the need should arise."

The Professor suspected what was in the works, even though the VP had yet to detail it. "What may I tell the Soldier?" he inquired.

"We'll have an AWAC surveillance aircraft off the Air Force record, high over the capital, should we enact the plan. It will direct two drones by remote control. We will have switched them with commercial airliners after they have taken off and their flight plans have been recorded. Their transponders will be disabled before the switch, so the FAA and the public will think the drones are the original airliners. The first drone will be flown toward the Capitol building, followed about thirty minutes later by the second drone."

As the VP unveiled his plot, the Professor was genuinely surprised at the sheer gluttony of his power grab. "But the Congress and Senate are both . . ."

The VP patted the air with both hands, continuing, "Yes, the entire legislative branch of the United States is housed there. I will, in addition, arrange for the President to be meeting with Congress at that time. On May 9, 2007, Presidential Directives NSPD51 and HSPD20 were issued. They provide that in the event of a national emergency, the President's office is given virtual dictatorial powers. If and when Plan B is enacted, the full power of the nation will rest right here in this office."

The Professor's heart hammered in his chest. He felt more alive than he'd felt in years, as with bated breath he waited to hear more. His fingers unconsciously stroked the wood carving on the arms of his leather chair. A question arose, which, in his excited state, he uncharacteristically blurted. "But won't the Air Force intercept commercial jets flying toward the Capitol?"

The VP waved off the Professor's concern. "We'll have war games going at that time, including Watchful Guardian, Northern Vigil,

Northern Safeguard, and Vigilant Denial. Fighters will be stationed away from their normal D.C. protection stations, pulled up to Canada and Alaska for a simulated Russian attack. Those remaining will be kept busy by the Northern Vigil drill that will include false radar blips generated by the FAA and DOD software.

"Don't worry, they won't interfere. *We* have it under control. That's not *your* concern."

The Professor felt the sting of condescension in the VP's last words.

The VP glared at the Professor for a long moment and then continued his business-like explanation of the attack on the Capitol. "The first plane will narrowly miss the Capitol building, in order to get every media camera in the world focused on it. But the drone will be filled with ordnance designed to burn and smoke furiously, providing brilliant footage for the television media.

"Then about thirty minutes later, the second plane will be sent directly into the Capitol rotunda for maximum shock effect. The image of that plane exploding into the iconic rotunda, signaling the death of the President as well as the entire Congress, will play around the clock on media worldwide.

"We'll be working on many levels. The decapitation of the legislative branch will effectively put the White House in charge, which, of course, I will inherit. The 2007 directive will enable us to avoid the reemergence of a legislative branch with any real power for years into the foreseeable future.

"But, most importantly, the images provided to television screens and newspaper headlines worldwide will dam up this gamma wave flood you've described that is poisoning the minds of the people. Once and for all, they'll know they have much to fear from the world, and that *we are here to protect them.*"

The VP rose from the chair behind his desk and came around to sit closer to the Professor. "Your Soldier's job will be to coordinate a small team of demolition experts, which we have already assembled, to plant cutter charges throughout the Capitol support structure prior to the day of the operation. A select group of Capitol police in charge of security will enable him and his team to work undetected by extending routine security power downs."

The Professor, fascinated, waited eagerly to hear more as the VP continued. "The cutter charges will be set to bring down the entire Capitol about one hour after the plane strikes the rotunda. The total destruction will be blamed on fire and will cover up evidence of the controlled demolition. Secure cleanup crews will be brought in for national security reasons, and the debris will be destroyed quickly so that no lingering evidence will remain. With no evidence, the truth will be whatever we create."

With some effort to control the trembling of his fingers, the Professor raised a hand in question. "Who will be blamed for this?"

"That depends on how the future plays out. The Chinese have been troublesome regarding Syrian and Iranian oil claims. As you know, your Soldier's foray into Tibet caught the media's attention, and we planted stories with the media about China's possible involvement to cover that situation. They backed off their oil claims after that.

"However, the scuttlebutt is that China's considering selling off U.S. loans as revenge, which would plunge the U.S. dollar into utter chaos, as China now owns most of our national debt.

"Therefore, for this job we'll leave open the door that it could have been Islamic terrorists who moved through China with or without their permission. This leaves us many options. With that kind of leverage, we can whip up support for our occupation of Islamic nations, or we can manipulate China with a possible public declaration of their involvement. We can play them like a flute.

"The Chinese have spent years creating a new face since the 2008 Olympics, and all those years of PR would be lost if we intimated in any way that China was connected with the horror the world will see on TV. Plus we'll count on you to whip up the key Christian fundamentalists to renew their push to get their people to turn away from Eastern mind/body techniques, and to continue their role in keeping it out of public schools. It's a win-win all around."

The Professor could barely catch his breath, his heart was pounding so, but he gathered himself to speak evenly. "When will this occur?"

"We only have a general possible date scheduled. Not everyone involved understands what it takes to do what is best for the homeland, and there are those who want to exhaust other options first.

"You say this woman you spoke of earlier may hold possibilities for us to understand and reverse what is happening to the people. We need to know how that progresses. Our decision rides on your success with her. I want to hear from you the moment you have her. Use this number." The VP handed him a heavy cream-colored card on which was printed only a 10-digit number.

The Professor's mind raced as his jaw tightened. This put him in a position to be the one who personally changed history. *He* would be the one to break this chain, to break *her* and this feminine mental force, so dangerous to the structures of control they had meticulously built. There was much to be done.

# 14. The Hounds Unleashed

*I say we nuke the bastards. In fact, it doesn't have to be Iran, it can be everywhere, anyplace that disagrees with me.*

– Glenn Beck, *The Glenn Beck Program,* May 11, 2006, Premiere Radio Networks

*The Central Intelligence Agency owns everyone of any significance in the major media.*

– William Colby, Former Director of the CIA

———————

FAX News was the first on the air that morning to use the phrase *promoter of forced bi-sexuality* when referring to Ravi's plea to the world to teach mind/body techniques in public schools worldwide. Within minutes, all the major networks' breaking news stories followed suit, and as America sleepily trudged out to their stoops to pick up the morning papers, headlines of the country's largest newspapers used the same term – *forced bi-sexuality* – demonstrating conclusively that both scripts and print stories had been written before FAX threw down the gauntlet.

Most Americans are unaware that nearly all U.S. print, radio, and television media are owned by only five mega-corporations. This means that vast media assaults issued on individuals, which may appear to be in the news because the story has its own newsworthy momentum, actually may have originated from only five strategically placed memos.

Phil O'Leary, FAX's opinionated talking head, ranted, "Who does this bimbo think she is, this Robbi, or Ravi, or whatever? *Where's she from, anyway,* with a name like that? She thinks she can just waltz right in here and tell us what our kids should be learning in school. But, even worse, *she wants to make all our kids BI-SEXUALS!* Well I'm here to tell you, that ain't gonna happen on my watch. You're not spinnin' that anti-Christian propaganda on this show, lady. And you can take that to the bank, America!"

Talk radio quickly took O'Leary's talking points and ran with them, resulting in ditto-heads across America mindlessly parroting the attacks around water coolers in thousands of work places throughout the day.

Ravi was stunned by the lightning speed and lock step of the American press in their vitriolic attacks on her statement at Folsom Prison, twisting the essence of her spiritual appeal into a sexual statement.

Rachel, who usually functioned as Ravi's assistant, became her counselor at critical times like this. Holding Ravi's hand as she spoke, she advised, "Ravi, our best action is to disappear for a few days. Let this take its course. It does no good to speak reason during a riot. You must give the planted media time to be answered by cooler, truer heads in the media. Then you'll have space from which to speak to this issue."

Ravi had challenged her plan, insisting that she wanted to go on the media today to clarify her position. But finally she capitulated, seeing the wisdom of Rachel's strategy.

Ravi nodded silently as she watched the city recede from her view. Their limo pulled into the parking lot of a private airport outside the city. Ravi needed to get away from the city, away from the media. She needed seclusion and sanity for a few days while Rachel strategized a game plan for their return. Rachel had arranged for the most dependable small plane known, a Beechcraft King Air 100, twin turboprop, with two highly experienced pilots.

One of the pilots turned to welcome them to the flight with a distinctly southern drawl. Noticing Ravi's obvious tension, he smiled. "I saw the preacher-man go after you today on the news, and I want you to know that I get what you're talkin' about. I know you weren't talkin' about sex when you said people need to find their balance. Since my daughter was born and I've become a father, I've learned a lot about needing to get in touch with my compassionate side. You can call it feminine side if you want, it's all the same cat no matter how ya skin it."

Ravi reached out to touch his shoulder. "Thank you."

With a smile, the pilot continued, "Wanna hear a good joke? I think it'll help ya put the preacher's rant in perspective. I grew up in the south, with some o' these preachers, who talked and talked and talked about sex, poundin' their fists on the pulpit every Sunday." With a wink he added, "Kinda made you wonder just where their heads were at, ya know? Anyhow, when I heard this joke in the Air Force, I nearly broke a rib."

Ravi nodded, so the pilot continued. "You see, there's this man who went to see a shrink, a psychiatrist . . ."

His co-pilot, who'd obviously been subjected to this story many times before, grinned and shook his head with mock resignation.

"So, the shrink starts to show the guy those ink blot images, Rorschach tests, I think they call 'em. The shrink holds up ink blot images of two birds flyin' and asks the guy what he sees. The guy says, 'Two people havin' sex.' Then the shrink holds up an ink blot of two flowers and asks the guy what he sees. The guy says, 'Two people havin' sex.' The shrink's perplexed, so he asks the guy, 'Has anyone ever suggested you may have an obsession with sex?' The guy gets all huffy, and says back to the shrink, 'Whaddaya mean, Doc? Yer the one that keeps showin' me all the dirty pictures!'"

Rachel smiled as Ravi laughed so hard, she had to grip the sides of the pilot's seat in front of her. She finally had calmed down, wiping tears from her eyes, when Rachel turned to the pilot and said, "Ya think she got it?" with such a wry look that the pilot and co-pilot both cracked up – starting Ravi up all over again.

The pilot mugged proudly at the riot he'd caused. He turned back to Ravi. "I thought you'd get a kick outta that, after the day you've had on TV." Ravi smiled as she remembered her father's belief in the power of humor. He was a cool diplomat on the outside, but the man was a natural comedian at the most unexpected and most needed times. She missed him dearly. She thanked God she still had Rachel as her world was turning upside down and inside out.

The pilots went back to business, checking and rechecking their equipment and instruments, as Ravi and Rachel settled into the back of the plane. Rachel had arranged lunch – tasty selections of Indian curry, naan bread, and other dishes the sisters had grown up eating in their parents' home. Rachel knew that comfort food like Father used to make would improve Ravi's spirits. It had always worked for Rachel when times got tough, which was why Rachel had always outweighed her little sister. They ate while the pilots continued their pre-flight tests. Ravi smiled at Rachel as she dove into the delicious food.

Eventually the lunch was finished, the pilots were ready, and the plane lifted off and up, pulling everyone back into their seats as they climbed rapidly to clear the trees just beyond the end of the rural runway. The engines whined, and only the perfect blue sky filled their vision outside the windows. The pilot angled the plane into a turn, then evened out toward their destination, a small cottage on the coast of Maine, a place for quiet and rest.

Ravi closed her eyes, and sleep quickly overtook her. The hum and vibration of the plane's engines were like a lullaby that gave her peace from the mental storms she'd grappled with all day. Meanwhile, Rachel alternately typed notes on her laptop and checked her email, as the beauty of New York, New Hampshire, and then Maine unfolded beneath them.

Rachel was relieved to be in the stillness high above the earth, headed for tranquility, after the roller coaster of their last few weeks. Even with all the turmoil, she wouldn't have changed this experience for her life, though she'd had doubts at the beginning. She believed in Ravi and was proud of what she was doing. She was grateful and glad to be a part of something meaningful and historic. During her musings, Rachel too dropped off into a comforting sleep.

Suddenly, the plane's vibrations and a steep turn awakened both Ravi and Rachel. With barely contained panic, the pilot wrestled with the steering mechanism, while the co-pilot flipped switches and tried to radio a distress call.

Rachel demanded, "What's going on?"

The co-pilot lowered his radio mic for a moment. "Something has got the plane. We've lost control of it!" He shouted into the microphone, "Mayday! Mayday! We are banking down and off course. We are out of control. I repeat, out of control!"

He hung up the mic as he spoke to the pilot. "We've lost radio. We have no access to the computer or data systems at all. We've been hijacked."

Ravi, frightened, asked, "What do you mean, hijacked?"

"The U.S. military has the capability to take off and fly aircraft, even large ones like commercial jets, by remote control. They can even land them with no one on board. Some planes have the capability built in, so the Air Force can wrest control of a plane from human hijackers. This feels like that."

Ravi cried, "You mean there is someone flying along beside us controlling our plane?" She looked to both sides frantically, whipping her head around to look out the windows. "Perhaps we can signal them!"

"No, it doesn't work like that. A mechanism must have been fitted to our plane. It uses our auto-pilot features and commandeers our database to tell the plane to fly from point A to point B." He joined the pilot, who was searching beneath and behind the dash and control panels to find something they could disconnect that would allow them to regain control.

The pilot spoke quietly to his partner. "The FAA will notice we've gone off course. We could have an interceptor tailing us within fifteen minutes."

Suddenly, the plane banked hard to the right and descended rapidly in a controlled dive into a forest below. A sliver of an opening emerged in the green. It appeared to be a small landing strip. The pilot yelled, "It's Canada! New Brunswick. Someone is bringing us down in Canada! Stow your bags and put your heads between your knees, NOW!"

. . .

The Soldier pulled his Hummer from the edge of the clearing into the woods to wait for the target's arrival. The boys in the control center would handle everything from the satellite. His job was to be ready to move.

As he waited, a vibration began in the center of his skull. His head wasn't right; something had been wrong ever since he'd offed those monks in Tibet. Uneasy sensations swelled in his heart that disturbed his focus. His focus was all he had. It was his skill – a skill he couldn't afford to lose.

His bag held the syringes and the meth-antidepressant solution that had become standard issue for every mission for the past six months. His scanner received the transmissions of the approaching plane, telling him that he had a few minutes before their arrival.

He stuck the needle into his vein. He watched the lazily drifting blood mix with the drug cocktail in the syringe before he plunged it into his body. Like the liquid, his mind flowed somewhere he couldn't see. The vibration in his head became the monks' droning chants. He saw them fall like dominoes in his mind's eye, and as the last monk fell, The Soldier also fell, tumbling down into an abyss – red and fiery, dark and deep.

As he fell, he reached out for the hand of a man whose face he couldn't make out. He screamed for the man to catch him, to hold him, to save him. Who was it? Who did he think could save him? *"Daddy!"* he screamed. The Soldier's chest heaved rapidly as sweat broke out on his face.

Frank's hand passed right through his father's image, as if he wasn't there, just like when he was a kid. His father's return from war had brought home only a ghost – a ghost who was blind both to Frank and to Mom. Dad looked right through Frank toward battles that no longer existed. Except in Dad's world they were the universe, and Frank was invisible to him.

*No, Dad, don't!* The Soldier gripped the sides of his seat so tightly, his fingernails bit into the leather. He began to bob and weave, as if he were dodging a blow to the head.

His father was huge, like on a drive-in movie screen, with large haunted eyes that for a moment almost responded to Frank's pleading, but then became blind to him again. He turned away to a distant war behind him, as in front of him, Frank remained, reaching. *Dad, wait!*

The Soldier's arms reached out toward the windshield – the syringe, still in his vein, wobbled as blood began to ooze from the insertion point. His muscles rippled as his fingers reached out, curling in, pleading.

The image of his father became the face of the last chanting monk he had killed in Tibet, smiling at him and reaching out to him. Then the monk's face transformed into his mother's face. As her fingertips almost touched Frank's, she morphed back into the monk, her soft eyes peering from his compassionate face, as Frank's gunshot felled him. Frank's heart was wrenched, as if he'd shot his own mother. Leveled by grief, he fell away from their searing eyes, as from one amorphous face they pled, *Love, Frankie.*

The radio scanner screamed, "We're goin' down. It's Canada!" and the Soldier bolted upright, suddenly awakened from his distant storms. The needle was still in his arm. He yanked it out and jammed the vehicle into gear, preparing for the attack. Cold sweat coated his brow, and his mind spun.

*Focus!* The Soldier slapped himself across the face – hard – and reached over to slam a CD into the vehicle's player. Pounding music blasted out of the speakers and exploded through the car. The Soldier watched the plane descend and jerked the Hummer forward. He drove in a beeline to where the plane would come to a stop at the end of the clearing.

. . .

The wheels of the plane slammed into the clay field below. The King Air bounced up into the air, before again dropping hard, this impact less violent than the first. Eventually the wheels found steady contact with the runway. Rachel's Indian cuisine was threatening to rise back up her throat.

As the plane taxied down the strip, a large Hummer jolted out of the woods directly into their path. The plane stopped with a jerk, and the Hummer slammed to a stop just in front of them. Loud heavy metal music screamed into the air. A large man emerged from the vehicle wearing fatigues with no insignias. He appeared to be in his mid-fifties, fit and hard. He strode purposefully toward them, ducking away from the dying but still spinning propeller, signaling the co-pilot to open his door. Having no recourse, the air crewman complied. As he opened the door, he shouted over the blasting music, "Who the hell are you?"

"You can call me Soldier. I'm sorry for the inconvenience. We'll have you on your way as soon as possible." As he spoke, he reached toward a small holster at his side. The Soldier raised a German Luger pistol and fired directly into the heart of the co-pilot.

Rachel screamed. Ravi gasped for breath, holding her own heart. Tears filled her eyes. The pilot struggled to unlatch his seatbelt as the man wielding the pistol coolly redirected his weapon and fired a second shot into his heart with pinpoint accuracy.

Rachel pleaded, "Oh God, oh my God, please, please."

Psychotropic drugs racing through his brain, the Soldier leaned into the plane, raised his weapon, and looked into the eyes of the panicked woman. "Yes, let me introduce you to God, up close and personal." He aimed directly at Rachel's pretty face.

The world went into slow motion, while inside the Soldier, thoughts moved at light speed. He winced in pain. Something, *a force,* seized him from within. That odd sound he'd been hearing since Tibet vibrated through him. The entire world oscillated and trembled. *The tuning fork of the universe had been struck.* He felt himself swoon, but regained enough stability to prevent himself from sprawling across the dead co-pilot. Only the pounding sound from his vehicle's stereo brought him back, as the singer screamed with primordial fury, pleading for his eyes to be nailed closed.

An instant before the Soldier released the shot, Ravi screamed, "NO!" and lunged at the gun. The shot pierced Ravi's left hand before penetrating Rachel's face and brain, killing her instantly. Bone fragments, blood, and fluid sprayed across the plane's interior and onto Ravi.

Ravi threw herself across Rachel's lifeless body. Wracked with sobs, she stroked her sister's ruined face and rocked her in her arms, as if soothing a hurt child.

Ravi's mind swirled. She no longer saw the gunman. Visions of the past exploded in her mind and howled from her heart. She saw young Rachel crying for her when other children teased her at school, and Rachel covering for her when Mother and Father caught her being naughty. With each scene that arose, Ravi's heart broke into a million new pieces, as if it were tearing apart. "Oh Rachel, my sweet. Oh my God! My God, *oh God!*"

Ravi began to pass out. Her mind screamed the thought that so often follows a dear one's death. *"I will never be able to tell you I'm sorry!"*

At that moment, Rachel's pretty undamaged face appeared before her from the gathering darkness. *"I am here.* I hear you. I am *fine,* Ravi. This is meant to be, just as what is happening to you is meant to be. I am with Father, and soon Mother will be with us."

As Rachel spoke of Father, Ravi saw him appear in her hazy thought. She watched as Rachel matter-of-factly reached over to straighten Father's rumpled shirt collar, as her take-charge sister had so often done in life. Rachel turned back to Ravi. "However, you, little sister, have a long journey before you. Sleep now. You'll need the rest. One day we will talk about how you handled your part of this quest."

Rachel's ethereal being smiled at Ravi, before turning to adjust Father's crooked tie. Father gazed meaningfully at Ravi, even as he patted her sister's busy wardrobe-tampering hands.

Their presence was so real. In Ravi's state of shock she lost the horrid reality she'd just experienced – her lips curling toward a smile at their familiar images – even as she fell toward darkness. From a murky distance she heard Rachel issue one final sober message that accompanied Ravi into the blackness of unconsciousness. *"This man is not your enemy.* The quest is greater than our lives. All of humanity has a part to play."

In her last moment of consciousness, Ravi's vision was filled with the hard face of the Soldier. She saw it for only an instant, but she knew in that instant that the man's face held a pained and haunted look, before all went black.

The Soldier watched the woman's attempts to revive her dying sister and felt a strange pain in his chest. It was a feeling he had felt before, long ago. But he couldn't place it, like a name right on the tip of your tongue that you know but just can't recall. It began to come into focus as he reached for the woman, who had now passed out. He had felt *sorrow,* just for a fleeting moment.

The pounding music enabled him to fend off this oddness and resume his mission. But the feeling had shaken him.

# 15. The Enemy Found

*The "Active Denial System," which may soon be used in Iraq, fires non-lethal microwaves that give an intolerable burning sensation . . . Iraq is becoming the proving ground for devices, some radically new . . .*
*– USA Today, July 24, 2005*

———————

Ian McDonald returned to the hospital after his briefing at the Data Collection Center with the migraine-tortured Mark Ratlig. As Ian learned the ropes of his daily duties at the hospital, he quickly realized that he preferred even the frenetic pace of the data center to the hospital.

Ian figured out that the reason he'd been recruited from the outside – from Naval Intelligence – wasn't because of the budget increases the Professor had told him about, although there probably was new money being pumped in. Through quiet conversations with other staff, he discovered that although the program had been going smoothly for decades, over the last months the attrition rate had been *horrendous.* Suicides and mental breakdowns had plagued the organization. Many had simply left.

However, except for one who remained on the lam, all personnel were eventually accounted for, because with an operation like this, agents weren't allowed to just quit. Somewhere in the Canadian hinterlands, a mass grave was piling up with company men and at least one woman.

He couldn't believe what he was witnessing at Taloncrag. The CIA – "the Company" to insiders – funded and controlled every aspect of the experiments, which included not only in-house re-patterning experiments using LSD and electroshock therapy and subliminal suggestion using video and audio, but also field experiments that were nothing short of bizarre. They were testing mind disruption weapons of the microwave kind that Ratlig had mentioned in his briefing, along with other new technologies on the cutting edge of mind control.

The Company rented cheap motel rooms that they fitted with one-way mirrors so they could videotape the subjects. The Company provided these free rooms to local prostitutes, who in turn provided massively dosed LSD cocktails to their customers. Everything was videotaped and archived by the men on the other side of the one-way mirrors.

It was a perfect setup. The subjects were wholly unaware they were involved in experiments, and even if they did figure it out, the Company had the blackmail factor as backup. Anyway, who would believe them if they went to the press with such an outlandish charge? Key media plants in both Canada and the U.S. were always available to kick into character assassination mode if necessary.

The goal, Ian was told, was to observe the sexual behavior of the male subjects while they were on LSD. Ian came to believe, however, that this was ultimately a recreational activity for the Company men, who clamored for this duty over the living hell of the hospital assignments.

There was no follow-up of the subjects once they staggered away from the motel, at least not formally. But it was common knowledge that many became psychotic or even committed suicide after their excursion into the hall of mirrors that was the Company's motel hell.

Ian had gone down a rabbit hole, and his world would never be the same. As the weeks dragged on, Ian eventually hired some of the hookers himself to distract himself from where he was and what he was doing. But when he was with them, he couldn't shake the feeling that someone was watching and recording what he was doing. These pathetic encounters were the nearest thing he had to human closeness, and as dismal as they were, he couldn't allow himself to lose contact altogether.

Ian's days mostly consisted of watching sessions during which the Professor administered LSD and electroshock therapy, followed by re-patterning video and audio therapies. From behind a one-way mirror in the laboratories known as Sleep Rooms by staff and subjects alike, Ian recorded subjects' responses. He was a clerk, filling out forms.

Once back at his hotel room, he drank until he passed out.

His life became a blur. Each day he arose amid the double racket of an alarm clock and a front desk wakeup call, to a bleary dose of black coffee and a half-assed shave. From there he moved in a state of minimal consciousness to Taloncrag, where he resumed his station behind the mirrors of the Sleep Rooms.

After years of military cuts, Ian stopped bothering to trim his hair. He didn't give a crap anymore, and no one else did either, so long as he checked the boxes and wrote numbers on the goddamn charts every time some poor SOB writhed or twitched on the Professor's table.

It became agony to be around the Professor, a man who took absolute delight in his work. Ian's blood ran cold when he had to speak to the man, or, God forbid, actually make physical contact. It was like maintaining a polite handshake with a venomous snake – all the while pretending that all was well. He'd never met anyone so cold. He'd worked with his share of jar-heads and military devotees who could commit atrocities by deluding themselves into believing it was for a glorious and patriotic cause. But he'd never worked with anyone who looked into the dark heart of abomination and savored it like a filet mignon and fine merlot. Ian had descended into the bowels of hell, and his co-worker was Satan.

One night, cocooned in his hotel room with his first drink in his hand, Ian caught CNN before the steady stream of alcohol could drug him into sleep. He saw a lovely young Indian woman with riveting black eyes and a colorful sari. He stopped on the channel because she was beautiful, but he stayed because he was fascinated with where she stood and what she was saying. The woman spoke to him from the exercise yard at Folsom Maximum Security Prison in California, surrounded by big tattooed prisoners who were hanging on every word she said.

As he watched the woman speak from within the high walls of incarceration, it was as if she were speaking directly to him from the prison his life had become. Her face was like a healing balm to Ian's tortured soul. There was something holy and pure about her that pulled like a magnet on his heart. The words she spoke melted the icy spikes of the screams that pounded his ears all day in the Company's hospital ward.

That night Ian drank, but less, and when he did sleep, it wasn't the teeth-gnashing, muscle-jerking sleep of an alcoholic. He experienced the sweet pure sleep of childhood. When he awoke, Ian remembered the woman's face and filed it in his mind so he could retrieve it again and again during the day.

The memory of her soft, lilting, yet powerful voice kindled a vibration that massaged Ian's troubled mind.

# 16. Worlds Collide

Sec. 102. (a) *The Congress hereby declares that it is the policy of the United States that activities in space should be devoted to peaceful purposes for the benefit of all mankind.*
— The National Aeronautics and Space Act of 1958

*It is possible to project power through and from space in response to events anywhere in the world.*
— Commission to Assess U.S. National Security Space Management and Organization, Donald Rumsfeld, Chair, January 2001

*[The] administration has approved a plan to expand domestic access to some of the most powerful tools of 21st-century spycraft . . . Kate Martin [Director of the Center for National Security Studies] said, ". . . laying the bricks one at a time for a police state."*
— *Washington Post,* Thursday, August 16, 2007

---

Ravi awoke to the drone of a car engine. For a moment she thought she had been having a nightmare, but a twinge of pain drew her eyes to her left hand. It was wrapped in layers of gauze. Blood spatters stained her clothing. It all came back to her – *Rachel!* – yet it wasn't as painful as it should have been. Her mind was thick, and her limbs were heavy. She had been sedated.

Ravi was lying in the back of the Hummer. The Soldier had field-bandaged her hand and placed her in the vehicle after he had injected her with a pain killer-sedative combination. The Professor would be furious that the woman had been physically damaged, as it might cause his experiments to be tainted.

He should be happy to have her at all, since his first plan had been to eliminate her, The Soldier thought, as he flicked his cigarette out the window. He would worry about that bridge when he blew the hell out of it. Time was of the essence, and he needed to get her from the airfield in New Brunswick to the Taloncrag Memorial Psychiatric Institute halfway across Quebec in Montreal. He could save time by cutting across Maine, but it was too dangerous to cross the border. He had to stay in Canadian territory and go around Maine – over 500 miles to go.

He was behind schedule because he'd had to supervise the disassembly and camouflage of the King Air plane. It couldn't be exploded or burned, as there would be air searches by the U.S. Air Force within a matter of minutes. For decades, U.S. Department of Defense policy has dictated that any time an aircraft goes more than 15 degrees off course and doesn't respond to radio, it is considered to be hijacked. The FAA immediately notifies the DOD, and then it takes an average of only 15 minutes for an aircraft to be intercepted by the Air Force. Interception has to be quick, in case the aircraft heads toward a populated area. If it does, it may have to be shot down in order to prevent even greater loss of life.

The Soldier had had to act fast. The plane's transponder had been remotely shut down the moment they took control of it. Once the plane was down and the inhabitants had been dealt with, he had signaled to his crew, who quickly emerged from the surrounding woods. Together, they had dismembered the King Air, using compressed air-powered jackhammers to knock the wings off. They'd shoved the pieces into the woods before the FAA had had time to determine the plane's location and dispatch the DOD search and rescue operations.

The Soldier had removed the plane's black box and had flung it from the top of a dam into a deep lake about 100 yards from the edge of the airfield. This woman had gotten too much publicity to take any chances, and they had a long drive ahead of them, during which they would be vulnerable to the Mounties or local cops who weren't in the loop.

He heard stirring in the back of the vehicle and paused at a rest stop just long enough to chloroform the woman back into silence. As blackness again enveloped Ravi, the Soldier's hard face was once again her last conscious vision before the void. As she drifted off, Ravi saw the man's face morph into that of a frightened boy.

. . .

The Soldier delivered his cargo, as ordered. The Professor complained about the goods being damaged, but the important thing was that she had been delivered. He was eager to begin his work. This woman presented a unique challenge that the Professor looked forward to dissecting and conquering. Finally, a real test of his powers of control – a challenge that could make history. Although those who wrote that history would never be aware of his role.

As instructed by the Vice President, the Professor briefed the Soldier on the backup plan, just in case his efforts with the woman failed. The Soldier left for Washington immediately.

The Professor pulled out the VP's card and dialed the number. *We've got the woman.*

He felt an uncomfortable urgency, but it was necessary to wait a few days for the woman's hand to heal to ensure untainted experiments. Achieving success before the VP's backup Plan B was enacted was critical.

The Professor had no problem with the backup plan. In fact, the idea of never having to appear before a Congressional committee to answer their inane and naïve questions was very pleasing. But even more important was that this tide of pathetic "free thinking" could be averted once and for all. The information that could be gathered by breaking this woman would be used to ensure that the problem was forever eliminated at its very root – within the human mind. Those who counted would know that *he* was the one who achieved this, thereby assuring his place at the head of the tables of power.

. . .

Ravi awakened to find herself wearing only a flimsy hospital gown, shivering in a cold room. She was strapped to a table. Leather straps bound her ankles and wrists. The table was elevated at a 45-degree angle, leaving her in a position between lying and standing. The Professor entered the room and walked to the sink without speaking or acknowledging her presence, any more than one would acknowledge a lab rat before beginning experiments. After carefully washing his hands and drying them, he turned to the subject and spoke.

"Good morning, Ravi. Welcome to Taloncrag Memorial Psychiatric Institute. You may call me *Professor,* for I am here to teach you."

Ravi stiffened. *How does he know my name?*

The Professor chuckled without humor as he saw her surprise. "Yes, my dear, we've been watching you for some time. More so since your dramatic rant at Oxford, but even before that, you were observed on a low level. When you dabbled with ending poverty you became of interest to us. Poverty is a necessary reality, as it ensures power, you see, to those who hold the wealth."

The man's calm and measured voice continued. "We allowed you a bit more rope after you received your Nobel Prize. However, I'm afraid you have been causing us no small consternation of late."

Checking the strap that held one of her wrists to the table, his brow arched in concern. "Are you comfortable, my dear?"

Something about the man's cool singsong words – he used them like a vivisectionist's scalpel, probing for a vulnerable point to cut into – rather than as communication.

"You see, dear, we had focused our microwave cognitive disrupting beams on you at your home and elsewhere, to no avail. After your appearance in Washington, we felt it was time to rescue you from your embarrassing diatribes."

His face brightened. "You should be proud. GPS efforts and satellite targeting, none of which comes cheap, were all directed at your insignificant little mind."

The Professor smiled at Ravi. "You received the greatest compliment of all by being given your own private assassin when all else failed to shut you up. To save you what little dignity you still possessed, we decided to give you the ever-effective face-saving device of sudden death." He spoke with magnanimity, as if applying his genius to her situation had been a generous offering of friendship.

His gray eyebrows raised in regret, which could have been mistaken for sympathy – if not for that voice – as he added, "You left us no choice, really." His brows dropped, and his face grew serious.

The man then abruptly chuckled in a bizarre emotional *non sequitur,* as if they were sharing a private joke.

Ravi felt sickened by the psychopathic twists and turns of his roller-coaster monologue.

Sensing Ravi's revulsion, he checked some meters on the wall, sighed, and continued the conversation while preparing his instruments. "All our efforts seemed to be for naught. Yet I am so very pleased that you foiled our fatal singing telegram, if you will. Apparently you suffer from some cognitive defect so unique that it prevented not only our microwave beams from helping you, but also affected our messenger of bad news at the Press Club." Again he feigned sympathy. Ravi's skin crawled as she observed this man's ease of duplicity.

With a shrug, he moved on. "After that performance, which simply ruined the auspicious occasion of your assassination, we decided we must for a time endure your rants about peace and love and human connection that are infecting weaker minds around you, so that we could find an opportunity to dissect your intriguing little psyche. All is well, for now we can finally work *together.* Fear not, my dear. We will find a cure for you, for much depends on it." With this hopeful prognosis for Ravi's condition, his face lit in a smile.

"Ravi, my dear, your mind's propensity for gamma wave emission is troubling enough in itself, as it promotes a clearer multidimensional perception of reality. But particularly alarming – and fascinating – is that quality you exhibit of also affecting the perception of others around you, and possibly even permanently infecting some with your defect."

His brow furrowed. "Reality perception is *our* business, my dear, not yours or anyone else's."

The Professor began to hook up sensors to Ravi's head.

As she watched him apply the sensors, something suddenly occurred to her. "But how did you . . .?"

"How did we know about your gamma wave production?" The Professor chuckled. "My dear, we do not require antiquated wires like these to know your mind. We have the ability to monitor anyone's mind, anywhere on the planet. With our satellite network and space shuttle program, there is no one we cannot know on a very intimate and personal level, right down to the waves emanating from your tiny insignificant consciousness."

"From the space shuttle programs? But they . . ."

"Yes, I'm aware that members of your precious United Nations and even the U.S. Congress have resisted space militarization for mind control. I believe U.N. members called for 'the negotiation of a comprehensive space convention, which could help prevent the militarization of space activities,' and some other claptrap about the betterment of humanity, but what they want and what they get are two very separate things in the real world."

The Professor adjusted the monitoring devices on her head. "We too have lobbyists, but our lobbyists have more tools in their tool chests, one might say," he added with a wink.

"Ow!" Ravi winced as the Professor tweaked an electrode pasted to her temple while he watched the wall of meters, observing her responses in the jumping needles.

"Some in your Congress have inklings of what we're up to, and in fact way back in 2001, language specifically prohibiting pyschotronic and mind control devices from space programs almost made it into a bill. But – well, I'm not one to brag, but let's just say the final bill did not mention our work here."

The Professor apologized. "But please forgive me. I digress. You're probably more interested in your own case. Yes, our technology has advanced since then, and we now have two-way capability – both projecting and receiving. We can, of course, project microwave, electromagnetic, radiation, laser, or sonic beams, and other energies to affect individuals across the planet one at a time or in groups. Our proud new accomplishment is that we also can sense brainwave activity from space.

"We have been increasingly concerned because brainwave patterns are jumping from 20 to 40 Hz more frequently, which shows new insights occurring in the mind. New insights are a very dangerous thing, as I'm sure you are beginning to realize by now." The Professor raised a syringe with a long needle into the light to examine it.

He continued, drawing a solution into the syringe. "Your brainwave patterns have often jumped to 70 Hz or even higher for some reason during your idiotic rants before the media lately, making you symbolic – no, I would say even *the embodiment* – of the problem we are facing, and therefore a perfect test subject.

"So, we felt we might kill two birds with one stone, so to speak, by taking you out of circulation, and rather than wasting your mental oddity by terminating it, using it to find a cure for the other hopeless souls who seem to be acquiring the same affliction. It may give us new insights."

Ravi's fright overtook her. The horror of her precious Rachel's destruction – the recurring hard face of the Soldier – and now being at the mercy of this madman. It was too much. Muscles tightened in her chest and her breathing became labored. She felt sure she would suffocate.

Suddenly in the midst of the storm of fear rushing through her, the vibration that began her journey – it felt like lifetimes ago – again thrummed through her being. A calm descended upon her. The reverberation of a choir of chants rattled the air. She watched the Professor to see if he was aware of it. He was not.

Just like that first time at the Oxford Club, Ravi felt the vibration increase and then listened to words flowing through her mouth. "You cannot stop this. It is bigger than you, bigger than me." Then Ravi fainted, as if the transmission had completely exhausted her. This time there was no one to catch her as she fell into the growing blackness.

The Professor, who had been arranging tools for his work, froze. The meters behind Ravi spiked, showing a huge increase in gamma wave activity. He turned from the meters and stared into space as the wheels of his mind spun furiously. Then he resumed arranging the instruments. Raising the long-needled syringe, he replied, "We'll see about that, my dear. Yes, we'll just see about that."

# 17. Breakdown

Entering the Institute, Ian stopped at the cafeteria, and rather than having his normal extra-large black coffee for breakfast, he sat down and ate real food. After last night's wonderful sleep, he felt like a new man, and the smell of bacon, eggs, and buttered toast was too good to pass up.

Ian hadn't felt like this since he was a child, when Mom would call him in from playing outside, and he'd bounce in with a ravenous appetite. Thoughts of his Mom's cooking, prepared with the seasoning of loving hands, brought memories of safety and warmth.

Ian spread the dishes from the cafeteria tray across the table, wanting to not just eat, but to dine. Food that smelled this good should not be devoured but should be a celebration of ingestion. Ian caught himself smiling. What a shock! This was an experience he hadn't had for quite a long time, and definitely not since starting his assignment at the hospital.

He mixed the over-easy eggs with the hash browns. The bright yellow yolks spilled over the crisp potatoes as he used his buttered wheat toast covered in strawberry jam to scoop them onto his fork. The smell was ecstasy, an olfactory heaven. Ian lifted the fork to his mouth, almost drooling. The taste! *Oh my God,* he thought, *I forgot what food tastes like!* For the first time in his life, he understood why people give thanks for their food. What a miracle, he thought. What a simple, innocent miracle and gift the sense of smell and taste are.

*How could I have been so asleep for so long?*

. . .

Ian strolled down the hall. He shook back his nearly shoulder-length blond hair. Ian had stopped caring about his hair, or for that matter, anything else, since coming here. But today he had actually washed and combed it. He liked the way it felt, free and flowing. Ian resisted the urge to hopscotch the floor tiles as he walked toward the lab to begin his long, tedious day of observing and cataloguing suffering. He actually caught himself whistling.

*What the hell is wrong with me?* Even as he thought the question, a grin spread across his face. *I'm whistling on my way to an inquisition.* Yet, in spite of his internal argument, Ian could barely keep from skipping into the observation room next to the Professor's dungeon of pain. There was a humming in the center of his brain, like chanting, massaging his mind. He couldn't shake the feeling that there was a God – a divine force in the world – and that there was a reason he was alive and breathing today – an inescapable feeling that there was meaning to his life.

He opened the door to the observation room, and his heart stopped. Through the one-way mirror, Ian saw the woman from the CNN news story. Her long black hair spread around her head where she lay on the Professor's steel table. He blinked and rubbed his eyes, thinking it must be his imagination. *No. It IS her!*

Ian couldn't breathe. His heart pounded like a savagely beaten drum. He wanted to run or break the window to save this woman from the beast. Adrenaline pumped through his body, making his senses more acute, intensifying his pain.

Ian's mind spun. He remembered what Mark Ratlig had told him: "There is *one particular person* who has risen to a level of prominence . . . We need to have a guinea pig, a quintessential guinea pig, and soon!"

Those words pierced him like an ice pick in his gut. *What have I been doing here!?* Ian held his breath to keep from puking.

# 18. The Experiment

*My feeling as a Christian points me to my Lord and Savior as a fighter . . . [not] the Jewish Christ-creed with its effeminate pity-ethics.*
  – Adolf Hitler

---

Ravi thrashed within the lightless depths of a bottomless well. Her hands clawed at the slimy walls, struggling to reach the surface where she could breathe. The cold water all around her was terrifying. It was a well long forgotten, with the bones of many lost souls decaying in its rancid darkness. Her lungs ached for air as her muscles clenched – reaching, gripping, slipping. At the moment death felt certain, a bright light burst through the liquid that held her. Her body exploded upward to break the surface. Every cell in her body screamed to suck oxygen into her lungs, brain, and body.

Ravi gasped for air. She looked up, blinking. She struggled to understand where she was. She realized she was not wet, and the walls of the well no longer enclosed her. Slowly she became aware of her surroundings. First, she saw the glint of a syringe and needle held above her by a tall man. Then the steel of her medical dungeon came into blinding focus all around her. The table was chilly and hard beneath her.

Ravi could hear moans and screams from beyond the walls. She couldn't be sure, but she was almost certain that screams of children were among them. The sterile order of the room heightened the horror of the seething chaos within this building. Ravi squeezed her hands tightly, and she curled her toes in as if she could pull back into herself and escape this nightmare.

Ravi made a great effort to place the face hovering over her and slowly remembered his earlier questions and lecture. But with a shock, another memory of him came to her. "You, *you* are the minister I saw on the news – the one who *attacked m. . .*"

The Professor cut in, "Oh no. It was *you* who attacked our work here, with your blasphemous ideas about transcendentalism."

The Professor held a small vial of clear liquid up to the light above the table so she could see it as the needle pierced its seal. He drew a small amount of the liquid into the syringe. "My dear, have you ever heard of scopolamine?" He answered himself. "Of course you have. Bright young girl that you are, you have a post-graduate degree in medicine, don't you? That was a silly question."

Ravi's mind gyrated madly, trying to make sense of this. She looked wildly about at the instruments around her, as she stammered, "But you are a minister! How can you be involved in *this?*"

Shaking his head, as if at a misguided child, the Professor explained, "This, my dear, *is* the work of God. Religion and the state have been married from the beginning. Oh, there are upstarts who defy that sacred union – Jesus, Buddha, and so on. But their ideas are eventually molded back into the one true religion, which, of course, is *power.* Look back at the wars, the holocausts – even slavery. All were justified by religion and supported by the churches who sided with the organs of power.

"It is futile to resist. Satan awaits the mind freed of the control of society. Your feminine, contemplative, transcendental sciences that seek to create a break from the patterns of control are illusions that have no place in this world. They defy God's will, which is the subjugation of mankind under the control of God's ministers who understand the sanctity of that control. Men like me.

"Women cannot understand God's will. That is why Jesus' mistake of passing the church on to Mary was rectified when the church exorcized that blasphemous chapter out of the historical record. The Gospel of Mary was cast out – just as you must now be cast out, my dear.

"Women's connection with the forces of nature and their willingness to admit the limits of human control have always been the enemy of order. How can the God of order reign when humans kowtow to the needs of other creatures or other forms of life? Control is dominance, not co-existence or mutual respect, for God is *The Father.*

"Most women are wise enough to keep their mouths shut about it, but there have been uppity women throughout history who were not. Hundreds of thousands of such women were burned at the stake or otherwise disposed of by the church in Europe and America. Their laughable feelings about humanity's connection with nature, their Wiccan pagan ways, were seen by the church for what they are – *wicked.*

"One day the church will return to the wisdom of the past, and today I will set an example with you, my dear. No, I will not burn you at the stake, but I am going to *burn your mind* as it roils within your pretty head."

The Professor meticulously wiped Ravi's smooth brown arm with an alcohol-soaked cotton swab and then used a rubber tube to raise a vein inside her elbow. Inserting the needle, he withdrew the plunger just enough to register the blood that indicated the needle was in the vein. The Professor then pressed it down, releasing the drug into her system, as he continued, "You know, of course, that scopolamine is a member of the Solanaceae family, also known as deadly nightshade or more accurately, *Atropa belladonna.* And it is native to Asia, just like you."

Ravi, looking down at her arm with large worried eyes, shakily protested, "No, I am American. I was born in Washington, D.C."

The Professor chuckled. "As you wish. But back to the point. You are aware that deadly nightshade is poisonous at certain levels, but we are very precise here and will not let you die. That would be far too easy for you – and would not serve the purpose of our work."

A betraying glint in the man's eye and a sudden jerk of the needle from her arm caused Ravi to recoil within her restraints. That painful yank had revealed feelings beneath the Professor's cool demeanor that ensured his implied promise of a fate worse than death.

The fleeting window into the Professor's emotions slammed closed as quickly as it had opened. He regained control as he explained, "We will provide you with a dosage that will have the strongest effect on the parasympathetic nervous system. The effects will be most marked in the subcortical and cortical levels of the brain and in the post-ganglionic nerves of the parasympathetic nervous system.

"You'll notice decreasing respiratory system secretions, decreasing heart rate, and dilation of your pupils. You have such lovely dark eyes – this will make you even more beautiful to behold as the terrible hallucinations begin."

Ravi shuddered as an icy chill ran down her spine. Her cranial muscles began to squeeze with relentless pressure before the drug had even passed her blood-brain barrier. The chemistry of her own fear pumped through her veins.

"You do realize, I'm sure, that the hallucinations associated with deadly nightshade are often horrible ones," the Professor said with a smile. "They should begin soon."

The Professor's smile grew wider as he observed the meters registering Ravi's physical responses to the onset of the drug. Ravi's panic caused her hands to clench and her back to arch rigidly. She squeezed her eyes shut and then blinked rapidly, trying to clear her vision – unable to believe what she was seeing. The overhead light blazed and intensified as the room split down the middle. The table she lay on fell into a smoldering abyss.

The screams and moans Ravi had heard before were now embodied by demons of horrific appearance. Putrid pus-filled wounds oozed on their scaly, ulcerated faces. Their desperate crack-addict bug-eye jitters revealed that even these demons were infested with tortured demons of their own. Rancid tongues slithered through sharp yellowed teeth.

The demons cursed at Ravi and taunted her. They howled that her dead father lived among them and was being forced into unspeakable perversions.

Self-doubt filled her heart, draining hope from it, as the demons, pointing long yellow-nailed fingers of accusation, hissed, "Your father blames *you* for Rachel's death! You could have stopped all this – *you were WARNED!*"

A voice that sounded like Rachel's, but hoarse and parched, screamed from far away, "Ravi, your ego put me here! Your egotistical ideas damned me!" The slithering tongues twisted, spraying putrid drool in an escalating frenzy. Ravi's growing agony fed the demons' hunger for her pain.

Ravi's mouth opened and wailed. Her mind shredded. Weeping wracked her body. Her sobs turned into physical spasms so violent they threatened to break her bones. The Professor watched the needles on the meters as they reflected Ravi's anguish.

Then suddenly, in the midst of her inner hell, a soft white light appeared. It pulsed against the fuming darkness that pressed in on Ravi, engaging the demons in battle. Rachel's cries and the demons' howls rose to a crescendo as the light throbbed beneath the torment, its pulsing growing stronger with each beat.

The membrane of this hallucinatory reality stretched thin until it burst wide open. The blinding white healing light flooded the world for an instant, expanding against the compressing darkness.

Ravi's father appeared to her. Then the light retreated as a great sucking pulled at the atmosphere like an inferno's back draft. The world of pain again exploded outward, drowning the light in its ferocity. The conquering demons in an instant convinced the exhausted Ravi of her father's horrible fate. She fell at their feet in subjugation, like a heavyweight boxer who could no longer hear the countdown of his demise.

Then within Ravi a shift occurred. A slight turning of her consciousness changed the vibratory rate of not just her mind, but her entire being. From utter hopelessness a light within Ravi stirred, as her heart somehow found the strength to lift.

Her lightening heart fueled the struggling glow – faintly, as if a weak breath had been blown to stir a guttering flame – but the flame grew. Ravi's hope fanned it. The light surged again and again, even as the cruel winds whipped at its fragile existence. With each breath of Ravi's hope the demons retreated further, slashing and wailing all the more wickedly as they receded. Yet, they did diminish, and the hell around her father faded into the luminous white light that Ravi's hope had breathed into existence.

Father spoke to her. "My dearest Ravi, it is not the drug that is causing this hell to come into being. It is your own fear that is causing it. Release your fear, and your reaction to the drug will change. Remember to breathe, my precious one." Ravi heard him and began to breathe from her diaphragm. Her abdomen rose first, then her chest, as she completely filled her lungs. Then she deflated her lungs, exhaling from the chest and retracting her abdominal wall before beginning the process again. She blinked, as the room came back into focus. *She was back!*

The Professor watched her respiration and saw the meter needles change. "Dear, don't try your cheap Eastern parlor tricks with me. They are futile here."

Ravi's conscious breathing persisted. The scopolamine was still in her bloodstream, but she was no longer experiencing it as the panicky hell it had been. It became a – a rather *pleasant* experience. Her hallucinations became *amusing,* as she saw the Professor's face begin to look very much like a pig's. A soft sigh, almost a laugh, escaped her lips.

The Professor's face hardened. "My dear, I assure you that this is no laughing matter. We are monitoring the gamma wave emissions from your mind, and we will know when you are pretending. I see by my readings that you are not."

He looked intently at the meters on the wall behind Ravi's head. "As you know, dear, we've utilized our microwave beams on you in the past, but I do believe that you will find them to be much more effective under the effects of deadly nightshade. Shall we find out?"

Ravi's vision became liquid. The Professor's words echoed through the room and became visual. She watched sounds as color and light, and the effect was pleasing. She realized she must be smiling when she heard and saw the Professor's tightening voice. As he placed a rubber tube between her teeth, he spoke, "Let's just see if we can wipe that smile off your face. The typical voltage for electroshock is around 150 volts. What if we begin with, let's say, 300 volts."

The Professor swabbed Ravi's temples with a conductive gel and clenched his teeth as he flipped the switch to administer the charge to her brain. The machine hummed to life.

The jolt blasted Ravi's mind. Her jaw clenched. Her entire nervous system electrified in pain that exploded through every corner of her being and erupted from her mouth. "Aaaaggggghhhhhhh!"

Ravi was slammed between the hard rocky shores of consciousness. Her throat gripped as thick spittle gagged her esophagus. The choking sent waves of panic crashing into electric swells of pain. Ravi rocked and reeled between these hammering forces. Unable to breathe, terrified and desperate, all was lost as the drowning experience returned.

From the depths of disaster, Ravi's father's face appeared before her once again. She felt his hand on her head as he spoke to her, just as he had when she'd awakened from bad dreams as a girl. "Breathe, my darling. *That is all.* Let go, let God, let go. *Breathe.* Do not try to control, it is folly. Let go, *let God.*"

The Professor saw the meter register a shift that he did not like. Irritably, he swabbed Ravi's temples with fresh gel and placed the electrodes on her temples once again. As he increased the dial's voltage and unleashed another shock, the Professor hissed between clenched teeth.

His eyes burned with rage as he administered a series of punishing electroshocks. A brilliant lightshow filled Ravi's consciousness. Rainbows of all-encompassing colors filled her mind, heart, body, and the universe she now floated in. She felt the vibratory rate of each color massaging the cells of her body as they cascaded through: ruby red, deep blue, royal purple – gleaming and glistening – until a golden radiance emerged. The new vibratory rate filled her and the ether around her, lifting her into a new level of being – charging her cells and atoms with wellness.

The meters showed the Professor that her gamma wave output had increased, not diminished.

Hours passed as he bore down on the woman. He was waging a battle, right here and right now, that meant *everything* to the world's future. He would not give an inch to this woman. This was a fundamental battle of the ages, between the human mind and heart and the machine of control which would always, always, *always* prevail over the power of the spirit. The angry machine hummed as he increased the voltage. He administered more drugs.

The Professor put in a long, hard day with Ravi. The intensity and duration of the experience began to wear her down. Pain overtook her consciousness. Finally the meters told the story the Professor had been determined to see. Ravi, in agony, was drenched in tears and sweat, urine and feces.

The rage that had roiled in the Professor for these long hours diminished. He had regained control and was once again the researcher.

He reached down and gently patted his subject's forehead. "Ravi, we have learned a great deal today. Tomorrow will be much more productive, don't you think?"

Ravi, pale and sweaty, breathed rapidly and shallowly, her eyes rolling back into her head as she drifted into the darkness of near mortal exhaustion.

The Professor turned away from his subject and meticulously washed his hands. He replaced all his instruments in their appointed locations, completed his clipboard forms, and exited the room.

# 19. Behold What Is Possible

*"When I hear my sergeants talking about slashing people's throats," he said, crying openly, "if I'm not a conscientious objector, what am I when I'm feeling all this pain when people talk about violence?"*

– Private 1st Class Agustín Aguayo, "U.S. Army Struggles with Soldier Who Won't Pull the Trigger," *Christian Science Monitor*, August 14, 2007

———————

Ian trembled as sweat trickled down his face. He stared through the one-way mirror. Ravi's exhausted frame lay unconscious on the table. She mumbled as behind closed eyelids, her eyes darted frantically in a fitful unconsciousness that couldn't really be called sleep. He had to get her out of here. Nothing else mattered. But how? Where to? There was nothing he could do right now. Security was highest at the end of the day as workers finished their shifts and left the hospital.

All day long, Ian had been forced to not only witness the woman's torture, but also to catalog the process and the measurements, just as he had for all the others. The Professor would look at the records.

Ian had known the instant he'd seen her this morning – no, when he'd seen her on television last night – that she meant something profound to his life, to him. He had to save her. This day had gone far beyond other horrible days in this room. He had witnessed her unrelenting agony. Now that the day was over, she would be safe until tomorrow. But the torture would begin again in the morning. He had to think, but he couldn't do it here. He had to get out of this place.

Ian returned to his hotel room. Instinctively he reached for the bottle of Johnny Walker by his bed. But when he raised it to his lips, the smell repulsed him. He set the bottle down on the night table. Sitting at his desk by the window, he gazed out, looking at nothing. He saw the Bank of Montreal across the street, and the wheels of his mind began to churn.

Ian had no money. He had lived on the Company's account and credit card. If the woman disappeared, the security frenzy it would set off would alert them that he too was gone. His credit cards would be shut off – or worse, tracked.

His pay had been deposited to his account in the U.S. during his time here. Ian switched on his computer to transfer funds to the Bank of Montreal, just across the street.

His heart froze when he saw that the bank opened at 9 o'clock. That was *after* the Professor would arrive at the hospital. If he couldn't get them out of here before then, Ravi would have to endure another day with the Professor. She had broken today. *What would another day do to her?*

Ian's head throbbed. He couldn't sleep or eat – or drink. Darkness fell, and he left his room, going nowhere in particular. He stumbled through the streets of Montreal, his breath visible in the cold night air. He wandered aimlessly through the alleyways and boulevards, heartsick, soul-sick – placing one stumbling foot before the other, seeing nothing but the bricks below his feet.

A squeal of tires biting into the pavement snapped him out of his daze. His head jerked up. Ian froze as he watched certain death explode toward him. Blinding headlights filled his vision. The car swerved in a locked-brake skid. It turned sideways, making it impossible for him to dive aside. In that moment Ian felt a lifetime of regret. He'd wasted his chance to rescue the woman. She, who had saved him from his spiraling deterioration without ever knowing who he was, just by her existence in the world.

Stunned by unavoidable oncoming death, Ian's swirling thoughts came harshly into focus: *So this is what it's like to die.*

In these last moments before impact, he was oddly mesmerized by the shininess of the passenger-side door handle that now shot toward his abdomen like a silver bullet with two tons of metal behind it.

A voice in the center of Ian's mind asked a simple question: *Are you done?*

In that split second, he had all the time in the world – even as the deadly silver handle shot toward his body. Its trajectory stretched as he pondered the desolation of his world, how easy it would be to answer yes, and just check out right now. Then Ravi's image arose. The question came again: *Are you done?*

"No."

The mind-splitting squeal ceased. The car shuddered on its shocks, stopping just inches in front of him. The driver's horn blasted into the night, followed by a string of vulgarities in French that Ian didn't understand, accompanied by a full complement of international sign language that he did.

His moment of insight was sucked away like oxygen in an inferno, leaving Ian once again in the cold damp chill of the Montreal night. His hands were shaking. He couldn't think. His ears were ringing as he back-pedaled out of the street. His stomach revolted, and he leaned against a brick wall in the alley and retched.

Ian's heaves subsided when he heard a sound that vibrated clear through him. The massive Le Gros Bourdon bell of the Notre-Dame Basilica, the largest bell in North America, rang through the falling night. Ian followed the reverberations.

He found himself walking through Metro Place d'Armes, where he looked up at the twin towers of the great cathedral. His mind pounded, emotions swirling, as he was pulled toward *something*. The 200-year-old Gothic structure was solid and inviting, huge and eternal.

As he approached it, his confusion grew. *Is this what I've become? A torturer? How can I live like this? Why didn't I die?* Ian's life had suddenly become unbearably real.

He passed by a bar, and the familiar urge to drown his feelings with a fifth of Scotch tugged at him, yet he moved on toward the resounding gong. He was walking into the heart of his pain rather than hiding from it inside a bottle. Ian approached the massive doors of the cathedral.

As he opened one of the enormous doors, suddenly his inner storm went silent. The relief was so overwhelming it took all he had to not fall down in the doorway and weep with gratitude. Years of anguish melted away. He could barely breathe, the feeling was so intense.

Incense filled his nostrils. He raised his eyes to exquisite stained glass windows that glowed silently. Gold-tipped polychrome carvings stood amid lavish altar-pieces and paintings and statues of the Holy Virgin. Christ and the saints welcomed him in. His schoolboy Catholicism and the feeling of awe it once inspired welled up within him.

Moving to the center aisle and kneeling, he crossed himself, something he hadn't done for decades. He moved deeper into the church, looking up at the old oak arches. The turquoise ceiling appeared so vast, it made his heart ache. Sliding into a pew near the crucifix, he unfolded the kneeling pad. His eyes fixed on the image of the crucified Christ, but his mind's eye saw Ravi strapped down on the table at the institute. He closed his eyes and clasped his hands, trying to squeeze the memory from his mind.

Ian prayed. He prayed like the innocent child he once was, asking for guidance. He offered all he was or would be, asking to be a servant, useful in something meaningful and right. He prayed until he felt a tap on his shoulder. The priest apologized, explaining it was time to clean the cathedral and that he'd have to leave.

Ian walked back toward his hotel. He felt calm. And there was something else – some distant forgotten experience. While he walked, the word for it bubbled to the surface of his mind: *faith*. He was experiencing faith, something he'd lost a very long time ago.

The moment he entered his room, exhaustion set in. He lay down, fearing that despite his fatigue he would not sleep, and the Scotch bottle would be his only solace. Ian looked over at the bottle, but when he closed his eyes, sleep took him immediately. Restful dreams of the beauty and calm of the cathedral filled his mind. He heard Ravi's resonant voice speaking from Folsom Prison. Visions arose – vague and undefined – perhaps previews of something about to be revealed.

The digital clock on the nightstand glowed red in the dark room. When it clicked from 2:59 a.m. to 3:00 a.m., a voice spoke in the center of Ian's brain: "It is time. Behold what is possible."

Ian gasped as a light illuminated his brain and skull. A touch illuminated his heart, and the muscles throughout his body sighed, released, and surrendered to the effortless swelling of the light. The radiance moved outward to encompass not only Ian, but also the room around him. Ian became the light, expanding outward with it.

It – *he* – outgrew the room. His lungs sucked in air as he watched the ceiling of his room rush toward him and saw the floors of the hotel as he expanded through and past them. Looking back and downward, he saw the hotel shrink behind him and then Montreal, Quebec, Canada, North America, and the Earth itself shrank below, as he and the limitless radiance he had become continued to grow.

In the midst of this miracle, he became afraid. *What if this is death?* That moment of doubt turned Ian's mind from the limitless wonder of possibility – to *fear*. In an instant, everything changed. His expansion began to collapse back on itself. Everything that had just been outward and limitless was thrown into reverse. In that moment, the voice came to him again and said clearly, "Remember this. Fear closes all doors. *Fear closes all doors!*"

With finality, like the door of a cosmic vault slamming shut, Ian found himself slammed back into his body. He sat upright, back in his hotel bed, gasping for breath.

He sat in the dark room. *What the hell was* that? So much, *so big,* all at once. It was incomprehensible to his logical mind. To understand it was impossible. He could only breathe and feel it.

Ian suddenly knew what to do. He didn't need the money or the plans he'd labored over earlier. The answers would come as he let go of control. *Remember to breathe,* he told himself. He had just experienced a miracle. When he felt fear, he tightened with the need to rationally plan and control every detail. The need for control was the polar opposite of faith.

*Breathe, release, open, and trust* became his mantra, as he drifted back into sleep.

# 20. Descending

*My God, my God, why hast thou forsaken me?*
– Matthew, 27:46

———————

Ravi registered the flash of fluorescent lights above her as she was wheeled from the Sleep Room where the Professor had broken her. She felt the motion of the gurney. With each click of the wheels and each passing light overhead, the screams she had heard from other Sleep Rooms grew fainter. The sounds grew calmer. A proper hospital began to appear around her.

For the most part, the personnel working in the recovery area were legitimate nurses and doctors, unaware of the activities of the Professor and his associates in the special wing. Occasionally, patients like Ravi were sent here for recovery from traumas they'd suffered in the Sleep Rooms. Thorazine was usually prescribed to keep recovering patients from communicating with the staff. Enough of that drug would leave the sharpest mind catatonic.

Ravi's IV drip ensured she would not be able to talk with anyone. For the first time since her ordeal had begun, Ravi felt hopeless. Her eyes leaked tears as the gurney was rolled down the hall toward her room. The Professor had promised another day of torment. This was not salvation, but only a respite.

Rachel's shattered body filled her mind, then the explosions of pain she had felt in the Professor's lab, and horrible visions of more to come. Ravi was too numb to sob. Drool oozed from the corner of her mouth and down her neck, joining the puddle of tears in her sweat-drenched hair.

She felt strong arms reach beneath her body and lift her onto a softer surface – a hospital bed. The room almost came into focus before her mind returned to the pain. Her heart felt skewered by an icy terror that froze her even as she tumbled backward into the fuzzy realms of Thorazine dreams.

Ravi had never in her life felt such utter hopelessness, not only for herself but for all of humanity. Her father's world of compassion simply did not exist. It had all been a fanciful dream that could never be real in a world like this. Her silent streaming tears were the only indication of the aching sorrow she felt within her paralyzed body.

A hand dimmed the lights of her room, a voice said, "Get some sleep, hon," and a door clicked shut. In the gloom Ravi's body clenched and jerked beneath the bonds of the drugs. Her father had been such a fool, she now realized with utter certainty. All trust, all faith was gone. There was no need to resist any longer. The hope of death was the only hope her withered heart could afford.

Her last thought before she lost consciousness was that she had killed her precious Rachel. Her idiotic blathering rants for the television cameras had been pompous acts of self-importance, nothing more. Her father's pathetic need for a better world had infected her, not blessed or bolstered her. She felt hatred for all his hopes and dreams, for herself, and for the world they lived in, as she fell into the abyss of total blackness.

# 21. Out of Control

Ian stood outside the Institute at 6:45 a.m., breathing, waiting, feeling. The moment arrived. It was right. He walked past the guard at the entrance booth, casually nodding good morning. He strode briskly down the hall, and, looking to make sure no one was inside, stepped into the nurses' locker room.

Ian left the room with a nurse's uniform and a pair of white shoes under his arm. He turned down the hallway to his right and moved toward the Sleep Room section of the hospital, looking around and stepping up his pace. Ian turned quickly, ducking into the Sleep Room. *Ravi wasn't there!*

A chart lay on the stool beside the table. It was very unlike the Professor to leave a chart lying around, but apparently the exertions of the previous day had exhausted him, and he'd slipped up. Ian scanned down the chart. There! The last entry showed that Ravi was in Room 212, one floor up.

He charged out the door, turned right down the next hall, bounded up the stairs, then through the doorway onto the second floor. He slowed, trying to blend in with the ward's normal activity, catching his breath as he searched for the room.

The Professor would arrive as he always did, like clockwork, at 7:15. He had less than thirty minutes to find Ravi and get her out of the building. All hell would break loose when the Professor discovered she was gone.

A nurse was sitting at the nurses' station, *right across from Room 212.* He didn't know what to do. The clock ticked. Five minutes went by, and then another five.

A second nurse walked slowly toward the station. The rubber soles of her white shoes gave voice to her tired feet as they met the polished floor with each step – *squeak, squeak, squeak, squeak.* She stopped to chat with the nurse at the desk, leaning her elbows on the counter to take a load off for a few minutes. They giggled about their husbands' reactions as they had watched the Montreal Canadiens lose yet another match the night before.

Ian's body tightened with each inane comment the nurses made about their stupid husbands and their stupid sports habits. The clock ticked, ticked, *ticked*. Ian reminded himself to breathe and to let go. Soon after, the nurses finished their conversation with wishes that hockey season would end soon. Ian silently concurred. Finally the squeaky nurse ambled on down the hall to make her rounds.

Ian gave a small prayer of thanks for the squeaky one's exit. The wall clock said 6:57. Eighteen minutes left. A phone rang softly, and the station nurse picked it up. Ian couldn't hear what she said, but as the nurse stood up, Ian took the opportunity to race past the nurses' station and into Ravi's room. Ravi's eyes were closed, but as Ian burst in, she slowly opened them. *Thank God!*

Ravi looked much better now than she had after the Professor's high-tech dungeon session. Someone had sponge-bathed her and washed her hair. Ravi was still groggy but clearing by the minute. As instructed by the Professor, the nurses had stopped the Thorazine drip so her senses would be clear and vulnerable to stimulation when he resumed his work this morning.

Ravi's eyes widened as, seeing Ian, she shrank back against the bed. Because she had been so much on his mind, Ian had forgotten this woman didn't know him. Ian spoke quickly as he leaned over her to look into Ravi's eyes. "My name is Ian McDonald. You don't know me, but I'm a friend. Do you believe me?"

The thick fog of impending doom that had enveloped her in the night lifted. A surge of life coursed through her heart and body. Ravi looked up at the man. Her icy heart of darkness melted, and she responded with certainty. "Yes, I do believe you." There was still hope. Her hands trembled as she took the stack of clothing the man offered.

"Put those on. Quickly." Ian turned his back to allow her privacy. He bit his lip. Would they be able to escape? His heart pounded and his mind doubted, until he remembered again: *Breathe.*

"What now?" Ravi stood small and fragile next to Ian, wearing a white nurse's uniform and white shoes, both of which were a little too big, but looked authentic enough.

"We've gotta get out of here. Now!"

Ian peeked out the door. The nurse was back. Damn! 7:05. Only ten minutes before the Professor would walk into the building. They couldn't wait for the nurse to leave the station. They had to move! His mind swam, finding no ideas worth latching onto.

Ian again peered around the corner, hoping the nurse had at least turned away from Ravi's room. The nurse was looking down, buried in a celebrity gossip rag. Ian heard the wall clock ticking. This would have to do.

As they took their first step out the door, the duty nurse raised her head to stare right at them, her eyes widening with interest.

There was no turning back. Ian slipped his arm around Ravi, positioning her so that the nurse would see as little of her as possible, and staggered forward. Leaning on Ravi, further shielding her from the nurse's line of sight, he called over his shoulder, "I've injured my knee. This nurse'll help me down to Emergency." Ian hoped his white lab coat would sell the fraud for the few minutes they would need. There was no other choice.

They moved slowly around the corner and then rushed forward as Ian saw the opening door of the first of the two elevators. Ian pushed the ground floor button. The doors closed at a pace that made Ian want to grab them and muscle them together. Finally the doors met, and the elevator began its descent.

. . .

The Professor came out of the first floor canteen with a cup of French roast coffee. He savored it as he walked, anticipating today's work. He would make new breakthroughs with Ravi in the Sleep Room. Punching the elevator's *up* button, he checked his watch. 7:07.

. . .

Ian's heart thudded audibly. The time it took for the elevator to descend was interminable. Finally, the door opened and Ian's heart leapt to his throat. He couldn't believe what he saw. *The basement!* Ian panicked as he realized the elevator had gone past the first floor and on down to the lowest level. He reached out, carefully pressing the first floor button as a face appeared through the door.

"Morning. Going up?" A worker from the basement laundry positioned her cart against the elevator door to hold it open while she loaded sheets and towels onto it. "This'll just take a second."

Ian's mind spun as he eyed the large stacks of linens. They couldn't wait for her to finish. They had to get out of here now. *7:10. Five minutes!*

. . .

The Professor looked at his watch, cursing the elevator. 7:10. With a beep, the doors slid open. He entered and punched the button for the second floor. Slipping through the opening doors, the Professor walked briskly down the hall toward Ravi's recovery room.

As he was about to enter the room, he was knocked aside by a fast-moving nurse whose head was down, reading a chart. French roast coffee splashed from his cup onto his suit coat. The nurse froze, realizing who she'd bumped – and the quality of his suit. The Professor glared at her.

Looking up into his furious face, the nurse stammered her apology. Running to the nurses' station, she got a box of tissues and sprinted back to mop the liquid from the Professor's expensive jacket. The red-faced nurse blocked him as he reached for the door handle. "I'm sorry, I'm so sorry. Jesus, this suit looks expensive, I-I-I'm sure I can get this out." She dabbed furiously at his lapel.

"I hope so, because I assure you, you could not afford the cost of getting this suit cleaned," the Professor said icily.

. . .

Ian took Ravi's hand and hurried her out of the elevator past the slow-moving laundry worker. They ran down halls and turned corners, going on Ian's instinct alone, when he saw a shaft of daylight. Its source was a ramp near the freight elevators where delivery trucks unloaded hospital and cafeteria supplies. Ian nearly dragged Ravi off her feet as he ran at full speed, pulling her behind him. 7:13.

. . .

The nurse pulled out another tissue, pressing hard into the Professor's lapel. She thought of the new school clothes her kids needed that she couldn't buy if she didn't get this bastard's suit clean. The Professor's scowl moved from the nurse's bowed head down to his watch. 7:13.

When the nurse spit on the Kleenex to use saliva as a cleaning agent like she did with her children, that was the last straw for the Professor. He grabbed her wrist and twisted. He hissed, "That is quite enough!"

Pushing the stricken nurse out of the way, the Professor snarled, "You'll get a bill for the cleaning. Or maybe a bill to replace the whole damned suit."

The nurse glared, rubbing her hurt wrist, as the Professor opened the door to reveal an empty bed.

. . .

7:14. An alarm in the hallway blared. The Professor must have gone straight to Ravi's room to start another day of degradation. Security guards secured doorway exits. Ian and Ravi burst around the corner into the concrete loading area as a steel gate began its descent from the ceiling to seal the loading dock. They were still thirty feet from the gate. If it closed, there was no hope of escape. They *had* to make it. There was no choice. They flew across the concrete floor.

Ian threw himself under the gate, and crouching, reached back for Ravi. Ravi stumbled over her too-big shoes and fell, sprawling forward. The momentum of the gate increased as it descended. With only inches to go before it sealed, a voice in Ian's mind screamed, *DO IT NOW!*

He grasped Ravi's slender wrists with both hands and yanked with all his might. She slid forward. Her trailing foot was caught as the heavy metal gate settled with a clang. A loud crack issued through the freight dock as the sole of her shoe broke in two from the pressure.

Slipping her foot out of the broken over-sized shoe, Ravi was already moving to gain traction. Panting, she scrambled to her feet on the free side of the sealed gate with Ian. As they ran up the ramp toward the street level, Ravi kicked off the other shoe to run barefoot.

Alarm bells and shouted orders filled the air with noise and confusion. Ian peered around the corner of the wall that sloped up from the subterranean loading dock. A dozen guards ran out the front doors, only yards to the left of the ramp where they stood. They would be seen, but that couldn't be helped. They had to run.

Ian and Ravi dashed across the street. A Guinness beer truck slammed on its brakes, sliding across the pavement where Ian and Ravi had crossed only a second before. The driver cursed at them in French, but the large truck blocked the view of the security guards, giving them another precious moment of cover before the driver ground the gears and stomped on the gas.

In that moment, Ravi had hailed a cab and they jumped in. Sirens sounded all around as police cars moved into the area. Driving down McTavish Street, the cabbie looked into the rearview mirror, suspicious about his breathless, wide-eyed passengers. He demanded the fare be paid up front. Ian had no cash, and neither did Ravi. Turning off the main street and pulling over to the curb, the cabbie angrily ordered them out.

A hospital security car roared by. A moment later, from around the corner, Ian and Ravi heard its tires squeal in a locked-brake stop. They heard its engine roar back to life in the whining scream of reverse gear. The sound grew nearer.

"CHRIST! They saw us!" Ian yelled, looking up and down the street for somewhere to run. Panicking, Ian suddenly remembered the events of the night before and told himself to breathe. The brakes of the hospital security car squealed inches from the corner where Ravi and Ian would have become visible to the driver. There it remained stuck, the driver angrily honking at a car that had blocked its reverse progress.

A semi-trailer truck approached; the driver didn't register their waving pleas for a ride until he looked down and saw Ravi. The driver was an Indian man. He pulled over and threw open the passenger door. In a Canadian-Indian accent, he asked, "Need a ride, eh?"

"Yes, thank you!" they replied in unison. Ravi and Ian climbed up, slamming the door behind them.

"I'm going all the way to Vancouver. Where are you headed?" the trucker asked cheerfully, as he shifted the big rig into gear. Ian and Ravi smiled at one another. The opposite side of Canada sounded good.

Behind them, an expanding web of security personnel shifted into emergency mode, taking names and recording testimonies.

# 22. The Iceman Cometh

*. . . America's top military leaders reportedly drafted plans to kill innocent people and commit acts of terrorism in U.S. cities to create public support for a war.*
– ABCNews.com, David Ruppe, New York, May 1, 2001

---

Since delivering the woman to the Professor, the Soldier had been working in Washington, D.C. with certain Security insiders and a demolition team. He and his team had moved quietly within the walls of the Capitol building, placing explosive charges fitted with remote control detonation devices. At this moment, the Soldier hung suspended from a caving harness and climbing ropes, carefully inserting a detonation charge between the inner walls of the Senate Chamber.

This vertical crawlspace had been created to hold the wiring for electrical lighting fixtures and ductwork for a modern air conditioning system, part of the Capitol's 1949 reconstruction, although the need to install steel support structures to bolster the heavy crumbling dome had been the initial impetus for that upgrade.

He could barely hear a session of the Senate just beyond the plaster wall. A small ray of light beamed into his dark workspace from the Senate chamber. The tiny point of brilliance, so luminous – it reminded him of something. *What was it?*

The young monk's face in Tibet – so singular and fragile like the beam of light – came back to him. He remembered how the boy's mouth had issued the thunderous chant of a thousand monks. The painful memory of the dying monk's metamorphosis – the experience that had leveled him like an uppercut to the chin on that haunting day – rattled him.

He forced his mind to focus on the work at hand. The Soldier's demolition training had begun decades ago in EOD when he was a Navy SEAL in Indian Head, Maryland. Explosive Ordinance Disposal had been about taking bombs apart, but it was a short stretch from there to learning how to put bombs together. He had a knack for it – and the nerve to place them wherever they were needed. From then on, when there was a need for someone who could do the job and keep his mouth shut, the Soldier had often been the one chosen for the assignment.

The Professor's obsession with the woman had stirred a covert ops hornets' nest. The Soldier's rapid shuttling between Canada and Washington on these missions created pressure that was wearing, even on his steely nerves. He hadn't been the same since the mission in Tibet, and yet he needed all his precision and focus now. This assignment demanded it.

He quietly placed the thermate-based steel-cutting demolition charge on a strategic load-bearing beam. Steadying himself with his climbing winch, he used the other hand to begin the most delicate part. His fingers trembled. *My fingers do* not *shake and it can't happen now!* He bit down on his tongue, using the pain to sharpen his focus and willing his hands to steady.

He carefully placed the wireless detonation device to the charge and – *an electric vibration exploded through the silence.*

It was his cell phone in the pocket of his shirt. His last remaining nerve jangling, he sucked in with an open mouth the small amount of air that was available in the hot, dusty crawlspace. Sweat trickled from his armpits as he grabbed for his phone.

The Professor spoke as the Soldier clicked it on. *Christ, the woman had escaped!* He had to go back to Montreal immediately.

In a rare act of contrition, the Professor admitted to the Soldier that he had panicked. He conceded that he had gotten the Montreal Police – the Service de Police de la Ville de Montréal – involved. The Professor promised the angry Soldier he would call them off immediately.

As the Soldier made his way down, silently rappelling between the walls, he muttered that the *last* thing he needed was local yokels across Canada getting involved in his operation. The CIA had already riled Canadians by shipping innocent Canadian citizens of Middle Eastern descent off to Syria to be tortured years before the U.S. had invaded that country.

The Professor felt stupid because he had not smelled out Lieutenant McDonald as a limp-wristed rat from the beginning. But these were difficult times. The attrition rate had skyrocketed, and he had to take whatever personnel he could get. Beggars can't be choosers. Worse, the attrition rate could get much higher if they didn't get the Indian woman back in the lab and learn how to stop this disease from spreading. The Soldier was his only hope of salvaging his place in history, before the VP resorted to Plan B – outright martial law.

The Soldier took control upon his arrival at Taloncrag. He quickly figured out what had happened through taxi records, eyewitness accounts gathered by Security, and satellite images. In a matter of minutes, he had the make, model, and license plate of the semi, as well as where it was headed. According to the trucker's manifest, his final destination would be Vancouver, but the first stop was Detroit.

A quick MapQuest showed he would likely take Autoroute Ville-Marie to Autoroute 20 O, which became Provincial Route 401 W, for nearly 500 miles west through Ontario, before crossing into the U.S. to Detroit. If he couldn't catch them before they left Canada, he could arrange for them to be stopped at the border. But he much preferred to deal with the escapees himself.

On the road, he pulled his Glock 34, an Austrian-made military semi-automatic side-arm, out of his glove box to check his ammo. He'd had to dump his German Luger after he'd eliminated the King Air crew and the woman's screaming companion. God, that had ticked him off. He felt an ache in his chest. It was such an odd feeling. It must be because he lost his favorite side-arm. He shouldn't have used the Luger for that.

Yeah, he had loved the Luger, but he liked the Glock as well. You didn't have to cock it, it had internal safety mechanisms instead of external, and most important for his line of work, if the gun exploded on you, it was designed to make sure the gun went, but not the shooter. As much as he used his weapons, that was a must feature.

Having no hands was a major drawback for future employment opportunities.

But why did he feel so bad about losing the Luger? He'd lost weapons before. Was it something else? Images and sensations of emotion tangled in the Soldier's mind, until with an act of will, he shook them off. Back to the task at hand. He had to find this traitor, Ian, and the woman.

It would not be hard to find them. He was cruising in his Hummer with a high sensitivity fuzz-buster to avoid any squabbles with the local cops. He accelerated to close the gap between himself and Mr. Ravi Singh, the Canadian trucker who'd immigrated from India twenty years before. He made a mental note to talk to Canadian immigration about this foreigner. Unfortunately for Mr. Singh, he'd picked up the wrong hitchhikers. He should have known better. It was, after all, against his company's policy.

His cell phone rang. He laid the Glock on the passenger seat, reached into his pocket, and flipped open the phone in one smooth movement, like a gun-slinging cowboy. "Yeah?"

The Professor spoke. "Listen, I want you to do something really special for our friend Mr. McDonald. He definitely deserves something . . . *appropriate* to his betrayal."

"Done." Ian's fate was sealed. The Soldier picked up the Glock from the passenger seat, tossed it into the glove box, and slammed the lid shut.

# 23. The Noose Tightens

Just as the Soldier knew he would, the trucker exited Montreal and took Autoroute Ville-Marie to Autoroute 40 O, crossing out of Quebec into the province of Ontario. The road, also known as Autoroute 20 O, was the main highway, which then became Provincial Route 401 W.

Ian and Ravi did not realize that the trucker's route to Vancouver was via Detroit and they would be crossing the border into the United States in a few hundred miles. If they had, they would have parted company with him, for there was a great likelihood that the U.S.-Canadian border guards had their photos by now.

Ravi had many questions for Ian that could not be asked in front of the truck driver. Questions like *Who are you?* and *Why did you save me?* For now, they would have to wait.

The trucker was from Pune, the village where Ravi's father and mother grew up. His name was Ravi as well, and he was amused that this lovely young woman had been given a boy's name. When she explained that her mother named her after the famed Indian sitarist, Ravi Shankar, trucker Ravi boasted that he was quite a singer himself. Ian watched Ravi's beautiful face as it glowed with the excitement of finding someone who made her feel close to family and home. She looked like a girl, beaming and laughing. Ian's heart melted. He wanted to keep this woman safe, if it was the last thing he ever did.

Ravi and Ravi sang through the morning, while sunlight streamed in through the window. Hearing sounds in a language he didn't understand soothed Ian's heart and mind. He didn't think about the words – he didn't know what they meant. He just felt the vibration of the sounds.

Watching these two people rooted from a culture so far away, sharing common childhood memories, moved Ian. This companionship offered both of them healing in a land and at a time when difference often meant alienation.

The drive across the Ontario plains was mesmerizing. Ravi the trucker promised them that further down the road the beauty of the hills and forests would become magnificent – more than they could even envision. He loved driving the open roads of Canada and could imagine doing nothing else or being anywhere else but here with the unfolding mountains, plains, farmland, and rivers, all so different and exquisitely beautiful. He said, "Canada is definitely God's country. Of course, all countries are God's country." He added with a wink, "When one is thankful for their home, God glows from within it."

Ian gazed out the window at the passing fields, woods, and occasional hills. The morning sun grew higher in the sky and warmed the cabin of the truck with its light. Ian dozed to the sound of a merry melody sung by the now renowned duo, *the singing Ravis*. Their songs were like lullabies.

Ian slept and the singing Ravis sang, until the trucker revealed his other love: eating. He knew the best truck stops on their route. As he pulled in at a diner whose sign advertised an enormous breakfast buffet, he declared proudly, "All you can eat!" He jumped down from the truck.

Ian and Ravi exchanged glances as they remembered they had no money. They sat still. Ian said, "We're not really hungry, we'll just wait here."

Ravi the trucker, a short, roundish man, looked up at them through the cab's open door. He studied their faces for only a moment before discerning what was going on, "Nonsense. Do not worry, my friends. Lunch is on Ravi today, and maybe dinner, too!" He added with a laugh, while patting his small frame's lateral girth, "Ravi cannot miss meals. I might destroy my perfect profile. Besides, I digest much better when eating with friends. This place is the best. Twenty-four hour breakfast!"

Ravi still did not move, looking self-consciously down at her bare feet. The temperature had dropped as the truck had gradually ascended to higher elevations. Ravi looked from her feet to the piles of dirty snow on the edges of the parking lot.

The trucker nodded as his eyes followed hers. He leaned in and rummaged around beneath his seat. "You will be very happy to know that, as my mother always said, I was blessed with small feet."

He produced a pair of slippers he used to get from cold roadside trucker showers to his truck's sleeper cell. "Cinderella, I think you'll find these a perfect fit." With that, the trio was on their way, following their noses as much as their eyes toward the aromas wafting from the diner.

The waffles, pancakes, scrambled eggs, cottage fries, and hash browns all lay steaming before them. They had their choice of coffee, tea, orange juice, tomato juice, grapefruit juice, and on and on. All three performed balancing acts, their plates piled high as they carefully walked back to their table.

Ian had a strange feeling that he couldn't quite identify. It was when Ravi-the-trucker said in order to avoid confusion, they should call him Ravi, and this lovely young woman, "Ravi*shing*," that Ian laughed with recognition. He was *happy*. It had been so long since he had felt joy that he hadn't even noticed when he'd lost it. *That is how we cope,* he supposed. *If we remembered happiness when our lives were devoid of it, it would drive us mad.*

Ian looked out the window at the passing cars and wondered how many of the drivers were unwittingly living lives of quiet desperation. What miracles lay waiting for those people, if they too could just learn to breathe, to let go of control, and move in faith.

The trucker paid the check and handed out toothpicks to his new friends. Filled and over-filled, the bloated trio hobbled out into the parking lot. As the trucker walked around to his side of the truck, Ravi spoke under her breath, "Should we go to the media?"

Ian quietly responded, "No, we don't know who can be trusted. Some are on the Company payroll."

"What about the internet?"

As the trucker reached across to unlock and swing open their door, Ian answered, "The internet is too highly controlled. Mind-Net is probably watching for keywords about you."

Ravi thought about the fierce media attacks on her just before her kidnapping. Were they orchestrated? They climbed up into the truck. The engine revved. All three held their hands by the heater before again hitting the road. Young Ravi sat quietly, thinking.

. . .

Forty-five minutes later, a Hummer pulled up to the diner. The Soldier ordered a large coffee to go and questioned the waitress about a threesome including a middle-aged overweight Indian man and a pretty young Indian woman. His waitress remembered them.

*The noose tightened.*

# 24. Still Breathing

They had driven all day long, and Ravi the trucker had seen to it that they were all well fed. A couple of weeks of this truck-stop food, and Ian and Ravi would have the same profile as their friend. It was soul food, stick-to-your-ribs food.

The sun had begun its descent in earnest. The warm cab, the low lights of the dashboard, and the gentle tunes of the singing Ravis left Ian dozing yet again. He was making up for the many ragged nights of sleeplessness inflicted by the torturous Sleep Room duty.

They drove into the deepening Ontario night. It had been a long time since he could relax like this, and he enjoyed the feeling of his arm touching Ravi's arm and his thigh touching Ravi's thigh. The truck hummed down the road, and dreams overtook him. In the dream, he heard the voice that had spoken to him after his return from the cathedral. It touched the center of his mind and set off a glow. It touched the center of his heart, and his lungs filled with air. As he exhaled, the glow spread.

Ian's mind traversed a universe of flowing consciousness. He saw the earth from far away, a blue orb cradled in darkness, fragile in the vast expanse of space. The earth became his heart, and he felt the pulse of humanity flow through him, the pain of losing loved ones to death, the joy of mothers holding their newborn babies to their breasts, with umbilical cords still connecting their bodies.

He felt great hope, and then suddenly the agony of war, precious children being lost, and a feeling of being hated by the world, by God. Ian gasped loudly in his sleep. He saw the U.S. Capitol building explode in a raging fire and then an enveloping darkness spread across the bright white-blue planet, covering it like a thick smog of hopelessness. Ian began to moan.

The two Ravis stopped singing and looked down at his troubled face, lit by the dashboard's lights. Tears spilled from his eyes. He sobbed softly, still dreaming. Ravi wanted to touch him, to console him, but she somehow knew that it was important for Ian to experience whatever pain he was feeling. She put her finger to her lips, signaling to the trucker to let Ian sleep as they drove on into the night. They resumed their singing, more softly now, while Ian continued to dream.

Ian's vision turned from the heavens down toward the earth. He saw tree tops and rivers. He saw a great fire and people dancing around it. A silvery platinum dome hung over the entire scene, a bulwark of protection – yet it seemed to offer sanctuary beyond physical safety. He heard vibrations – *chants* – emanating from the dome.

Abruptly, the vision turned westward. Everything went into fast-forward, jerked out of the slow, smooth dreaming reverie of a moment before. His vision screamed over the treetops, down the road, and to a place where many electric lights shone with shrill brightness, lights that screamed at the eyes. Many cars and trucks were stopped at a roadblock. He saw uniformed men and handcuffs being snapped tight on wrists. He felt the pinch of them. He saw a door open, a uniformed man waiting behind it. Through that door, he saw – *oblivion.* Ian's heart turned to ice. He tried to scream but could not, as if he were drugged. His heart beat wildly as he made vain attempts to speak. He groaned and struggled.

The blue digital dashboard clock clicked from 2:59 a.m. to 3:00 a.m. Ravi looked with worried eyes from Ian to the trucker. He pulled over to the side of Provincial Route 401 W as Ravi reached over to shake Ian's shoulder.

# 25. The Kill

*Activists behind a website dedicated to revealing secret documents have complained of harassment . . . detained for 21 hours by police . . . followed on a flight from Reykjavik to Copenhagen by two American agents . . . thinly veiled threats, he says, from "an apparent British intelligence agent" . . . "Computers were also seized" . . . another member of Wikileaks said on Twitter . . . "If anything happens to us, you know why . . . and you know who is responsible."*
– The Sunday Times (UK), April 11, 2010

Descending a steep incline, the road ahead curved around a series of S-shaped bends. Trees blocked the Soldier's view of the oncoming highway as his headlights strained to pierce the darkness. As he sped around the last of the curves, his pulse quickened. He was close.

The Hummer rounded the corner onto a straight stretch of the highway to reveal an 18-wheeler climbing the next hill. He pulled out his binoculars to look at its license plate and then hastily threw them down and gripped the wheel, accelerating. It was them.

This was perfect. Now there'd be no need to complicate things by involving immigration agents at the U.S. border, with their choking traffic, bright lights, curious eyes, and meddlesome questions. He thought about the Professor's demand that Ian, the traitor, get something very special. He could fulfill that request with the care and the time it deserved in the desolate woods just off the road.

The highway was under construction here, leaving only two lanes open for vehicles, his and the lane for oncoming traffic. Two cars separated him from the semi. But all was well; he had them now. He reached over to pull his Glock out of the glove box.

Looking up, the Soldier slammed on his brakes just in time. The car in front of the Hummer had begun to slow down, putting on its emergency flashers.

The Soldier pulled to his left to pass. Just as he did so, an 18-wheeler rose over the hill from the opposite direction like a blazing super-nova. The headlights blinded him. A horn exploded in the night. The Soldier wrenched the wheel back to the right just in time to avoid destruction as the big rig screamed by, only inches from his side. "CHRIST!" Sweat beaded on the Soldier's forehead.

The target's truck had disappeared over the hill, and he still couldn't pass this asshole in front of him, because suddenly it was Grand-friggin'-Central-Station here. A steady stream of traffic from the opposite direction was coming at him. The ditch to the right was far too severe to attempt passing on that side. *It'll be all right,* he told himself. *It ain't like that rig is gonna outrun me. And they don't even know I'm here.*

He lit a cigarette and settled into his seat. He had meant to savor the coming kill. *I need to get this back on track.* The Soldier watched the exhaled smoke plume across his windshield, an ominous smoldering lit by the glowing red dash lights below. His stomach churned as if he'd swallowed something tainted. The sweat on his brow intensified. He drew another deep drag on his smoke, trying to dull his unease.

# 26. The Woods

Ian jerked awake. Emerging from his vision of capture and oblivion, he struggled to right himself from his cramped position and gasped, "Whooaaa, wha', *what happened?*" He blinked, trying to make sense of the dreams he'd just left and trying to reorient himself. Ravi's soft concerned eyes looked into his. "Breathe," she said. She gently stroked his forearm. He inhaled deeply and relaxed the breath out.

Ian looked at the dashboard clock and saw the softly glowing *3:00* in the darkness. Suddenly, he knew. He looked at the trucker and said firmly, "Ravi, this is where we must get out."

The truck driver, surprised, pulled on his brake as he exclaimed, "What do you mean, my friend?"

Ian took Ravi's hand. "I can't explain, but we must leave NOW. Hurry!"

Ravi jumped out of the truck with him. She looked back at the trucker, as Ian shouted to him over the passing traffic, "Ravi, put your truck in gear right now, RIGHT THIS MINUTE! Thanks for everything. We love you. You must go, *NOW!*" Ian slammed the door and pulled Ravi toward the woods.

The trucker grabbed his gearshift, grinding the multi-ton 18-wheeler into gear. He stepped on the accelerator, and the great engine whined into motion.

Ian and Ravi ran down the ditch, up the other side, and into the woods – just as headlights bent around the last curve, its high beams raking the trees as they dove for cover.

# 27. Dropping the Trap Door

The Soldier finally blew past the jerk with the emergency flashers, fighting an urge to squeeze off a round into the driver's window as he passed. But he was a professional, and that woman needed to be back in the lab, *ASAP*.

He rounded a long curve. His lights flashed on a movement in the woods just off the road. As he started to slow down to investigate, the big rig appeared just ahead. The Soldier floored the gas pedal as he realized the road was suddenly deserted except for him and the semi. *Finally some good luck.* The night was black, and when he noticed that the hill to the left offered both a clear path with no oncoming traffic and a smooth incline for a relatively safe crash path for the semi, he moved into action.

The Soldier pulled up to the left of the rig and sped ahead of it as he pressed the button to lower the right rear window. His plan was to blow out the two front left tires of the rig, causing the truck to sag to the left, climb the slope, and come to a stop in the trees just beyond. It had to be a controlled accident; he needed the woman alive for the Professor. He swung around to fire a round out the open window.

The bullet cut through the outside tire, but it didn't penetrate the inside backup tire. The cab lurched to the left. Inside, Ravi gripped the wheel and yanked it to the right, heading for a deep ravine.

Ravi's frantic attempt to right his truck after the shocking bright flash and shot that rang out from the passing Hummer caused his heart to seize. All those years of truck stop food had taken a toll on his arteries and heart.

As Ravi slumped over the wheel, the truck veered off the road, careening off a steep shoulder and down into a gully far below. Crashing through the saplings all the way down reduced the truck's speed, but when it hit bottom, the sound was thunderous.

"DAMN!" The Soldier could see the Professor's face when he told him he'd killed the woman. Slamming on the brakes, he leapt out and ran as fast as he could, slipping down the slope into the ravine, grabbing saplings as he went. He skidded down, reaching from one to the next. At the bottom, he placed his boot on the overturned semi's inside front wheel and crawled up the truck's undercarriage, finding footholds where he could.

Standing on the driver's side of the cab, which had now become the top, he lowered himself through the window and found the trucker – alone. In the glow of the truck's one remaining headlight and yellow side lamps, the soldier scanned the immediate area and saw no bodies.

He knelt down beside the trucker, gently cradling his head. He spoke softly to the dying man. "I'm a Mountie. We'll help you, we've got an ambulance coming. But the two young folks – are they okay?"

Ravi was only moments from death. He registered the Mountie's concern and sought to reassure him, even as he fought for breath. "Yes . . . fine. I let them out . . . just . . . before."

The Soldier dropped Ravi's head with a thud. Bracing his hands against the window frame, he hoisted himself out of the window. Climbing up the hill, he looked back toward the dying trucker's overturned rig and felt a pain in his chest. He touched his Glock, and its smooth surface brought him back to the task at hand. He moved on up the hill to his vehicle.

The Soldier wheeled the Hummer around in a U-turn, gravel spraying and tires squealing. He roared back up the highway to where he'd sighted the motion in the woods. He crossed over to the other side of the road. With the driver's side window open, he crept at a snail's pace along the shoulder, shining his spotlight on the brush.

Finally he spotted a broken branch and what looked like two sets of footprints. Not much foot traffic out in a place like this. *This might turn out just fine after all.*

# 28. Shadows Cast

The night was lit only by stars. Ian's fear crept up his spine to grip his brain. He remembered his vision in Montreal. He breathed.

Ravi followed closely, her hand in Ian's. It was good to let someone else find the way. The last few weeks had been exhausting. The public attention, the media attacks, the self-doubt — and then her heart broke as she thought of Rachel, poor lovely Rachel — and the psychiatric institute. Fear crept up inside her, but as Ravi exhaled, she *let go*.

Allowing Ian to chart the way — it felt like the flow she'd experienced when she had begun letting the messages pour through her. It felt right, as if this was the time to release control. She was learning a dance of action and non-action, control and non-control, like the waves of the ocean exerting force and then receding. A rhythm was out there, and she sensed it wasn't only she who was opening to it. Something larger was occurring. Right now, in this moment, her part was to trust Ian's movement, to ride the wave that flowed through his heart. She squeezed his hand as they made their way through the forest. His touch was warm and sure.

Ian felt — no, he *knew* — that this was the way. Out here the stars were huge, casting far more light than in urban areas, yet the overhead forest canopy thickened with each step they took, leading them into growing darkness. Even so, Ian moved forward with speed and purpose. The path they took was slightly more illuminated than the surrounding shadows.

They forged ahead deeper into the forest. The night air was chill, yet both Ian and Ravi had become drenched with sweat, dodging and weaving between the branches of the dense trees. Ian had increased their pace after hearing a thunderous crash in the distance only minutes after they'd fled the highway. Ravi advanced as well as she could in the slippers the trucker had given her, but the mud of the forest floor had found its way into them, making her footing more and more treacherous. She was still exhausted from the ordeal of the previous day. Ian slowed as Ravi struggled, but urged her on.

The forest became ever more dense as they moved further into it. The devices of man receded behind them. They might be heading to death from thirst, starvation, or even hypothermia if the weather turned. Over and over, fear clenched Ian's muscles, and over and over the voice of his visions spoke softly. *Fear closes all doors. Fear closes all doors.* He breathed deeply, and the path became a bit brighter.

In the distance, wolves began to howl. Ian and Ravi froze. The shadows of the forest were dark and deep. Ian's path was no longer lit. Oblivion had swallowed them without a sound.

Faint stirrings in the brush startled them. *Probably just animals,* they both hoped in unison. Suddenly the rustling intensified, and from the shadows, movement exploded toward them. Both were thrown to the ground, gasping for breath. In a flash, their feet were bound, their hands held behind them. Ravi wrenched one hand free, reaching toward Ian. She wanted her last experience to be touching him. "IAN!"

Ian's thought was the same as Ravi's, as he too stretched out his hand toward her. Their fingers nearly touched. A charge ran through their hearts. After all they had been through, for it to end like this was too much to bear.

Ian's mind churned in a torrent of thought. How his years of sleepwalking through life had ended only yesterday. How this magical woman had affected him through the television screen, and then in life – years of soul sickness had been healed in a matter of hours. His heart broke. So many years of secrets and regrets. He needed to express his heart, even if it was the last thing he did.

"Ravi, *I love you!*"

"Ian!"

They were pulled apart into the shadows of the forest. The starlight was blocked out. Only darkness remained.

# 29. And This Too Shall Pass

*The use of antidepressants and other mind-altering drugs among school children has more than quadrupled in the last decade, it is revealed today.*
— *London Telegraph,* July 23, 2007

*Dr. Peter Breggin, often referred to as the "Conscience of Psychiatry," [warns] "We're bringing up a generation in this country in which you either sit down, shut up and do what you're told, or you get diagnosed and drugged."*
— *The Psychiatric Drugging of Children,* Counterpunch, April 21, 2010

*The problem with being a child in America today compared to 20 or 30 years ago is that if you are different, if you are agitated, if you are extremely active, you will fall under the gaze of the helping professions, the so-called helping professions.*
— David Cohen, M.D., *The Drugging of Our Children*

---

Ian and Ravi sat on either side of a large man who looked much like a character from an old western movie – clad in buckskin clothing, a bone warrior plate on his chest. Flickering red and yellow firelight played across his face.

Before them, Indian men and women danced around the fire to subdued chants and quiet drumming, while others sat and watched. Ravi, Ian, and the Indian sat in the large circle of observers who surrounded the dancers and the bonfire at the circle's center.

It seemed like a dream. Ian's eyes shot upward. Just for a moment, he saw a silvery platinum light. Then it was gone. *Was this the gathering covered by the dome of light in my dream?* No one else reacted to it. Perhaps it had only been his imagination.

The man between Ian and Ravi, his warrior plate rattling on his chest, opened his arms and spoke. "My mother named me *He Who is in the Stars* in my ancestor's language. Here I am known as the Healer – a term our ancestors used for those with awareness of the spirit world."

Ian and Ravi stared, speechless. They had been marched for an hour in silence by shadowy figures they could barely make out in the darkness. Their captors had led them ever deeper into the dark foliage of the forest until they had suddenly stepped into a clearing, and this settlement had appeared before them. They still struggled to understand where they were and why they had been brought here.

The Healer continued. "I apologize for your capture and for frightening you. The Great Spirit gave me a vision of your coming, but as often happens, I saw only images, like slices of what was to pass."

Turning to Ravi, he said, "I was unsure if the Lieutenant was your captor or your protector." He smiled at Ian. "I ask for your understanding, Lieutenant. The Great Spirit always reminds us he has a sense of humor." He added, "I hope you can laugh with him."

Ian's body had become taut and his breath had become rapid and shallow during the terrifying moments of their capture and long march. Sitting here now, unbound and unguarded, he felt himself beginning to loosen as the man spoke. The man had a powerful aura that spoke more loudly than his words. "Call me Ian."

"As I said, we have been expecting you for some time, many weeks, in fact."

Ravi's mouth dropped open. "But we escaped only yesterday. How did . . . ?"

The Healer continued, "I've had visions, little sister." Ravi's eyes misted at his words. Fusing Rachel's memory with this large, gentle man, she felt drawn to him. Though she had just met him, when he reached out and lightly stroked her cheek as one would to reassure a child, it felt right. It wasn't just his words. It was something about *his presence*.

The Healer explained, "My visions are not linear. The Great Spirit isn't big on details, but is perfect with the big picture, you might say."

Smiling, he continued. "What I know is that you have been through a great deal and you have many questions. I also know that you are in grave danger. Tonight we will begin with your questions. You are safe here with us, for now. You met some of our young men in the forest. They are ever vigilant. We can talk now by the fire. I will share with you what the Great Spirit has shared with me."

As the Healer finished speaking, Ian again glimpsed the enormous silvery dome of light encompassing the forest, before it disappeared. The Healer spoke again. "In this place we have created a spiritual circle. For many years our people have come together in this forest for a sacred purpose. Here, what the world calls miracles can occur. Consciousness can evolve much more rapidly. This is a microcosm of what the larger world will become, as human beings realize the power of their consciousness."

Stunned by this revelation, Ravi burst in. "Who are you – and, er – your people?"

The Healer swept his hand toward the people dancing and sitting around the fire. "We are the First Nation of Canada and the original people of America. Many are people of the Tsleil-Waututh Nation, my father's people. However, many original peoples have learned of us, and from the south we have Shawnee, Kick-a-poo, Lakota, Wyandot – my mother's people, who long ago lived here and were the native people of this place, and others as well. We have taught each other much. All who wish to honor their ancestors and maintain the old ways are drawn to our community. The Great Spirit has told us that it is important to maintain islands of people who remain close to our mother earth spirit."

They sat silently watching the dancers for a moment before he spoke again. "My people have endured great suffering, many trails of tears. Through this we have learned what your Bible teaches: *This too shall pass.* You have been called to us, little sister, so that I can tell you that. I know you have seen great suffering lately. I saw your own sister depart this world, and you should know she is among us now to comfort you on your journey before she crosses over."

Ravi began to weep as she felt Rachel's embrace. It was as though Rachel's arms had been around her all along, but the Healer's words had allowed her to feel them. The Healer and Ian sat close but did not interfere as she wept.

Ian observed how those around them sang and danced on, allowing Ravi's feelings to have space. In this place, feelings were not judged or ridiculed. The quiet voice in the center of his mind whispered: *Profound is a way of life here.*

As the drumbeat increased in volume, Ian's fear returned. He asked the Healer, "Are we still in danger?"

"Not tonight. Tonight we have been given protection while a process is playing out." The drumbeat subsided. "You saw the dome of light when you came."

Ian's surprise crossed his face. The man had not shown any indication that he had witnessed the extraordinary light. "You saw it?"

"Not with my eyes, but with my heart. I felt your heart's vibration – it told me you had experienced it visually. There are many more than five senses, young brother. The one your books label simply as the *sixth sense* is vast and wide. There are many languages of the heart and spirit that offer information far beyond what your current world thinks is possible."

Ravi wiped her eyes and looked up at the Healer. "*Current* world?"

"Yes, little sister. The world is in great flux. This is the reason you are here tonight – to understand better what has been happening to you. I know the Great Spirit has been speaking through you. You have been a great Voice, and many people around the world are grateful to you for allowing the Universal Mind to speak with your tongue. The words have been welling up through all of humanity but have been waiting to find a voice for their travels.

"I have experienced the same self-doubts that you have. I know it can be troubling to speak great truths that seem to percolate up from within and then spill over like boiling water, without understanding what they mean. It is a hard thing to speak the heart language when the meaning is too large for the brain. The vulnerability of such speaking is difficult to bear. To move in this way is what the Bible would call *faith*.

"The world is going through great change. As you said at Oxford, we are leaving one age and entering a new one, Aquarius – the Age of Man –that requires us to find our faith. This is larger than the changing of ages, for this is the completion of the *great cycle.*"

Ian was confused. "Wait, you mean your people studied astrology?"

"No, we have no history of astrological wisdom. But like Ravi, I have been called a genius and have studied many cultures, including the White Man's ways. Astrology offered a larger context through which to understand the progression of man.

"My first days were not as a First Nation warrior, but as a schoolboy in Kansas. I knew that my skin was darker than most, but I had little awareness of who I truly was, or of my original people, whose blood ran in my veins. My journey eventually led me back to my people and my ancestors.

"When I was in school, I was much like you, Ravi, in that my mind wanted to embrace many things very quickly. My teachers felt that I had a sickness they called Attention Deficit Disorder. My visions tell me this happened to you, as well."

Ravi looked into the Healer's eyes, which were moist and shining with emotion in the firelight. They had shared the pain of having their gifts misconstrued as defects. Their hearts had endured the desolation that outcasts know.

The Healer's eyes shifted to the dancers, twirling and stamping their prayers and visions of hope down into mother earth. He spoke. "I was forced to take the White man's medicine. It cut me off from the words of the Great Spirit. I knew then how it felt to be truly alone. I know now it served me in the same way a vision does, so that I could understand many in the world who are feeling such alienation."

Ravi's breath caught as she thought of a time when she sat alone at school, feeling like a stranger in a place where everyone else seemed to belong. She remembered the pain of being different when the school nurse called her to the classroom door for her medication as other children giggled and pointed.

"I know what it is like to be a stranger in one's own homeland, my precious little sister." The Healer put his big arm around Ravi's shoulders.

A boy danced before the Healer with arms spread open like an eagle as the warm firelight seemed to lift him in flight. His young face beamed with wonder and joy.

"This pain and the loneliness we felt, Ravi, is being felt by all God's children now. Just as we were drugged into normalcy, millions today feel pressed to deny their gifts. That is why your voice – the voice of the Great Spirit – has been so well received. Many have been lifted on the breath of the Great Spirit since you have loaned him your lungs and lips.

"Of course, the machine turned on you. But those you touched who work in the media have done what they could to share your words and lift you to prominence. You should know, it is enormously important that they do their part, as you do yours. Your collective acts have eased the passage of many lost souls through a dangerous valley of the human journey.

"Earth's children today feel so very out of place in a world that no longer makes sense." The Healer paused. "To understand how vital your role is, you must know the depth of the loneliness of the people.

"The emerging world, so wide and deep, is being ushered in by our expanding souls. To bring a new reality into a constricting world that worships and is built upon the altar of control – without context for what is happening – one can only feel as though they *do not belong in this world.* There is no more lonely a feeling.

"You comforted many that first day and since. The dogma of society and religion is the only reality they have known. It has no place for who they are becoming. Their broken hearts long to know why they are here, and you reminded them . . ."

Ravi's shoulders sank under the weight of her responsibility. The Healer squeezed her arm reassuringly. "Little sister, they think they thirst for your return. I think you know that it is not really *you* they long for, but for their connection to the Great Spirit. The time – the age we are entering – is a homecoming for which the children of light have been waiting many lifetimes. Your voice has helped them remember much of what they have been awaiting. Tonight I will help you remember more. I will tell you now what you came to hear: the history of man, the long journey of man."

# 30. Fingers Clench

Ratlig's reports were now being sent to both the Professor and the Vice President. The VP wanted to know every hiccup in the status of the gamma wave threat. He had become obsessed with the loss of control portended by a changing of consciousness of the masses.

This was a new world. The domination he envisioned – absolute control of the material world's resources – was something he could understand, but controlling *shifting consciousness?* It was like trying to grab water.

What was driving him mad was that without control of the mind, nothing could truly be controlled. Not in a world where eighty percent of the people own little to nothing, and particularly not in a nation where twenty percent of the people own a staggering 85 percent of all of America's wealth. Given enough clarity of thought, the other struggling eighty percent of the people would eventually begin asking some very tough questions about the rules of the economic game they had been playing.

The twenty percent of the population who own virtually everything can maintain such a tilted scale only by having a thumb squarely upon the global consciousness. Now that the consciousness seemed to be shifting, it needed to be – it *must* be – set back in place. A form of global electroshock therapy was required to burn this gamma phenomenon out of existence. There was no turning back.

The Vice President fed Ratlig's report into his shredder and picked up the secure line as the red light silently flashed. "Yeah?"

He nodded as the Air Force Four Star General spoke.

"We have dispatched teams to finalize the war games orders. We're about to lock them into the DOD and FAA systems." The General hesitated for a moment. "They will occur day after tomorrow, upon your order."

Hearing doubt in his voice, the Vice President demanded, "Any questions, General? Any problems?"

The General shifted in his seat. "Well, sir, if we have Watchful Guardian, Northern Safeguard, and Vigilant Denial all going on at the same time, that will leave the northeast corridor virtually defenseless."

The VP tightened his grip on the phone. "Your point?"

The General stared intently at his assistant, who had explained the problem with the war games to him only moments before. "Well, do you think that is wise?"

The Vice President tossed a piece of bait, to see if the General would bite. "Would you like to be a Five Star General?" This could only happen if the United States were under direct attack, as four star generals in the Air Force only become five star generals in times of war.

The General, taken aback, mopped his brow with his handkerchief. *That could happen only if the homeland were under attack! What the hell is going on here?*

The General's assistant pointed to his notes, directing his superior's eyes to another issue. "Mr. Vice President, there's another problem. The Northern Vigil drill will cause false radar blips on all FAA and DOD radar screens. The fighters still in the northeastern quadrant would be blind if any air attack were to occur."

"General, do you go both ways?"

"What!?" The General shook his head in wonder, as his assistant watched with concern. *Is this man insane?*

"Are you a pillow biter – a faggot?"

"What is going on, sir?" *Is he joking?* "Sir, this isn't funny."

The VP's voice grew cool and menacing. "General, you have your orders. We have intelligence that is way above your pay grade. These war games are necessary to enable our forces to protect our homeland."

"But sir . . . "

The Vice President's eyes flashed behind his glasses as he leaned into his telephone. "There is no room for dissent. You either find your gonads and march in step, or you will find yourself cut from the pack. Is that clear, General?"

The General was a year from retirement and a cushy job waiting for him as a military analyst for Mind-Net Broadcasting. "Yes, sir. Loud and clear, sir."

# 31. Expanding Souls – Constricting Worlds

*We want to fill our culture again with the Christian spirit . . . We want to burn out all the recent immoral developments in literature, in the theater, and in the press – in short, we want to burn out the poison of immorality which has entered into our whole life and culture as a result of liberal excess during the past . . . [few] years.*

– Adolf Hitler, *The Speeches of Adolf Hitler, 1922-1939,* Vol. 1 (London, Oxford University Press, 1942), pp. 871-872

———————

Young men fed the fire. As they threw dry logs onto it, flames licked up toward the heavens, great geysers of sparks flying up into the black night. The light and shadow danced across the Healer's face, changing it, transforming it into something more than human.

His brown eyes became golden as they followed the flickering sparks to the sky above. He continued, "The Great Spirit kindled the fire of life many ages ago. Your cosmologists call it the Big Bang. The hopes of the Great Spirit became manifest, exploding out across what would become the universe. The dark and the light, the hot and the cold, the full and the empty began to grow like a large flower opening its petals from a singular point of what we could only call nothingness, because we cannot understand how great and limitless it was.

"The singular and united became split into the duality of the yin and the yang that our Eastern brothers and sisters have explored for centuries – what we might call the male and the female.

"Your physics explains duality as positive and negative polarities. All things in this world have both sides of the force of life within them, and all things always, *always* seek balance.

We – humanity – now, in our lifetime, are finally experiencing the beginning of the reunion of the full power of the universe. The male expansion that has connected our planet through exploration and exploitation is now folding back into the feminine contemplative consciousness, which is why you are here tonight: to play your part.

"Many First Nation peoples honored the human beings that your world calls homosexuals. We saw them as people who had a knowing in both worlds and had much to offer those tipped more toward one polarity. When your world has rejected these people, it has suffered. The great Holocaust targeted homosexuals for destruction. They were crushed, not just by hobnail boots and gas chambers, but by something more pervasive and complete that has echoed far beyond those times. Their spirits were crushed by fear, a fear that still prevents many from truly being the human beings the Great Spirit made them.

"These two-spirit people have known the loneliness that you have experienced, Ravi. I know, because *I am one of them."* The Healer paused as a man with dreadlocks and dark skin stepped into the firelight and handed the Healer a hot drink. Their touch lingered for a moment as the Healer smiled up at him. The two exchanged a fleeting look before the Healer continued. "Those of us, like you, who have known the pain of being different are more likely to open to the vision now dawning on humanity."

Ian broke in. "No disrespect, mind you, but are you saying you have to be gay to see a larger world?"

The Healer laughed loudly and clapped Ian on the back. "No, my brother. I'm saying that when societies have not allowed those who are different to be themselves, then no one could truly be themselves, because we all have unique gifts to share. When societies suppress those who are different, the iron vise of conformity crushes all diversity.

"Please wait. I want to show you something." The Healer rose and disappeared into the woods.

The fire dancers' chanting had grown louder. The eerie synthesis combined a low vibrating sound not unlike Gregorian religious chants with a high-pitched, driving rhythm – like some ethereal punk rock. It tore at the fabric of the heart and soul, as if urging it to break apart, to be reborn into a new language of life.

# 32. The Medicine Wheel

*Roughly 16.5 million people were practicing yoga in the United States early last year, in studios, gyms or at home, making yoga practice up 43 percent from 2002.*
— *Yoga Journal* Study, 2006

*. . . relaxation techniques (primarily meditation), used by 16.3% of the [United States] population (up from 13.1% in 1990).*
— *The Journal of the American Medical Association,* 1998

*While crime rates in the United States reached an all time high in the 1970s and 1980s, they have drastically declined since 1991.*
— U.S. Bureau of Justice Statistics

---

The Healer reappeared as the chanting reached a crescendo. Men and women danced with mesmerizing intensity, as the chanters screamed out their sounds, and drums pounded fiercely. The colors, fire, and shadow throbbed with the force of the sound. It was all encompassing – psychedelic. The vibrations radiated within Ian and Ravi as they lost themselves in the tumult. They opened to what was about to be revealed.

The Healer stood above them, illuminated against the dark sky. He held something about two feet wide, leather stretched across a round wooden frame. The music subsided as he spoke, becoming a background rhythm like a cosmic heartbeat. "Our people have long revered the image of the Medicine Wheel. It contains four color quadrants." He held it up for Ian and Ravi to see.

"The colors, as you see, are yellow, red, black, and white. These represent the original peoples of the world, the four original races. The limitless power of unity, which existed before the Big Bang, can be brought into manifest reality when balance is achieved. Wise men among our people know that each of the original peoples have brought particular skills and talents into the world necessary for all humanity to find its balance.

"The Eastern people – represented by yellow – have brought to us an infinite knowledge of the inner world, the contemplative nature of humanity. The aboriginal people, my people – represented by red – have brought great wisdom of man's relationship with the physical world, the animal world, the plant world – what some today call the environment. Southern people – represented by black – have brought connection with the emotional world, often expressed through art and music, but also through great oration and other expressions. The Northern and Western people – white – have brought into existence great curiosity, wanting to know all things about all things."

The Healer paused thoughtfully, and then directed his words to Ravi. "The great loneliness we felt as children when our gifts were seen as defects is not unlike what the peoples of the world are now feeling as the vibrational rate, the very foundation of their existence, is shifting beneath them and within them. They feel that what they are deep inside does not fit the dogma of society and is not appreciated."

Again, he held up the Medicine Wheel. "Our people have long thought that the homecoming of all earth's people will happen when each of the four original peoples recognizes the gifts of the others as equally important as their own. This is happening. The gifts of the Southern people have permeated into the psyche of the entire planet through art, music, oration, and spirit, or *soul,* as some call it. Think of this. Martin Luther King, Jr., Nelson Mandela, and Desmond Tutu have become voices of conscience and hope for billions of people worldwide across the entire spectrum of humanity: all cultures, all races.

"The Eastern people, including your parents and your people, Ravi, have shared great wisdom of the inner world through meditation, yoga, and tai chi that is being practiced in corporate board rooms, churches of all faiths, schools, and health care institutions around the world. Millions are being educated in self-healing and inner wisdom.

"The White people's endless curiosity has caused a technological revolution across our planet that has explored every corner of the globe and even outer space. And Western science is beginning to understand the importance of our people's reverence for mother earth, and also the profound health and mind benefits of the Eastern inner technologies.

"These meditative gifts from the East spreading through the planet are accelerating people's ability to open to greater wisdom from all the original peoples and to the reality of the masculine-feminine nature of the universe. We are completing the vision of the medicine wheel."

They sat transfixed by the dancing flames. Their gaze was returned through the flames from the other side of the circle, where the men, women, and children now sat quietly.

Ravi spoke the question that burned in her mind. "But if we are finding balance, why is there so much pain?"

# 33. The Pain of Losing Oneself

The Soldier was back on the trail again. He had lost their track for a time in the growing density of the forest. But it wasn't just that. He'd earned his salt in the jungles of Southeast Asia and understood how to track in foliage perhaps as well as any man.

The problem was not with the trail – nor was it with his night vision goggles. It was with his mind. He had been distracted by shadows, faces that appeared – no, they did not appear. He could *feel* them. The forest whispered. *God's eyes.*

He shook himself, casting off the strange thoughts that invaded his psyche. He was back on track. He bore down and moved more quickly to make up the lost time. He knew it was them – two pairs of tracks. One larger, one smaller.

It was only a matter of time. The young traitor's hours were numbered. And he would bring the woman back. He would not lose them again. *But you have lost yourself.*

The Soldier stopped. He looked up through the murky canopy to the North Star. He felt a swirling in his chest, like a virus crawling inside him. He couldn't stand this sensation. Feeling anything was alien to him. He lit a cigarette and inhaled deeply. Reaching into his backpack, his fingers found the loaded meth-antidepressant syringes.

The wind blew, shifting the trees. The starlight disappeared. Darkness enveloped him. He dropped the needles back into his pack. This mission would require keen senses. The trail was difficult to follow here, even for him.

Touching his revolver inside his pack refocused and reassured him. It was cold and lifeless, deadly and effective. He resumed the hunt.

# 34. The Illusion of Pain

*There are three great oppressions:* Government *because it is based on materialistic values which don't include any spiritual values and doesn't look after people;* religion *because it created a fear in people. Most religions built up a fear of God rather than building up a firm relation.* Hollywood . . . *gave us an awful image of one another — all those negative things.*

— Chief Leonard George, Tsleil-Waututh Nation

---

Ravi looked up, awaiting an answer to her question. Why is there so much pain in the world, if indeed humanity is entering a time of achieving balance?

The Healer sat down beside Ravi, setting the Medicine Wheel aside. "Ah, the illusion of pain. Changes come. The question is, how much pain must we endure before we loosen and breathe into the inevitable birth of new worlds? Just as the physical body tightens and health suffers when we resist the Great Spirit flowing through us, so does the world. To answer this question of our great transitional pain, we have to go back to the origin of the journey of earth's children.

"Your Bible speaks in metaphor so that our brain-minds can comprehend a spark of much greater truths. The Bible tells us of the Garden of Eden, the origin of man and woman, and a time when our Eastern friends would say the yin and yang were one. In the garden, all needs were taken care of. No thought was required beyond gratitude for the sustenance that God provided all creatures great and small.

"Then the fruit of knowledge appeared. The serpent, we are told, is God's *fallen* angel, who tempted woman and then man with a succulent taste of the apple of knowledge. The bite of that knowledge was the beginning of the age of technology, agriculture, social structure – all the things Eastern wisdom would refer to as yang or male consciousness.

"The yin or feminine consciousness of receptive gratitude, or *faith,* was supplanted with a fear of scarcity and need for endless control and accumulation."

Ian asked, "Are you saying that technological advancement is evil?"

The Healer looked at Ian as he clarified. "This was not good versus evil. Both forces were created by God, just as his fallen angel was. These were forces, or engines set in motion to foster our evolution of consciousness over the coming millennia, you see. Humankind could not simply be grateful bovine creatures grazing mindlessly on God's bounty. They had to step out of the Garden in order to appreciate the greater meaning. God did not want sheep, but co-creators.

"The stretching of this yang or male muscle of consciousness extended throughout every corner of the globe."

Ian's mind spun. "So we should turn away from technology worldwide, like you have here? Is that even possible?"

"We do not need to turn away from technology, but we must see it for what it is and decide what we will make of it – a god or a plowshare. Now is when all the millennia of yang development must fold back into the feminine – the passive, the receptive – so that we can rediscover our wholeness with the Great Spirit – and let technology become a tool of our spirituality."

The fire was fanned by a breeze. The Healer's illuminated presence seemed to grow as the blaze lifted him from the shadows and the darkness behind him was conquered by the light.

"What holds back our evolution to wholeness now are the last dying throes of male control and dogma's rebellion against relinquishing its virtual domination of humanity's consciousness. Forces of control are attempting to demonize our natural evolution of becoming whole again, because control by its very nature is a dividing force."

The Healer pondered the sky above him before speaking again. "People are controlled by dividing them from one another with fear. But worst of all, people are divided from their spirit nature by rhetoric that makes them feel that they must depend on others – on dogmatic hierarchies – for their truth and salvation.

"This was why both Buddha and Jesus eschewed institutions and dogma as God, but rather turned to contemplation within for their answers. This was a very yin, or feminine, act of receptivity and intuition. The admonition to *turn within* set the wheels of change in motion so that over the next two thousand years, God's children could truly absorb and make part of themselves the feminine wisdom that Buddha and Jesus planted like a seed."

Ravi interjected, "But why did we need two thousand years to learn these lessons? And again, *why so much pain?*"

"The Great Spirit does not communicate in words. Words are only glimmers of knowing, because intellectual understanding of truth is but the tiny molecule that holds the atom at the very tip of the iceberg of knowing. True knowledge is a vast experience that can take many lifetimes of poor choices that grind truth into the flesh and bones of the people. Each incarnation's end drives home what we have done, so we can know the feelings of all those we've touched and harmed. That embeds the knowledge into the essence of our spirit being, our consciousness. This happens only over many lifetimes – as we experience many wrongs done to us and by us, and also the pain they cause."

The Healer paused, carefully selecting his words. "But now human beings have enough accumulated wisdom. Ravi, your question, *why so much pain?* This is no longer a question for God – it is a question for humanity. We can end the long trail of tears that all the people of the Medicine Wheel have suffered – but we must no longer continue to repeat the same mistakes, for we are entering the time of what my Mayan brothers long ago foretold as *the quickening.*"

# 35. Quickening

As the Soldier moved stealthily through the virgin forest, the tracks led deep into old growth timber. The dark columns reached far above the damp floor, an organic cathedral.

The darkness that had already seemed absolute suddenly became pitch black. The night vision goggles became necessary for any movement at all. In the eerie green world of the goggles, images became distorted. Flashes of reflected light from the moist leaves of flora became eyes, staring at him. *Back off. What the hell are you looking at?*

The mirages dissolved when he moved through the leaves and felt the moisture touch his skin. But the feeling of judgment did not. The slip of the plants' blades across his skin and clothing became whispers. *What have you done?*

The Soldier's pulse accelerated. It wasn't from the movement – he could haul a 50-pound pack all day long. The air surrounding him was cold. Yet he was drenched in sweat.

The brush became thicker. He could not focus his eyes on the trail. The sliding leaves whispered. *What have you done? What have you done?*

He could hear nothing but that sound. *What is it? What is happening?* His heart thudded in his throat. His stomach churned. He moved forward, one foot in front of the other.

Memories – no, not really memories, he had murdered those long ago to make sure they would never return. Yet, here they were – ghostly apparitions. *This isn't real! I am not hearing this!*

*What have you done?*

*Nothing. Leave me the hell alone!*

*What have you done?*

# 36. Priests of Disunion

*I do not think the measure of a civilization is how tall its buildings of concrete are, but rather how well its people have learned to relate to their environment and fellow man.*

— Sun Bear, Chippewa Tribe

---

Years of catechism study as a good Catholic boy caused Ian's mind to recoil when the Healer mentioned reincarnation as if it were a fact. "You're talking of *reincarnation,* when you said we have many lifetimes to grind Jesus's lessons into us. Doesn't the Bible say we only have one life, and that life ends with heaven or hell?"

The Healer's dark eyes reflected the endless field of stars twinkling above, like souls passing through the vastness of existence. He retorted sharply, "Dogma! Rigid dogma that squeezes down and holds back our natural flowing evolution."

The Healer paused, reconsidering his outburst at his guest. He reached to touch Ian's shoulder as he added with a smile, "You must have been impatient with me in another life, my brother. I apologize for returning the favor."

Ravi suppressed a laugh at the look on Ian's face. She interjected, "The Bible does not definitively deny reincarnation. In fact, Orthodox Judaism, which the Christian faith is built upon, accepts reincarnation. In the Book of John 1:21, Jewish priests asked John the Baptist if he was Elijah. In other words, was he Elijah, reincarnated into his present form as John the Baptist? Even Christ himself said that John the Baptist was Elijah."

The Healer nodded in agreement, continuing, "The Biblical challenge to the idea of reincarnation is not substantial. It boils down, mainly, to one passage, Hebrews 9:27. There is great controversy over the authorship of the Book of Hebrews."

Ian insisted, "I'm sorry, but I still don't understand. Why is it so important that reincarnation be established, and uh, well, like I said, didn't religious scholars already disprove it?"

The Healer became animated, speaking with his hands as he talked.

"In 553 A.D., at the Fifth Ecumenical Council of the Catholic Church, most of the Christian scriptural references to reincarnation were purged from the teachings. But a church leader named Origen had taught four centuries earlier that reincarnation was part of Christianity. In fact, Pope Vigilius had refused to sign a papal decree condemning Origen's teachings on reincarnation, but he was eventually forced to do so because of political pressure from the emperor.

"Many accepted truths in today's Christianity are based on one obscure line, often in books of the Bible that are controversial. Reincarnation is one, condemnation of homosexuality is another, and the worst of all is the dogma of creationism. These obscure lines have been used to alter the thinking of hundreds of millions of Christians. They have been used in a war to control men's minds.

"How do they do that – control minds, I mean?" Ian asked with curiosity. Having seen what real mind control was in the last few months, such a benign thing as religious doctrine didn't seem all that big a deal.

"The denial of reincarnation is anti-evolutionary. The essence of evolution, which is required of us now more than at any other time in our history, is fluidity of spirit. The rejection of reincarnation rigidifies people, causing them to grit their teeth and resist who they really are, in order to follow dogmatic and arbitrary rules so they can avoid eternal damnation when they die. They stop evolving and live in obedient fear of a wrathful, vengeful God – who will either give them a *not guilty* sentence for their self-denial, or will damn them to eternal suffering for stepping outside the rigid lines.

"Squeezing society into constricting models of obedience for fear of damnation results in the rejection of those among us who are different, as in the case of homosexuals."

The Healer's eyes closed for a moment as he touched his fingertips together. He appeared to go within himself, as if waiting for a deeper truth. Opening his eyes, he spoke.

"But this does much more than reject gay people. It fosters a mentality that suppresses many of the differences and gifts we all offer the world. It denies the tolerance at the heart of the Gospel of Jesus."

Opening his arms to the group, the fire, and the universe expanding above them to make his point, the Healer explained, "It is important that we understand the dynamics of false prophets who deny that we are growing, changing spirits, free to explore who we are. Fundamentalists of many faiths are fond of claiming that all of the truth in this vast universe is found within a few hundred pages of a three-pound book. This insults the vastness of the Great Spirit, as it flows and changes with the winding rivers and blowing winds, as do the creatures and consciousness of our world that are ever changing – *ever becoming* – as are we. Remember, the worship of books was not the way of Jesus.

"The purpose of the Gospel, or the Good News to humanity, was to empower us to let go of our pasts and be forgiven for our mistakes so that we could ever evolve into more and more potential. Jesus promised this. *These and greater things shall you do,* he said, meaning we would evolve to do even greater things then he."

The wind suddenly howled through the trees as the Healer spoke these words. The few people still dancing grew quieter. Ravi watched as the tongues of the flames reached upward toward the endless heavens. Beyond the fire circle, coyotes howled in the night.

Ian watched as an insight appeared to spark behind Ravi's eyes. She spoke. "I understand what you've said about reincarnation and rejection of homosexuals and people who are different. But you also said creationism holds back evolution. How?"

The Healer listened to his sister the wind and his cousins the coyotes before answering. "Yes, fundamentalism not only denies its followers the ability to see themselves as ever-learning, reincarnating beings, but it also disconnects them from the *web of life* in this current lifetime. Creationists sneer at the idea they came from monkeys.

"The fact is that the chimpanzee and human genomes are more than 98% identical. In fact, to understand just how close we are to our brother chimpanzees, realize that the DNA of chimps and humans is only 1.5% different, while the DNA between women and men is 1% different. Fundamentalist creationism seeks to separate man from his animal cousins, nearly all of which share tens of thousands of the same genes."

Ian asked, "Yes, but why does *their* refusal to admit connection to the animal family present a problem for *us?*"

"Spiritually, it breaks the Medicine Wheel and denies humanity's wholeness. It dishonors my people's wisdom. The denial of humanity's connection to the web of life dismisses centuries of collective wisdom that my First Nation people and all Aboriginal people assimilated and passed down — wisdom created for the benefit of all humans. Just because our people did not write it down but shared it verbally does not make it less important to humanity than mathematics or psychology.

"But also, the mass denial of humanity's part in the great web of life harms you physically and directly, because it harms your home — Mother Earth. It harms your body by affecting the food you eat and the water you drink."

Ian was intrigued. "How can a belief do that?"

"When humans remove themselves from the web of the Earth Spirit, it allows men to become capable of treating precious Mother Earth as a wastebasket — *because they are not connected to it.*"

The Healer paused, picking up a leaf from the ground. As if he were not in the midst of a conversation, he slowly broke the leaf open and inhaled its sweet, pungent fragrance. He offered it to Ian to smell. As Ian took it and put it to his nose, Ravi thought, *Now the leaf is part of him.*

The Healer continued, "Your body is damaged as creationism's disconnection with earth's life enables men to treat earth's creatures and other life forms with no dignity or honor. They say man *is not of this world,* which allows them to rip apart elegant DNA constructions that took millennia to unfold in their perfection. Like infants wielding a scalpel, they perform surgery on our Mother Earth as if she were a lab animal, having no idea what the outcome will be. They create Frankenstein foods, combining animal DNA with plant DNA. The testing lab they use is your body.

"Another result is the gruesome factory farming of God's creatures and the chemicals, fear hormones, and literal dis-ease these practices pump into the bloodstream of the web of life. Those who consume these terrorized, mistreated animals are contaminated and sickened, physically and emotionally by their fear. Their poisoned waste contaminates the land and water."

The Healer's voice rose in both volume and power. "This mentality that creationism fosters – that man is not a part of this world . . ." He had to stop, not from a loss of words – just the opposite. The Healer's eyes moistened, as if the emotions roiling within him were so overpowering they could only spill out through his eyes.

His voice broke as he expressed what flooded through him. "In such a world, *how can anything be sacred?*"

# 37. Owning Control Itself

*China has the potential to build a "green economy" over the next decades, said a report on energy and the environment by McKinsey & Company, a global management consultant firm.*
— *China Daily,* December 27, 2009

*War is a racket. It always has been. It is possibly the oldest, easily the most profitable, surely the most vicious. . . . A racket is best described, I believe, as something that is not what it seems to the majority of the people. Only a small 'inside' group knows what it is about. It is conducted for the benefit of the very few, at the expense of the very many. Out of war a few people make huge fortunes.*
— Maj. Gen. Smedley Butler (U.S. Marine Corps.), 1935, recipient of 16 medals, and the only person to be awarded the Brevet Medal and two Medals of Honor.

———————

On the Vice President's desk, the cover of *Economic Journal,* Britain's famed financial magazine, blared a headline about rumblings within China to disinvest themselves of American debt.

The VP fired off instructions to the official who had brought this latest report to his attention. "We will connect an attack on the homeland to China. Prepare the press releases. I want corroborative reports prepared in advance from both the CIA and FBI. You know who you can trust there."

The senior official nodded. "So you've settled on them as the villain in the attack. The dollar would tank if . . ."

"That's not the real problem. They are moving too quickly on green technology. We must cripple them internationally."

The Vice President sat back to let this sink in before continuing. "Our only ace is energy dominance. We control the world militarily, but . . ." Trying to be helpful, the official interjected, "Yes, but the Russian and Chinese militaries . . ."

The VP waved his point away. "Peanuts. We invest 41.5 percent of the global military budget, the Russians only 4 percent, and the Chinese only 5.8 percent.

"The only thing that can recoup our heavy investment in raw power is to use that power to control global energy resources. If we can isolate the Chinese politically by pinning this attack on them, we can push for sanctions, cripple their economic trade, and hobble their green revolution."

The VP stared at the official for a moment. "Are you taking note of all this? When the storm hits, things will have to happen quickly. We are hours away from the zero point."

"Yes sir. I've got it. We'll be ready."

The Vice President moved on. "We'll also need corroborative reports on Venezuela's involvement. Chavez must be isolated and then removed. There is too much oil down there to leave in that Indian's hands."

He sat back and folded his hands with finality. "With China's green economy retarded and control of Venezuelan oil, our Middle East reserves will keep the Europeans and Russians in tow."

The VP stared at the air, pondering any loose ends for a moment before turning back to the senior official. He concluded, "Everything must be in place by the day after tomorrow. Will there be any problems?"

Responding briskly, the official replied, "No, sir."

He directed the man out the door with his pointing finger. "That will be all. See yourself out."

When the door closed behind him, the VP picked up his phone and punched in the Professor's number. "Day after tomorrow – everything is go, unless you can perform some miracle with this woman." He added with a sneer, "Have you even been able to reacquire her yet?"

The Professor flinched. *The ingrate wouldn't even be at that desk if not for my efforts.* With a tight mouth and controlled voice, he replied, "Our man has reported in. We are only a few hours away from retaking her. I will break her this time. I assure you, she *will* enable us to regain mass control."

"Keep me posted." The Vice President hung up.

He now actually *wanted* the Professor to fail. He didn't care for the pious prick, and Plan B was all set. He'd had enough of the Congress, the Chinese, the Europeans – the whole lot of them.

He mused. Mind-Net may own words – but in a few short hours he would be the sole owner of control itself. He would never again have to consider other, lesser opinions. The machine would be complete.

When chaos filled the world's TV screens, his calm voice would be the sound of safety. He would concede – nothing.

# 38. Self Forgiveness –
# The Power to Be Wrong

*As soon as . . . even a glimpse of right on the other side is admitted, the cause for doubting one's own right is laid.*
  – Adolf Hitler

———————

The Healer listened to the coyotes' howls for a time, as if considering their opinion, before continuing. "Only a humanity who sees itself as growing and evolving can open and embrace the other three original people's gifts."

He stroked the four quadrants of the Medicine Wheel in a circular motion as he spoke. "This honoring of all of our people – north, south, east, and west – is necessary for our current transition. Separation and intolerance closes doors.

"The fundamentalist rejection of homosexuals is at the core of this."

Sadness crossed the Healer's face, as boyhood memories crossed his mind. He touched a ragged scar on his neck as he resumed. "A wise man once said you can measure the evolution of a society by how they treat their homosexual people. Because they are different than the majority in any society, they are like the canary in the coal mine. When they wither and diminish, it is an indication of the state of that society as a whole.

"The same fundamentalist proponents who deny that humanity is here to evolve and learn and to become more effective stewards of our mother earth, are often the ones who teach their flocks to deny the power of the feminine and denigrate the unique perspective that homosexuals have to offer our world. They are unable to see spiritual gifts, focusing only on sexuality.

"The most intolerant and closed societies promote fear of difference and deceive followers into believing they will save them from the evil of all those who are different, such as homosexuals. They paint those who are different as embodiments of Satan. This is what the Nazi Reich did.

"People are drawn to this madness, because by doing so they can leave behind the pain of introspection. They can ignore the beam in their own eye by focusing on the speck in the homosexual's eye, to paraphrase Jesus. Of course, this mentality of intolerance is a wildfire that quickly excludes more and more people who are unique in other ways, leaving society diminished and our evolution curtailed. Nazism's violent suppression of such gifts left a very bleak reality in its wake.

"In reality, lives of difference often lead to fresh perspectives. In some homosexuals, for example, such insight cultivated in them gifts for art and décor which actually lifted the communal spirit. My own ancestors viewed the two-spirited people among us as seers and visionaries."

As the Healer spoke these words, Ian's eye was caught by a spider web barely illuminated by the firelight. A lightning bug was caught in the web, struggling. Its yellow light blazed and then faded, then blazed again. Ian watched as the spider, attracted by the firefly's struggles to be free, closed in. Its glow suddenly died.

The Healer expanded his point. "Why does humanity repeatedly turn on precious illuminators like Jesus? We do it for the same reason that we reject our brothers and sisters who are different from us. Because to acknowledge new insights calls into question everything we have been, all we believe, and who we are. It exhorts us to open to different realities than we know, to evolve into a new consciousness. This is threatening because it holds a mirror up to us and asks us to look into ourselves.

"So in order to avoid the discomfort of introspection, seeing clearly who we are, regretting and repenting when needed, and thereby *evolving*, we turn on our visionaries and avatars, making *them* the evil ones who must be destroyed.

"When we become dogmatic and reject new views in favor of those that are familiar to us, we become closed and rigid, as the fascists epitomized. In the Gospel of Judas, Jesus rejected dogma and . . ."

Ian protested, "But Judas *betrayed* Jesus!"

The Healer spoke to his concern. "Ian, the Gospel of Judas revealed that Judas was a *most* trusted apostle, entrusted by Jesus with secrets that none of the others were given. This may be why Jesus chose Judas to bear the most horrible and important of all tasks – to turn him in to the Romans."

Ian's mind was spinning. "A Gospel of *Judas!?*"

Ravi interjected, "The last known copy of the Gospel of Judas was saved from an Egyptian artifacts dealer in just the last decade. He was allowing the gospel to disintegrate in a bank vault while he haggled for more money. But it was saved and authenticated by teams of experts in religious history."

The Healer picked up Ravi's thought. "And there was a reason that the Gospel of Judas was saved. It told of a *mystical* Jesus that the world needed to know.

"The Gospel of Judas told of a Jesus who had a grand vision of spirituality, and who dismissed dogmatic religious rituals in favor of a mystical connection with God. This threatened the entire hierarchy of organized religion. That is why Judas was demonized and his Gospel excluded."

Ian leaned forward to breathe and steady himself, as the Healer's words rocked the very foundations of his religious upbringing.

"This Gospel revealed that when the Apostles were practicing the holy Eucharist, Jesus laughed at them. They became angry with him. Jesus asked them why they were angered and explained that his purpose for laughing was to make the point that they were worshiping a *shadow* of God. Jesus' point was that the dogma and rites, even of religion, were shadows – straw dogs – and that the real spiritual experience was far beyond such actions, more expansive and fluid than physical rituals could contain.

"You see, institutions used the dogma and ritual to gain power and control, making the faithful believe they had to come *to them* in order to reach God.

"Judas was the only one who stood and acknowledged Jesus' lesson. Jesus took Judas aside, saying, *Step away from the others. I will tell you of the great and boundless kingdom. So great no angel's eye has ever seen it. No heart has ever touched it. Boundless beyond imagination.* Judas' Gospel revealed the ultimate truth that to know God was not dogmatic, but transcendental.

Ian's mind swam. Suddenly Jesus had become more than a martyr on a cross. The Healer had breathed life into the man.

The clouds parted, and moonlight bathed the woods in a comforting illumination. The Healer raised his eyes to behold the magnificent luminance as it spread across the clearing. Then as dark clouds again drew in, shrouding the forest in darkness, he continued. His voice too, was darker. "Religion has hidden this truth and demonized Judas throughout the ages. In time, this externalizing of Judas became a tool for demonizing Jewish people, who were always a minority in all lands – people who were *different.*

"Passion plays over the centuries in Europe pounded this lesson home, culminating in a huge production of the Passion Play in Germany, attended by Hitler. Judas was a caricature of 'the Jew' who betrayed Jesus, while Jesus was portrayed by an Aryan-looking actor. Judas, according to these passion plays, betrayed Jesus for money, which was not the case. Judas turned Jesus in to the Romans only because Jesus instructed him to, to give humanity a lesson about not destroying the visionaries among us."

Ian wondered, "You mean Jesus' great lesson was not to destroy those who were different than us, because we might be destroying something sacred?"

The Healer replied, "Yes, that is the essence. But it was also about our tendency to demonize others because of the discomfort their differences cause us internally. It is a way we avoid dealing with our own internal struggles. What was the effect of these passion plays? *To externalize evil.* The result was that people completely missed the lesson Jesus offered. That lesson was to look inside ourselves at our own tendency to kill our avatars and visionaries and to once and for all understand that it is our own self-rejection that causes us to repeat this behavior.

"This is why forgiveness is key. The Gospel, or *Good News of Forgiveness,* enables us to forgive ourselves and to evolve. The teaching was to help us be more fluid and flexible, because as we've seen, when people get rigid and dogmatic, precious beings die, again and again and again."

The night around them had grown silent as he spoke. The only sound was the crackling of the flames. They sat staring into the fire, the center of man's insights since prehistoric times.

Ravi's face was lit by a flame that crackled into life as she broke the silence. "But what is causing the disruption in people around the world *now?* Why are these forces trying to examine me in order to control others? *What do they fear?*"

# 39. Coven of Fear

From somewhere very far away, an alarm was sounding. The woman – his place in history – *gone*. He tried to turn away from the noise, but could not. In fact, he could not move. He was bound! Unable to move his arms and legs, he struggled against his bonds like a drowning man struggles for air.

The Professor's eyes opened. His phone had been ringing. In his turmoil, he'd wrapped his body in the linens and covers of his bed. He grabbed the phone and sat up. The time and the originating number on the phone came into focus as he clicked it on. It was 4 a.m. *What the hell could he want at this hour?*

"Yes?"

"I've been thinking. We need the woman, even if Plan B is enacted."

The Professor had begun to feel like the Vice President's nanny. He'd become increasingly neurotic and paranoid as the implementation date of Plan B drew nearer. "We will have her soon. The Soldier has never failed me. He is relentless."

The VP removed his round wire-rimmed glasses and rubbed his eyes and face as he spoke into the phone, "Where is he? Canada?"

"Yes. As I said before, he is indeed in Canada."

*Of course. The pompous ass already told me that.* He had not slept all night. His fifth or sixth glass of Scotch sat before him. He was beginning to lose control of his memory. Insomnia had become a nightly ritual. This loss of mental control was unbearable. Years of political combat had left no time for family, for love. His control was all he had. For the first time in as long as he could remember, he was afraid. He felt alone.

He wanted to stay on the line with the Professor, who was at least another human being. "So, how are you doing?"

The Professor drew back and looked incredulously at the cell phone in his hand. The VP sounded like someone making chit-chat at a dinner party. He was unsure quite how to respond. "Well, he has pursued them west of Montreal. They appear to be headed toward Vancouver, but they'll never make it past Detroit."

The VP's sleep-deprived, Scotch-induced moment of humanity dissipated at the mention of the woman – *the problem*. His paranoia reignited. "Detroit? How long will that take? Get him to move on them, NOW!"

"I assure you . . . "

"I do not want assurances. I want control of this situation, dammit!"

The Vice President regained his composure. Lowering his voice, he spoke menacingly and clearly. "If we can't cure this problem, we may be haunted by questions rising up from the graves of the victims of Plan B. Control of the government is not enough if the minds of the people are not controlled. Get her, now!"

The Professor's line went dead. His jaw tightening, he punched in the Soldier's number.

The VP stared at the wall in front of his desk. This office, where he had once felt omnipotent, had begun to close in on him. The quiet despair of the dead of night – the silence – opened the door to too many feelings. He had no one else to call and awaken.

He looked at the empty liquor glasses and candy wrappers on his desk and slammed a button on his console. "Get a janitor in here. This place is out of control."

He awaited the maintenance man, trying to suppress the unsettled feeling in his gut. Without control, he felt only fear.

# 40. This is Much Bigger than You

The Healer's face glowed as he pondered Ravi's question. *What is causing such disruption in the world – and why would they need her to help control it? What is it they fear?*

"The alarm clock set 52,000 years ago at the beginning of our technological age is going off in the form of an energetic shift that can enable us to thrive creatively and compassionately. In a world simultaneously competing for overtaxed resources and wielding unimaginably destructive hair-trigger weapons – this shift is absolutely essential. The timing is perfect.

"As the vibration of the planet rises, the gamma waves of humans are stimulated." He looked at Ravi. "In my vision I saw your consciousness forcefully raise the meters in the laboratory. This is not happening just to you. It is happening to millions."

A rumble of thunder rolled across the forest. A bolt of distant lightning arced, illuminating the clouds. The huge thunderheads took on the appearance of giant enlightening brains, as exploding electricity roiled within.

"This awakening today is becoming global, but its seeds have sprouted in many lands in many ways for many centuries. This broad swath consciousness has been the enemy of dogmatic control, not just in the Western or modern world, but throughout the history of all civilizations. Philosophies that promoted such thinking have always been suppressed.

"In China the teachings of Confucius were celebrated by governments and institutions because it taught people to be obedient to a hierarchy of order and control. However, Lao Tzu's wisdom, recorded in the *Tao Te Ching – The Way of the Universe –* was never promoted with such fervor. Why? Because it taught people that each of us has access to the truth of the universe *within* – in the quietude of mind and heart, beyond any dependence on institutions or governments. This knowledge was suppressed, just as the transcendental messages of the Gospels of Judas and Mary were suppressed in the West."

The rages of flashing light behind the cumulus brains above went dark. The air grew still, and the Healer's voice lowered. "Today, there are false prophets who frighten their followers into believing that the great gifts of the East, to go within and contemplate our personal connection to the Great Father, are not of God and are even Satanic."

Arcs of lightning created a vast lightshow of illumination across the sky as the Healer continued. "In reality, the Eastern meditative arts are closest to what Jesus was really teaching. Jesus himself studied with Eastern masters."

Ian interrupted. "Wait. Jesus was in the *Middle* East, not . . ."

The Healer delayed his larger point to satisfy Ian's query. "Ian, your Bible has a gap in Jesus' life between the ages of 12 to about 30, with no explanation of what Jesus did during those years. This gap was explained when a Russian doctor named Nicolas Notovitch, who journeyed extensively throughout Afghanistan, India, and Tibet, published a book in 1894 called *The Unknown Life of Christ*. It resulted from his stay in a convent, where he discovered a Tibetan translation of ancient documents known as *The Life of St. Issa*. Other scrolls had before revealed that this St. Issa appeared, in fact, to be Jesus, who spent 17 years in India and Tibet, from age 13 to 29, where he was both a student and a teacher of Buddhist and Hindu holy men."

While Ian struggled to digest this huge chunk of new information, the Healer resumed his discussion of the attempts to demonize Eastern practices designed to expand consciousness. "These false prophets who teach their followers that the wisdom of the East is Satanic seek to break the great Medicine Wheel by dishonoring the rainbow of humanity and the wisdom it offers. But they cannot stop it. The people are not listening to them anymore. The people now sit in their churches to go within, to gather with their brothers and sisters, and to lift their consciousness to a higher vibratory rate."

The lightning extended across the sky in huge spreading branches of interconnecting light, cracking sharply with each new explosion of luminescence, climbing and swelling throughout the heavens.

"Ravi, you asked earlier, *What do they fear?*"

He turned to her. Knowing he was about to remind her of a painful memory, he spoke gently. "Those who worship control and not the Great Spirit are measuring what is happening to human consciousness, as the Professor told you, in the form of gamma wave emissions. They see the results of these gamma wave increases in the form of people becoming liberated from their control. That is why they labeled you *the new enemy.*" The Healer looked at Ravi with a sad smile.

The Healer noticed Ian's startled response to the term. "Ian, I believe you heard Ravi referred to that way, before you knew who she was."

The Healer turned back to Ravi and instructed her gently, "Do not hold this heavily on your shoulders, little sister, for as the Great Spirit spoke through you to the tall man in the laboratory, *this is much bigger than you.*"

# 41. Someone Will Pay

Whispers from the woods were disrupting his tracking ability. *Whispers from the woods? Christ, get a grip!*

He had lost the trail three times in just the last thirty minutes. At the rate he was going, he might contaminate the trail with his own footprints. The deeper he had gotten into these woods, the crazier it – *he* – had gotten.

He squatted down and pulled a lightweight nylon tarp from his pack. Shoveling leaves with his hands, he formed a makeshift mattress, spread the nylon across it, and then lay down and pulled the extra material over him. He took a cigarette from his pack and listened to the distant rumble of thunder.

The storm was far away. He had to be getting close to the pair. Dawn would bring them within his grasp. He lit his cigarette and watched the smoke curl upward as he settled back into the leaves.

His phone vibrated.

"Yeah."

"Do you have them?"

The Soldier spit on the ground. "If I had them, you'd know it."

"When will you?"

"I'm close. I'll have them by daybreak."

Remembering the VP's erratic fuming, the Professor pushed on. "Not good enough. Move on them *now!*"

*What a piss-ant.* "Look, I'm the tracker. The morning is when I'll have them. It's pitch black out here. I'll move in a couple of hours. Until then – piss off and good night."

The Professor stared at his phone. He'd been hung up on twice in one night. His fury flared. He would not tolerate this loss of control. Soon, someone would pay, and order would be restored. Ravi and Ian would pay first.

# 42. Little Sister, the Forces are Amassing

The forest was silent, except for the occasional pop and spark of the fire.

"Ravi, you asked, *Why so long, why so much suffering?* And I told you of the *illusion* of pain which remains so long as we resist where the river of change carries us. Windows open constantly that offer humanity a quicker, easier transition, but the collective consciousness – the vibratory rate of the whole of humanity – must be ready before that can happen.

"If human consciousness remains tight and fearful, the birthing of a larger reality becomes increasingly painful. But, as any mother knows, you can't stop a birth. You can only fight it or relax into it.

"Remember September 11, 2001, and the attacks on the World Trade Centers and the Pentagon? Looking back now, what would have happened had the people of the United States embraced the admonitions of Jesus: *Do not resist an evil person, if someone strikes you on the right cheek, turn to him the other also,* and *Treat others as you yourself would be treated?* What if they had looked within and noted that almost all of the weapons in the world at that time – causing untold misery and destruction – were produced and distributed by the United States?

"If they had looked within and then announced to the world: *This way of behaving must stop. Weapons and violence have injured our people, and we do not want to contribute to this happening anywhere else to any one else, so we hereby declare a one-year moratorium on weapons production and distribution from the United States. Furthermore, we will offer to extend that moratorium indefinitely if the major powers of the world will follow our lead. AND we will use a tithing of one-tenth of what we would spend on weapons to raise the $20 billion per year necessary to end global starvation. We invite other powers to join us in this effort.*

"If that had happened, where would the U.S. be today? Would it be weaker? Would it be more in danger? Hundreds and hundreds of billions of dollars would have remained in the U.S. coffers rather than having been squandered on endless wars that accomplished nothing. Tens of thousands of maimed U.S. soldiers would still have their limbs, their traumatized minds would still be healthy and whole, and they would be living normal lives with families they love and care for.

"The good will that would have resonated from a world that saw the U.S. disengage from such an attack with humility and humanity, as Jesus implored, would have been infinitely more powerful than the most destructive weapon. The world would have clamored to ensure the hopeful future of the United States of America.

"The reality is that we as a people cannot step into the next era and accept the bounty that technology and creativity offer unless we can let go of our burdens of blame. So long as we seek to demonize others rather than seeing their challenges as an opportunity to open to a larger view of reality, we will be killing Jesus all over again, snuffing out his light, again and again."

The gathering storm erupted with a ferocious blast of thunder, exploding huge lightning bolts across the sky, illuminating the Healer and then plunging him into utter darkness, then brilliant light, then darkness again.

"For humanity to walk into the Aquarian Age of Man, we must not only drop the burdens of our blame, but we must also face the discomfort of self-awareness and find the humility to ask forgiveness of ourselves, because the Great Spirit has forgiven us long ago."

The thunder and lightning from the west diminished, and a gentle shower began its cleansing dance.

The Healer sat in silence, as if awaiting clarification of his final message. The firelight, streaked by sparkling lines of rain, shone upon him. Centuries of sins seemed to wash from the world, as they all inhaled deeply the purified air.

. . .

The Healer's face lifted to be bathed in the soothing rain, until his melancholy eyes again lowered to gaze directly at Ravi. "Abundance hangs like a ripe fruit before our blind eyes, if our focus can be turned from destruction to compassion – even when, and *especially when,* we've been wronged."

The first rays of sun were not yet visible, but a distant glow of a new dawn, pregnant with potential, announced itself faintly beyond the eastern horizon. The Healer stretched his arms, turning his face up to the raindrops. "We should find some sleep this morning, before the day grows long. We have much to do in this new day."

As Ian walked back to the shelter provided for the travelers, the Healer spoke quietly to Ravi. "Little sister, great forces are amassing against you. We must find a way for you to speak to the world without being censored by the media who will twist your words beyond recognition.

"I have a plan, but its success depends on your ability to traverse the treacherous thickets of those gathering against you. This journey will sorely test both you and any hope of this vision becoming manifest. Do not despair, for I sense a great ally coming to your aid, one who knows the ways of the dark forces. He is being prepared for a new mission as we speak."

In the deep slumber of exhaustion, Ravi dreamed. Rachel's face came to her again. *The man is not your enemy. Breathe – have faith. The man is not your enemy.*

# 43. Forgive Them Father

*The brain is designed so that acts of charity are pleasurable; being nice to others makes us feel nice. [In an] elegant brain imaging experiment . . . When they chose to give away the money [they'd been given], the reward centers of the brain became active. Dopamine flooded their synapses, and they experienced the delightful glow of unselfishness.*

— Jonah Lehrer, Neuroscientist and Editor at Large, *Seed Magazine*

———————

The dome of silvery light shimmered over the Soldier as he slept in his hastily built campsite. It was not the dreamless slumber he had trained his mind and body to fall into. It was a lucid dream state in which he knew he was dreaming and knew he had a choice whether to remain in it or to come to waking consciousness.

In his reverie, Frank's mother appeared, urging him to stay with her in this silvery mind-field, this field of awareness. The wind had risen, and the whispering leaves again spoke to the Soldier. *To stay here is your choice — and the decision you make now will mean everything.*

The Soldier answered the whisper's challenge without words. Normally he slept on a razor's edge, alerted easily to any possible danger. But he remained asleep and unaware as someone approached his encampment. As Frank slept, a hand reached from the foliage and removed the packet of syringes containing the psychotropic-meth cocktail – his enabler – from his pack. For the last few months, he had relied upon the drugs to complete missions that had become more and more difficult to perform. The hand withdrew into the forest with the syringes.

Mother's presence was soothing, so alien to the hard life Frank had built. Like a ragged world-weary Prodigal Son, he fell into her embrace.

As comforting as the dream of his mother was, it was an act of will to stay here with her. In order to truly surrender to this all-encompassing spiritual state, he had to let go of all the thought forms — the judgmental rigid views of himself and life — that had gripped his mind and body for so many years. But he was ready. Here in this place, he could acknowledge the truth. *He was bone-tired of his hard life.* It had not led him to what he sought. Each door he had walked through had thrown another bolt, closing him in. His spirit was suffocating. He could no longer stand this state of being.

To stay in this peaceful place, his mind had to unlock, and his heart had to relax open to *everything-ness,* where limits, boundaries, command structures, and protocol made no sense. His soul and mind drifted laterally, and then expanded and swirled, washed like a tumbling surfer at the mercy of the waves of the infinite and powerful ocean.

A white light filled Frank's heart. He felt his heart expand in rhythm with the light as it began to pulse. Frank was experiencing his ethereal body, the energetic template upon which his physical being was constructed – what some people called the soul. His opening heart became vulnerable and permeable. Feelings and images found space in his being, which began to tremble at a higher vibratory rate that rattled him like a struck tuning fork.

Sounds echoed through him – the chanting in Tibet – the falling monks, and the last monk's plea . . .

The hard edges of Frank's ethereal body were coming *unglued,* dissolving into a velvet lightness of being, limitless and free. He felt a oneness with all that passed through his expanding mind and heart.

Images more real than real began to rise through Frank's consciousness. Beings appeared – people that he did not recognize – yet he somehow knew they were an essential part of him. His past transgressions had fused their spirits together – *but how?*

The spectral beings were children. Latin American, Southeast Asian, and African children all stared solemnly at him silently, mournfully, without judgment, but with the abject sadness of broken souls. The air was thick with judgment, but it was the cloistered air of self-judgment. Frank fell into their eyes, drowning in their sorrow.

Frank's heart joined theirs as they reached for the comfort of those who were beyond their grasp. He felt their fear, their desolation at being alone forever, having lost the ones who'd loved them.

Frank longed to reach out and comfort these children, to hold them and tell them that everything would be all right. If they could feel safe and loved, his own heart would release this agony of despair. But Frank could not reach them. A field – a surface – both imprisoned the children in their solitary suffering and separated Frank from them. This division was also the source of his own enormous suffering, and he strained with every ounce of his consciousness to touch it, feel it, and see it.

As he and the children reached toward each other, he heard their whispers. *Frankie, Frankie, Frankie . . .*

In the silver shimmering light he was horrified to see what divided them: an angry beast of a man with a slashing knife and blasting weapon. The beast he saw was himself.

The sound of his mother weeping, mingled with the moaning of the children, washed through his heart, melting him. Her tears dissolved everything he thought he was. Frank felt himself tumbling into an abyss of pain. These children's parents, unable to reach them. Frank's own father, fading into oblivion. Frank wept uncontrollably. Waves of feeling wracked him so violently they almost ripped him apart.

The Soldier awakened suddenly as the sun cracked the dawn. His face was damp. His collar and the leaves beneath his head were wet. Everything was still.

He did not arise immediately as he normally would have. Through the foliage overhead, the blue sky winked at him from between the rustling leaves. He lay still as a memory floated from a tiny point before blossoming to fill his waking mind – *the dreams*.

He tried to remember what he had dreamed. Most of his life, for better or worse, he had not experienced dreams, so it was difficult, now, to recall them. A faint image of the dome of light he'd seen glimmered in his memory.

Frank lay still, trying to piece together all that had happened. He remembered the hunt of the night before, and how it had ended. Last night he'd seen that the targets' direction was leading them away from civilization, and it was obvious he needed to wait for daylight in order to track them.

But in this nest of leaves, his mind – his very consciousness – had shifted. Slowly, pieces of what Frank had witnessed in his sleep began to come together. The unfolding memories coming to him in the light of day awakened him further to the web of agony he'd caused. The dream world began to merge with his waking world.

As the Soldier lay in the twilight between sleep and waking, he felt the agony of those he had vanquished, just as he had felt the pain of their children the night before. As he experienced their sorrow at leaving wives and children too soon, the spirits of those he'd murdered did not curse him – but, as their children had the night before, they called him *Frankie*. Frankie – the name he'd left behind when his mother kissed him goodbye on the day he walked out of her life forever. The day he'd walked away from love.

A sensation – unfamiliar, yet haunting – rose from a part of his body he'd thought was long since dead. The pain in his chest – he now recognized it. *His heart was aching.*

Frank tried to shake himself out of these thoughts, but unease shuddered through him. He reached for the packet of drug-filled syringes. They were gone.

Frank touched his Glock in its holster, and its hard familiarity brought him back to his mission. His mind and body moved back into the groove of habit. He arose and again picked up the targets' trail. His night dreams of inner self, despair, and compassion faded with the increasing glare of the light of day. The hunt resumed.

The Soldier found it easy to follow their tracks, but suddenly his heart raced. The trail abruptly ended where an altercation had obviously occurred. He kneeled down to look more closely. The ground showed the markings of a jumble of many feet. But the other feet were not wearing normal shoes. The indentations were softer with no pronounced heel.

At a sudden rustling, he looked up, but it was too late. A blow to the back of his head sent him reeling down to the ground. He felt warm blood. His body would not respond to his mind's command to move. He felt nausea. His hands were pulled behind his back and bound. The world grew dark as if the pixels of daylight had been supplanted with expanding dark spots. His ears rang, and the world tunneled. He watched the dark spots as they expanded until his vision was completely extinguished. The Soldier passed out.

# 44. Redemption

*Paul, devoted to destroying those challenging the powers of his time, went to Damascus to persecute Christians. On the way he was struck down seeing a brilliant light from heaven, and he heard the risen Christ, and was blinded. Then Paul was taken to the city where he was healed by a Christian . . .*
– Acts, 9:1-30 (The Conversion of Apostle Paul)

––––––––––

The Soldier regained consciousness in fits and spurts. His dreams of the night before returned like waves crashing upon the shores of his mind, only to recede as the world began to come into focus. Then another wave crashed, sending him reeling back into his memories. Frank had experienced torture. This was worse.

Finally his vision adjusted, and his surroundings became clear. The Soldier felt bindings around his wrists, ankles, and head. He was tied to the trunk of a thick tree behind him. A young man with braided hair was examining his face closely. The young man turned as an older man spoke to him.

The older man appeared in the Soldier's line of vision and moved close to him. The man wore deerskin clothing and what looked like moccasins. He was conscious enough to know he was still in Canada and was aware that Hurons had settled near here, but no one wore this kind of clothing anymore. It had to be a costume. He prepared for the worst, his body tightening.

The Healer, sensing Frank's fear of torture, looked deeply into his steely blue eyes. Veins bulged on Frank's temples as he strained against the head bindings that forced him to look back into the Indian's steady brown eyes. "My brother, we will not harm you. We only seek to keep you from harming others. Great sorrow would come if you completed your mission, not just for us and the world, but for you. The Great Spirit connects us all."

The Soldier gritted his teeth and offered nothing. He urgently catalogued options and tactics, and quickly realized he had none –

except that his global cell phone was turned on. The GPS would tell them that he was no longer moving. They might move in if they sensed there was a problem. The target was too valuable for them not to be paying close attention.

The Healer walked around Frank waving a burning weed, smoky in the morning air. The Soldier at first feared it was a torture device, but then realized that the Indian was moving the plant around to allow smoke to drift toward him. The smell was not unlike marijuana, but as the Indian wafted the smoke toward Frank's face, he could see that it was sage.

Native Americans had used sage for centuries. Elders taught that before a person can be healed or heal another, one must be cleansed both physically and spiritually – of negative thoughts, destructive spirits, and divisive energy. In this way healing can come through clearly, without distortion in either the healer or the one being healed.

The Healer chanted softly as he moved around him, brushing the smoke toward Frank as he moved. Then he spoke. "The elders tell us that all ceremonies, tribal or private, must be entered into with a good heart so that we can pray, sing, and walk in a sacred manner. Then the spirits will help us enter a sacred realm."

The Soldier said nothing. His jaw tightened.

After circling Frank with sage smoke, the Healer repeated the process with cedar bark, and then with sweet grass braided like hair. When the Healer reached toward him, the Soldier recoiled, straining against his bindings to escape the Indian's touch. The Healer placed his open palm over Frank's heart, drawing his face near to Frank's as he spoke. "My brother, you do not need to pretend with me. The Great Spirit has shown me your journey of pain. There is no judgment here. We have all lived many lives, and we all have much to regret. We have restrained you only so that you will not regret more."

The silvery dome light of his dreams shimmered around them for an instant. Frank blinked and it was gone, leaving him to wonder if he had imagined it.

The Indian disappeared from Frank's vision. Minutes later a young woman with long dark hair appeared carrying a bucket of water. It was the target! The Soldier stiffened, anticipating some kind of water torture.

Ravi looked at the man directly. "You killed my sister." Ravi's eyes, only inches from Frank's, filled with tears. "When my father died, he begged my sister and me to watch over one another no matter what. I promised . . ." Ravi's voice broke.

The Soldier tried to look away, but he could not. Ravi filled his field of vision. His heart swelled with the feelings of the night before. He could not stand this; he'd rather have his fingernails torn out.

Ravi continued, "This morning when I heard you had been captured by the sentries, *I hated you.*" Her face and heart tightened as she remembered how easily Frank had taken her sister's life. Angry tears filled her eyes as her heart exploded in a storm of sorrow and fury. She struggled on, looking directly at Frank.

Frank's hard face was betrayed by his pain-filled eyes that longed to look away in shame. But they remained locked on her own, as if surrendering to the just sentence of her damnation. That instant of vulnerability shifted Ravi's heart.

Ravi breathed deeply. Her lips quivered with emotion as she exhaled a halting breath, and her tight voice loosened as she spoke. "Then I had a dream – a vision – and I saw you as a small boy. A woman – I think your mother, called you *Frankie.* I saw a man, a hard man full of rage and bitterness. You saw your own reflection in him. You loved him, Frankie, even though he was cruel to you. He in turn saw himself in you, a self that had died in a long pitiless war where many men he'd loved had died horrible deaths, and some because of mistakes he had made."

Ravi wet a cloth in the bucket and dabbed at Frank's perspiring brow as she spoke. Ravi now wept not only for Rachel, but also for the little Frankie of her dream. Their faces became one. The sorrow of broken hearts lost definition, co-mingling, no longer defined by Rachel or Frankie, becoming a universal sorrow.

"Your innocence reminded your father of what he had lost, and the fury of that knowing came down on *you,* little Frankie. He *did* love you. This life of hardness you have lived was to make him proud, even though you have never spoken of it. But Frankie, when he passed from this world, his heart broke because of what he'd done to you – to his precious one, *his own reflection.*"

Tears filled Ravi's soft brown eyes as she felt Frank's heart break even before he felt it himself. Without self-consciousness or shame, Frank cried, *"Oooowwww, God help me. This is too much. I can't bear this."*

Frank wept like a child, his chest heaving. Ravi placed her hand on his heart. She welcomed the spirit that was reconnecting with itself. As the tears flowed, Ravi's heart broke open, and Frank's loss and pain merged with hers. She felt release in his regret as if it were her own. The alchemical miracle of compassion empowered Frank's tears to cleanse and unburden her breaking heart as well.

Ravi dabbed his face clean with the cloth and offered him a cup of water. As she turned to leave, Frank croaked, *"I-I-I'm so sorry,"* and again the tears flowed. Frank's body was wracked with emotion as if every cell were electrified and then drained of its charge again and again.

Ravi turned back. She stroked his face and through her own tears, saw Rachel's death in his haunted eyes. She felt Frank's regret. Stroking his face, she crooned, "I know, I know, I know." She allowed space for Frank's heart to empty its jagged shards. Between their sobs, their breathing became deep and then became one.

Frank looked into Ravi's eyes. "How can you forgive me?"

Ravi replied, "In my dream, after I watched your father betray the child you were, I remembered who I have been. We have all lived many lives, Frank, and we . . . *I* have been a killer as well. There is nothing anyone has done that everyone has not experienced.

"Every emotion we feel reflects a different vibrational rate. Hate is the lowest vibration; compassion is the highest. Outcomes of mutual benefit can only be achieved when people rise to higher vibratory rates.

"All of humanity is struggling to choose the vibration at which their mind, heart, and soul will operate – whether it will be the low vibration of hate, fear, guilt, and shame, or the higher ones of love, acceptance, joy, and peace.

"When we forgive, we choose a higher vibration. Righteous revenge only makes killers of us all, spreading the vibration of murder. Within me is a hatred for you and what you've done to my precious Rachel, but also within me is a knowing that in past lives, I, too, have murdered – ripped people away from those they loved. I felt your agony, regret, and despair as you felt it, as I do now.

"I am choosing to allow my heart to vibrate at the rate of compassion. We have a joined life now. We are co-conspirators of hope, meaning that we have joined, breathing together to bring something meaningful into this life. If I chose to vibrate at the rate of hatred, we would not be able to complete our mission."

Suddenly, the omni-octave chants seemed to fill the woods around her. She again heard her lips voice a truth that came from beyond her. Ravi spoke forcefully and with urgency, her voice rising. "This isn't just about us. *This is the state of the world.*"

Frank's eyes focused on the woman. Her last words had shaken him awake. A larger reality opened before him.

Frank's mind snapped back to a memory. "I have to speak to the Indian, quickly, *please.*"

Ravi disappeared, and the Healer reappeared in Frank's vision. He began removing Frank's bindings. "I can see, my brother, these are no longer necessary."

Frank said urgently, "I have to tell you, there will be others here soon. My cell phone has GPS, and they will fear I have failed when they see I've not moved during daylight. Many will follow me."

"Thank you my brother. We will prepare."

# 45. New Friends

*Peace is not achieved by controlling nations, but mastering our thoughts.*
– John Harricharan

---

Ian, Frank, Ravi, and the Healer warmed themselves near the morning fire. The black man with long dreadlocks placed steaming cups in their hands. The Healer thanked him in his own native Tsleil-Waututh Nation tongue. "Thank you, my brother, you are good to me." The black man smiled lovingly at the Healer as he withdrew.

"My dear brother has brought us this Jamaican Blue Mountain coffee, a delicacy from his land."

Warmth spread through Frank as he sat with his – *friends*. Strange. He had been either in the military or the Company nearly his entire life and had never considered one co-worker as a friend. Well, there may have been *one*. But, today, as the sun rose, *his friends* – people he had known only for a few hours – sat around him.

"Only for hours in *this* life, my brother. We go way back in the Great Spirit's infinite plans." The Healer patted Frank's shoulder with a knowing wink, watching Frank's eyes widen as he heard his thoughts being spoken aloud.

. . .

Just as Frank had suspected, the troops had honed in on his phone's signal once his position had frozen. The Professor's call hours before explained the Soldier's stationary GPS signal, but when his daylight movement suddenly stopped with no report, the Professor knew something was wrong. He had called Ratlig at the monitoring station, and the data showed that something very odd was occurring at the targets' location.

The gamma waves were off the charts, out in the middle of bum-sug-nowhere, where no civilian population was known to exist. They'd zapped the area immediately with electromagnetic pulses, but the gamma waves remained at unbelievably high levels. The images had given the appearance of a "dome" of energy over the area, unlike anything they had ever detected before. Troops were dropped into position just beyond where the chopper's noise would be audible to the targets.

They had skillfully moved in from three directions, their triangulated formation stealing through the thick woods. They met no resistance. Apparently no guards had been posted. Just before they made visual contact with the targets, the silence was broken by the hooting of an owl.

The Healer heard the sentry, who had sent the message in the voice of cousin owl. He gave no indication of it and continued to enjoy quiet conversation and coffee with his new friends.

# 46. What Do You Mean "WE," Kemo Sabi?

The troops moved in – two angling in from the front, one approaching directly from the back. A small hill covered with boulders near the back of the clearing stood between the group of friends and the troops moving through the woods behind them. The two forces advancing toward them from the front became visible as they emerged from the brush into the clearing.

The Healer stood and stepped toward the approaching troops, stopping just in front of the fire. Ian, Ravi, and Frank backed up toward the hill. With gun raised, the troop leader moved in, stopping only a few feet from the Healer. Moving the barrel of his gun toward Frank, as if pointing to him with his finger, the leader spoke to the Indian. "We're here to take these people in. We can do this hard, or we can do this easy."

The Healer smiled at the group leader. "What do you mean 'WE,' Kemo Sabi?"

The Healer raised his arms to the heavens, and a great flash filled their eyes, white and blue like lightning, followed by a huge plume of white smoke. When the smoke cleared, only the Indian stood before them. *The others were gone.*

The Indian spoke. "Your crude technology does not work here, White Man. You walk in our world today."

# 47. Moving through Miracles

*Unless we wake up to the damage that the gadget-filled, pharmaceutically-enhanced 21st century is doing to our brains, we could be sleepwalking towards a future in which neuro-chip technology blurs the line between living and non-living machines, and between our bodies and the outside world.*
    – *UK Daily Mail,* Saturday, May 10, 2008

---

When the flash powder hit the fire, Ian, Ravi, and Frank stepped back into the cavern entrance hidden among the boulders behind them. The young man waiting above heaved the boulder that was poised to fall into place, sealing the entrance. The Healer, who had trained as a chemist and had even once worked in pyrotechnics, supplied the flash powder which until now had been employed only to entertain the children from time to time with fireworks magic during the long Canadian nights in the First Nation lands.

Leaving the Healer's engineered chaos above, the trio descended from the mouth of the cavern into a cave. Frank led with a crude wooden torch, prepared and placed at the cave's entrance by the Healer's people, igniting the pitch-soaked rags wrapped around one end of the stick with his lighter as they walked. They moved quickly to put distance between themselves and their pursuers into a depthless black, ever extending just beyond the edge of the torch's light.

The path sharply descended, and the walls tightened. The incline was so severe at times that they had to sit on the smooth floor and prop their feet and hands outward against the narrowing walls of the passage in a rough approximation of rappelling without ropes, sliding inches at a time before again pressing their feet into the walls. The steep angle of their movement continued for over thirty minutes, and they became more daring, sliding several feet at a time, then digging in to stop themselves before they could fall God knew how far below.

Little by little the incline lessened, and the walls of the cave expanded from a suffocating fissure in the earth into a grand expanse whose ceiling loomed high beyond the range of the torch's illumination. Only the hanging daggers of the longest stalactites shone in the light. The shape of the blackness hovering above was detectable only by the sonorous echoes of their footsteps and those of the faint dripping sounds of white liquid that fell from some of the jutting stones. These sounds became fainter and they lost even this reference point as they moved forward into the expanding vastness.

Frank unfolded the map the Healer had given him, raised his compass into the flickering light, and then moved purposefully forward again.

The endless silence of this great cathedral of inky gloom was disquieting. They moved several hundred feet across the level expanse, never seeing a wall surrounding them. Their torch appeared more and more feeble with each step, as the darkness around them seemed to grow deeper and wider.

Then the swath of the torch's illumination came into focus with the appearance of a great wall looming high overhead as they approached. The wall became concave as they neared it, growing even brighter to their dilated, light-starved pupils as its reflective surface closed in all around with each step forward.

The silky white surface of the wall, surrounded by crystals that brightly reflected the flame's light, was split in the center by a dark narrow opening. The sudden constriction of their pupils in response to the brilliance left what lay beyond the approaching passage in utter blackness.

They passed through the tight opening in single file, each turning sideways to get through it, to find themselves in another cave whose walls and ceiling drew close around them.

As the three pressed together, suddenly Frank stopped. A loud *click* echoed through the dark caverns as Frank turned to face Ian. Frank held the switchblade the Healer had returned to him after untying him from the tree.

Ian's heart froze. He lost his balance and stepped back into Ravi, who stumbled behind him. Ian's mind swirled as he tried to remember all that had transpired in the hours since Frank's transformation. What had he missed? It had seemed so real, so honest. Maybe it was naïve to think people could change, but *hadn't he himself changed?* Maybe all he'd seen and felt had been a hall of mirrors. The speed with which miracles could become mirages, in which the mind could fall out of grace and back into old patterns of fear and mistrust, was staggering.

Ravi fell back against the cavern wall. Her fingers spidered out, trying to grip before she slipped down the smooth wall. She had lost her balance at the shock of seeing Frank wield the long sharp silver blade, which flickered dangerously in the dancing torch light. Her mind spun back to her ordeal in the Professor's lab — to cold steel and sharp instruments that had gleamed under the hospital lights. Her mouth gaped open, yet she could not draw in breath.

His face lit by the flame of the torch, Frank spoke to Ian. "I need you to cut me."

"What?" Ian could hardly get the word out.

"There's a GPS chip buried beneath the skin on my left shoulder. SOP, Standard Operating Procedure for agents at my level. It's about a third of an inch under the skin. Down here the signal may be undetectable, but when they find the entrance and follow, they'll pick it up. And if they don't get it then, they'll pick it up when we come out on the other end."

Frank sat down on a rock and held the knife back over his shoulder, handle first, oblivious to Ian and Ravi's moment of doubt.

Frank passed the torch over his other shoulder, wanting to be sure Ian could see what he was doing when he cut into him. Ian and Ravi both took a deep breath and almost laughed at one another's relief. They stifled their nervous laughter, to spare Frank their mistrust of him, of the different person he'd become under the Healer's dome.

The blade gleamed sharp and long in the torchlight. Ian took it hesitantly, burning the blade with the flame to sterilize it. Ravi took the torch from him, pointing the light at Frank's shoulder. Frank pulled off his shirt and waited. Ian looked at Ravi. She nodded toward Frank's shoulder, encouraging Ian to get on with it. Time was short. She could feel their pursuers closing in.

Even in the dim light, Ian could see many scars on Frank's war-ravaged body. He felt around on the shoulder until Frank identified the spot where the chip was implanted. He placed the knife tip lightly on that point. Frank reminded Ian, "Like I said, it's about a third of an inch in. Don't saw on me, just poke down into it with a solid thrust. But don't go too deep."

Ian realized he wasn't breathing. He inhaled and blew his breath out in a rush as he buried the tip of the weapon into Frank's shoulder. Ravi gasped as blood spurted from the wound.

Frank sat motionless, emotionless. He'd endured much greater pain over the years and impassively allowed Ian to do his work. He didn't want to make Ian any more nervous, even though it hurt like hell.

Once in, Ian prodded with the knife tip until he heard the tap of the blade on the silicon. He slid the tip to one side to pry the chip out of Frank's shoulder. Blood began to stream in earnest down Frank's back. Ian clenched his teeth and squinted his eyes as he worked. In the absolute silence of the cavern, they heard a quiet sucking sound as he pulled the chip to the side and then up and out. Frank shuddered. He reached up quickly to compress the wound with his shirt, then stood and took the torch from Ravi.

Without a word, he continued through the cavern as quickly as the dimness would allow, and Ian and Ravi followed. Danger was closing in, fast.

# 48. Let There be Light

After they had taken one turn after another and had put some distance between themselves and the cavern entrance, they felt the panic of their flight begin to diminish. Frank stopped and stood in the silence to listen for any sounds that would indicate pursuers. There were none.

In that moment of relief, Frank's mind flashed back to the disappearing act they'd pulled to begin their escape and the last words they had heard the Healer speak as they "vanished." He imagined the looks on the faces of the strike force when they had heard, *What do you mean 'WE,' Kemo Sabi?* and he laughed out loud. He leaned against the cavern wall as his laughs became belly laughs, then snorting and choking. He was unable to stop.

Ian and Ravi looked at him in the light of the torch, perplexed, until they made out through Frank's snorts the words *Kemo Sabi.* All three leaned on the walls to howl uncontrollably, interrupted only by snickers and desperate gasps for breath. Life was good. Cold-blooded killers were on their trail, and they had a thin shred of a chance to avoid oblivion – but life was good.

These caverns had been used for shelter in pre-White Man times by the Wyandot nation when they settled in what would eventually become Canadian territory. The dolostone caverns were made of a sedimentary rock that was not only resistant to erosion but also eerily beautiful. Over the centuries, acidic groundwater had created stunning stalagmites and stalactites. Crystals composed of calcium magnesium carbonate were plentiful. The Healer's people were drawn to this area because they considered the crystals sacred and capable of amplifying higher consciousness energy – not unlike the way crystals focus radio waves in a radio.

The tunnels they had passed through up till now had been smooth and milky white and had seemed benign; however, the walls here had the sharp and disturbing appearance of sharks' teeth. It was as if they were descending into a set of jaws. The passages were again becoming narrower and more confining as they moved steadily through them. Hollowed places appeared in the walls that overflowed with a bacterial slime the locals called *moonmilk*. The floor became more slippery and treacherous.

Until now, they had progressed through a single tunnel. But now they began to encounter a matrix of intersecting tunnels. Using his military compass and the map, Frank led Ian and Ravi through the winding passages.

They were headed for an exit from the caverns at a point in Michigan, across the U.S.-Canadian border. Without the map, they would have been lost. It was surely accurate; each turn appeared where the map said it would. They needed only to follow it correctly. They appeared to be just a couple of hours away from their goal.

At this point, their focus wasn't on their pursuers, but on the more immediate danger of inaccurately traversing this subterranean network of intricate passages. Even after the strike force discovered the caverns, it was unlikely that they would be able to follow them through the labyrinthine tunnels. There were just too many forks and side-trails. One could easily end up lost in this maze of connecting caves, rooms, and tunnels – some of which required crawling on hands and knees. If the trio chose the wrong path, they would never be found.

The caves led under the Detroit River, known in Ontario as *Rivière du Détroit,* which connected Lake St. Clair to Lake Erie and divided Canada from the United States. They were crossing underneath the river at a point where it was about two miles wide. As they descended, they could feel a building pressure as if the weight of the mighty river were bearing down on them. As a substantial flow of water dripped and sometimes poured through fissures hidden among the smooth white stalactites above them, the three exchanged nervous glances.

The combustible material of the torch was rapidly nearing its end, and the flame was getting smaller. Despite Frank's efforts to protect it, from time to time, drips of water landed on the flame. Each of them silently flinched when they heard the sizzles. Whether their trek would outlast the light was a question none of them wanted to ponder. The march into darkness went on.

The torchlight began to flicker. Frank quickened the pace. Ian and Ravi panted with exertion, concentrating on keeping their footing as they tried to keep up and stay on the path, now illuminated by what had become a dying strobe light. Their pupils dilated with trepidation and adrenaline as they scurried through the passages.

Frank moved even faster. The light was dimming. Without the torch to light the way, he doubted he could accurately follow the map, even if he could read it with his cigarette lighter.

Even with the map, it was impossible to tell how far they were from the exit, with all the twists and turns. They could be close to it, yet it could take them hours to get there if they had to move in darkness.

The light of the torch flared brightly for a second – its dying gasp. Then it was gone. Instantly the shadows that had stalked them from the edges of their only source of light swarmed in on them. They froze, their eyes straining against utter darkness.

Frank took Ian's hand and placed it on his shoulder, telling Ravi to place hers on Ian's. Much more slowly, they moved on. Frank felt the walls with his hands, trying to decipher if there were turns opening ahead of them. He wanted to reserve what was left of his lighter for brief glances at the map. If he couldn't do that, there was no hope at all.

The dying of the light had cast them into a sensory deprivation chamber. The sound of their shuffling steps and the touch of their hands were their only sensory information. Phantom sounds and a sense of lurking danger thickened around them as they moved in short hobbled steps. *How much farther?* The inky blackness pressed in on them.

Ian and Ravi stumbled to an abrupt stop behind Frank as he thumbed his cigarette lighter and his dark silhouette appeared. Then the blackness enclosed them again as he snapped it shut. He moved on, making a severe turn into an opening to his right. They shuffled forward, descending a narrowing slimy moonmilk-covered path. They heard only the sound of their feet grasping for traction as the passageway narrowed. They were squeezed between the walls. Frank froze. His mind spun. *This isn't right!*

Ravi and Ian were fortunate that they were behind Frank and were therefore spared the look of doubt on his face as his lighter flared again. The tapering passageway had become so constricted that he could barely get the lighter up past his waist so he could see the map. Water was running freely down the walls around them. The musty air was thick and hard to breathe. The map had grown damp and limp, and droplets splashed from the closing walls. Despite Frank's protective hand covering the lighter, the water dampened the wick and extinguished the flame.

Frank spoke. "We have to go back." The tunnel was too narrow for them to turn around. He directed them to retrace their steps walking backwards. Frank quietly blew on his extinguished lighter to dry the wick as they moved. He tried to remember how many steps they had taken down this path.

Only Frank had seen that the lighter's flame had become smaller, just before the moisture had put it out. *I'm out of lighter fluid.* He suppressed his panic. If his lighter was dead, they were screwed.

When they reached the point where they'd last turned off, he directed them to the right, back down the previous tunnel. *This better be the one I think it is.*

The increasingly frightened convoy moved on through the gloom, their sweaty hands gripping the shoulder before them more tightly. Step by step, yard by yard, they moved farther into the murky depths. Frank stopped again.

He sensed more than saw an opening on their left. They stood together at the Y juncture of their current path and the new one. Frank pulled out his lighter and grazed the flint wheel against the fabric on his thigh. Perhaps it would light just once more. *It has too!* The tiny flame seemed brilliant as the three huddled around the minute point of illumination – holding their breath for fear of blowing it out.

Frank checked the map. He stepped into the left side of the Y, still looking at the map. He had to be absolutely sure.

A feeble light shone far ahead of them. Perhaps it was an echoing flare of Frank's lighter from some particularly reflective crystal formation. The lighter died – yet the glimmer far ahead of them continued to glint faintly.

The path was leading distinctly upward now. The light increased, and as they approached its source, a resplendent radiance expanded. Sunlight, still a hundred yards away, entered the cave, illuminating the crystal-laden walls in a welcome translucence.

As they drew nearer, dancing rays starred off millions of shiny crystals to *explode* in their dilated eyes, flooding their hearts and minds with excitement and hope. Squinting, they held their hands up as visors to block some of the light from their eyes.

They felt along the smooth walls of the cave as blind people would to find their way toward the exit. Visually the walls no longer existed – their light-starved eyes were now overloaded with brilliance. Pure radiance inflamed the space. It was a child's image of what heaven might be like, less the harp music and choir. *Salvation – for the first time – was truly possible!*

# 49. Plan B – The End of Democracy

*Fascism should more properly be called corporatism because it is the merger of state and corporate power.*
    – Benito Mussolini

*The operation . . . was the blueprint for a succession of CIA plots to foment coups and destabilize governments . . . The coup had its roots in a British showdown with Iran . . . The prize was Iran's oil fields . . .*
    – Secrets of History: The CIA in Iran, James Rison, *The New York Times,* April 16, 2000

*We have created in the United States, largely in the last thirty years, a whole series of programs, a few of them explicit, many of them deeply hidden, that take money from the pockets of the poor and the middle class and the upper-middle class and funnel it to the wealthiest people in America . . .*
    – David Cay Johnston, Pulitzer Prize-winning Investigative Journalist, *Democracy Now* Interview, January 18, 2008

*Today's [Supreme Court] decision [that corporations may spend freely to support or oppose candidates for president and Congress] . . . imperils our democratic well-being.*
    – Robert Weissman, President, Public Citizen, Associated Press, January 21, 2010

---

The Professor let the phone slip from his hand. His face drained of blood as the full weight of the unthinkable news settled upon him. *The Soldier had deserted.* With these four words, the Professor's world collapsed.

His eyes stared blankly as his mouth fell open. That *SON-OF-A...!*

A man like the Soldier could bring down governments if information he carried got into the wrong hands. And in this information age of YouTube, blogs, and a nightmarish list of other uncontrollable media – the ramifications were too horrible to contemplate.

The Professor's fingers felt numb as he dialed the VP's number to report this catastrophe.

Almost 500 miles away, the Vice President's inner sanctum was inflamed with activity. Since the Professor's call, the high security phone on the VP's mahogany desk had been used more this morning than it had since its installation. The messages that sizzled through the wire were both dangerous and violent. An empire of control was slipping through their fingers, and fists tightened in an iron grip, attempting to seize whatever still lay within the machine's panicky grasp.

Everything was falling to pieces. The Professor no longer had the woman, and any hope of dissecting the shift in human consciousness had rested on the Professor's ability to break her. Even more immediate and cataclysmic was that the fallback, Plan B, could not be enacted so long as the Soldier's breath remained in his lungs.

The demolition charges, meticulously set within the Capitol building, could not be used as long as the Soldier was alive to testify about their plan and his part in it. With Congress still in operation, the belly of the beast lay open and vulnerable to the disaster of committees, subpoenas, and investigations. *What if the woman and the Soldier went public together?*

Decades of development of systems of thought control and manipulation of laws devised to end democratic rule and empower the final solution of absolute corporate control of the world – now so close at hand – could end overnight if together they unleashed a public awakening.

Once awakened, the public would demand to know – *everything!* Laws, media, and government designs to pull the wealth of America and the world away from struggling masses and into the bank accounts of a tiny yet monstrously powerful elite, would be exposed. If tales were told by insiders, enticed by offers of immunity or reduced sentences, war crimes would come to light. Past criminal destabilizations of governments – Guatemala, Iran, Chile – would all pale in comparison to the operations of recent decades. The illegal arrests, the torture, the spying on innocent Americans – all of it would be laid bare. The corporate media would not be able to hold this information back. The more the public learned, the more information they would demand.

*This would not stand!*

The entire might of the most powerful covert operations machine in history began to turn like the eye of an angry behemoth toward the trio fleeing invisibly beneath the flowing river of Detroit. No expense would be spared.

All resources that could be used without raising the suspicion of government outsiders – those who were not in the inner circle of control and deceit – were mobilized. Satellites – the behemoth's eyes – turned in the heavens. Data monitors, radios, and telephones crackled as information shot from one to another. People were captured and torture was unleashed. No care was taken to leave only invisible wounds. No holds were barred. This was fourth down on the one-inch line. Eyes would be gouged and kneecaps would be shattered. Anything that was required would be done to keep the light of truth from crossing the goal line.

*A way of life was at stake.*

# 50. Windows

Blinded momentarily by the shrill sunlight, the three ragged and dirty companions emerged from the gloomy depths of the caverns into sunny Michigan. According to Frank's map, they were 23 miles southwest of Detroit, about five miles inland from the river. They followed a road east back toward the river, until they were able to hitch a ride in the back of a pickup truck into Detroit.

As they passed through the countryside, Ian, Frank and Ravi reflected. The events that had brought them together were not accidental. The three had become part of something profound and sacred. Warmth and calm excitement spread through their hearts and minds as they remembered their last encounter with the Healer. They would carry this memory like a talisman. It was his vision that was leading them south.

The Healer had told them what he could about his last vision before they left. Over the rich vapors of the coffee they had shared like a sacrament to their friendship, he'd told them of his plan to connect them with his friends in Kansas City. Although his vision wasn't completely clear, he felt there was a small window of opportunity that might save them, if the timing was just right.

Now they faced the challenge of heading south to the home of the Healer's trusted friends of the Wyandot tribe – the people of the Healer's mother. Years before, Liam and Oi Yue Douglas had taught tai chi to troubled Indian youth through a program sponsored by Haskell Indian Nations University in Lawrence, Kansas. This work had eventually led them to the First Nations people in Canada, where they had met the Healer. Quickly recognizing their common vision, they had become fast friends.

Thinking it might be easier to move without being spotted in an impoverished neighborhood, Frank asked the driver to drop them off a few blocks south of Martin Luther King Boulevard, in this poorest part of America's poorest city – the Midtown area. Frank, ever prepared, "like a good soldier" – he smiled as he savored the words –

was carrying cash. They walked through the streets of this largely abandoned post-industrial area of Detroit. Ian and Ravi were wearing the deerskin clothing the First Nation people had given them when they had arrived at the encampment. The stares of people who passed them on the street made them self-conscious, though the garments had seemed so natural before.

Inside a Goodwill store, Ravi donned well fitting jeans and a blue cotton blouse. As she emerged from the changing room, Ian found himself seeing Ravi in a new light.

Ravi noticed Ian's lingering gaze and blushed, but a small smile curved her lips as she looked away to hide it. Her heart fluttered. Before Ian had entered the changing booth with his new clothes in hand, still in the buckskin clothing – his long blond hair touching his shoulders – Ravi too had seen Ian in a different light.

All three emerged from the store wearing jeans and shirts. Ian's t-shirt read, "Have a nice day!" They stopped at a filthy phone kiosk and Frank flipped through the tattered Yellow Pages to get an address. After asking several pedestrians for street directions, they found their way to the Greyhound bus station and purchased tickets to Chicago. From there they would transfer to St. Louis, Missouri, before heading across the state to Kansas City.

With an hour and a half until their bus was scheduled to leave, they sat in the café on the upper balcony level of the terminal, looking down at the bustling crowd below. They ordered coffee and sandwiches and exchanged the casual small talk of friends.

They'd known one another for only a matter of hours. The intensity of their shared struggle had compressed lifetimes of experience into this short timeframe. It was not the length of a relationship that mattered, but the willingness to give oneself completely over to the will of "the Great Spirit," as the Healer would say.

Ravi's mind returned to the Healer's last words as she sipped her coffee. "What do you mean 'WE,' Kemo Sabi?" Ravi said with a lilting, slightly British accent. Ian and Frank burst into sweet laughter, a flowing river in the desert that had been their lives – *before*. Their souls were returning home.

Their conversation turned to their shared odyssey. Frank wanted to know how Ravi had survived the attempt on her life at the National Press Club, explaining to her how the Professor had unleashed one of his pathetic Manchurian drones upon her.

Ravi was not familiar with that phrase and wanted to know what it meant. Frank described the Company's Manchurian programming project – how the consciousness of the "patients" was systematically erased from their minds, leaving them automatons. Ravi's eyes moistened as memories of her own terror and feeling of helplessness on the Professor's table fused with the sadness in the eyes of the young man with the gun.

The waitress came with their food. She placed a plate on the table in front of Frank. He looked up at her and said, "Thank you." No one else noticed, but Frank's world stood still. How long had it been since he'd uttered those words?

The waitress smiled at him, lightly touched his shoulder, and replied, "You're very welcome."

Frank turned back to Ravi. How had she avoided assassination? Ravi struggled to find words to explain what had happened. "There was *a vibration* in my mind – I had felt it before when all this began months ago at Oxford University."

Frank interrupted, leaning in. "A *vibration?* What do you mean by that?"

"It was a sound, resonant and deep, that vibrated right through me, and I think also through the man who was programmed to kill me. I can't exactly describe it. It was so all-encompassing – but if I had to name it, I'd call it *a chant.*"

Frank's jaw went slack. His mind spun back to the mountain in Tibet, the monk's murder, and his own breakdown. Ravi's reference to the chanting sound as *a beginning* shifted Frank's memory of his brutal act followed by his own collapse. He suddenly realized this horrible experience, which had seemed like the death of who he was – had actually been the moment of his becoming – *becoming what?*

Like the forest's whispering foliage, a rushing waitress's apron slipped across the back of Frank's chair with the answer: *Chrysalis: A being in transformation.*

Frank froze. He'd forgotten what he was about to say. As he struggled to remember, a series of tumblers unlocked other chambers within him. He needed to – he was supposed to – *what?* Unload another burden from the vault of his heart? *What? What is it I must express?*

As Frank started to ask Ravi a question, the now familiar vibration spread through him. It took his breath away. It was urgent that he tell Ravi about his demolition work at the Capitol.

Frank quickly unfolded the story of his mission inside the walls of Congress just days before. He gave an overview of the demolition charges, the installation of the wireless detonators, and what he knew about Plan B's intention to destroy global democracy.

Ian and Ravi stared at one another, their wide eyes shining with fear. The deep horror Ravi felt was reflected in the turmoil showing on Ian's face as he flashed back to his dream in the trucker's cab. *The burning Capitol building – was that what I saw?*

Hungry as they'd been a moment before, the food now sat before them untouched. Their nebulous quest suddenly took on an enormity that weighed heavily upon them all. Their mission to fulfill the Healer's vision was vital. It had to work. *It had to.*

Ian was about to describe his dream to Ravi when suddenly Frank grew taut and alert, like a jungle cat sensing danger. It took Ian and Ravi a moment to notice the intensity in his face as he stared at the lobby area beneath them, but when they did, they watched Frank for instruction. He abruptly turned and picked up a menu, popping it open to use the unfolded pages to hide Ravi's face from the crowd below.

Under his breath, Frank snapped orders. "*We've got to move!* One at a time, and don't look down. Just move away from the table, away from anybody who could see you from below. Go to the bathrooms in the back."

He threw some money on the table as they rose.

As they approached the bathrooms, Frank stepped ahead of them. He looked around, scanning the restaurant behind them, before ducking into the men's room. He found no one inside, and as Ian walked past him, he reached across him to grab Ravi by her t-shirt, pulling her in with them.

The bathroom door had no lock, so Ian stood guard to prevent anyone from entering while Frank used his knife to cut through the thick layers of paint that sealed the window shut. With great effort, Frank lifted the stubborn window. The cool air rushed in.

. . .

Below the balcony, a man in a black trench coat spoke into a microphone on his lapel as he turned to scan the crowd in the bus station. All bus stations around southwestern Ontario were now covered, including Detroit. They had just arrived after receiving a civilian tip about people possibly fitting the description in a ghetto area not far from here. It shouldn't be hard to spot two Caucasians and a pretty Indian woman. Besides, several of the men knew the traitor's face.

The Soldier had some explaining to do, and the Professor was eager to give him a place in the Sleep Room where he could dissect his consciousness before brutally ending it. His session would not require as much finesse as Ravi's, for there was less need to keep the Soldier in that delicate balance – that painful purgatory between life and death. The woman had been a test subject. He could indulge in pure revenge with the Soldier.

Catching a glimpse of sudden movement out of the corner of his eye, the trench-coated sentry looked upward and spoke urgently into the radio mic on his lapel.

# 51. Oh Lord, Could You Spare Me a Mercedes Benz?

The door of the men's room burst open. With revolver in hand, the agent kicked each stall door open before noticing the window was slightly ajar. The jagged paint chips on the floor below it told the story.

. . .

Once out the window, down the fire escape, and in the alley behind the bus station, Ian, Ravi, and Frank stopped abruptly at an unoccupied bread truck. The keys dangled from the ignition.

Ian clambered into the passenger side as Frank flung himself into the open driver's seat and snatched the delivery man's cap from the dash, pulling the bill down low over his face – an instant too late. As Ravi grabbed the side mirror to hoist herself in beside Ian, she saw a man in a suit and trench coat emerge from a doorway on Frank's side of the truck.

Ravi yelled, "Frank!" pointing at the man, just as the agent raised his right hand to click on his communications mic. Frank's hand chopped out sideways at lightning speed, knocking the man to the ground before he jumped out and slammed his knee squarely into the center of the man's chest, pinning him. Ravi climbed over Ian to emerge from the driver's side, just as Frank pulled his knife open and was arcing it down toward the man's heart.

Frank's arm froze in midair, and as he twisted around to see what force had stopped him, he saw Ravi's hand gripping his wrist. Ravi's years of balance and energy training had given her physical power far beyond her slight frame. Ravi did not speak, only looked into Frank's eyes, but Frank heard the message clearly in his mind. *No more regrets, Frankie.*

In that moment of hesitation as Frank and Ravi's eyes met, the agent saw his chance. He brought the short-nosed revolver up toward Frank's chest.

Without thought, Ravi swung down, using the truck's door frame as a fulcrum. Her body extended out and around, flying through the air like a gymnast's. Ravi's motion had further distracted Frank, and when he looked down, his heart stopped, realizing there was nothing he could do to prevent his own destruction.

The man's finger, a microsecond shy of the pressure needed to send a .38 slug ripping through Frank's chest and into his pumping heart, squeezed as Ravi's shoe made contact with the tip of the gun. The force was unstoppable.

Fire roared from the gun as it blasted its payload. The breath rushed out of Frank, and he instinctively grabbed his chest. Ravi's foot had changed the trajectory of the bullet just enough for the shot to miss him, sending the bullet between his arm and body. The gun flew across the alleyway, clattering to a stop on the bricks.

Frank's mouth opened in amazement. "Wow!" he said, as he pulled his wondering gaze from Ravi back to the man beneath him and brought his right hand down to grip the agent's neck tightly.

With his left hand Frank loosed a judo chop to the side of his neck, putting out the man's lights. He went limp. Frank jumped up, pushing Ravi in front of him into the truck. He fired up the engine and hit the gas. As the truck rumbled to life, Ravi searched Frank's face. "Did you . . .?"

Frank shook his head, as he looked down the alley before him. Behind the truck, the downed man slowly began to stir, still disoriented. Buzzing on the edge of consciousness, he struggled to lift his head off the pavement.

. . .

The Company man who'd first spotted them in the café was now speaking into his radio. Forces moved rapidly through the immediate area. One agent turned the corner and peered down the red brick alleyway behind the bus station, where steam rose from the sewers beneath the street. Seeing nothing other than a bread truck slowly ambling away from its delivery, he turned to move on.

. . .

Ian and Ravi peered out from behind the panel dividing the truck's cab from the storage area. Their eyes darted nervously as the truck turned the corner out of the alleyway and pulled into the street.

. . .

Using his lapel radio, the agent reported in to the group leader. "Nothing. Just a delivery truck."

As the truck passed him and turned onto the street, he spotted his fellow agent lying on his back where Frank had left him. The truck had hidden him. He screamed into his mic, "Dammit! That was them!" The man whirled around to see the truck turning another corner, and he broke into a full run while shouting frantically into his microphone.

In his rearview mirror, Frank saw the man running a moment before his turn took him out of view. He stomped on the gas, roaring the old truck for all it was worth down the street, cutting left down another street, over a set of railroad tracks, and into a residential district. He slammed on the brakes, abruptly stopping beside a BMW parked at the curb. He jumped out, speaking urgently to Ian. "Take the truck up there two blocks, turn left and park a half block down. I don't care where you park it. Just hide it – and stay there!"

At the bus station, cars squealed around corners, hesitating for only a moment as agents yanked open doors and jumped in. The cars roared into motion, all headed in the direction the bread truck had been going before it disappeared.

Frank crouched beside the BMW and watched the street until Ian made the turn and the truck vanished around the corner. Already hearing the acceleration of an approaching sedan, Frank quickly ducked lower on the curb side of the BMW and pressed himself against it until the car thundered past at high speed.

With any luck, it wouldn't slam on its brakes and turn to follow the truck down the side street. Frank could only wait and listen.

A half block from the corner, Ian pulled into a driveway, cut across the neatly mowed lawn, rolled over two rose bushes, and squeezed the truck into the narrow gap between two houses, breaking off both side mirrors in the process.

The agent in the racing car hesitated as he looked to his left, surveying the street Ian had just turned onto, before continuing straight ahead.

Frank held his breath as he heard the sedan slow. When the car accelerated, he went to work. He pulled a thin instrument from his wallet, and within seconds the door was open. The car alarm burped briefly before Frank reached under the dash, and, with a sharp pull, abruptly killed the sound.

Ian and Ravi froze, ready to bolt, as a dark BMW raced up the street toward them. It screeched to a stop at the end of the driveway. The smoke-tinted passenger window eased down and Frank stuck his head out, waving his arm at them. "Get in! Hurry!"

Ian and Ravi flung open the rear door, jumped to the ground, raced down the driveway, and leapt into the backseat of the BMW. Frank mashed the gas pedal and skidded around a corner as a Hummer turned onto the street from the other end of the block. The occupants of the black-windowed Hummer slowly and carefully surveyed the street just seconds after the end of the dark BMW disappeared around the corner.

Frank turned a few more corners through the residential streets before entering a main boulevard. They pulled onto I-96, heading west toward Lansing. They would take the I-69 southwest to I-94, which would take them almost all the way to Chicago.

The bus station incident had been a close call. They stopped only briefly to get food and coffee to go at McDonalds, since they still hadn't eaten after their narrow escape. It was going to be a long, demanding day.

When they neared Lansing, Frank turned off the highway, drove to the airport, and found the long-term parking area. He got out and lit a cigarette, walking casually until he spotted a white Mercedes showing a long-term parking ticket with today's date stamp. Within minutes he pulled up behind the dark BMW, motioning for Ian and Ravi to join him in their new Mercedes. Ian rode shotgun, and Ravi jumped into the backseat.

Frank pulled up to the parking lot booth, smiled at the parking attendant, paid the parking fee for the gleaming white Mercedes Benz, and encouraged the attendant to have a nice day. Then they were on I-94, moving toward Chicago in a car that the police wouldn't know was stolen for at least a day – maybe two.

The road droned beneath, the white lines hypnotized, and the others dozed, as Frank gradually relaxed. After a while, he thought about pulling over to let Ian do some driving so he could catch a few winks himself. Frank eyed a truck stop emerging on the horizon as a possible place to make the switch, just as he saw the helicopter.

His neck hairs bristled. Maybe it was a highway patrol helicopter clocking speeders. Its flight pattern showed it was doing general surveillance.

But as it bore down on the highway in front of them over the opposite lane, Frank recognized the helicopter's markings and realized that a brainwave scanning was in process. He knew what was happening – he could almost see Mark Ratlig's sickly pale face as he turned his dials and watched his computer screens. "Ratlig, you geek spying son of a rat!"

The Company analyst's smell was all over this. He was zeroing in on Ravi's consciousness. If the satellite had isolated their car, *the show was over.*

# 52. The Eye Goes Blind

At the satellite receiving station in Canada, Ratlig squinted through the smoke of the cigarette dangling from his mouth as he punched fiercely at his telephone keypad to get the Professor. "We tracked the roads they might use to get out of Detroit, like you ordered. We've sensed higher gamma waves near Lansing, Michigan, on I-94. I've dispatched a helicopter, but they haven't found the exact source yet. We're photographing all the passing vehicles."

The Professor sat grim-faced, staring blankly out his office window. A faint red fire seethed behind his dark pupils before he spoke through gritted teeth into the phone. "We NEED the woman alive! This disease is spreading too quickly. But the Soldier, *the Soldier must be eliminated!* Listen carefully to what I'm saying. The Soldier cannot survive. Your career *and your freedom* depend on what happens today. *GET THEM!*" The Professor leaned over his desk, physically pressing his full weight into the threat he had unleashed upon Ratlig. He slammed the phone into its cradle.

Mark flinched as the connection broke, just as a blip appeared on his screen. He screamed at his assistant, *"JESUS,* get the Professor back! *WE'VE GOT SOMETHING!"*

. . .

The helicopter changed direction in mid-air and banked left to buzz low just as Frank drove through an underpass. The concrete and steel overpass caused Ratlig's signal to blur at the crucial moment when it would have isolated their car as the target.

Frank turned and reached back over the center console to squeeze Ravi's hand in a vise grip. Ian whipped his head back toward Ravi when he heard her yelp in pain.

As the signal faded, the copter pilot began a U-turn to backtrack to where the radar flare had been, hoping to recover it.

Frank released Ravi's hand to maneuver the car through traffic toward the nearest exit. He dumped his soft drink onto a sweater that had been left on the console by the Mercedes' owner. Ravi, shocked and confused, watched through eyes tearing with pain.

The helicopter had disappeared from Frank's vision, but its sound told him it was wheeling around on the opposite side of the overpass to reconnoiter. He had only seconds to act.

If the craft isolated Ravi, hell's fury would descend on them from every direction. Ravi gasped as without warning, Frank turned again and wrapped the cold dripping sweater around her head. "Hold that there!"

Frank broke open his satellite phone on the car's dash and ordered Ravi to touch the prongs of its 9-volt battery against her tongue. "Shock your tongue with this NOW! Keep doing it. They're scanning for your brainwave emissions. Did you see the helicopter?"

Frank turned back to negotiate the off-ramp coming up on their right.

Ravi nodded, eyes darting with fear to the sky, searching. Memories of the Professor's lab merged with the sound of the returning helicopter pounding low overhead. Quickly, Ravi touched the battery to her tongue as Frank had instructed. Frank reached around again and grabbed her hand, while cutting through honking traffic. "Don't do it rhythmically. It's more disruptive when it's erratic. Ian, you do it for her so she doesn't know when the shock is coming."

Ian remembered the chain-smoking analyst poring over endless lines of data code. Ratlig had explained that the technology could not only track higher gamma wave emissions in general areas but was so highly refined that it could zero in on individuals. The memory propelled him into action.

Ian took the battery from Ravi's hand as instructed – then rocked sideways as Frank jerked the wheel toward the off-ramp. He lost his grip on the battery. The helicopter's blades above them pounded deafeningly.

Ian fumbled the battery in his fingers before steadying himself. He leaned over the back of his seat and tapped it in erratic patterns against Ravi's tongue. Flashing back to his participation in the Sleep Room torture, he murmured, "I'm so sorry."

Frank got them off the highway, and running a red light, floored it, putting distance between them and the searching aircraft as quickly as he could.

Ravi sat back with eyes closed, as the sticky cold soda dribbled down her face and neck and the maelstrom swirled around her. Her mind was indeed distracted. Suddenly, over their car's roaring engine, something was different. She could no longer hear the helicopter. *There was hope.*

Looking at his roadmap, Frank furiously punched numbers into the car phone of the stolen Mercedes. Frank's cryptic conversation with someone on the other end was brief and caused him to whip the car into a quick right turn so they were heading east again toward Lansing. He couldn't reenter the interstate, as the aerial surveillance might still be there.

Frank spoke over his shoulder to Ravi. "There's a doctor who used to be in the program with me. He may be able to help us lower your gamma wave emissions temporarily, so we can avoid the watchers long enough to get where we're going. We'll never make it without his help. They're scanning the roads all around us, and this wet-head battery trick won't work for much longer. I think we can trust him, but I have to warn you, the man is unusual." Ravi opened her eyes wide. *How much weirder can this get?*

After twenty miles on surface streets, Frank reentered I-94 East. Although surface streets would be less likely to be watched, getting to their destination quicker would be the safest bet, so he was taking a chance on the highway.

Frank pressed on, opening up the Benz's powerful engine, while craning his neck to look for aerial activity above them. When the car's cell phone rang, Ian and Ravi looked at one another in fear. It was a stolen car. But Frank saw the caller ID and picked up.

The voice said, "They're tightening the noose. Homeland Security has blocked off I-94 ahead. Get off at exit 110 South and take US 27."

Frank wrenched the wheel, cutting across traffic to exit the highway. The tires squealed with the hard turn, as other cars braked and fishtailed to avoid hitting the *damned maniac* in the white Mercedes careening off the freeway.

If they missed this exit, there'd be no others before the roadblock. Ravi and Ian bounced around in the car as Ian hung over the back of his seat, struggling to keep touching Ravi's tongue with the battery, while trying not to poke her in the eye.

Off the freeway at last, they drove deep into an industrial area that appeared to be nearly deserted. They passed decrepit corrugated steel warehouses surrounded by decaying corpses of equally dilapidated trucks and cars, rusting side by side in a silent mechanical death pact.

The sky had become overcast with a greenish tint, ominous and foreboding, as a storm gathered. A group of Mexican workers stood in a shop yard looking up at the sky. As they drove past, Frank heard one solemnly predict that *la tormenta* was approaching.

The word triggered memories of his "work" in Central America during what had come to be known as *the Dirty Wars*. The U.S. had destroyed peasant revolutions by training government goons and death squads, arming them with the best weapons gringo dollars could buy. The Soldier had trained thugs in the Contra army, who, when their U.S. trainers unleashed them like pit bulls to dismantle the "Poets' Revolution" in Nicaragua – had raped children.

Frank fidgeted in his seat, his thoughts a maelstrom of regret. He drove on. What else could he do?

They turned off the two-lane blacktop onto a smaller oil-treated dirt road. The approaching storm became more threatening as they headed into the countryside. There was nothing to block its sick greenish embrace and no place to seek shelter if it let loose its fury upon them. They were utterly alone and exposed. *La tormenta* gathered around them.

The oil road became a dirt path of two earthen ruts. Tall grass grew all around, whispering against the sides of the car. The empty prairie extended as far as the eye could see. Frank recognized a landmark: A dead tree stood alone, its naked branches jutting out toward the sky, as if pleading for an end to its desolate existence.

Frank turned right to pass through an overgrown bramble of bushes, pulling into a short section of crumbling asphalt that dead-ended at a fence. He stopped just short of the rusted barbed wire. Ian and Ravi suspected they were lost. As Frank pushed the "redial" button on the car phone, the barbed wire fence began to shake and shift. The dirt around its posts crumbled, and the entire section of fence slid slowly off to the left as if some subterranean force were pulling it. There were no tire tracks or path before them, only open prairie. Frank pulled the car through the opening into the field and to the top of a gently sloping hill.

Below the crest, a deserted farmhouse sat in the sweeping meadow, almost hidden by a barn that appeared to be near collapse. Great holes gaped in its gray, weather-beaten sides and roof – toothless mouths frozen in a cry of loneliness. The structure was surrounded by equally ancient trees. The largest among them was long dead and bleached by the elements.

Black clouds thickened above. Perhaps fleeing the gathering storm, a murder of black crows cut erratically across the dark greenish sky before flowing into the hole in the barn's roof. They disappeared, swallowed by the blackness of the hole.

Frank drove down the slope and through the open door of the barn. Thick cobwebs and dust motes puffed into the air all around them. Their tires stirred chaff and dirt that, by the looks of it, hadn't been disturbed for many years. The crows cackled angrily and swarmed around them before swooping out into the thickening air.

Frank pulled the car into a tight slot, perhaps once used for milking cows, at the rear of the barn. A heavy metallic groan issued through the silent pre-storm air. Suddenly the entire barn shifted around them. Ian and Ravi instinctively ducked, raising their arms to protect their heads – the barn was collapsing around them! Their entrance must have been the straw that was breaking this old structure's rotten back.

# 53. The Chemistry of Obedience

*A vast array of pharmaceuticals . . . including . . . mood stabilizers . . . have been found in the drinking water supplies of at least 41 million Americans . . .*
— Associated Press, March 9, 2008

*. . . a quiet, picturesque village in southern France was suddenly and mysteriously struck down with mass insanity and hallucinations. At least five people died, dozens were interned in asylums and hundreds afflicted . . . an American investigative journalist has uncovered evidence suggesting the CIA peppered local food with the hallucinogenic drug LSD as part of a mind control experiment at the height of the Cold War.*
— *The Daily Telegraph* (UK), March 11, 2010

---

The noise changed to a clanking, mechanized hum. It was not the barn moving at all, but rather their car descending into the earth. Riding an elevator mechanism, their car was being gently lowered through the floor of the barn into a subterranean garage, where a large man stood beneath a bright fluorescent light.

The doctor, as Frank had called him, leaned on a wooden staff like some towering primeval wizard, observing their descent. Adding to his wizardly appearance were wildly disheveled shoulder-length gray hair and a long coat that hung down to his calves. Round wire-rimmed spectacles perched on his nose.

As Frank opened his door, a rat ran out of the hay at his feet and scampered across the room, which was uncomfortably bright after the darkness of the sky and the barn. A black cat sitting by the wizard's leg charged forward to pounce on the rat. Emerging from the car, Ravi winced at the sound of snapping bones as the cat tore the rat apart. The wizard seemed not to notice.

Ian and Ravi exchanged nervous glances. This was a very weird place, and its silent owner seemed even stranger. Perhaps Frank's trust of his former colleague had been a mistake.

Then the man's face cracked open into a huge grin, as he opened his burly arms and laughed out loud, embracing Frank. Smacking him loudly on the back, he said, "I always knew you had a spark in you, Soldier. But I never thought you'd leave the program. You were so committed. But you didn't turn me in, even though you knew where I was, and – well, you're here. What the hell happened?"

Frank flinched at the question. So much had happened in such a short time: Rachel's murder at his own hand, his dreams, the experience with the Healer, and their escape. Frank self-consciously glanced at Ravi. "Doc, just call me Frank. As far as how I got here, well, that's a long story, and I'm not sure how to . . ."

Doc patted Frank on the back again. "Forget it. You're no longer in the asylum of covert ops, and we have work to do, don't we? You can still call me Doc, and you two can as well. I feel more like a Doc than I ever did before, because now I'm taking the good advice, *Physician, heal thyself.* Welcome to my humble abode."

Doc motioned for them to follow him through a doorway into what appeared to be an underground greenhouse. After the stark, threatening world above and their descent into this netherworld, the bright lights and green plants were an odd but pleasant sight. The ceiling was completely filled with fluorescent grow-lights, and the walls were covered with aluminum foil. As Doc and Frank walked ahead talking of old times, Ravi and Ian followed.

Ravi looked more intently at the plants as they moved through the greenhouse. Some were garden vegetables, but many looked like weeds, their leaves long and jagged. Suddenly it dawned on her. "This is *pot!*" she blurted.

Ian laughed aloud as Doc turned. "Well, yes, it is, my dear. Surely you won't begrudge an old man a few eccentricities. I have many very old and very dark demons that pop into my mind at the worst possible moments. This lovely herb can be very helpful to me at times when life darkens. Plus it subsidizes my luxurious life style," Doc added with a wink, waving around at the dilapidated structure.

Ravi's face flushed in embarrassment at having spoken her observation aloud. She hadn't been judging the man, she was just surprised. Doc sensed her discomfort and patted her on the shoulder, motioning for Ian to come along as well. "Come, let's all have a cup of tea, while Frank here fills me in on your adventure."

They left the expanse of the greenhouse to enter a living space that was equally rugged, yet cozy and warm. A shaft of sunlight beamed from a skylight at the top of a long vertical tunnel reaching about twenty feet to the surface above. More sunlight shone from windows at the ends of round tunnels that opened where the meadow sloped down behind the old barn above them. Apparently the gathering storm outside had at least temporarily broken.

Ravi wondered at the room stacked with books, DVDs, and CDs on wall-to-wall shelves. Doc lived in an underground library of sorts, Ravi mused, a Hobbit hole. The view of the world through the tunneled windows made this place feel both safe and cheerful.

Doc, preparing the tea, noticed Ravi looking at the walls stacked with various forms of media. He smiled at her. "You see, dear, I don't get out much. There is not much out there for me anymore. This library I've accumulated keeps me amused and educated, and I keep it quite up to date." Noticing her inquisitive gaze at his tunnel windows, he added, "As for my underground taste in décor, I'll just say, I don't like the bastards knowing what I'm thinking. Or doing, for that matter."

After distributing cups of tea to the others, he handed Ravi something that looked like sherry. Ravi took the glass. "Why is my drink different?"

Doc explained, "I'm treating Frank and Ian to a taste of the lovely herbs from my garden, but you, my dear, must not drink that type of tea right now."

"Why not?"

"Research has shown that psychedelic substances may enhance one's psychic abilities, and I fear this could make you more vulnerable to detection by the watchers, given your excessively prodigious gamma wave production."

Turning to Ian and Frank, he answered their question before it was asked. "No offense, gentlemen, but fear not. According to my equipment's measurements since your arrival, your brainwaves are not in the same league as Ravi's. Your minds will blend with those of the crowd above quite nicely – whose levels, interestingly enough, are rising incrementally each day. I've been paying close attention to this trend, with great anticipation for the future."

Doc turned back to Ravi. "The eye-in-the-sky monitors will not detect you – not while you're down here. But when you return to the surface . . ." Doc completed his thought by extending the glass holding the ruby-red liquid. "Well, suffice it to say that this sherry is quite delicious. I made it myself. And it won't expand your consciousness at all."

Ravi's curiosity was sparked. "Really. I had no idea there'd been research showing marijuana enhanced psychic ability."

Doc replied, "The research is preliminary, and it doesn't say marijuana actually enhances psychic ability, but it does indicate that college students who smoked pot had higher incidences of psychic ability than those who drank alcohol. Those students' psychic abilities were actually diminished."

Doc continued with an impish smile. "You know, dear, I have a simple litmus test that often turns out to be correct, as to what substances limit consciousness and what has the potential to stimulate consciousness."

Ravi bit. "What test is that?"

"Well, if it is *legal*, it most likely *limits* consciousness and flat-lines creativity. If it is illegal, it is more likely to – if not expand consciousness in some way – at least not flat-line it. People with limited creativity and sedate minds are much easier to control, you see, than those whose minds are traversing the inter-dimensional realms of the universe."

The wheels of Ravi's mind were turning. "But what about heroin and cocaine?"

Doc threw up his hands in mock surrender. "Well, dear, you got me there. No system is perfect, right? However, in the case of those commodities, it is simple market share or turf battles that make them illegal. If federal agents can be unleashed on drug dealers, then that makes less competition for covert government operators who would use drugs to raise money to finance illegal wars around the world, and for their friends and independent contractors in the shadow world of drug running."

Ian and Ravi looked lost. Doc explained further. "I'm sure you are aware of the charges that the CIA ran heroin to finance illegal wars in Southeast Asia in the 1960s. I assure you those charges were true."

Both Ian and Ravi still looked puzzled, so Doc referred to another event that had happened more recently. "Perhaps you heard about cocaine from Latin America being run into the inner cities of America in the 1980s to finance the illegal wars in Nicaragua and throughout Central America?"

Frank nodded. He had known about this operation firsthand.

"Of course, before the U.S. invasion of Afghanistan, the fundamentalist Taliban, for all their faults, had almost completely eradicated the opium poppy production there. But within a year of America's invasion, opium and heroin production was breaking new records.

"Hundreds of billions of drug dollars are laundered through U.S. stock markets every year. The drug wars are a dog and pony show so that Americans remain blissfully ignorant that their children are often being poisoned by shadow elements of their own government."

Ravi was still thinking about how drugs affect cognition. "When you said that legal drugs often flat-line consciousness, what did you mean?"

"ADD and ADHD drugs, for example, can have a side effect of suppressing the creativity of children who use them."

Ravi nodded as she remembered taking the drugs during her own childhood. Doc continued, "Psychotropic drugs used for anxiety and depression can have the same effect. When people's innermost being is rebelling against lies and distortions they see all around them, a pressure builds that will eventually become the engine for change, both in their lives and society.

"The only way to stop evolutionary change is to stop people's higher consciousness. Of course this has consequences. The health of

257 The Awakening   257

the body may break down, tumors may sprout in the brain, or explosive episodes of suicide or violence may occur, as has happened in the past, when kids masterminded student killing sprees."

Doc waved his arms animatedly as he made his point. "Oh, we could talk all day about serotonin levels as excito-toxins, and all kinds of other scientific stuff, but the bottom line is that experience and feelings have a purpose and cannot be erased chemically without disastrous results. Our feelings prod us toward truth and authenticity, and that can be as uncomfortable as it is necessary. Chemical suppression of feelings is unwise."

Ravi fell into her listening position, her chin nestled into her open palms, propped up by her elbows on the arm of the sofa. Doc was riveting! This was cutting edge information that her university lecturers never told her about, and maybe never knew themselves.

"Think of the body and psyche as a teapot, and think of truth as a cooling agent, and lies as chaotic heat. When the mind is agitated by distortion – like the atoms in the tea are excited into chaos within a heating teapot – pressure builds. That pressure can power the engine of healthy evolutionary, revolutionary change, or it can be suppressed until it explodes in one form or another, internally or externally." Doc threw his hands up and outward, miming an explosion.

Doc noticed his apt student's sherry glass was empty. "May I refresh your glass, my dear?" He disappeared into the kitchen. The three sat in his living area, hearing the comforting sounds of a good host's domesticity as a cabinet was opened and sherry was poured.

Doc returned with her drink, continuing where he'd left off. "Oh, researchers are working on circumventing the natural processes of fear and regret, even as we speak. They want to enable people like me to do horrible things to people in distant lands, and then come home, pop a pill, and never again think of what we've done. *No, thank you,* I say."

Doc waved his hand toward his underground pot plantation. "My herbs have helped me through dark times, but they haven't erased my memories, my fears, or my regrets. I wouldn't want that, because my journey has been one of *the spirit,* you see. Those in power who worship only control will never understand that. They don't want to understand that. They think everything is mechanical, including you and me.

"They are about to release a new drug that inhibits an enzyme called Cdk5. Cdk5 leaves the residue of fear in the mind from past trauma. Their studies found that Cdk5, when paired with p35, helped diminish learned fear by erasing the chemical residue from past experience. What they are planning to do is chemically remove the trauma of past experience.

"What a monstrous idea, to create a society without guilt and regret. Every feeling we have is part of our becoming who we are." Doc shook his weary old head. "They can't see or comprehend grand designs. They see only mechanisms, just as engineers rip apart genes that took millions of years to evolve, to mix and mash them together. It's like an infant humanity is wielding a razor-sharp scalpel over its horrified adult patient known as the *web of life.*"

Ravi looked at Ian to see if he noticed – the Healer had invoked this same disturbing image to describe humanity's hubris.

Doc had said enough. He wanted Ravi to get the short bit of rest his underground shielded home could afford her. But before that, he needed to do one last test.

The equipment in the kitchen had remotely monitored the effects of the sherry on Ravi's brainwaves. While Doc was in the kitchen refreshing her drink, he'd checked the instruments and saw that the sherry was not producing the desired results. Her second glass, dosed with a psychotropic drug, showed only minimal results. To acquire the most accurate results for those tests, Doc had had to keep Ravi ignorant of what he was doing. However, this last test required her cooperation.

Doc stood up, patting Ravi on the knee. "You should get some rest, my dear. But right now, could you spend a few moments talking to Ian about something inane?"

Ravi looked at him with a puzzled smile. "What?"

Doc explained. "I know it sounds silly, but I need to monitor your brainwaves, and if you could just humor me and talk to Ian about something meaningless for a few moments, then I'll let you rest."

"I mean, what should we talk about?"

Doc pondered, looking up at the ceiling for a moment. "Why don't you talk about the latest Hollywood blockbuster movie, or perhaps a popular sit-com. That should do it. Yes, just talk for about five minutes, and then you should catch a nap, if you can. You'll need your rest." Doc looked over, nodding his head toward Ian. "You, too."

Doc noted Ravi's sticky hair. It was coated in dry sugar from its encounter with the soda-soaked sweater. "Before your discussion, feel free to use my powder room. Its amenities are limited, but you will find soap and hot water and towels, should you want to freshen up a bit from your journey."

He nodded toward a door just beyond the row of round window holes. The sun had descended since their arrival. Time was precious. Doc left them to join Frank in the kitchen – and to check his instruments.

Ian and Ravi took turns using Doc's shower as he and Frank chatted quietly in the kitchen.

When he heard activity in the living room, Doc peered in from the kitchen. "Ready?"

Looking at each other with only partially suppressed smiles, they haltingly began the conversation that Doc had suggested.

# 54. Breaking the Shell of Understanding

Leaving Ian and Ravi to their conversation, Doc settled his large frame into a squeaky wooden chair in the kitchen. He explained to Frank, "Research indicates that viewing or even talking about insipid, meaningless entertainment, such as much of what Hollywood pumps out, can diminish states of higher consciousness, so I thought I'd see how it worked on Ravi."

After a few minutes, Doc rose and opened the overhead cabinet that held his electronic measuring devices. He silently observed the meter's needles, which were bouncing slightly. Doc shook his head. "No luck."

He poked his head around the corner, into the living room. "That's fine, you two. You've suffered long enough. You can let go of the Hollywood drivel you've inflicted on one another. Get some rest."

He turned back to Frank, who was looking at him with admiration. Frank grabbed his old friend's shoulder. "Doc, you are amazing. You seem *so alive*. What's happened to you?"

"I felt better the moment I left the program. Not being part of a murderous organization was very refreshing from the get-go, I discovered. But once my life calmed down, the stress of all those years began to infiltrate my mind. And for a long while, life was very hard. So many nightmares, so many regrets. A bad case of post-traumatic stress disorder. I didn't think I'd make it. Thought I'd end up being one of those poor bastards who eats his gun while sitting on the crapper in the middle of the night.

"But over time, things began to change. I monitored global media and began to see a shift in the pattern of people's needs and wants. When I saw the worldwide anti-war efforts expand, I actually began to hope. Oh sure, the cops beat the hell out of them, and the wars went on anyway, but that shift I saw in people's hearts helped heal me. A few media people risked their careers in order to actually do their job —

they reported real news. I saw possibility for the future. Of course, I also had my herb farm here, and that added a bit of joy to my life."

Doc chuckled, choking a little as he took a hit from a freshly rolled joint, and offered it to Frank. "But, Frank, the truth is, I'm healing. I don't even want this as much as I used to." Doc held up the joint, and then chuckled again as a smoky cough escaped through his lips. He reached out to touch Frank's arm as he spoke under his breath, "Mate, yer not gonna believe this, but I'm actually learning *yoga!*"

Frank burst out laughing as he watched this exuberance bubble out of his old comrade, and he tried to imagine Doc's hulking frame in colorful yoga tights, with his large hairy bare feet sticking out below.

"So, where're your yoga tights?"

Doc collapsed into marijuana-enhanced hysterics as he realized what Frank was laughing about. The two men fell against each other, trying to hold themselves upright, as waves of laughter nearly caused them to collapse.

Doc had been transformed. When Frank had worked with him years before, he'd been a hard, emotionless man. Their work had required it. Yet, Frank had always felt as close to Doc as anyone could feel to another in that monstrous machine. Even through the madness of their work, there had always been an air of authenticity about Doc.

When Doc had left the program, all of Frank's training urged him to turn him in. Deserters were poison to the Company's carefully guarded secrets at the illegal operations levels in which Frank and Doc functioned. No one walked away from the Company with the kind of information they both were privy to and lived to tell about it. He knew where Doc was, because he had taken the dangerous step of contacting Frank after his desertion. Frank had fought against himself to not betray his friend.

Seeing Doc like this now, living with humor and ease, was something Frank *needed* to witness, and he said a silent prayer of thanks that he'd resisted his urge to rat out his friend as the deserter their superiors had labeled him. His own demons were as deep and dark as Doc's had been – maybe more. Frank had experienced a taste of the malignant memories he was going to have to face in order to find the level of peace that Doc was slowly and surely achieving. Seeing the man Doc had become gave him hope for his own future. The very concept of *future* was something Frank had not considered for a long time. It felt terrifying – yet exciting and good.

As if Doc had sensed his thoughts, he reached out to pat Frank's back, but his hand instead found the fresh wound where the implant used to be. "I knew you'd removed it, or you'd never have gotten this far. Frank, I'm not sure you know – the implant was not just a tracking device. They used those implants to manipulate us. They could remotely activate it to emit signals that would disrupt our thought processes, affect our nervous system, amplify our violent tendencies, and affect our consciousness in other ways as well.

"Now that you are free of this," he said, indicating Frank's incision, "you too will see and feel change percolating from within you. It will not all be pleasant. You will wrestle your demons for the rest of your life, but . . ." Doc swept his arm toward the adjacent room filled with books. "I've been doing a lot of reading since I left, and I've found some comfort there."

He rose from his chair, scanned a shelf, and pulled a slender book from it. He handed it to Frank. "An Arab poet named Kahlil Gibran wrote, *Your pain is the breaking of the shell that encloses your understanding.*" He added, "You keep this. I believe you'll find the truths imparted within it will lighten your burden."

The word *burden* hit Frank like a blow to the chest. He remembered how he had cruelly told Rachel that he would introduce her to God, just before he killed her. Frank looked over at Ravi, and began to sob. *"Rachel* . . . her sister. Doc, I . . ." He choked on the words.

Doc reached out, stroking Frank's rough face. "I know it's hard. If it's any consolation, I believe you will never add any more nightmares to the vaults of your consciousness."

Doc looked at him intently, beyond Frank's eyes, deep into his heart. "I believe in you, my friend. You are not what they made you. They didn't make you become the Soldier, but they made goddamned sure you stayed that way. But even when they had you, you didn't betray me after I left. That was not easy for you, I know. I always felt there was something genuine in you. That is why I maintained contact, even though my training told me it was folly. My heart told me something else."

Frank wept out loud at Doc's kind words and gentle touch. Doc *knew* how he felt. Frank's heart swelled with vulnerability, both exquisite and agonizing.

A tear spilled from Ravi's eye as she sat quietly in the semi-dark of Doc's living room, listening.

Doc inquired gently, "Frank, what led you into the program in the beginning?"

Frank thought. "You know, if you'd asked me that not long ago, I'd have thought you were crazy for even asking that question. You know how it is – you put one foot in front of the other and complete the mission. You don't reflect much when you're in the program. But I've done a lot of remembering lately.

"My father and I were close before he went to 'Nam, early on after the French pulled out. When he came back from war, *he couldn't see me anymore.* He'd look at me and be seeing something beyond me that I couldn't touch. Sometimes he'd look at me and see an enemy, and he hurt me many times, but mostly he couldn't see me at all. I wanted to be where he'd been, so he'd see *me* again. I wanted him to respect me. And I wanted to kill the enemy who took him away from me. Once I got in, the enemies kept coming. Overseas, at home – they were everywhere.

"Of course, if there weren't any, the machine created them out of whole cloth, so they could keep the machine running. Once I began working with the Professor, my *purpose* became so clear. There were no doubts, no regrets – only missions and enemies."

"What broke the spell?"

"Many dominoes fell. As you know, a lot of other agents left the program before and after you did. But when you contacted me a few months ago, and I learned that you, unlike the others, had not only left, but had actually *survived* your departure . . ." Frank struggled to put his complex reasons into words. "Well, I guess that got me thinking that what we were doing maybe wasn't all there was. You know, *a bigger world,* or some crap like that. But the program runs deep, even if they don't manipulate you with the electronics."

Frank's eyes grew distant in memory. "It began in Tibet, on a mission. A monk I killed spoke to me in my mother's voice before he died – he called me *Frankie.* After that, I had to use the needle for every mission. I was being rattled apart for months, but when I came to Canada to capture Ravi – when she touched me, *forgiving me for killing her only sister* – everything shifted. I had a complete breakdown." Frank remembered the Healer and felt a hitch in his heart. With a tear in his eye, he smiled sadly at Doc. It had been his salvation. "Doc, it was the best damn thing that ever happened to me."

Doc returned the teary smile. "I know, mate, funny how the worst things can evolve into the best things, the *real* things. Some day I'll tell you my story. The thing we all learn in this lifetime – or over many – is that human beings are capable of such horrible things and yet also such extraordinary goodness.

*"Stay open,* my friend. There's much more to you than the creature they sought to create."

. . .

Ravi's heart was moved by what she'd heard, but exhaustion overtook her, and she returned to the land of nod, as Doc and Frank's voices murmured in the kitchen.

They got down to the business at hand: getting Ravi to their final destination undetected. Doc leaned toward Frank, peering over his spectacles. "She cannot go far without being detected once she leaves this shelter. The dose of antidepressants I gave her was not capable of suppressing her gamma emissions. I just checked the meter again. It diminished them, but not enough."

Doc saw the question in Frank's face. "Yes, yes, I dosed her sherry. We can't give her any more, safely. I can give you something to treat her, but only as a last resort to suppress her consciousness. It will work for three or four hours, at best. Any longer and her mind may resist it."

Frank lit a cigarette and squinted through the smoke, searching for an answer. "How can we suppress her higher consciousness activity until we reach our destination? We have to get to Kansas City by morning. If we don't, the window closes, and it's all over."

Doc leaned in to explain quietly, just as Ravi stirred in the living room. She stretched luxuriously on the comfy tattered sofa, turning her head toward the kitchen light, beyond the darkness of the living room. As Doc slid a laptop computer across the table to Frank, Ravi heard only, "Take this, it's fully loaded."

Doc nodded toward Ravi, unaware she was watching from the darkness, and in a whisper offered an explanation. "We know it works, the research is conclusive. I pilfered this collection from the lab. I'll admit to ya, mate, originally for my own distractional recreation. I *needed* distraction back then. But, like I said, the shop analysis showed it'll work. The only question is, do you think she'll use it?"

Frank turned to look at Ravi, pondering his answer to Doc's question, to find her awake and watching them. Frank quickly stood with the laptop under his arm and turned to Ravi. "I hope you're rested. We've got a long hard road ahead of us."

The trio followed Doc back through his underground plantation to the garage where they'd left their car. Doc tossed Frank the keys to another vehicle, a white BMW, stating without ceremony, "I'll trade you. They're sure to have tagged your car by now. They had cameras shooting everything from the copter. It'd take 'em a while to analyze down to yours if they hadn't zeroed in on you, which obviously they hadn't yet. But by now . . . just take my car."

Doc handed Frank a map. "By now they've almost completely enacted the Homeland Security Presidential Directives – military checkpoints all over the country. This map should help you avoid them."

Frank's jaw dropped. "The whole country? But how . . .?"

With a wink, Doc cut in. "As I said, I've got a few contacts here and there, and a few tricks up this old sleeve."

The three got into their new car and Frank started the engine. Doc pushed a button, and a steel garage door slowly lifted. Behind it was what appeared to be a one-car garage. On the floor were two metal conveyer tracks. Doc pushed another button, and another garage door opened at the back of the space, revealing a dark tunnel beyond it. Frank looked at Doc through the window with a smile. "Do I get a free car wash with each visit?"

Doc laughed softly. "You know me mate, 'never in and out the same way twice. Old habits die hard. Pull forward and turn off the engine once you settle on the track there. It's automatic. It'll take you down a 50-yard passage to the grove of trees across the meadow. When the conveyer stops, it will lift you back up to the world above. The map'll get you back to the highway from there. You have about five minutes to brief Ravi before you reach the lift."

Doc grabbed Frank's forearm and bent to look into his eyes. "God be with you, my friend. When this is all over, I want to have you back here as a guest. We'll watch my yoga DVD together."

Frank smiled, reaching up to squeeze Doc's arm. "Thank you – *for everything.*"

Once they were parked on the track, Frank turned off the engine, and the conveyer began churning, taking them deeper into the darkness of the tunnel. He turned on the dome light, and twisting around to face Ravi, he handed her the laptop computer and accessory bag Doc had given him.

Ravi's eyes filled with a question, and Frank answered, "Ravi, I didn't want to tell you this before I had to. I don't have time for explanations, so I'll just say it. This laptop is filled with pornographic films and clips. You have to watch them."

# 55. The Metaphysics of Power

*It's not that pornography acts on the brain like a drug . . . It is a drug . . . an enormously powerful, stimulant, which triggers such a rush and such a high.*
*— Deseret Morning News,* Wednesday, May 5, 2004

---

Ravi and Ian shouted in unison, "WHAT!?"

Frank made a patting motion with his hand. "Calm down, calm down. Doc worked in the Analysis department when he was with the Company. Over a decade or so ago, they learned that hard-core pornography limits consciousness on some levels, particularly creative consciousness."

Ravi scowled, and her face hardened. Frank rushed on. "Ravi, Doc tried the antidepressants on you in as large a dose as he could without risking permanent damage. It didn't work. It reduced your gamma wave levels a little, but your mind somehow overrode them. He gave us more pills, and we'll use them, but your mind is too powerful for antidepressants alone to control."

"What about the wet cloth on my head, and the battery jolts?"

"That was a quick fix, with no guarantee it would work at all. I was desperate when I saw the helicopter. Over time, your body and mind would adjust to it.

"The only thing that can guarantee your brainwaves will not betray our position is opiates. But we have a lot of hours of driving ahead of us, and your mind could escape the opiate suppression even in your sleep if you remain sedated for many hours. This is the only fix we have available. Really, the research proves this works in controlling thought waves."

Ravi protested. "But PORNOGRAPHY! That controls men, not women!"

"Ravi, we don't have much time before we come to the surface. Statistically, a majority of women now view pornography, so apparently, it does have some effect on them. We're almost there. Turn it on. You'll need to flip through the programs to find the ones that are most, er, stimulating. You can't let it get boring. Hurry! We're there!"

As the clanking mechanism of the conveyer lift slammed into position, Ravi, red-faced, snapped at Ian and Frank, "Well, turn around and mind your own business then, dammit!"

She turned on the computer, and the sound, already at full volume, blasted through the car. Heavy breathing and moans vibrated the air, as Ravi scrambled to turn down the volume. She pressed the wrong button and accidentally turned off the computer completely. Ian couldn't help laughing at her predicament.

Ravi shot Ian a cold look, as Frank spoke. "Ravi, I'm sorry, but you were right about men and women being different in one respect. Sound is more exciting to women, whereas visuals are more stimulating to men. You'll need to turn up the volume. You've gotta turn on the computer *right now!*"

Ravi's fuming glare filled Frank's rearview mirror. Then her face turned upward. She saw an aircraft cutting across the sky beyond the sloping hill before them. She scrambled again, this time to turn the computer back on.

Frank added, "You'll find headphones in the accessory bag. You can use those so the sound doesn't carry."

Fumbling for the headphones, Ravi mumbled, "Thank God for small favors."

Following Doc's map, they drove across the prairie toward the access road. Ian and Frank settled into an uneasy silence. Finally, when they turned onto the two-lane blacktop that would lead them back to the highway, Ian could no longer pretend he didn't know Ravi was in the backseat, watching God-knows-what on the screen. He distracted himself with conversation. He asked Frank, "Did you learn about this stuff while you were with the Company?"

"Yeah, some, but it was Doc's field. He was a contract psychiatrist. As you know by now, Doc loves to talk, and he explained some of it to me."

"His field?" Ian recalled the Company stake-outs observing prostitutes and clients in Canada. He had always assumed that operation was more for the agents' entertainment than for gathering any useful intelligence. "Why would the Company monitor pornography use?"

Frank replied, "They monitored many aspects of human behavior. But the short answer is that pornography is a distraction. It serves the power elite to have millions using one hand in front of their computer, rather than both hands searching the internet to amass information about what's happening in – and to – their society.

"A few minutes of internet surfing shows the savvy user that the corporate news media is aligned with the military industrial complex, the petro-chemical industry, and drug companies in twisting the news to suit the needs of multi-national corporations. But the internet is too big a money maker to shut down or restrict, so the solution is to allow mass information exchange, while offering tantalizing distractions to the masses to keep their minds less inquisitive about things that really matter.

"Which segues into the long answer to your question about why the powers-that-be would be interested in pornography. The longer answer – and the more important one – is that it affects human consciousness, resulting in diminished gamma wave activity."

"So, what is it about hard-core porno that disrupts gamma wave consciousness?"

Frank, too, was relieved to be distracted by conversation as he drove. He lit a cigarette and took a deep drag, expanding his explanation as the smoke drifted from his mouth and out the window. "Are you familiar with yoga and the Vedic chakra systems?"

Ian had thought of yoga and chakras as new age concepts. It was strange to hear this combat-hardened soldier talking about them. "I've seen stand-ups joke about yoga in comedy skits, but not much more than that," Ian replied.

Frank shrugged and went on. "Both ancient traditional Chinese and India's Ayurvedic health sciences were based on observation of the behavior of conscious energy in the mind and body. In the Chinese energy system – which acupuncture is part of – the main focus is a pelvic area energy center called the *dan tien*. In yogic Vedic energy medicine, a major energy center just below the dan tien is called the *root chakra*. The dan tien is three or so inches below the navel, about three inches inside the body from the front, and the root chakra is just below that, inside the body at the base of the spine.

"Dan tien energy is called generative energy, and its job is to recreate cells throughout the systems that keep everything new and fresh in the body and mind. The root chakra's energy is called procreative energy, associated with creation, like the procreation that sex accomplishes in producing children."

"Well if it's energy for sex, then how could pornography limit it?"

Frank flicked his cigarette butt out the window as they sped past golden prairie. They almost forgot about Ravi as their conversation continued.

At first Ravi had been self-conscious about the presence of her companions, but as she flipped through the programs, finding ones that stimulated her, she completely tuned out her surroundings. Her initial resistance to watching the films lessened as she was drawn into the scenes.

Despite her medical background, Ravi was not aware of the physical changes her body was going through as she became engrossed in the pornography. Powerful physical, emotional, and mental effects went unnoticed as the tunnel vision of narrowing awareness drew her in.

The veins in her temples became visible as the steamy scenes unfolded before her fixed and dilating eyes. The pressure rose in the tiny blood vessels in her retinas, as the biochemical effects of viewing pornography spread through her body. Adrenaline's amphetamine-like rush pumped from her adrenal glands, and her glandular system screamed into action, producing a heavily dosed drug cocktail resulting in the mass release of the hormone oxytocin.

The chemical release created a hyperactive need for bonding. When normally released, this would activate to bond mother to child, friend to friend, or lover to lover. But in this razor's edge of chemical explosions produced by the pornography, the squeezing hunger of all the cells to obtain and entwine became powerfully intensified, because it reached for something beyond grasping – something that did not exist.

And this was only one of the drugs released. Dopamine, serotonin, and testosterone were also produced in copious amounts by the pharmaceutical factory of Ravi's body, each affecting her psyche through her body's physiological response to the chemicals. All were geared to rein in her psyche, to focus it ever more intensely on the experience, squeezing her down physically, emotionally, and mentally. This downward spiral resulted in a continually diminishing field of awareness, pressured by the gravitational black hole of her narrowing focus.

Only because of Ravi's years of training in the energetic nature of the mind and body was she able to register at all what was now happening to her.

The cells in her body were going through a transformation. The energy of her being and tissues of her body began to tighten, as if gripping at the erotic concepts flashing through her mind. The squeezing of her mind and body left no room for anything else. There was no *space* left within her for – for what? This process was squeezing something out of her.

Ravi had spent years expanding her being through the practices of meditation, yoga, qigong, tai chi, and contemplative prayer. This growing tightness pressing within and throughout her – it extinguished something that was so familiar, and yet it was quickly becoming so foreign. Something was being lost. *What was it?*

Then it dawned on her with absolute clarity. She was experiencing her soul being removed from her physical being – torn out cell by cell, the tension of her muscles increasing as it was squeezed out.

Ravi realized that, as long as her thoughts were holistic and multidimensional, her soul was part of her experience, and viewing the purely mechanical pornographic scenes was uncomfortable. A part of her was rejecting the soullessness of what she was seeing.

However, as she allowed herself to be drawn deeper into the scenarios on the screen, she became less averse. She could feel a separation of her ethereal soul perception from her physical animal perception, like a skin being peeled away from her body.

Something else was occurring on an even larger scale. A part of her was being pulled into a matrix consciousness, snared in a mind net that had been created in the collective ether by many millions of people using these media. She felt energy swirl around her, as if the agitated psyches of all who'd been involved in or affected by the pornography now swarmed like ethereal bees. The flowing and buzzing grew tighter. The sinuous energy became a grabbing, clenching force that pressed in on the trillions of cells of her body, her mind, and her heart. Ravi's energy field clutched in a desperate but futile attempt to hold onto these scenes that were not even real, but part of a sad mass hyper-sexualized social delusion.

Ravi had become oblivious to Ian and Frank's conversation, not just because of the sounds blasting through the headphones into her ears, tweaking the tiny aural hairs that led sound images into her brain. Her consciousness had so gripped the images there was *no room* for anything else – no room for real human contact.

· · ·

Frank checked Doc's map ever so often, avoiding the Homeland Security checkpoints along the highway. Once he realized he had missed a turnoff miles back and had to drive off the highway, down a grassy embankment, and then accelerate through a barbed wire fence to get to a gravel county road. The abrading sound of barbed wire scraping the perfect white paint job was sickening. Frank winked at Ian. "Doc's gonna love what we've done with his car."

Ian smiled at the change in Frank's demeanor since they'd left Doc's. He couldn't put his finger on exactly what it was that had changed about him, but he sensed in Frank a new lightness. Even through the urgency and mortal danger of their plight, there was an easiness – even *joy* in him.

As he cruised through the county road system avoiding the highway road blocks, Frank took up their conversation again. "You asked how pornography could limit sexual energy. It doesn't; it supercharges it. But the procreative aspect of the root chakra energy is not just about the sex that results in creating children. It is about all creative energy: composers, architects, artists, orators, ministers of the cloth.

"All types of creative human endeavors are powered by the generative and pro-creative energy centers in the pelvis. That is why mystics often practiced celibacy – to enable all their sexual energy to become creative energy they could channel into higher consciousness.

"These energy centers are like generators that power a home with electricity. What is done with the electricity is not determined by the energy centers, but by the consciousness of the mind."

"Jesus, I can't believe the Company studies mysticism!" Ian exclaimed.

"You'd be surprised at the amount of interest those in the business of power have shown in mysticism over the centuries. Have you ever heard of the Spear of Longinus?"

Ian shook his head.

"According to the Gospel of John, it was the actual spear that pierced the side of Jesus when he hung on the cross – a spear thrust into him by a Roman Centurion named Longinus. It has also been called the Holy Lance, or the Spear of Destiny."

Ian looked up at Frank with an *Is there a point to this?* expression. "Okaaay?"

Frank acknowledged Ian's skepticism with a nod, but continued as he drove. "This spear was controlled or sought after by dozens of leaders and conquerors including Adolf Hitler. When Hitler was 21, he saw this Spear of Destiny while visiting the Hofburg Treasure House in Vienna.

"He wrote about it in *Mein Kampf.* We had to read that in training when they taught us about Eastern mysticism so we'd take this stuff more seriously. Young Hitler wrote that hearing about the legend changed his life. He wrote, *There is a legend associated with this spear, that whoever claims it, and solves its secrets, holds the destiny of the world in his hands for good or evil.*"

Ian's jaw dropped. "No shit!?"

"It gets more bizarre," Frank assured Ian with a darkening look. "In 1938 after the Third Reich annexed Austria, Hitler triumphantly entered the Treasure House where he'd become obsessed with this spear years before. According to reports, he ordered everyone out of the room, and he spent a long time with it by himself. He then took it to Nuremburg, where it remained until the American Army took possession of it on April 30, 1945, when General Patton's Third Army took it into U.S. custody. Legend held that those who possessed it died soon after losing control of it, and in fact, Hitler killed himself in his private bunker within ninety minutes of when U.S. forces seized it.

"While the spear was in U.S. possession, the United States unleashed the atom bombs on Hiroshima and Nagasaki, killing more civilians in two attacks than any army in history, and because of that, the U.S. was recognized as the world's greatest superpower."

"You are creeping me out, big time." Ian fidgeted, pulled out one of Frank's cigarettes, and lit it. He exhaled smoke, looking out his window with a troubled sigh. Nervously tapping the ashes into the ashtray, he looked back at Frank. "There's *more?*"

Frank nodded. "In the spear's dark history, dozens of rulers and conquerors laid claim to it – among them Charlemagne and Otto the Great. Each one carrying the spear into battle knew great victories. But again, just as with Hitler, when each lost possession of it, he died straight away. Charlemagne dropped the spear while crossing a river and died shortly thereafter. Even Napoleon tried to acquire it.

"Patton was the only American who really believed in the Spear of Longinus. Soon after the spear was returned to Austria to the very same spot where Hitler had first seen it, Patton died in a mysterious car crash."

A silence fell between them. Frank and Ian were startled out of their solitary musings when Ravi reached up to tap Frank on the shoulder. "Pull over somewhere. I need to use the restroom."

Relieved to return to the mundane physicality of life, Ian gave a nervous laugh and reached for another cigarette from Frank's pack. Frank nodded at Ravi, who could see but not hear him because of her headphones, and scanned the horizon for a rest stop.

He pulled over at the next rest area, barely coming to a stop before Ravi hurriedly opened her door to get out. As she stood, Frank spoke to her. "Ravi, I'm sorry to tell you this, but it needs to be said. Don't masturbate while you're in there. It'll change your biochemistry and calm your mind from the agitation, and you'll become detectable again."

Ravi sniffed as she raised her chin in insulted defiance, calling over her shoulder as she walked away. "Oh, *screw you,* Frank!"

# 56. Marketing Social Descent

Seeing how upset Ravi was, Ian determined that he would talk to Frank about finding some other way to shield her from gamma wave detection.

Just as he began to speak, Frank turned to Ian with a serious look on his face. Ian braced himself. "My, my, our little girl has developed quite the *potty-mouth*. I think we're going to have to pay closer attention to what she's watching on TV."

Ian blew the Pepsi he was drinking right out through his nostrils. He choked on the acid soda in his throat and sinuses as he struggled for breath amid his laughter. All the tension that had been building released, and his body shook with hilarity. His laughter was contagious. Frank and he fed off each other like schoolboys trying not to laugh in class but absolutely unable to control themselves, as Ravi turned to shoot an annoyed look at them before disappearing into the women's restroom.

"Oh, boy! We're in trouble now!" Frank snorted anew, with Ian now holding his sides in pain. Finally, Frank was able to stop for a moment. Wiping tears from his eyes, he announced, "Christ, I'd better go to the can, or I'll wet my pants."

Ian erupted again as Frank got out of the car and hobbled to the bathroom.

Hearing Ian's laughter all the way to the bathroom, Frank smirked, just as Ravi emerged from the ladies' room. Ravi, now completely out of sorts, assumed Frank was laughing at her. As Frank entered the men's room, he turned his head to see Ravi place her arm behind her back and extend her middle finger at him. Her years of yoga stretches enabled her to do it very impressively.

Ravi heard Frank's choking laughter echo from the men's room. She silently sat down in the backseat and glared at Ian. "I'm sorry, Ravi. This situation is so ridiculous, what else can we do but laugh?"

Ravi flashed a hard look at Ian as she jerked on her headphones and switched on the computer, mumbling something under her breath.

A few moments later, Frank settled into the car. He and Ian exchanged raised-eyebrow looks. They'd better not laugh, if they knew what was good for them.

The powder keg of Ravi's volatile mood and frustration level was best left alone, so Ian resumed his earlier conversation with Frank. "You said these pelvic energy centers generate creative energy. So, if your sexuality gets all steamed up through pornography, wouldn't that make you more creative all around?"

Frank, putting the car in drive and heading toward the on-ramp, responded, "It's complicated. Sexuality and creativity are not mutually exclusive. Some of the most creative men that were monitored became highly sexualized when they had creative breakthroughs in their art or work. For these men, their creativity and their sexuality became simultaneously hyper-stimulated."

Ian nodded slowly, still trying to reconcile the fine distinction between normal heightened sexuality found in creative men and hard-core porn's creativity-diminishing effect.

Frank, seeing Ian's puzzled frown, continued. "The problem with hard-core pornography is that it is designed to pour all that energy into sexuality, thereby shutting the gates or closing the switches that might lead to creativity. That hyper-focus channels energy into a direct current, occupying all the mental facilities with lust and taking it away from other creative processes.

"It's just like in a home, where different breakers channel electricity to different parts of the house. Pornography would be at the breaker box turning off all the switches except for the one hard-wired directly into the lust appliance. The rest of the house goes dark and cold. So, if a population is busy pouring their energy into sexuality like a hamster on a wheel going nowhere, nothing else gets energy for creativity.

"If Dr. Martin Luther King, Jr., or Mahatma Gandhi had spent hours watching porn rather than writing the speeches that changed history, or Einstein or Edison had been drawn away from their work, distracted constantly by other thoughts, the world would be a lot different than it is."

"But it seems like you're saying that the powers that be are behind the porn industry."

"Well, I'm not saying they direct, or act in, or even produce porn. But they do endorse it and facilitate it, because it serves the purposes of the power elite to keep people less creative and aware. If those powers didn't want porn to exist in such readily available ways, trust me, it wouldn't."

"I'll give you that. But what do you mean they facilitate it?"

Frank lit a cigarette and flung the match out the window. "Well, we all know that people like sex. It's a natural part of who we are, and therefore we're all drawn to watch sex. It interests us. The powers that be are great networkers. They know that people like sex, that they like to watch sex, and that corporations like to make money. So, if market forces provide people with a steroid version of what they like, people want it very badly, and someone makes a lot of money giving it to them – and the industry grows, and the money wheel turns round and round, and on and on."

"What do you mean, steroid version?"

Frank exhaled smoke through his nose and mouth, checking Ravi in the rearview before continuing. "Think of cocaine distributors. Coca leaves have been chewed by Indians in South America for centuries without harmful effects, as the leaves only act as a mild stimulant – just like sex has been a healthy part of art and literature for ages. But developed nations like America took those benign leaves and processed them into cocaine, which has ruined thousands of lives by cultivating that razor-edge, thermonuclear intensity of desire in the mind and body – just the same as in the case of hard-core pornography."

Ian's eyebrows rose. "Sex in art and literature of the past was healthy? And didn't do the same thing?"

Frank exhaled another puff of smoke and went on. "Countries have had nudity and sex in their entertainment for decades, even centuries. But America's ability to take something natural and hone it to a dangerous edge of effectiveness, whether it be weaponry, technology, entertainment, or pornography – becomes a problem.

We're good at seeing what makes things tick and then tweaking it to maximize the effect until you could split atoms with it."

Ian took a drag off his cigarette. "So America makes good porn, or at least highly effective porn, and corporations make money off it. How does that work? The corporate part, I mean."

"Back in 2000, *The New York Times* reported that AT&T, Time Warner, General Motors, EchoStar, Liberty Media, Marriott International, Hilton, On Command, and LodgeNet Entertainment all had big financial stakes in adult films. We're talkin' *big* money. Hell, early in this century, Americans were already spending $8 to $10 billion on porn every year. That was bigger than the combined gross income of ABC, CBS, and NBC. Sixty percent of all website visits were sexual in nature, even back then."

Ian frowned, "Was it legal? I mean if it was legal, why would the government stop it?"

Frank lit another cigarette. "Look, I'm not moralizing here. God knows, I'm not qualified to be a moralist. I'm just telling you what I know. I can think of much worse things people could do than watch other people have sex. On my scale of concerns it's very low on the totem pole." Frank's eyes went vacant as his mind digressed to his own mortal sins.

Finally Frank realized Ian was still waiting for the rest of his answer. "The corporate establishment *did* work hand in hand with the moralists to infuse guilt on the millions who do what people do, which is look when someone is having sex. Corporatia makes pornography more and more accessible, while the religious moralists most often allowed on corporate TV and radio stations make those tens of millions using the porn feel like "perverts" who must keep their behavior secret and hidden. We know from history that even some of the religious moralists with their own media shows have been secret porn users, unable to disclose who they really are.

"In this way, no one exchanges experiences or feelings, or brings their 'secret lives' to light in any way. It makes people feel more and more alienated from one another and less able to act collectively. People feel less and less empowered, and more and more guilty. The result is that human potential is being limited and manipulated through the hyper-sexualization of society's entertainment."

A new insight came to Frank, as he added, "It's not just pornography. It's wider than that. Everyone accepts the constant use of seduction as a normal entertainment and advertising tool, but no one admits to being aroused by it or affected by it."

"Affected by something wider than pornography?"

"Oh, yeah. People are affected by the vast array of seductive illusions created by the media. Do you know that in some advertising, those seductive women are actually pre-pubescent girls made up and dressed to appear as sexual beings? We're talking ten, eleven, twelve years old. There is a significant effect from this, which has been noted by those in the business of consciousness control."

"Which is . . . ?"

"Older men – who could be focusing their energy on wisdom and contribution to society – are obsessed with chasing their lost youth embodied in younger and younger women. It's an illusion – just as an addict sees salvation in just one more hit of cocaine.

"The powers that be have the ability to stop this sexualizing of society – just like they stop the use of the f word on network TV – if they really want too. When politicians get on TV and moralize about it and then do nothing to stop it, that means that somebody in power wants it to be there."

Ian gazed out the window at the passing hills and trees. "But maybe they can't stop it."

"Movie ratings once prohibited children from seeing excessive blood from a gunshot wound. They could see all the war in the world – so long as they were kept ignorant of its damaging results on the body. Yet, using minors to entice older men into buying things can't be restricted? Do you actually buy that?"

Ian pondered the question. "Maybe that could be stopped, but not pornography, since the internet's outside the jurisdiction of the FCC."

"In the case of internet porn – everything on the internet is traceable if the required amount of resources are applied to the task. The U.S. Customs Service said years ago that more than 100,000 websites offered child pornography, which was illegal worldwide even back then. It could've been stopped, but it wasn't, because the true powers didn't want it stopped. It served a purpose for them. It helped them control people's consciousness more effectively, and it also provided a great tool for blackmailing people they wanted to silence or manipulate."

Frank and Ian wearied of their conversation, and both grew silent in contemplation, as they passed through the darkening hills of the Midwestern countryside.

Ian chewed on the avalanche of disturbing facts Frank had unloaded on him. Frank drove effortlessly between the never-ending white lines of the freeway, his mind drifting back to his own source of endless guilt.

Those he'd killed and the last words they'd said, some pleading that their children not be left fatherless or motherless, stabbed at Frank's heart. Ian slept and Ravi receded into the realms of lust, and his torture went on. But as it did, Frank observed his feelings.

For years, Frank's reflexive reaction to feelings had been to crush them by an act of will. More recently he ingested chemicals to eradicate them. Feelings inside the intelligence machine were *verboten,* and as long as the Soldier was part of it, he wanted no awareness of emotions that could impede his work.

Frank viewed his feelings differently now that he'd stepped beyond the machine. Instead of seeing them as something that interfered with his mission, now he saw them as purposeful – even sacred.

He had begun to perceive them as part of a healing process. It was as if the cells of his body had been poisoned by years of violence and by suppression of any sentiment about his actions or the losses they produced. Becoming conscious of them was a painful side effect of the toxins evaporating from his cells – and it was also a trigger to further release more poisons. By acknowledging the terrible consequences of his actions, he was experiencing the pain in his heart and mind and relieving the pressures within. But as each layer released, he was also unveiling ever deeper layers of shame and regret.

Frank knew that in order to be cleansed of his sins, he had to truly *feel* what he'd done. In this light, the pain became bittersweet and precious as it led to further unburdening. Silent tears rolled down Frank's rough face as he drove and remembered – and regretted.

For a long time Frank rode through his purgatory, until a familiar face returned to his reverie. He thought it was Ravi, but his heart froze when he realized it was Rachel. He glanced in his rearview at Ravi. Trying but unable to hold back, afraid Ian or Ravi would see or hear, Frank sobbed audibly. Tears streamed down his face. He swept them off with the back of his hand.

Hearing Frank, Ian awoke, but allowed him privacy by feigning sleep. He had been there. He had seen what his ship's missiles had done in the Gulf Wars years before.

When Ravi heard Frank's sobs, for a moment she pulled her mind out of the laptop's program, but she too pretended not to notice. She tried to leave Frank to his feelings by immersing herself in the laptop's endless library of videos. But the intensity of his feelings had broken the spell of the magnets of lust that had pulled her mind into an ever-smaller universe.

. . .

Frank had tried to give Ravi privacy as she did what she had to do, but he tensed each time he saw an aircraft in the sky. He glanced in the rearview mirror ever so often to check whether she'd fallen asleep or grown bored and immune to the videos. For hours, when he occasionally looked back, he'd see her eyes dilated and fixed on the glowing computer screen, sometimes fidgeting in her seat. But looking back now, he noted the videos were affecting her less. She was becoming bored – more easily distracted by the world outside the computer screen. This was a problem.

Frank pulled over at the next rest stop and found an isolated parking spot sheltered by two large fir trees. Opening the glove box, he retrieved the gear Doc had given him. Frank turned back and tapped Ravi on the arm, motioning her to take off the headphones. As Ravi removed them, Frank spoke. "You can turn off the computer now. We only have a few hours to go, and Doc gave me something that can control your gamma waves, if you don't mind using it."

Ravi, experiencing the second most bizarre day of her life, exasperated and highly suspicious of what might be next, threw up her hands and demanded, "Okay, what!? *What is it?*"

Frank pulled out the syringe, spoon, and the small packet. "This will suppress your consciousness until we get there. It's heroin."

# 57. Oblivion's Relief

Ravi had had enough, *more* than enough of the last fix, and, at this point, would move on to anything that worked. Her body felt tight, clutching, and weird, as if her inner being needed a long, cold shower. Without a word, she held out her arm between the front seats.

Frank rolled up the car windows and then carefully spilled the heroin into the silver spoon, adding a few drops of bottled water before stirring the solution and heating it with his lighter. He turned to Ian. "Take off your belt and wrap it around her upper arm. We need to raise a vein."

Ravi flinched as Frank inserted the needle into her blood vessel. He withdrew the plunger to register the blood from her vein, and then pressed it down to inject the solution into her bloodstream. Ravi's eyes began to flutter as she slumped back into her seat. Her breathing became shallow, and her mouth grew slack. "Oooohhhhh."

"How do you feel?" Frank inquired.

All the cells of Ravi's body that had just experienced hours of squeezing and clutching caused by the porno-biochemical combination now let go – of anything and everything. Her mind drifted and flowed on cool currents and loose, graceful tides. Ravi gazed up, working only slightly to focus on Frank's soft, fuzzy face. With half-lidded eyes and a goofy grin on her face, Ravi pondered his question before answering. "How do I feel? I feel goooooooooooooood." And with that, Ravi was sound asleep.

Ian reached back to position her more comfortably. Frank turned and instructed, "Don't lay her down. She's probably going to puke at some point."

Just as Ian took Ravi's shoulders, she suddenly awoke from her opiate sleep. Looking up at him with a sincere, dreamy-girly-crush kind of look, she crooned, "Know what, cowboy? *You're kinda cute!*"

The instant she finished the last word, Ravi burped, and a tiny bit of vomit dribbled from her mouth. Ian reached back and opened her door as she began to choke. He pushed Ravi over to lean her out the door just in time for the projectile vomit to spew out across the parking space rather than in the car.

Ian thanked God Frank had warned him, as he saw little bits of road snacks stream across the pavement. Road snacks that hadn't really looked all that appetizing *before* being partially digested.

As Ian was cleaning Ravi off with a napkin, Frank said, "She's probably done now. Close the door and let's get on the road. We need to get there while she's still out."

Frank backed out of their parking space as Ian closed the door. Frank dropped the car into gear. As he accelerated, he looked over at Ian with a grin. "Oh, by the way. Did I tell you?" He batted his eyelashes coyly. *"You're kinda cute, cowboy!"* He sped onto the highway, hooting with laughter.

# 58. Entering Babylon

Once in Chicago, Frank pulled over to let Ian take the wheel for awhile. Ian turned south on I-55, cutting across the state toward East St. Louis, Illinois, then over the river to St. Louis, Missouri. From here they could go all the way into Kansas City on I-70, unless they had to use county road detours to avoid Homeland Security checkpoints. Things looked fine, assuming Doc's checkpoint maps were still accurate. They had been so far.

Finally, they had what appeared to be a free ride, nothing but smooth straight asphalt into Kansas City. The Healer's vision was coming true.

Ian relaxed his hands on the wheel, breathing easier in his delusion, for they were nearing the end of a temporary calm that had only been the eye of the hurricane.

. . .

Many miles away in Montreal, in the bowels of the Taloncrag Psychiatric Institute, the Professor bent over the Healer. He had spent nearly twelve hours administering the scopolamine that had worked so well on young Ravi days before. With over a dozen electroshock jolts through this Indian's brain, each one weakening his resistance more than the last, the savage was close to breaking. Unlike the Professor, he was a lesser man, not noble in the least, but a savage who knew only his primal urges and incapable of higher consciousness.

Looking down at the red man, the Professor spoke. "My friend, we are about to break through together, so that you can help us help Ravi."

The Healer, covered in sweat, lay ragged and exhausted after the last jolt of electricity had wracked his mind and body. The drugs were taking a toll, and he could barely make out the tall man standing over him who called himself the Professor.

Through the haze of pain and mental strain, the Healer cried out, "Owwww . . *please* . . . wait, I have . . . something . . . to tell you." The Professor's pulse quickened with anticipation, as the Healer spoke slowly and with hesitation. He bent low near the Healer's face to be sure to hear his words, as with great effort and trembling, the Healer whispered, enunciating carefully, *"What do you mean 'WE,' Kemo Sabi?"* A weak smile spread across the Healer's face as he closed his eyes, exhausted. He passed out.

. . .

In the Sleep Room next door lay the young warrior who had pushed the boulder into place. He had been strong. But in the end, the Professor's work had broken him. The young man prayed to the Great Spirit that his pain had bought the seekers enough time to complete the Healer's vision. He had not heard all that was said that day in the village. He did not know why they were headed to Kansas City, only that they were headed there. In a moment of agony and weakness he had revealed this to the Professor.

. . .

Since they'd lost any signal they could trace with the brainwave monitors, they had to rely on old fashioned intel, and the Indian's Kansas City tip was their best bet.

Within moments, key individuals had been notified, and jets were in the air. They could not depend on local authorities – there would be too many questions to be answered. It was better to keep it in-house. Private jets would be landing in Kansas City's downtown airport within the hour, and cars would be stationed and waiting at every westbound freeway exit on I-70.

Frantic calls between Mark Ratlig and the Professor and from the Professor to the cars dispatched to the freeway off-ramp positions sizzled like an electricity fire spreading through a house. The Professor screamed at everyone, *"Everything* depends on stopping them. I will *ruin* every last one of you if that woman and the Soldier are not stopped. And THAT *is a GODDAMNED PROMISE!"*

. . .

Ian drove through the dimness of predawn as Frank slept. Ravi was still on the nod from her dose, although her sleep had become increasingly fitful. They were nearly there, and soon the sun would crest the horizon.

Daybreak was minutes from illuminating Kansas City. Many miles above, in the high altitudes, the sun glared brightly. Shining gears whirred and bearings turned in the soundlessness of space, where a satellite with a mammoth gaze encompassing many hundreds of miles focused its watchful eye on Ian, Ravi, and Frank.

Ian turned the Beamer off I-70 at 435 South and headed toward Blue Parkway, which would take them directly to the Nelson-Atkins Museum of Art. Only a few miles remained between them and the place where they hoped to find salvation.

With the breakdown and confession of the warrior in the Professor's lab, the city had become the epicenter of a massive machine of observation and control. Windows of hope closed all around them. Frank and Ian did not know. *But Ravi did.*

For hours, Ravi had remained unconscious, as far as her traveling companions could tell. However, within Ravi's heroin nod, she had traveled universes. The humming of the road under the tires became wind blowing through her hair, lifting her upward through thick white clouds and into the ethers beyond. Doors appeared as worlds sped by. As she reached for them, they flew open. In the beginning, attractive men and women reached out to draw her toward them, calling like sirens with irresistible propositions to seduce her away from her journey. Ravi felt drawn to them, as if she had become iron dust and their calls were a magnetic force pulling at the center of her being.

Then a door opened that caused her to gasp and choke. Behind that door was Rachel's shattered body. Blackness filled her heart. FRANK! That *bastard* had murdered her precious Rachel! Ravi's heart shrieked in a voice filled with hatred, "I'll KILL him!" Every cell of her body was electric with hate, like millions of slicing razor blades. Her heart was black and thick as hatred pulled her away from her true journey. The weight of her loathing began to pull her from the sky.

Yet deep within the heavy desolation of her heart, a light glimmered. An image, so small and so bright, grew into Rachel's broken body and face. It began to shift and move, as if a film of her death were spooling in reverse. The pieces of Rachel's shattered form began to flow back together. Bits of flesh and bone coalesced to become her uninjured body and face.

*Rachel was alive again!* Undamaged, her image glowed. The shining rays reached out to encircle Ravi, drawing her close, until she could smell Rachel's sweet warm breath on her face as she spoke. "Ravi, I am all right. *This man is not your enemy. All things have purpose.*

"In Babylon, mankind reached for God with technology – with a tower that scraped the sky. God humbled man by painfully separating humanity – dividing the people by giving them different languages."

Rachel's healed form, sweeping her arm and bowing as if to usher Ravi toward a deeper meaning, continued. "But Babylon also means *the gates of God,* where all things return. I am with you. I will *always* be with you. You are entering Babylon, where all God's children will come together to awaken. Hate will not save you – the people yearn for a vision of hope. Have faith. *Have faith.*"

Ravi's heart lightened, and she once again was flying through clouds and sky and doors. She felt a great vibration throbbing through the universe, and she looked for its source. There at the end of the sky, at the end of everything, Rachel again appeared – this time in front of a door.

Frank and a small orange-robed monk stood with her, arm in arm, all three opening the door for Ravi to look inside. Ravi peered through the doorway to see multitudes of people of all races and nationalities looking at her, waiting for her to speak. Frank, Rachel, and the monk bowed slightly, beckoning her on toward the multitudes as a butler might offer a doorway to an honored guest. Ravi blinked, and when her eyes opened again, the people were looking at her from television screens. They were all on TV, endless rows of televisions hovering in space. Millions of faces watched her with anticipation from the screens.

The universe swirled. Now she was encircled by the faces in the screens. Then Ravi saw the scene from far away, looking at herself in the middle of the circle, but then she was not there. A beating heart had taken her place. When the people saw the beating heart, they wept joyful tears, as if they had found a missing part of themselves.

The millions of televisions became beating hearts, all connected to the center heart by wires — no, they were arteries, pumping the blood of life to one another. It was a web of life, each heart supporting and being supported by the others.

Ravi dreamed in the backseat as they approached Kansas City, while in Canada, Mark Ratlig leaned into his bank of computer screens, staring at a blip that had just appeared. His hands moved frantically across his console. Dials turned and switches flipped at amazing speed. Ratlig's heart pounded.

Within moments, phone connections were made. The contagion of Ratlig's pulsing heart soon spread to the Professor, and then to the VP, as Ratlig rattled off satellite readings over the phone. The Professor and VP gripped their phones in white-knuckled rage and terror. Everything was riding on this! Mics were clicked on and transmissions were fired off through an expanding chain of command. Superiors barked orders, sending their subordinates reeling like over-whipped frothing horses being ridden to their death, in this last surge toward gaining absolute global power.

Ravi's dreams suddenly froze. An ominous shadow fell across the world of beating hearts as the heart in the center went still. The faces on the televisions looked toward the source of the shadow in horror, and their mouths opened in silent screams. The endless rows of screens turned to static.

And then horrific images emerged, first coming slowly, then accelerating madly as sounds of violence grew to a deafening thunder. Tanks rolled over cities. Jets unleashed missiles and bombs. Oil derricks pumped furiously, as first oil and then blood spurted from the ground. Mothers of all races wailed over dead children. People with emaciated bodies searched for food. Barbed wired prisons held millions of hopeless people.

Suddenly, all the screens switched to *one image,* a familiar balding man with glasses, in a fine suit, living in a white house. With clenched teeth, he angrily clutched a telephone to his ear.

Static exploded from the televisions. Ravi squinted at a blinding light that consumed the man's image. The mushroom cloud of an atomic blast filled every screen. Then everything went black and silent. Nothing existed. The dreams of man had come to an end.

Oblivion settled upon a mortally wounded world. All the long struggles and accomplishments of man – nurtured by so many for so long – were erased. The elegant and meticulous process of evolution – decimated.

. . .

A faint glow pulsed in the center of the screens. With each new pulse, the face of Ravi's father emerged a little more clearly. He reached out. Then he was gone. The screens were dark.

From the endless rows of silent screens, masses of people reappeared. They were straining to communicate something. Pointing to Ravi, they frantically urged her to look behind her. A great shadow lurked – she felt its presence. Terror filled her.

Ravi slowly turned. She couldn't make out the source of the shadow, although *she knew* she knew. Then recognition struck her like a freight train, spilling her out of her dream into a full ice water awakening. Her body clenched and gasped in total panic. "THE PROFESSOR!"

Ravi sat up with a jolt as she screamed the words. Her eyes, urgent, darted in all directions. Her head jerked around, searching. Her heart pounded as she screamed, "THEY ARE NEAR! THEY ARE NEAR! *I FEEL THEM!*"

. . .

The agent ran down the steps of the private jet with the others and slid into the driver's side of one of the small army of sedans waiting on the tarmac. Tires smoking, the fleet of sedans peeled away from the airport in different directions.

With GPS, the agent quickly arrived at the I-435 and I-70 intersection. He waited just off the right side of the I-435 southbound lane, where I-70 off-ramped from the east. Moments later, a white BMW turned off the exit onto I-435 South from I-70. First in his rearview, and then as the car passed him, he saw a Caucasian man driving – no passengers.

It was at that moment that Ravi's head whipped around to look out the rear window of the car, searching for the source of the fear exploding in her mind. The quick motion in the back of the BMW caught the agent's attention. Although the sun hadn't yet risen, the faint light of approaching dawn allowed him to see what looked like a young woman with long hair sitting in the back seat. If she was there, *who else was in the front seat?*

At that moment the analysis station in Canada detected a gamma projection moving from westbound I-70 onto I-435 South. Ratlig's voice screamed through the agent's earpiece, "We've got something big – *it must be them.* THEY'RE ON TOP OF YOU! Do you see them?"

It had to be them. The agent slammed his car into gear, spraying gravel until the wheels gripped the asphalt shoulder. He flipped open his cell phone.

. . .

Frank jerked awake when he heard a screech of tires behind them. He spotted the sedan as it wheeled into traffic too hard and too fast. He yelled at Ian, "Step on it. We're not far from Blue Parkway. Go west on it! There!" Frank pointed to the exit. The tires squealed as they took the corner much too fast, the car beginning to tilt up on two wheels.

They were very near their destination, but as they took the corner, a black unmarked helicopter hovered fifty feet above the ground directly in front of them. Black and foreboding against the awakening sky, the dark predator had been waiting for them.

Inside the helicopter, the pilot shouted into his mic, "We've got 'em! We have a signal! It has to be them!" He pushed the control stick forward, accelerating. The sound of the blades exploded through the air, pounding down upon the approaching BMW.

The Beamer roared down Blue Parkway directly toward the descending aircraft – barely missing the bird's runner. The helicopter rounded in the air, reversing direction to give chase as the car and the pursuing agent's sedan sped beneath them. Ian drove faster than he'd ever driven, negotiating the narrow winding boulevard even as the car behind them began slamming into their rear bumper.

The screaming helicopter tracked them as the two cars barreled down the parkway, now side by side. An agent in the aircraft raised a weapon. The large Brush Creek spillway paralleled the parkway on their left, its wide concrete bottom about twenty feet beneath the roadway.

The three were jolted as the dark sedan rammed them. Ian slammed on the brakes and turned the wheel hard to the left onto a side street that passed over the concrete waterway below in a desperate attempt to shake their pursuer.

Ian couldn't control the hard turn onto the overpass as the car behind accelerated and the helicopter bore down. The Beamer careened and struck the guardrail on the right. Sparks showered as metal ground against metal in a hellish squeal, before the car slid into the concrete barrier of the overpass.

The car in pursuit was right on Ian's tail as he rounded the corner. It hit the sidewalk of the overpass, jumped the curb, and slammed directly into the concrete wall. The impact lifted the car up and over the guardrail. It landed upside down on the concrete spillway below, crushing the driver's skull and snapping his neck.

That impact was instantly followed by a great metallic groan. The BMW, which had become tangled in a concrete barrier farther along the bridge, now lifted in slow motion. Its rear end rose up, sending the car somersaulting over the rail and plummeting into the concrete spillway. The three of them were thrown up to the roof of the car and then slammed back down into their seats as the car did a complete 360. It landed right side up with a deafening crash a few feet from the agent's mangled car.

# 59. Fallen

A 15-year-old boy wearing a black doo-rag sat on the edge of Brush Creek's wide concrete riverbed in the shadows of the overpass. Jamal had been out all night again with his fren's. Since Momma would have to catch the bus fer work in 'nother hour, he might avoid a whole world o' pain if he waited till she lef'. He could watch the sun rise and then go home.

So he sat in the silent chill of the early morning gloom, waiting. The approaching lights of two fast-moving cars racing westbound on Blue Parkway caught his attention. Their headlights grew brighter. The wail of the cars' engines caused him to stand up in alarm. Under his breath, Jamal exclaimed, "Goddamn!" as the cars roared closer, shattering the pre-dawn silence with the shriek of burning rubber as they rounded a corner, coming straight toward him. Although he couldn't see them, it sounded like they'd turned left onto the very overpass he had been sitting under.

From the bridge above, he heard the scream of squealing tires, telling him that the cars had indeed turned toward the overpass. Experience told him that to be where trouble was, *was trouble.* Jamal looked for a way to get out of there.

He was near a large storm drain opening about five feet high and four feet wide that led into the angled concrete side of the riverbed, part of a large network of tunnels that carried Kansas City's rainwater from its streets into Brush Creek's flood prevention system. He had often used the tunnels to get from one part of town to another without getting hassled by the graveyard shift of Kansas City's finest.

Jamal edged toward the tunnel. He froze when a dark helicopter exploded across the sky, flying directly toward the overpass. With wide eyes, Jamal repeated, more loudly than before, *"God-DAMN!"*

Jamal's heart stopped as a sound like a screaming mastodon ripped through the air, for a brief moment even drowning out the heavy thumping of the helicopter blades. Then the scream abruptly stopped.

Jamal was still looking up at the helicopter as a silent dark shape rapidly became a sedan that slammed down onto the concrete. It landed upside down, crushing the driver right before his eyes. Jamal's heart stuck in his panic-closed throat, then hammered in his chest as he heard a heavy metal groan just before a *sweet ride white BMW* came crashing down from above. The Beamer did a complete 360-degree flip in the air before it too collided with the concrete. With a deafening slam and spraying sparks, this one landed right side up, all four of its tires exploding on impact. This time Jamal jumped and yelled, "GODDAMN! GODDAMN!"

He watched, dumbfounded, frozen in his tracks as if his feet were buried in the concrete he stood on, as the people in the car began to stir. Two men in the front seat struggled against jammed doors and then pulled themselves out through the windows.

A really old dude with short dark hair reached in through the back window to pull out a pretty woman, not as old as the old dude, but old, maybe 20 or even 30. She was Mexican, maybe. Just as the man pulled her out, a red ray lit up the dust raised by the car's collision. Jamal watched the laser light, mesmerized by the sharp red beam as it swept across the concrete spillway.

He heard a crack from above, followed by the sound of metal being pierced by a bullet as it penetrated the roof of the car. The girl had been *right there* a second before. Jamal recognized the sound of a bullet striking – he had heard these sounds in his neighborhood plenty of times before. Although he lived less than a mile from the resplendent wealth of the Plaza area, he might as well have lived a million miles away, because you saw things there that Plaza people don' *nevah'* see.

However, Jamal had never seen anything like what he was seeing now. When the bullet ripped through the roof of that fly BMW, and the pair tumbled away from the car just in time, Jamal screamed in a high-pitched panic, "GODDAMN! Goddamn! Goddamn! Oh sweet mutha' fuggin' Jesus! Goddamn! *GODDAMN!*" Jamal's feet were suddenly unstuck from the cement below him. He flew toward the drain tunnel.

Ian saw the boy disappear into the opening. He sprinted after him, right on his heels, yelling for Frank and Ravi to follow. As Ravi entered the tunnel, Frank looked up to see the helicopter swirling around into position. A red dot appeared in the middle of Ravi's back.

Frank put his hands on her shoulders to shove her forward. A sharp crack from above followed by a thud sent Ravi stumbling forward into the tunnel as Frank's weight fell on her from behind.

Panic roared through the drain tunnel. Ian had gone ahead, following the boy, who seemed to know where he was going. Ravi tried to lift herself from the ground, but she could not move. As she struggled to free herself, Frank's limp body rolled off her. Rays of light from the laser streamed through the dust and morning mist outside, and fresh bursts of dust sprayed up as blasts erupted from the dancing red dots.

Between the rising sun and the laser, there was just enough light to illuminate Frank's body. Ravi screamed, "IAN! FRANK'S HURT!"

# 60. The Promise:
# No One Gets Out of Here Alive

The VP was apoplectic when he heard the report of the trio's escape into the sewer system. With the slam of a button on his console, he switched channels to learn that as planned, the Plan B drones had swapped with two commercial jets that had taken off as registered flights. Using anti-hijacking control systems, the team had already commandeered, downed, and disposed of the jets in remote areas, effectively erasing them from existence. The drones, heavily laden with explosives, now flew in the air in their place. The FAA thought the drones *were* the planes. There was no turning back.

The commercial flights they had chosen were those with light passenger loads, but the unfortunates who had been on them were no more. The drones were on their way toward D.C., not far outside the capital.

The detonators within the Capitol rotunda's walls were in place. Demolition cleanup crews were awaiting orders to begin moving debris out of the Capitol once it was destroyed. It would be recycled immediately in order to eliminate any forensic evidence, in case any investigative commissions might be demanded.

The Air Force war games had been enacted at the VP's command, and military interceptor jets that normally protected the capital were now far away from D.C., chasing phantom radar images.

Plan B would afford spectacularly visual news that would drown out any public appeal the woman might make. There would be no room in the media for her rants, once a "terrorist" attack on the nation's capital hit the news.

But in order for Plan B to work, the Soldier must never be able to tell about his part in it. So long as he remained alive, he could blow the whistle on the Capitol attack, and all would be lost.

Slamming his hand on his console, the VP switched away from the Plan B team and back to the crew in Kansas City. With a controlled voice that thinly veiled a primal scream, the VP unleashed the deadly order. "The Soldier, *the Traitor,* MUST be terminated. Everything rides on this. Get men into those sewers, NOW!"

The VP switched back to the Plan B team with a slam of his palm. "Stand by for the order! Be ready to go when I give it!"

Then back to the Kansas City crew. "The second the Soldier is terminated, I want to know. Immediately. I repeat, IMMEDIATELY!"

. . .

Frank lay on his back. He could not move his head. He strained to look down at the dancing red lasers near his feet – feet that he could no longer move.

Ravi grabbed him under the arms and dragged him deeper into the drainage tunnel. Frank groaned with the movement. Ravi's heart pounded as she gasped from the effort and the horror of seeing Frank helpless and broken.

Bullets hissed and thudded into the moist soil of the tunnel's entrance just inches from Frank's feet. "Oh, Frank," she cried, looking down at his broken body. The bullet had shattered Frank's spine as it entered below his shoulder blades and exited through his left lung. His entire lower body was dead weight. He coughed a spray of blood onto his chest as Ravi cradled his head in her lap.

Ravi's mind spun as her heart raced. Wiping the blood from Frank's mouth with her shirt tail, she again murmured, "Oh, Frankie."

Oddly, in the midst of this hopeless destruction, Frank's face lit up. A blood-smeared smile spread across his face as he choked out, "You're only the secon' person to call me that 'sides my mom."

Ravi stroked his face and looked into his eyes, as Frank struggled on. "The other was a monk I killed, not long before I – murdered Rachel." Frank cried the last word, as his voice became childlike and fearful, like a boy confessing a sin to his mother. His torso quivered as sobs wracked his tortured body. He spoke in a red foamy whisper. "I'm sorry, I'm sorry, I'm sorry . . ." he whispered like a penance, spit and blood bubbling from his lips. Tears spilled from his eyes.

Ravi, choking back emotion, yelled loudly into the tunnel, "IAN! HELP!"

Frank's upper body suddenly stiffened and his mind became clear. His eyes darted around the tunnel, taking in where he was. He took command and spoke clearly and forcefully. "Ravi, I'm done. You have to go! GO, *NOW!*" His hand gripped her arm as he spoke, before it released and collapsed onto his chest.

She turned toward the black tunnel, screaming at the top of her lungs, "IAN! Ian, we need you! *Frank's hurt!*" and her voice broke as tears spilled from her eyes onto Frank's increasingly pale face.

Ravi held Frank's head and felt the first shudder go through him, as his eyes clouded and he looked not at her, but through her. "Daddy? Issat you? Wha . . .?" The thickened blood streamed from his top lip down over his teeth as he tearfully whispered the words. His chest whistled loudly as he labored for another breath. A large clot of blood choked from his throat. Frank again spoke – his voice fragile and soft. "Whadja' say, Daddy? Ya *s-s-s-ssseeee me?* Ya been waitin' for me?" Then Frank's fogging eyes cleared, and he saw Ravi again, but still in an excited voice cried, "My daddy's been waitin' for me. He's *always* seen me."

"Of course he sees you, Frank. *You've done good, Frankie.*" Ravi stroked his sweat-beaded forehead with her hand, as he wept quietly. Frank was smiling as his trembling fingers fluttered weakly. She took his hands into hers. Frank's smile grew as his sobs did, tears streaming from his eyes. Ravi wept with him, holding him to her breast as their chests heaved in unison. Blood soaked Ravi's shirt as Frank's warm life oozed out. Ravi knew she was watching him die.

Frank choked heavily, spasming with each cough. Ravi raised up and sat back to give him more air. His eyes again had that far-away look. There were no more tears in his eyes, only excitement. "I've gotta get home for supper now. My mom's makin' a special supper tonight, 'cause my daddy's come home from war. He's gonna play ball with me after supper. Momma said he would."

His eyes focused on Ravi again, yet maintained the child's excitement. Frank's hand squeezed her hand. He spoke in a strained whisper, even as the blood, thick and clotted, gargled from his throat and mouth with the words. "Ravi! There's Mom, and Daddy's waitin' too! Jus' like she said he would be. *I see him.* They're standin' with some fren's, an Indian man and a Chinese man in an orange robe, and a pretty girl — *she looks like you, 'cept bigger'n you. I've seen her before."* Frank's excited smile remained as his body went limp and he exhaled his last breath.

Ravi knew he was gone, but held him nonetheless, until Ian appeared in the tunnel behind her.

Adrenaline pumped through Ian's body. He'd seen death before, and he knew Frank was gone. With the chopper pounding the air outside the tunnel, Ian grabbed Ravi and lifted her to her feet, pulling her down the tunnel behind him.

# 61. Subterranean Blues

The helicopter, unable to land, hovered and fired into the tunnel. The pilot clicked on his mic. "Somebody get a sewer system map of Kansas City, NOW! I don't give a damn what computer systems you have to hack! *GET IT!*"

He whirled the chopper around to peer into street drains on the south side of eastbound Blue Parkway. "I want to see the tunnels in every direction." The pilot motioned frantically to his shooter, who was punching up a street map on the computer screen in the craft's dash. He scrambled for their location, and finally pointed to it on the map for the pilot, who shouted into his mic, "West from The Paseo and south from Swope Parkway – any drainage tunnel that connects with Brush Creek. Get an agent covering every outlet! Get those cars moving – *NOW!*"

. . .

Jamal scurried down the concrete passage, his head bent to avoid the low ceiling, his Nikes slapping water with every step. "Hell, I know ya'll ain't guilty o' nuthin.' I been hauled in five damn times and I ain't nevah been guilty o' none o' those muttha' fuggin' chahges. My brotha' got 'rrested las' nigh', cause some brotha', six feet tall, robbed a Gas-n-Sip on Paseo. My brotha's on'y five feet five. Oh, he's guilty awrigh', guilty a bein' black!"

Jamal held up his hand to signal Ian and Ravi to stop as he poked his head up to the edge of the street grate. He immediately jerked it back. "Damn! Tha' helicopta's right out der! Git *down!*"

The trio ducked down under the grate to move past it and on through the tunnel, as a red laser beam darted around over their heads. The shooter in the helicopter spotted Ian's head just as he ducked. Jamal continued talking as they crept. "Don' you worry none, I'll git ya to da museum, jus' like da man said. I got der many times tru dis tunnel. One o' my girl fren's lives by it. Hell, this creepy li'l cave is the safest way for a brotha to git anywhere once da sun go down. Too *nasty* down here fer da man, ya see." He pointed to a rat scurrying past them.

Ravi didn't see the rat, as she stolidly stumbled forward. Too much had happened too fast, and there was still too much to do. She had nothing left for anything but putting one foot in front of the other as she followed Ian's steps, who likewise followed Jamal's.

. . .

The helicopter dispatched cars to cover both the tunnel opening where the fugitives had been spotted and the next opening a mile down the riverbed. The plan was to come from both ends of the drain toward the targets, now trapped somewhere in between those two points.

Men entered the tunnels from both openings, progressing toward one another in a pincer move on Ian, Ravi, and Jamal. Red lasers flashed down the passageway before the armed men, who moved methodically to squeeze the targets between them.

. . .

The VP cleared his communications for only the Plan B team and the crew in Kansas City. Nothing else mattered. A light flashed on the console, and he punched the button for reception from the Plan B team. "Sir, the drones are circling the capital. Fuel may become an issue. Are we good to go yet?"

"Hold!" the VP yelled, as he slammed back to the Kansas City crew. "What's the status of the Soldier?"

"Sir, we're closing in on them. We've spotted them in the sewer and dispatched men to cover exits on both sides of them. We're moving in."

The VP slammed back to the Plan B team. "Keep those drones in the air. This has to happen. The flight plan records of the passenger jets cannot be undone – those aircrafts have already been destroyed. We are at a point of no return. Keep my channel clear. *Any moment now.*"

. . .

A member of the A-Team in Kansas City, Agent Blackman, separated from his group in the tunnel to search the street above. He was going back over the tunnel sections they had already passed, peering down into them from the drainage grates on the street. Examining one of the drains, the agent froze. The beam from his flashlight revealed something his crew had missed – a thick smear of blood on the drain's concrete wall.

There the blood ended. *Why?* Was it the blood of those they pursued – *or of someone left behind?* Blackman needed to check all the way back to where the targets had entered the tunnels after fleeing their wrecked car.

He turned quickly, charging back down the street to the spillway, where steam still fumed from the car's shattered cooling system. Agent Blackman now moved more slowly, surveying the scene. Catching his breath, he quickly surveyed the crash scene before turning to the drain tunnel opening – where Frank's corpse lay only inches from the agent's line of vision.

# 62. Drowning on Air

The VP waited at his console, blood pulsing in his brain as he anticipated notification of the Soldier's death. His other hand was poised to enact Plan B.

Unknown to the VP, one very thorough agent – Agent Blackman – was only moments from raising him on his radio to deliver that eagerly-awaited report. Each step the agent took toward the tunnel entrance dropped another domino leading to the enactment of Plan B – the biggest coup ever perpetrated in human history – a subjugation that would unleash misery beyond imagination.

Blackman's heels clicked faster and faster as he approached. He thought he saw something. Reaching the entrance, he saw – *the Traitor!* The Soldier's inert body lay on the ground.

Blackman's mind swam. He'd be friggin' rewarded big time for this! He stood over the body in the tunnel. With trembling fingers he raised his hand to the microphone at his mouth. Agent Blackman clicked it to the "on" position, to deliver to the Vice President of the United States of America his triumphant discovery.

The VP heard the click opening the channel to the Kansas City crew. Frantic, he couldn't wait for the communication. Demanding, screaming, "Yeah, what the hell you got!?" His other hand touched the button to give orders to the D.C. team.

. . .

The sun had now broken over the horizon. On the campus of the University of Missouri at Kansas City, students filled the streets heading for morning classes. Two coeds walked down the sidewalk beneath towering green-leafed trees. They were giggling about their most recent horror-show dates, until suddenly one screamed. As she pointed to the drain across the street, her companion joined in. Jamal was peering out through the sewer opening to get his bearings. When the women shrieked, a shocked Jamal screamed right back at them. But he recognized the campus behind them and ducked back down.

Turning to Ravi and Ian, he told them, "We almos' der. Da nex' openin' is our stop!"

Quick-stepping down the tunnel, they heard the helicopter patrolling up and down the length of Brush Creek, where cars hissed by. They did not hear the men they moved toward, who were within a hundred yards and closing fast. Hearing the chopper and seeing a light about thirty feet ahead, Jamal urged them on. "It's gittin' thick out der. I don' like it. *Move yo' feet!* Momma's awready gonna kick my ass. If I get capped by some monster mutha' she goin' kill me *fo' sho'.*"

Reaching the street drain, where the morning light rayed down into the tunnel, Jamal announced, "Heah's our stop." He boosted his lithe form up the wall and out through the street grate. Ian wove his fingers together to give Ravi a boost up. She bumped her head on the concrete top of the drain before reaching out for Jamal's hands with tearing eyes. Jamal pulled her easily up onto the street. Ian then boosted himself, sticking his head and shoulders out of the drain, so Jamal and Ravi could grab his torso to pull him up and out.

Ian was too big to pass through the drain. Ravi and Jamal pulled and grunted, and Ian sucked in his gut and wiggled and squirmed, but to no avail. He couldn't get his hips through the opening. He dropped back down into the tunnel. Jamal was frantic, almost bouncing on the street, his eyes darted back and forth and up and back down at Ian. Ravi urged Ian to try again.

Ian heard sounds in the tunnel, shuffling feet and heavy breathing. The sounds came closer until far down the tunnel Ian saw the now familiar flash of red laser dots dancing faintly across the walls. Jamal demanded, "Take yo' pants off! Take yo' damn pants off! Hurry up! My cousin's behind is way bigger'n yo's is. Thas' how he got out one nigh'!"

Ian frantically pulled his jeans down to his ankles, as Jamal directed, "Thas' 'nough, now get some o' that silky mud off da flo', and smear it all ova' yo' white ass! HURRY! That helicopta's comin!" Jamal's head swiveled up and around, then back to Ian.

Ian could hear the copter closing in as he smeared the goo from the sewer floor over his buttocks and belly before jumping up to extend his head, chest, and arms out of the street drain, reaching up for help from Ravi and Jamal. Ian wiggled and twisted wildly as Ravi and Jamal each grabbed a hand. Because the mud Ian had smeared on his body was also on his hands, their grip slipped again and again.

From the direction of the flashing dots, Ian heard a voice say, "What was that? Did you hear that? Look, his ass is stuck in the drain! Fire, NOW!"

Ian's eyes showed sheer terror as he yelled up at Jamal and Ravi, "Get me *OUT OF HERE!*" The red lights flashed across the wall. Wiping their hands frantically on their clothes, Jamal and Ravi gripped Ian by the forearms and tugged ferociously. The laser sight flashed on Ian's kicking lower body. Two shots rang out, one after the other. The first bullet caught the edge of the drain's steel frame and pinged loudly before ricocheting past Jamal's head.

The second bullet ripped through Ian's pants bunched around his ankles, but missed his flesh. The high-pitched sound of the bullet ricocheting on concrete echoed from farther down the tunnel, followed immediately by a heavy groan and the sound of a body hitting the ground.

. . .

Far beyond, the A-Team, who had entered the tunnel from the opening just beyond where Frank had died, hit the floor when the ricochet whizzed between and past them. They yelled down the tunnel at the oncoming B-Team, with many colorful words and their own weapons raised in case the dense sacks-o-crap did something else stupid.

In their panic, they ducked and froze, yelling toward the *friendly-fire, loose-cannon SOBs* coming in from the opposite end to pincer the targets between them.

. . .

The VP's hand wavered over the Plan B communications button. Once the kill confirmation was given by the agent in Kansas City, the VP would launch the coup with the drones and the demolition charges. With Congress in full session and the President arriving right on schedule for his speech – everything was set up perfectly! His heart pounded.

"Yeah, what the hell you got!?"

Agent Blackman could not respond. His larynx had been ripped from his throat. The stray bullet that had ricocheted past the other pincer team had mortally wounded him.

His finger slipped off his bloody mic button, closing the channel with the VP before he could utter one single word. The only sound that carried to the Vice President was a moan escaping from the lungs of his collapsing body.

The VP heard the breathy sound and the closing click and shouted, "Who opened the channel? Where are you? Identify yourself immediately! Come in, come in, over!"

The A-Team leader, listening on his own earpiece, was confused by the VP's words and tried to clarify. "We did not, I repeat, *did not* open the channel, sir. Over."

Blackman heard his team leader and the VP as he struggled for air. Sprawled only inches from Frank's body, he summoned all his strength to again press the mic button and open his channel with the Vice President. He held the mic to his mouth.

The VP, hearing the new click, demanded, "Yeah, *who the hell is this?*"

The A-Team leader shrugged his shoulders at his team. Fifty yards down the tunnel, Blackman's open mouth strained to confirm what the VP was waiting to hear. The B-Team leader at the other end of the tunnel, equally ignorant of Agent Blackman's struggle, shrugged as well.

Blackman, like a goldfish out of its bowl, drowning on air that it could not breathe, worked to form the air from his lungs into words. It was futile. His lips opened and rounded, forming the proper shapes to make sounds, but there was no larynx in his throat to mold the air. Blackman struggled for endless moments, while deep within the VP's gut, what would eventually become a peptic ulcer sprouted as he waited.

Finally, the agent, drowning in his own blood, expired. His hand went limp, and Blackman's channel closed forever on the seething VP, who was now pounding his fist into his console, screaming, "GODDAMN IT! *Who the hell IS this?!*"

The A-Team leader, hearing the VP's rant, again looked at his team with raised eyebrows and shrugged.

. . .

Emerging from the drain, Ian stood naked before the world. The University students across the street gawked. He raced after Jamal and Ravi, struggling to pull up his pants as he sprinted. They left behind them the gunmen in the sewer, working to get themselves and their equipment out through the drain. While his fellow agents struggled, one of them had the sense to raise the nearby aircraft on his radio.

The helicopter, which had been farther down the concrete river bed watching other possible exits, roared toward the fugitives as they pushed to reach the lawn of the Nelson-Atkins Museum of Art.

The pilot described the scene into his radio mic. Several hundred people had gathered for what was apparently a media event of some kind. Television cameras, microphones, and a large crowd were gathered around someone under the trees' canopy in front of the museum.

The pilot, still reporting in, jammed his first finger down toward the ground to direct the shooter next to him to stop the fleeing targets before they could enter the crowd.

Ian and Jamal, both sprinting hard, reached back to help Ravi keep up. Just a few more feet to tree cover. Turf erupted around them as shots rained from above. They reached the heavy ring of trees surrounding the museum lawn. The helicopter pulled off and away, trying to spot them beneath the foliage from a side angle. But the trio was already absorbed into the milling crowd.

Ravi and Ian looked like war refugees. They walked more slowly now that they were in the safety of the crowd. The sprawling lawn covered a hilly expanse that led to the massive Romanesque columns guarding the museum's entrance.

The helicopter pilot spotted them among the crowd in the shadows of the trees, and the shooter quickly took aim. His crosshairs danced around Ravi's moving form. As he zeroed in on her, a police helicopter, alerted by dispatch of low flying craft, flew toward the copter. With a quick tap on the shooter's shoulder, the pilot gave a kill sign – hand across his throat – and pointed to the police aircraft.

The dark unmarked helicopter hesitated for a moment before reluctantly pulling up. It darted away from the museum, like a hungry lion who realized his prey might suddenly become the predator.

Jamal followed Ian and Ravi to collect the cash payment Ian had promised him upon their delivery to this place. The crowd parted as the ragged and dirty trio, who looked like they had passed through the gates of hell, moved toward the heart of the assembly pressed around the museum's reflecting pool.

Ravi and Ian scanned the crowd for someone who appeared to be in charge. They did not know this Liam Douglas the Healer had sent them to. They only knew from the Healer's vision that he would be the person to connect Ravi with the eyes of the world through a corps of assembled media – if they survived.

Half a dozen television cameras set to broadcast live from this happy-sunny-day-human-interest event turned from the congregation of people toward the approaching war-ravaged trio.

# 63. Closing Doors

Two cars careened up onto the south lawn of the Nelson-Atkins behind the approaching trio. The first car skidded sideways to a stop a few yards from the hundreds gathered there. A second pulled up just behind it. The perplexed pursuers jumped from their cars and stood, scratching their heads, wondering what to do, as the crowd closed around Ravi, Ian, and Jamal. Unsure how aggressively they should pursue the targets now that they were in public, they pressed their tiny earpieces to their heads, trying to get instructions.

Television cameras rolled footage of the crowd and the strange people in the center. Some of the cameras turned toward the pursuers, who quickly looked away when they saw they were being filmed. The men reported into their headsets that some kind of media event was taking place. And that TV cameras were recording them.

. . .

In Washington, the VP motioned frantically toward his office wall, as if clicking an imaginary remote control with his hand. An aide promptly responded to his unspoken command, punching a series of keystrokes into a desk console. A bank of televisions sparked to life, displaying broadcasts of all the major national and international news networks.

. . .

The A-Team Leader reported into his headset that the Traitor, the Soldier, was not among the group who arrived at the Nelson, and the woman was covered in blood. From Washington, a harsh and panicky voice screamed into his earpiece, "Is she hurt? Is it her blood?"

The A-Team Leader reported that it didn't appear to be, only to hear the voice scream back at him, "GET MEN INTO THOSE TUNNELS, *NOW!* Find out if the Soldier was left in there!"

The VP waited, his security line cleared. The Professor was already out of the loop and had fled Canada, as loose ends were being tied up at the speed of satellite communication waves. If the Soldier were recovered, the Capitol could be blown, and he would control the day's media coverage. Explosive cable news pronouncements would lead all broadcasts: *"The President and the entire United States Congress killed by Muslim terrorists, perhaps with Chinese support — more on this as the story develops."* This would drown out anything the woman might say today.

But they couldn't proceed with the plan if the Soldier were still alive.

She was only steps from the microphones.

All the VP could do as the men searched the tunnels — was wait.

. . .

Liam Douglas, the Healer's friend, was up ahead. He was speaking excitedly to supporters in the assembling crowd. It was one of the best attended events they had ever organized, and the media had come out in force today. He turned as he sensed someone approaching him. His eyes widened and his mouth opened in shock as he saw the three travelers. He took in Ravi and Ian's sunken, exhausted eyes and the blood covering Ravi's shirt. His voice quivered as he spoke. "My God, are you all right?" He searched Ravi's face as he held her shoulders with both hands.

Ravi nodded that she was okay. "This, this is not . . ." A sob shuddered through her as she finished, "This is not my blood."

Liam beckoned for his wife, and when she saw Ravi's condition, she gasped in horror. Liam quickly explained, "She's all right, that's not her blood. But give her your sweater, would you?" Oi Yue wrapped her sweater around Ravi and hugged her with one arm while offering her a drink of water with the other. Ravi accepted the water bottle with a shaking hand, as Liam continued. "Ravi, I recognize you from television. The Healer got word to me you were coming." Looking down at Jamal, he continued. "But his message didn't indicate any of your party was so young." Looking at Ian, he ventured, "You look like a fellow Scotsman, so I assume you are Ian, but is this young man — Frank?"

Ian started to answer as Ravi burst into tears. The weight of all she'd been through crashed down on her as she spoke. "We have to *hurry!* Frank — Frank is dead. We, we . . ." Sobs wracked her small frame, and she couldn't speak.

Ravi's broken heart unfroze, and the feelings poured through. *Rachel,* sweet Rachel. Frank. The Professor, the drugs, the torture. It all swirled in a kaleidoscope too intense and horrible for her mind and heart. She sobbed.

Ian asked Liam, "Can we hurry? Can we talk to the media now?"

Liam shook his head. "Not yet, but soon. There are satellite feeds, and connections like that take hours to arrange. Everything's set for the top of the hour. We've got five minutes until they're ready to go live." Liam motioned to the group to ascend a small speaker's platform in preparation for the press conference.

. . .

The agents on the lawn had received their orders from the VP. Their cars spun around as they tore away from the museum, back toward the spillway.

All along the south bank of the Brush Creek channel, dark-suited men scrambled down the concrete walls toward the drain entrances like swarming rats.

Liam patted Ravi's back, holding her head to his shoulder while she wept. "Ravi, the Healer told us that you must speak *live* today to the world media. It must be you who speaks in order to capture their attention. I know it's hard. But can you be ready in – " he looked at his watch – "one minute?"

Multi-octave chants began to hum around her. Ravi remembered Frank's horrifying announcement in the bus station about what he'd done at the Capitol, and she nodded emphatically. Her heart quickened. Time was of the essence, and this was more important than her personal pain.

Liam's wife dabbed water onto a napkin to clean the tears and dried blood off Ravi's face and neck as Liam turned back to address the crowd and the media.

"We have a very special guest speaker here today who you will all recognize once I introduce her. But while we wait to go live in a few seconds, let me begin by . . ."

. . .

The VP slammed down his palm, ending the conversation with Kansas City. Just as he pounded another button on his console to open another communication, a figure appeared on the screens of all the televisions simultaneously. It was *the woman.*

# 64. Now! Now! Now!

The VP screamed into the microphone on his desk, *"Are the detonators in place?"* Before the answer could be given, he ordered, "Stand by!"

His mind spun furiously through options. Then he slammed another button on his console, shouting, "Contact the media, IMMEDIATELY! Tell them to cut away from the Kansas City event. We have an emergency announcement from the Office of the Vice President!"

A voice spoke into his earpiece, and the VP screamed, "ALL OF THEM, DAMMIT! ALL OF THE DAMNED MEDIA!"

Another console button was slammed, and the VP's voice squawked viciously into the cockpit of the unmarked helicopter. "Eliminate the woman! I repeat, terminate the woman! NOW!"

The pilot responded, shouting over the sound of the blades, as the shooter opened his door and pointed the barrel of his scoped rifle out the side. "They're under tree cover! We can't place the target visually. Our gamma wave sensor is showing a broad swath among the crowd. We cannot, I repeat, cannot isolate her!"

Mark Ratlig, his line opened by the VP, heard the exchange. He furiously punched up screens, using the satellites to assist in isolating the woman. He could not believe what he was seeing! The white dots of higher gamma wave consciousness on the radar-like screens expanded as he watched. Points across the globe began to pulsate with light.

He spoke to the VP with a quavering voice, "Sir, something is happening globally. We cannot isolate any of our targets worldwide. I don't know . . ."

The VP slammed Ratlig's channel shut, terrified, staring at the television screens on his wall. His voice now shrill, he screamed to his aide, "THE MEDIA! Get those goddamned TV cameras focused on the White House, NOW!"

. . .

The Healer had realized on that dark magical night by the fire that Ravi's only chance of survival was to speak through *live, unedited* media to the world.

But the Healer had not known of Frank's work in D.C. The need for live coverage had become urgent. Whereas once it was necessary in order to save Ian and Ravi and Frank, it was now needed to save the very foundations of global democracy.

Liam Douglas had organized dozens of media events over the years. Many months ago he had told the Healer of this special global media event he was developing. The Healer's consciousness had seized upon this bit of memory which had fit like a puzzle piece with the time they would arrive in Kansas City – and it came to him in a vision that he had shared with his friends on their last morning together.

He knew the odds were slim it would come together, considering the challenges the trio would face on their long journey south, but it offered a window of hope. Experience told him that his memory about the approaching media event and the timing of this chain of events had not come to him by accident. The White Man called this *synchronicity.* First Nation people called it *the way of the spirit,* a way of life.

The cameras' red lights flashed, their monitors sparked to life, and Liam brought the crowd to order.

As he spoke, Ravi's emotional torment grew. The familiar vibration that had begun the day she first embarked upon this journey, so very long ago at Oxford, became a consummate force, rattling her with urgency. The horrific images from the thousands of television screens in her heroin dream that morning ignited in her mind.

From the rattle and hum of this force, a voice slowly came into focus like a radio tuner zoning in on a band wave. It was Frank's voice. "NOW! NOW! The Capitol! Ravi, you must speak NOW!"

The red lights blinked on the surrounding cameras; the satellite feeds were now live. Liam began addressing the assembled media. "Before we begin our Global World Healing Day events, we have a special treat for you all."

The crowd's cheering intensified as Ravi stepped toward the cameras. As the chaos swirled in her mind, the television monitors facing Liam and Ravi began to change. All of them had shown Liam's face. But suddenly, the White House appeared on the FOX monitor. And then on CNN's, then on the BBC's. Ravi watched in horror, her heart pounding furiously as the vibration screamed like an oncoming freight train in her mind. Out of the nearly twenty monitors, four had already switched programming to the White House. She saw her image on yet another monitor replaced by color bars.

. . .

Three armed men entered the tunnel from the spillway and found Frank's blood-soaked body, as well as Blackman's throatless corpse. Pressing his headset, the man closest to the opening charged out of the tunnel, screaming into his microphone, "Agent Pestis reporting, the target is expired. He's dead, he's dead, I repeat, the target is dead!"

. . .

Ravi pushed forward. Liam turned, bumping into her as she reached up to take his microphone even as he spoke, "Please welcome *The Honorable Ms. Ravi Shyamalan . . .*" Liam's voice trailed off as Ravi grabbed the mic.

The crowd roared its approval, many having come to know Ravi from her C-SPAN appearance at Oxford and her CNN appearance at Folsom Prison. The attending minor media personalities, mostly lesser known weekend reporters sent to cover a human interest story, smelled opportunity. This event, publicized as a worldwide healing day gala, had turned into something far more newsworthy. They now had access to a controversial international hard-news celebrity, recently reported as killed after her disappearance in a plane accident. Visions of Peabody awards and Pulitzer prizes danced in their heads as they closed in with lenses whirring and cameras clicking. Ravi extended her arms, frantically trying to quiet the cheering crowd.

. . .

The VP, hearing the agents yelling that the Soldier was dead, suddenly could breathe again. The gates to his plans blew wide open. He was saved. The masses would beg for war. This long-awaited communication would make it possible for him to give the "go" order for the destruction of Congress – of democracy – and set in motion the pretext for energy wars that would last for decades to come. Control would be his.

A moment later, Ravi's tearful voice – broadcast through the networks still focused on the event in Kansas City – filled his office.

. . .

The vibration of chants pounded through Ravi's body as she opened the sweater Oi Yue had given her, exposing her blood-soaked shirt to the cameras. Her tears flowed as she fiercely spoke through them. "This is the blood of a covert government agent named Frank Delaney, who saved me from torture and death and got me here today.

"Before he died in my arms moments ago, he told me and Naval Intelligence agent Ian McDonald that he'd planted explosives in the United States Capitol building as part of a homegrown false-flag operation designed by the Office of the Vice President in collaboration with elements of the CIA to destroy the halls of democracy, to blame it on foreign terrorists, and use that attack as an excuse to end American democracy employing Presidential Directives NSPD51 and HSPD20."

. . .

Blood drained from the Vice President's face as Ravi's words echoed off the wood panels of his office.

In that moment, as global media carried Ravi's words of truth, Ratlig watched his screens as a thousand points of light flashed across the planet. Dumbfounded at what he saw, he knew it signaled the end of the world he'd known.

Within seconds, empires were collapsing upon themselves as files were being deleted and destroyed at the speed of light. Loose ends were being tied, and potential witnesses were being vanquished – but there was not enough time. The damage was too vast. It was the end. All that had been built crumbled beneath them. The vast power structures who had quietly supported the Vice President's ambitions from behind the scenes for their own varied reasons and ultimate benefit folded like a house of cards.

In the end, the VP had only been an errand boy for a behemoth economic force vastly beyond his limited power. He was now on his own. After firing off a dozen well-placed calls to hold back the flood for as long as possible, the VP said in a hoarse whisper into the microphone to the Plan B team in D.C., "Abort."

He passed through a recessed door in the wall of his office into an elevator that led to a rooftop helipad, where a waiting helicopter thumped in anticipation. The VP climbed aboard, and the chopper ascended slowly into the sky, circled once, and disappeared from sight.

# 65. Do You Feel It?
# It Is Happening!

*There is immense silent agony in the world, and the task of man is to be a voice for the plundered poor . . .*
– Rabbi Abraham Joshua Heschel, Jewish Mystic (1907-1972)

*We must cut the number of anti-depressants prescribed by doctors. Pills must not be a crutch for the wider issues in our society . . .*
– Liberal Democrat Leader Nick Clegg, BBC, February 8, 2008

*Spirituality is not only for the saints; it is for everybody . . . we must bring spirituality into politics, business, industry, agriculture, and into our homes.*
– Satish Kumar, Founder of London School for Nonviolence

---

The pounding chant vibration within Ravi shifted, and the words flowed through her.

"Although our fear has created a fearful world in our time, there is no reason to cower. In fact, those in the halls of power have *used* our emotions to suppress a mighty part of who we are. Now is the time in history when we must become bold in voicing what has been suppressed for too long. What is this power within us that I speak of?"

Ravi covered Frank's blood with the sweater to bring the listeners' attention directly to her words. "No institution or revolution can save us from our future. Only an evolution of consciousness within each of us can do this. We are each part of the awakening. *We ARE the awakening.* The world will change around us as we open to the truth now expanding within each of us.

"It is time for all of us to see earth, not as a battleground, but as *our home.*

"My father was a government man serving in the halls of power, yet he deeply believed in the subtle power of the feminine. He believed that the maternal nesting power found in our feminine nature – *in both men and women* – must emerge from the background into the foreground of history. We must become earth's homemakers seeking order in our world that can only come about through empathy, care, and nurturing. It is time for us all to come home to our feminine nature.

"My father often said to me, 'As a boy, I watched my mother and was always amazed that she found such profound satisfaction in nourishing and nurturing those in her home. Her greatest desire – her greatest ambition – was to nurture.'"

Ravi's eyes over-spilled as her heart did, remembering the beautiful simplicity of her father's spirit. She completed her father's thought, overcoming a hitch in her chest and her voice, "– and then he would look into my eyes with such sincerity and ask me, 'Ravi, can you see the power of that? Can you understand how profoundly beautiful that ambition is?'"

Young Jamal stepped behind Ian, where he took off his doo-rag and self-consciously mopped a tear. He thought of his li'l over-worked Momma's struggle to hol' him and his brotha's in line, washin' their clothes and cookin' their food, after long days at work. His mind's eye saw her at this moment takin' the long bus ride, with its many waits and transfers, to that lousy job she went to ever' single day so she could pay the rent and buy the food.

As she spoke, Ravi sensed a shift within herself. The struggle and challenge of her experience had changed and empowered her. She no longer spoke with the bookish, tentative voice of the untested scholar who had walked into Oxford a lifetime ago. Ravi no longer experienced the vibration as interference. She had *become* the vibration. It was now part of her. Her feminine voice had become a smooth powerful *roar*.

"A lioness within us awakens!" Ravi's stance before the cameras became as commanding as her voice. "She has been hungry, prowling behind a world of locks – behind bars of control. Hungering within her cage, she has been ravenous for *compassion* and *justice*. She will slash our hardened hearts until they finally *open*. Our world can NEVER be the same!"

Cameras closed in as Ravi continued, her authority building with a force reflecting that fierce lioness. Those watching felt an electric charge with each of her words. "A spell cast over humanity is breaking. I have walked through the torment that all of humanity is experiencing. I have been strapped to the table that is the torture humanity is feeling through manipulation, fear-mongering, and war. I have experienced my consciousness being numbed and suppressed just like millions have experienced for years, in many, *many* ways.

"We are separated from who we are. *We all feel it!* False gods are sold to us through religion, media, and government. These false images are tearing me apart, and it is not just me. *You feel it too!* You too feel the strain, the pressure." Tears fell from Ravi's eyes, as she heard many in the audience sob aloud. Their hearts swelled in the glow of Ravi's emerging power. She remembered the Healer speaking of people being hungry for the comfort of validation. She remembered the massive wave she'd ridden in her dream, a wave leading to multitudes who were parched for truth.

Ravi wiped her tears with the back of her hand and inhaled deeply, continuing with greater strength. "The long journey of humanity through our planet's evolution has seen the expansion of male controlling energy. The greed and conquest of those ages, driven by a need to control the world around us, all had a place in bringing us to where we are today in a fully developed, fully inhabited, and interconnected world. The masculine was not wrong, but it will no longer suppress the feminine. The days of the subjugation of the feminine are over, *forever!*"

Ravi's heart was breaking from all she'd seen, and she wanted to mourn all she'd lost. But those she'd left behind pushed her onward with a force that would not be denied. "That way of living has been honed to a razor's edge. Now it is time for humanity to learn to use all those millennia of development with wisdom. This can only happen by learning to *let go of control.*"

Ravi's images, both soothing and hopeful, were nonetheless delivered with a force that could drive nails. "The male energy of conquest and domination must now at long last embrace the feminine power of contemplation, receptivity, and compassion. The man whose blood I wear lived this change. He proved that the shift I am talking about *is possible* for ALL of humanity. Within him," Ravi put her hand on Ian's shoulder, "and within this man, the lioness roared, enabling them to wield the power of their hearts, breaking the chains of their masculine world's prison. Just as we, collectively, must now re-direct our masculine power to build a world of balance, where nurturing and compassion can take their place on the thrones of power.

"The feminine force of *faith* is the opposite of fear and control. Faith is not an emasculated force. Faith is a storm, savage and relentless in its quest for truth and justice, and it will no longer bow to anyone! In our emerging new world, institutions must release their grip on resources, so that *all* can have access to the abundance our technology brings. Otherwise the world's people will collectively suffocate from the death grip of control, in a violent and miserable future."

Emotion roiled through Ravi, as the frustration of ages of suppressed energy burst through. She wiped her eyes and stood tall and strong. "These two men I've spoken of had been a part of the covert mind control operation from which I just yesterday escaped. Ian McDonald of U.S. Naval Intelligence now stands beside me, but Frank Delaney of the CIA was lost from us today." Through her tears Ravi spoke forcefully into the cameras.

Determined to represent Frank's journey to the world, she continued. "I tell you this because I want the world to know what these men have done, so that you can shine your light of awareness on Ian – and on others who may come forward as he and Frank did."

Ravi looked directly into the eyes of those watching on television to emphasize her point. "Through the power of your awareness, this man can be protected from harm. Do not be seduced again by the siren call of popular culture. Remain focused on what matters. Whether these men are rewarded or punished for their actions depends entirely on your paying attention. You, your attention, your consciousness, and your focus are more powerful than you imagine. Let your heart open to them, and to your own power! Never again be diminished!

"Many of you throughout the world have felt an increasing sense of depression and alienation. Fear not. This is as it should be. A phenomenon is occurring in our world, as the vibratory rate of global consciousness shifts, according to a timetable established long, long ago.

"Just over two thousand years ago the young Buddha lived in his parents' compound, where he was shielded from all the suffering and loss in the world. When he emerged as a young man and saw the suffering of the world, it broke him to pieces, and from those pieces he became more than he had been. He became enlightened. He learned compassion. Today the world is reaching Buddha-hood. We will no longer be able to turn away from the world's suffering, for we will feel it in our very cells, just as Jesus wept with empathy for those mourning the death of Lazarus.

"The depression you've felt – a depression that no amount of antidepressants, overeating, binge drinking, or compulsive shopping could ever overcome – is the effect of our global consciousness rising to this cohesive state.

"The half of the impoverished world that hungers when they go to bed at night is part of the global brain. As our minds become attuned to the consciousness that connects all parts of the human mind, we attune to the global brain – and we feel within us the impoverished half of our global mind. Rather than fighting these feelings with drugs or consumerism, we can open our heart to our feelings, and as the Dalai Lama said, *Our tears of compassion will feed the well of hope.* Never be ashamed of tears of compassion, for within them is great and eternal power!

"The growing loneliness and alienation you have felt is humanity being rattled apart from old patterns and systems in a society that no longer works. We feel alone and unwanted in the dying, dysfunctional system. But the inspiration of our global mind is bringing in wholly innovative new systems that work for everyone.

"The manna from heaven is falling all around us, and we need only open our eyes and hearts to it. We will do what is right, no longer because some institution or book says it is right, but because doing so nurtures the atoms and cells of our being, and relieves our fear and stress.

"We will see our earth transform very rapidly now that we have remembered *who we are*. We are homemakers on this precious fragile blue orb we call earth, *our home,* the home of God's children. Homemakers do not look into the cabinet and claim its contents as their own, but rather seek within it ways to nourish and nurture everyone at the table of their love. We have within us the power to transform our world from this dysfunctional hungering house of competing forces, into a real home, a *palace of love.*

"This feminine force within us now will wield the power of 52,000 years of masculine technological development – and the balance created by this profound marriage will transform *everything.*"

Ravi's eyes widened as a shudder of energy coursed through her spine. The vibration that had begun it all stretched through her being like an exquisite light. Breathlessly, she cried to the people and cameras surrounding her, "*Do you feel it?* It is happening! We are *becoming!*"

Ravi saw others in the crowd looking around for the source of a sound that was within their own minds, as only she had done before.

Many miles away, Mark Ratlig sat alone in his analysis center, staring open-mouthed, cigarette dangling, at screens of maps worldwide. Pale and exhausted, he watched in horror as the brilliant points of light that had webbed through the maps earlier now intensified, and with an almost audible surge, pulsed outward to illuminate entire nations in spider webs of light.

# 66. Ian's Vision

*All the resources we need are in the mind.*
– Theodore Roosevelt

*World Tai Chi Day is a part of World Healing Day, which was born out of research at Princeton University [that] found that during times of great tragedy human consciousness focuses to such a degree that it actually affected their computers physically all around the world.*
– *The Evening Sun*, April 18, 2010

*Working together, World Healing Day seeks to accomplish collectively the true power of a global human consciousness.*
– *Pakistan-Asia News.com*, April 24, 2010

*World Healing Day recognizes various religious and spiritual practices with celebrations addressing world healing including World Prayer Day, World Yoga Day, World T'ai Chi Qigong Day and World [Healing] Meditation Day.*
– *Agence France Presse*, April 16, 2010

*[The last Saturday of April] is World Healing Day, plus Adam Yauch (Beastie Boys) and Yoko Ono are meditating twice daily for world health . . .*
– *UK Independent*, April 23, 2010

———————

Ravi wiped her eyes with the back of her hand and smiled through tears into the cameras. "And now, without words, I want to enjoy, receive the joy from, and participate in this 15th annual World Tai Chi Day, expanded to include World Yoga Day, World Healing Meditation Day, and World Prayer Day, all now celebrated as *World Healing Day.*

"Tai chi's purpose is to loosen our grip on who we are, so that we can open to a new reality where our masculine and feminine energies can find balance within, and thereby manifest equilibrium in our world. By finding balance we become one. Let's all join in to celebrate the motto of World Healing Day, 'One world – one breath.' Yahweh is the breath, Qigong is the breath, to respirate is to re-invoke the spirit. Let us breathe together."

Ian watched Liam, Oi Yue, and Ravi lead multitudes of people across the planet – via the internet and media – in taking a deep breath together before flowing into tai chi forms. The mystical, slow-motion movements unfolded before him like a healing balm, massaging his mind with the sounds of *only breathing*. Ian noticed Jamal beside him, equally captivated by the scene. Suddenly remembering the reward he'd promised him, Ian pulled some wadded cash out of his pocket – change he'd never given back to Frank.

Jamal, hearing Ian's rustling dollar bills, turned and immediately shook his head no, waving the money off with his hand. "Naw boo. *This is fly!* I should be payin' *you!* Like da homegirl said, us peeps gotta stick tagetha. Homegirl is da trufe, da sistah is *da real thing."* Jamal took Ian's hand in a thumb-lock handshake while he spoke, patting Ian's shoulder with his free hand.

Ian and Jamal stood together, enchanted by the shifting, flowing tai chi forms of the hundreds around them on the sprawling lawn in the morning sun. Along with them, tens of thousands in other cities around the world were coming together to breathe – to heal.

Mesmerized by the changing forms, Ian saw a vision of the whole of humanity. As the tai chi players' bodies loosened and flowed, he saw a glimpse of whole economies and political powers releasing their grip on the status quo, enabling them to re-form in evolutions of graceful transformation. A global metamorphosis had begun as all things in human history begin. He remembered Ravi's words from Folsom Prison: *The loosening of the human central nervous system will make everything possible.*

Behind Ravi, high in the blue sky, Ian thought he saw a silver light shimmer for just a moment, and then it was gone.

# 67. These and Greater Things

*Behold, I have become human.*
*If you should not want to join me in becoming God, you would do me wrong.*
– Meister Eckhart, Master Preacher Friar of the Dominican Order

―――――――――

Agents of the FBI and the Royal Canadian Mounted Police burst through the door of the Sleep Room at Taloncrag, where the Healer lay. The FBI agent checked his pulse. He was gone. Only minutes before the agents had arrived, the Healer's heart had burst from the strain of resisting the Professor's efforts.

. . .

Other agents entered the mental hospital's adjacent Sleep Rooms. In one of them the young warrior was strapped down, unconscious. His eyes began to flutter open at the sounds of the agents who bustled through the room, gathering and noting evidence, examining instrument tables and charts strewn haphazardly as if a rushed exit had been made by those in charge.

. . .

The media explosion caused by Ravi's revelation of Frank's participation in the plot to destroy the Capitol had immediately launched an investigation, beginning with an inspection of the Capitol building. The discovery of the thermate cutter charges and explosives in the walls validated her claims.

Capitol police who had not participated in the security breaches that allowed Frank and the demolition crew to plant the charges came forward. They reported security irregularities they had noticed in the period prior to the day in question. Once the lower level participants were threatened with prison, the investigations quickly moved up to higher echelons.

Although the VP was AWOL, the VP's press office, out of force of habit, made a weak attempt through the White House spokesperson to intimate that Ravi may have had something to do with the discovered terrorist plans, but it had no wheels and died an instant death. Nobody was buying it.

Within hours, the legislative branch of the United States had more power than it had had in many years. The law enforcement and intelligence branches of the executive – the Justice Department, the FBI, CIA, and NSA – would go through massive shakeups in the following days and weeks as purer hearts within those structures would demand that truth be told. Within hours, the leadership in these departments scrambled to be cleaner than the proverbial whistle, even before the housecleaning began. They climbed all over one another to dig out every dirty aspect of the covert programs, taking no chances of being tinged by the scandal.

. . .

At Taloncrag Memorial, an agent bent down over the Indian warrior who was slowly returning to consciousness. He asked the young man, "Who are you, son?"

A vibration filled the young man's mind and heart with a light, a hope, and courage. As he breathed into this vibration, his lips uttered the words in a hoarse whisper: *"I am the Healer."*

. . .

RCMP and FBI agents descended from the woods into the area where Ian, Ravi, and the Healer had not long ago watched his people dance around the fire, on that magical night when they had heard the Healer explain the good news about what was happening to them and to humanity.

The area looked deserted. Morning sun shone down through leaves. The mist was so heavy that the terrain was difficult and unpredictable. The silence was deafening, and when a twig broke somewhere out beyond the fog layer, the sound that would normally have been barely audible was as loud as a gunshot. The agents froze in their tracks.

Suddenly all firearms cocked in an orchestra of fear as a young black man with long dreadlocks, dressed from head to toe in Indian-style buckskin clothing, emerged from the lifting mist. The entire village slowly came into view as the sun turned the fog into wisps of vapors dancing like ascending spirits. The people looked up from their morning work at the approaching agents.

The agents blinked, trying to understand what they were seeing. As if they had passed through a time machine, a scene from history appeared. Before them stood an Indian village – or as the RCMP were thinking, a First Nation village – with bark houses and people wearing buckskin clothing and moccasins.

An RCMP agent asked the approaching young man, "Who are you?"

A faint lightness, a hint of a silvery dome appeared over the buckskin-clad Jamaican man as he spoke. The words flowed from his mouth as if he himself were hearing them for the first time. "I am the Healer."

Agents asked others villagers the same question, hearing again and again the response, "I am the Healer."

"I am the Healer."

"I am the Healer."

The first agent squatted beside a young Indian boy, and with an air of authority ordered, "Son, this is important. Tell me who you *really* are."

The boy looked up into the agent's eyes, and with all honesty, in a clear voice, answered, "I, too, am the Healer."

. . .

Behind the RCMP agent, high in the blue sky, the young Healer saw a silver light shimmer for a moment, as if in a cosmic wink, and then it was gone.

# 68. Rattle and Hum

## Two Years Later, in an Undisclosed Location

*They must find it difficult . . . Those who have taken authority as the truth, rather than truth as the authority.*
– Gerald Massey

*There have been tyrants and murderers and for a time they seem invincible but in the end, they always fall – think of it, always.*
– Mahatma Gandhi

———————

The physician walked into the hospital room where the Professor lay attached to an intravenous drip and monitors that measured his heartbeat and other vital functions. The physician sat on the edge of his bed. He took the Professor's hand and shook his head slowly. With a Spanish accent, he said, "I'm sorry, Malcolm. The news is not good."

Malcolm remained stone-faced, but looked up, moving only his eyes, as the doctor continued, "We can't identify exactly what is causing it, but your organs and system functions are breaking down. It is as if you've aged twenty years on the inside since you came here two months ago."

Malcolm croaked, "Why?"

"We don't know. We've seen a similar effect on the organs of amphetamine abusers and crack addicts, when the constant overuse of their systems resulted in a fast forwarding of their aging process, causing the organs to atrophy. They had learned to ignore their feelings, the signals of their systems' needs."

The doctor hesitated for a moment, unsure how to say what had to be said. He completed his thought with grim truth. "As connection with their feelings died – they perished, too."

"I can't explain why this has happened to you. But you might think about putting your house in order." With his pen poised to write, he asked, "Is there anyone we can contact – friends, loved ones, relatives?"

Malcolm stared into space as if reviewing a film spanning the course of his life, and answered flatly, "No. No one."

# 69. Futures Past – Rachel and Frankie

### Five Years Later

*The past is a foreign country. They do things differently there.*
– L. P. Hartley

*I like the dreams of future better than the history of the past.*
– Thomas Jefferson

———————

Ravi and Ian sat before the television set in the living room in a cross-legged yoga posture. Ravi turned toward the kitchen. "Hurry, it is almost time!"

Doc emerged from the kitchen with the hot cookie sheet of fresh cinnamon toast he'd just pulled from the oven. Ravi smiled at Doc's hulking frame in his electric blue yoga tights, his large hairy feet protruding from the leggings.

Doc smiled. "Now, we can't let the kids begin their first real World Healing Day celebration without breakfast. And I did promise them I'd make cinnamon toast this morning. I can't believe they've never tasted the delights of cinnamon toast before. You and Ian should atone for your austere ways by having a bite immediately," Doc added with a wink.

The children scampered from Doc's guest bedroom. Two-year-old Frankie toddled after his older sister. Rachel, now three and a half years old, bounced like an elf, Doc's colossal presence towering over her. The children were beside themselves over the smell of the cinnamon baked into the buttery, melted-sugar toast the Doc held above them. "Careful kids, this is hot. Let me get it for you."

Ravi said in her mother voice, *"Rachel, Frank,* you must eat only one piece now, and save the others for after we do yoga with the world to celebrate World Healing Day." Pointing to the television screen, she said, "Uncle Liam and Auntie Oi Yue are about to talk to us."

Doc winked at Ravi as he spoke to the children. "You heard your Mum. Heal the world first, enjoy the treats second. Trust me, your Mum knows about such things."

# Epilogue

*A nation that continues year after year to spend more money on military defense than on programs of social uplift is approaching spiritual death.*
– Martin Luther King, Jr.


*Rich western countries spend up to 25 times as much on defence as they do on overseas aid . . .*
– UK *Guardian* (Business Page), Wednesday July 6, 2005


*Nearly 70 percent of Americans believe traditional journalism is out of touch, and nearly half are turning to the Internet to get their news, according to a new survey.*
– Reuters, February 29, 2008


*Princess Diana has angered government ministers after calling for an international ban on landmines . . . Shadow defence spokesman, David Clark, said: "I think we should all welcome the fact she has . . . tried to warn the world of the dangers of these terrible weapons. I think we should be applauding what she's doing."*
– BBC News, January 15, 1997

---

Ravi's road was easier after her global media emergence – but the evolutionary world she'd spoken of in Kansas City did not come into being instantly or without trials. Some corners of the corporate media savaged her after her live guerrilla appearance on global television at the World Healing Day event. Ravi used that window of celebrity to start a media revolution, even as the backlash, vast and vicious, was set against her.

Ravi began anchoring and broadcasting cutting-edge internet news stories, interviewing many former employees of The Program, including Ian and eventually Doc and others. Her interviews uncovered in-depth exposés of The Program and what the whistleblowers had witnessed while working within it. Eventually Ian, Doc, and the other truth tellers told their stories before the U.S. Congress and the World Court in The Hague.

In her stories, the names of the Professor and Mark Ratlig were mentioned, as well as their part in the government propaganda and mind control efforts, and their revelations to Ian and Ravi during their time in Canada.

The Professor escaped to an undisclosed location in Latin America to live out his remaining days. However, Mark Ratlig disappeared for only a short time. His body was found floating in the Great Lakes shortly after Ravi's initial media exposé. The official explanation was a boating accident.

The former Vice President's whereabouts are still unknown.

But most of Ravi's time was spent in interviews and discussions with the many visionaries and inventors with whom she'd spent years creating connections back in her economist's life, before her long journey began. The controversy surrounding her awakened millions to the hopeful possibilities that her previous work had envisioned. Realities unfolded, one upon another, creating a force that eventually spilled over to positively influence even some in corporate media, fostering an unveiling of great promise for humanity, even as the darkest corners of human nature were revealed in the process.

Ravi's notoriety brought a huge number of Americans and others worldwide to the internet for news that corporate media would not tell, via channels outside the official internet portals that had been created to control information. The internet became a haven for hundreds of alternative news sites that eventually eclipsed the viewership of major network and cable news. An information revolution occurred without one gunshot or act of violence.

Through her alternative media stardom, Ravi's voice was a force in the world for those first few months, as investigations into the crimes she had revealed were expanded. But beyond that, she gave voice to the shift in humanity that continued to spread like wildfire. Over time, Ravi's notoriety faded, to her great relief, as like a rising tide, millions stood up to take her place. As the Healer predicted, it was not Ravi's voice that caused monumental change in the world; rather, it was the awakening of people across the world.

On many fronts – science, industry, media, and government – ordinary people began to reject policies that insulted their souls. Economic systems crashed and then began to re-form into whole new economies driven by the needs of people – not just the wealthiest and most powerful, but all people – and the web of life as well.

The awakening continued to spread. The viewership and readership of corporate media plummeted as millions created decentralized media institutions to spread information that affected the lives of people across the planet. Individuals became researchers and reporters as media technology became a participatory, empowering act.

As a result, the mammoth media conglomerates were eventually broken up into smaller companies. Local media control was expanded so that only residents could own media in their cities, as had been the case in the middle of the twentieth century. This engendered a renaissance in comprehensive coverage of local issues that spurred a massive shift in direction for cities worldwide toward meeting the local needs of citizens.

This new media promoted their area's farmers and renewable energy resources rather than the interests of large corporations. Costs of energy dropped, food nutritional quality bloomed, health costs lowered, and local employment with livable wages rose, now that giant corporations were no longer sucking money out of local economies as they had been doing for decades.

In the early throes of these changes, many big media celebrities quit their influential positions with major networks and opted to work for lower pay, lending their expertise and gravitas to the new media springing up everywhere. Applying their skills to actions that supported the web of life held more appeal than big paychecks.

The rising vibratory rate of global consciousness enabled the average person to feel with their heart and soul as well as think holistically. Propaganda became disempowered. The people began to turn off media that continued to tell them, in the words of George Orwell's novel *1984,* that "2 plus 2 did not equal 4."

This new ability the people had acquired – to think multi-dimensionally and thereby see through centuries of propaganda to the heart of reality – spilled over into religion. The investigations, televised globally, uncovered the mind control programs of covert agencies.

Similar investigations were carried out in other nations and in the world court. The role of religious institutions in supporting wars of conquest and an economy of oppression and subjugation were examined and exposed to the public, now hungering for whole truth.

New spiritual institutions arose that were based not on hierarchy, but on cultivating techniques that empowered individuals to go within to discover a personal connection with their God. Sermons were often replaced with group meditations, not unlike the services of Quakers or the Soka Gakkai Buddhists, where during meditations individuals stood up to share their own personal revelations. Religion became an evolutionary experience rather than one of dogma fed to people by a hierarchy of power.

The globe's trend, that of the richest western countries spending up to 25 times as much on defense as they did on overseas aid, not only ended but reversed. For the first time in modern history, spending on human needs and uplift eclipsed spending on weaponry and defense.

The result of this shift by first world nations was an outpouring of goodwill from people in developing nations, evidenced by diminished incidence of violent revolution. The people in those countries could now focus on development – no longer under the control of weapons-bloated, corrupt governments. They could now foment democracy and form labor unions, without fear of suppression by well armed dictatorships. Princess Diana's vision of global disarmament became a reality.

Change became the order of the day. Two engineers named Tom Franklin and Mark Dayton created a breakthrough in solar nanotechnology and unleashed a global energy revolution that enabled rich and poor alike access to virtually free, clean energy, forever.

Because of their breakthrough, renewable energy expanded rapidly as governments worldwide launched a Manhattan-type project to create a de-centralized renewable energy economy. The installation and work required to maintain the system boosted employment, thereby improving local economies.

Unfortunately, Tom and Mark did not live to see this happen. They were murdered by Dark Star Security agents, in the service of a vast energy consortium seeking to bury the technology to prevent the nuclear, coal, and petroleum industries from losing future profits. The remarkable story of these courageous young men became known to the world when it was revealed in a book entitled *A Conspiracy of Spirits*.

Investigations spurred by the engineers' demise revealed that long before their highly efficient solar-electric cars (SECars) breakthrough, General Motors had actually created a highly efficient electric car back in the mid-1990s, the EV-1. It was believed by some that it had been mysteriously destroyed, because such a low-maintenance car would have threatened future auto industry profits.

Plans for ethanol use ended, and farmland was once again used to produce food for a hungry, malnourished world, rather than fuel for wealthy nations. The production of food became more plant-based after a campaign to raise the public's awareness that it took more energy, water, land, and other resources to raise livestock than it did to feed people with vegetation and fruit. When the average person became educated that their high-meat diets were causing people in developing nations to starve, their eating habits changed quickly and dramatically.

As the feverish demand for meat and fish worldwide subsided, marine populations began to pull back from extinction, destruction of rainforests to create ranchland ended, and factory farming was outlawed worldwide. Massive programs were instituted to redistribute corporate cultivated land back to the families who'd lost their small farms – reversing years of legislation that had unfairly given corporate farming an advantage in the 1980s, 1990s, and beyond.

The children of farmers began to return to the land to reclaim the heritage of their fathers and mothers, bringing wholesome produce and meat to a population tired of tasteless, genetically modified foods and over-fertilized and insecticide-soaked food-like substances formerly pushed by factory farms.

Because the lifelong torment of restricted cages and pens was eliminated and range-fed livestock were given fewer hormones and drugs, their meat contained none of the stress-produced lactic acids and drugs that had been passed on to consumers in past decades. The anxiety levels of human beings began to diminish accordingly.

These changes, along with health care for all, affordable daycare for families, and more wholesome foods in schools caused stress levels to dramatically lessen.

As stress diminished, health care costs plummeted as well. The multi-trillion dollar annual costs of global healthcare was diverted into a plethora of visionary projects and programs that created urban communities that were greener, more breathable, and vibrant with community activities.

Youth incarceration rates plummeted, eventually leading to low imprisonment rates globally. Savings from police, court, and prison costs were used for job training, Head Start, and other educational programs. All students had access to free education through graduate school, in return for an equal time period of community service upon graduation, at fair wage rates.

Programs were launched to help foster home-based cottage industries, so that more and more people could work without having to "go" to work. This, along with flex jobs and more tele-commuting opportunities where people could work from home, translated into less traffic, less road construction and repair costs, less energy usage and pollution, and closer family units, as parents were able to be with their children more hours of the day.

As global media began asking real questions and governments responded to an enlightened citizenry, many truths came to light. Workers began demanding answers. Why was the current generation working longer hours for less pay – given the fact that, because of technological advances, they were thirty times more productive than their parents' generation? It was revealed that although the average worker produced many times more than their forefathers and mothers, over decades, unfair economic systems, tilted tax systems, and corporate-government policies had siphoned the increased profits into the pockets of a very few.

Employees worldwide demanded and achieved 30-hour workweeks, with ninety days vacation every year, in addition to sick time. Now that education was free to all, mass populations with increased leisure time became better educated and more free thinking.

These advances in equity were made possible when the massive wealth that had been tilted toward the top twenty percent of the population during the first twelve years of the new millennium began to spread throughout society.

As information flowed freely, a growing awareness of the high crimes committed by those who had held power in the past caused stirrings of trouble. People sensed that panic might cause the power structures to fight for survival, perhaps even attacking their own populations with false-flag terror strikes to frighten them into unconditionally supporting their government.

As a result, a global South African-style judicial system of pardon and forgiveness in exchange for truth was created. In the mid-1990s, after the fall of the white supremacist government in Pretoria, the South African black majority government had instituted such a program. They had advanced change by relinquishing revenge.

The success of the South African system, along with Ravi's world-renowned forgiveness of Frank after he'd murdered her sister Rachel, inspired the world to follow these historic examples. It was proposed that those who'd served in media, corporations, or government who had committed or covered up criminal acts would be completely forgiven with no prison time, so long as they exposed the truth.

In 2015, the world-wide *Truth, Forgiveness and Reconciliation Day* was established. On this day the entire planet agreed finally to acknowledge the simple and yet profound wisdom that Jesus had tried to impart to his fellow humans: that truth was most important, and that *forgiveness is the most effective way to enable truth to come out.*

Frank, Ian, and Doc became national heroes. Through their willingness to risk everything, everything changed. They demonstrated that the most powerful forces for truth in government and media were the whistleblowers within these structures who could not allow themselves to hide what should not be hidden.

# Closing Note:
# One World . . . One Breath

*And ye shall know the truth, and the truth shall make you free.*
– Jesus (John 8:32)

*A human being is a part of a whole, called by us a universe, a part limited in time and space. He experiences himself, his thoughts and feelings as something separated from the rest . . . a kind of optical delusion of his consciousness. This delusion is a kind of prison for us, restricting us to our personal desires and to affection for a few persons nearest to us. Our task must be to free ourselves from this prison by widening our circle of compassion to embrace all living creatures and the whole of nature in its beauty.*
– Albert Einstein

*Love thy neighbor as thyself.*
– The Bible

*Allah created nations and tribes that we might know one another, not that we might despise one another.*
– The Koran

*. . . never to turn aside the stranger, for it is like turning aside the most high God.*
– The Torah

*Full of love for all things in the world; practicing virtue in order to benefit others, this man alone is happy.*
– The Buddha

*The sage has no interest of his own, but takes the interests of the people as his own. He is kind to the kind; he is also kind to the unkind: for Virtue is kind. He is faithful to the faithful; he is also faithful to the unfaithful: for Virtue is faithful.*
– Tao Te Ching

*Seek to be in harmony with all your neighbors; live in amity with your brethren.*
– Confucius

*Let us walk softly on the Earth with all living beings great and small, remembering as we go, that one God kind and wise created all.*
– Native American Psalm

*Do not do to others that which would anger you if others did it to you.*
– Socrates

*A man obtains a proper rule of action by looking on his neighbor as himself.*
– Hindu Psalm

*Regard Heaven as your father, Earth as your mother, And all things as your brothers and sisters.*
– Shintoism, Oracle of the Kami of Atsuta

*And if thine eyes be turned towards justice, choose thou for thy neighbour that which thou choosest for thyself.*
– Bahá'í World Faith

*This is the sum of Dharma [duty]: Do naught unto others which would cause you pain if done to you.*
– Brahmanism

*Don't do things you wouldn't want to have done to you.*
– British Humanist Society

*In happiness and suffering, in joy and grief, we should regard all creatures as we regard our own self.*
    – Jainism

*The law imprinted on the hearts of all men is to love the members of society as themselves.*
    – Roman Pagan Religion

*Don't create enmity with anyone as God is within everyone.*
    – Sikhism

*We affirm and promote respect for the interdependence of all existence of which we are a part.*
    – Unitarian

*One going to take a pointed stick to pinch a baby bird should first try it on himself to feel how it hurts.*
    – Yoruba (Nigeria)

*That nature alone is good which refrains from doing unto another whatsoever is not good for itself.*
    – Zoroastrianism

*Act as if the maxim of thy action were to become by thy will a universal law of nature.*
    – Immanuel Kant

*May I do to others as I would that they should do unto me.*
    – Plato

*All things are our relatives; what we do to everything, we do to ourselves. All is really One.*
    – Black Elk

# Facts and Fiction

With the exception of the two newspaper articles opening the Prologue, all of the dated newspaper and scientific journal articles and references to the History Channel documentary positioned at the beginning of chapters are actual news reports. Media statements or reporting in the body of this book regarding the fictionalized events or characters in this book are, of course, fictional.

Presidential directives providing extraordinary powers to the executive branch referred to in the novel are actual administration directives.

All references to United States patents on mind control technologies in this book are U.S. patents on file with the U.S. Patent Office. Media quotes and Congressional record quotes regarding the CIA's MK-ULTRA mind control experiments are non-fiction.

References to scientific research on the positive effects of mind/body transcendental practices on human consciousness, individually and on a societal level, are real studies reported in mainstream media.

Quotes citing books in the Bible and other Gospels not included in the Bible, such as the Gospels of Judas and Mary, are actual quotes, as well as references to the ancient scrolls regarding Saint Issa, which some historians believe to be a partial chronicle of Jesus' lost years.

---

Learn more about issues related to the news articles cited at the beginning of chapters throughout *2012 The Awakening,* as well as a collection of short videos on various global healing concepts and movements, by visiting www.2012TheAwakening-TheNovel.com.

# Author's Note
## We All Can Be a Part of the Awakening

*Everything rides on a slight turning of the human consciousness, for . . . what we need has always been here. It is only our approach that must change, ever so slightly.*
– Ravi Shyamalan, Recipient, Nobel Prize in Economics

*Today . . . is World Yoga Day – a part of World Healing Day. Originally inspired by the Global Consciousness Project at Princeton University, World Healing Day seeks to unite healing intentions from a multitude of spiritual and medical practices.*
– The Huffington Post.com, April 24, 2010

---

Princeton University's Engineering Anomalies Research Lab (PEAR) gave birth to the Global Consciousness Project, designed to measure the effect of human consciousness on physical reality. It employed random number generating devices, which normally would achieve random results such as those produced by flipping a coin millions of times. However, researchers found results less random at times of great human tragedy.

The Global Consciousness Project found that human consciousness indeed appeared to affect the results of their random event generators during catastrophic events such as Princess Diana's death and on 9/11/2001.

What if human consciousness coalesced around a vision of healing intention rather than around great shock, fear, and suffering?

World Healing Day is a yearly global healing wave that begins at 10 a.m. on the last Saturday of April, with mass events in the earliest time zone of New Zealand, and then expanding with events in hundreds of cities across 65 nations spanning six continents. World Healing Day is comprised of global events including World Prayer Day, World Healing Meditation Day, World Yoga Day, World Reiki Day, and World Tai Chi & Qigong Day. All faiths, religions, and philosophies are invited to join in this unifying event – coming together as one human family, to beget *a global vision of healing.*

## "One World . . . One Breath."

Learn more about World Healing Day at
www.WorldHealingDay.org & www.2012TheAwakening-TheNovel.com

Become part of # The Awakening

**Organize your own** local World Healing Day event on the last Saturday of April each year. At WorldHealingDay.org find free Organizing and Media Kits to help you engage your local community to become part of a global wave of healing energy. Each year events are held in hundreds of cities in over 65 nations.

Past events have been held at the United Nations Building in New York and at the Nobel Peace Center in Oslo, Norway.

**www.WorldHealingDay.org**
www.WorldHealingMeditationDay.org
www.WorldPrayerDay.org
www.WorldYogaDay.org
www.WorldTaiChiDay.org
and more ...

2012 The Awakening and Illumination Corporation Publishing are proud sponsors of **World Healing Day.**

**You can wear** a meaningful piece of history ... Get your own The Awakening t-shirt.

100% cotton t-shirt is black with white text. Image on front is full color. Back of shirt says "One World ... One Breath" in 26 languages.

For more information, visit www.WorldHealingDay.org or call 1-913-648-2256

# About the Author of
# 2012 The Awakening

Bill Douglas has practiced and studied tai chi and qigong for more than 30 years. He now teaches and writes about tai chi for a living. He has also been both a professional and volunteer environmental and human rights activist for most of his adult life.

Bill is working with a Veterans Administration program to donate copies of his tai chi and qigong DVD to returning veterans in honor of his father, William Edward Douglas, Sr., who served in the 45th Infantry Division in Patton's army and many decades later experienced healing from PTSD when Bill introduced him to qigong meditation.

According to Bill, his main pursuit today is to love with extreme passion those around him and to cherish this life and the beautiful world that blesses us all.

Bill's upcoming novel, a technological environmental thriller entitled *A Conspiracy of Spirits,* will be out in 2011. Bill's third novel, *The Gardeners,* is on the edge of Bill's consciousness. It should arrive in 2012.

———————

Learn more about the author, the miraculous story of how his writing career began, and how this amazing novel came into being at www.2012TheAwakening-TheNovel.com.

See the next page for other world acclaimed non-fiction books and mind-expanding video/audio productions by Bill Douglas.

# Other Acclaimed Works by the Author of 2012 The Awakening

**Anthology of Tai Chi & Qigong DVD**
SMARTaichi.com

**A Conspiracy of Spirits**
A new environmental/spiritual
thriller from Bill Douglas

**The Amateur Parent - A Book
on Life, Death, War & Peace,
and Everything Else in the Universe**
(Illumination Corporation Publishing)

"An excellent introduction to Tai Chi"
- Booklist Magazine

"Extraordinary teaching tool. Well done!"
- University Professor, Pennsylvania

"The best Tai Chi video"
- Francesca Sato, Rome, Italy

"Bill Douglas is an incredibly skilled and
compassionate instructor"
- M. Bowen, Washington, D.C.

*Coming in 2011*

'The wisdom and simplicity of 'The Amateur Parent' may
profoundly enrich your life's journey."
- Christian*New Age Quarterly

"'The Amateur Parent' is about wisdom, courage, and beauty ...
If you only read one more book, make it 'The Amateur Parent'."
- Metaphysical Reviews, Sept. 2002

"Deeply introspective, soul-stirring, original visionary wisdom anyone
will enjoy. A work of profound wisdom ..."
- Lightword Publishing Reviews

"I wasn't able to put it down - each turn of the page unfolded a mystery"
- Jennifer Hollowell, J.M.H. Reviews

**The Complete Idiot's Guide
to Tai Chi & Qigong**
(Penguin / Alpha Books, New York)

"Visionary! If you buy only one
Tai Chi book - this is the book."
- Dr. Michael Steward, Sr. Senior Coach, Team USA

"Chinese culture can be difficult to explain . . . Sifu Bill Douglas
successfully uses American culture to explain the art of
Tai Chi Chuan. He simplifies difficult concepts."
- Hong Yi Jiao, USA All-Tai Chi Grand Champion

**Anthology of Sitting
Qigong Meditations CD**
SMARTaichi.com

**Qigong Meditation
for Children CD**

**ORDER at amazon.com, SMARTaichi.com, or by calling 1-913-648-2256**

# Acknowledgments

I have met many great Tai Chi and Qigong teachers over my 30 years of experience in the field of mind-body science, but I have met only a handful of true masters. Dr. Effie Chow is a master among masters. She is a rare treasure in our society and world. Therefore, my first thank you must go to Dr. Chow for being a shining light, so much like Ravi. Particularly I want to thank her for reminding me and thousands of others how miraculous it is to embrace the world, even in the darkest nights of our lives.

Dr. Chow, a pioneer of Qigong in America at its earliest days of development, was operating in a man's world at the time. Her compassion and humility for Qigong as a conduit to help us open to our divine connection with the higher power, was a very feminine approach to what ultimately is a very feminine-yin practice. Effie was undaunted in her mission, which eventually led her to create and found the world-altering World Congress on Qigong, East West Academy of Healing Arts, the American Qigong Association, and the World Qigong Federation.

Great thanks to my Lutheran Sunday School teacher for sharing the beauty of precious Jesus. I'm so proud that the Lutheran Church – my Lutheran Church – has now recognized the value of two-spirit Lutheran pastors and has finally welcomed them home.

A shout out to my friend Jeff Chappell for helping me see past a lifetime of homophobic propaganda with one simple act – by coming out to me.

God bless and keep my two personal feminine angels, Angela and Andrea Mei Wah Douglas. Angela, there is a special place in heaven for you, and it is you among all women in this world who have shown me the true elegant power of the feminine. You are a wise, beautiful and powerful woman. You have a skill that comes from within – if I were to give you a name, I would call you a "love factory" – because you infuse everything around you with love. From the flowers you nurture around our home whose value I was blind to for so long, to the people in the sphere of your household and world – you infuse all of us whom you touch with love. We, in turn, shine that love into the world around us. Without your influence, Ravi's father would not have been awed by the power of the homemaker. Without his awakening, Ravi could not have been. I owe everything in this novel – and in my life – to you.

Andrea – Mei Wah – my precious flower and my feminine warrior for fairness. You, more than anyone else, have drawn my heart out so I could become aware of it. I will always love you for that.

My two masculine angels, Michael and Isaac, you have taught me that being a man means being strong and caring rather than macho and aloof. I love and respect you both more than I can say. Bless you.

Mom, thank you for your unending desire to nurture all those you touched. Father, thank you for your valiant effort to heal from the lasting wounds of war. I love you both.

Norma Odell, my long-time, most interesting friend, what a joy and an inspiration you are to know. Thanks to you and to Virginia Haley for your help on this project.

Thanks to Edokko Japanese Restaurant in Lenexa, Kansas, for your healthy, delicious nourishment and serene atmosphere, which carried me through the heavy lifting of the production of this novel.

Lastly, I must acknowledge Julie Tenenbaum of Final Draft Secretarial Service. Julie is a meticulous editor, yes, but also a person of vision and heart whose goal was not just precision, but to give a tangible clarified voice to Ravi, Frank, and Ian on their journey to awaken feminine power in themselves and our world.

Editing, by its nature, is a yang-masculine act of definition, whereas creative vision is a very yin-feminine act. Julie embodies the balance the world so desperately sought in *2012 The Awakening*. This uniquely spiritual novel could never have truly manifested without her extraordinary skills. Anyone endeavoring to write a novel or non-fiction of an esoteric-spiritual nature would be crazy not to contract Final Draft to do their editing.

Thank you, Julie, for your part in giving birth to this epic tale of transformation and hope. I may have carried this baby for dozens of months, but you mid-wifed it and me through the toughest of the labor pains – the final editing process. Bringing a larger reality into a constricted world is perhaps the most massive project I've ever signed up for, and without your humor, skills, creativity, and spiritual wisdom – well, suffice it to say, I could not imagine ever writing another novel without the formidable talents you bring to the table.

# Acknowledgment to Groups & People Ushering in a New World

*Spiritual practices that involve the physical body, such as t'ai chi, qigong, and yoga . . . will play an important role in the global awakening.*
— *A New Earth,* Eckhart Tolle (an Oprah's Book Club pick)

---

Each year people all over the planet work together to organize World Tai Chi & Qigong Day events to further the health and healing of our precious planet. I want to thank each of you for your work in sharing these powerful mind/body tools with the world.

Aaron Angel
Abraham Ortiz, MD
Dr Aihan Kuhn
Ai Ping Cheng
Albert M Chuderski
Alena Beyer
Alena Nickos
Alexander Gómez D'Alemán
Alice Uchida
Alicia Kow Siaw-Khian
Alicia Lowry
Allan Kelson
Allen Naipo
Alvaro E Rivera Morales
Amanda Lan
Ana Mesquita
Ana Rezende
Andrew Dale
Angela López
Angela Soci
Anh Vo
Ann Colichidas
Ann Kirson Swersky, PhD
Anna M Pergola
Annette Eccles
Annette McKinney
Antonelli Carlo

Antonia Hendriks Antonio Delgado
Antonio Pereira
Aristein Woo
Barbara Gleisner
Barbara Grinter
Barbara Jennings
Rev Barbara F Matsuura
Barry Freeman
Bas Opdenkelder
Beatrice DeFranco
Beatrice Melendez Aleman
Becky Browne
Ben Serpas
Bett Lujan Martinez, MEd
Bev Abela
Bill Moore
Prof Bill Parkinson
Phil Pensabene
Bob Correll
Bob Weisbord
Bobbie Nixon
Brad Ferguson
Brad Holmes
Brian Bruning
Bryan Bagnas
Bryan Knack
CJ Rhoads
Camilo Sanchez, OMD, L Ac MQG
Carl Donaldson, Jr, ND, LMT

Carl Meeks
Carlo Mastrolacasa
Carlos Barreto
Carlos A Guevara
Carlos Rosales
Carol Henderson
Carol Ogilvie
Carol Stevens
Carolyn Cooper
Carolyn Hearn
Carolyn Perkins
Catherine Bigley
Catherine Downes
Cathi Knauf
César Antúnez
Charles Brynan
Charles Rivera
Charlie Schwab
Prof Cheng Man Ching
Cheryl Johnson
Cheryl Lynne Rubbo
Chris Bouguyon
Chris Headlee
Christine Milton
Cindy Cortez, DD
Colleen Thompson
Colin Berg
Colin Orr
Cootie Harris
Craig Ing
Criss xBearx Rosenlof
Cynthia Ming

Dada Inocalla
DahVid Weiss, LAc, PhD
Dai Shiang Ying
Dale Napier
Dan Ferrera
Daniel Brasher
Danielle Beauvais, PhD
Darwin Kwan
Dave Bucklow
Dave Johnson
Dave Pickens
David Christophy
Dr David Clippinger
David M Knibbe
David Larsen
David Mitchell
David-Dorian Ross
David Shaver CT
David Ward
David R White
David Wong
Dawn Weisbord
Deah Kinion, L. Ac.
Debbie Jacobs-Karlstrom
Deborah Adams
Deborah Moen
Debra Lin Allen
Debra Schumacher
Dennis Pounall
Dennis Watts
Diana Lau
Diana Steijn
Diane Gold
Dianna Cole
Dixie Howell
Dodie Amundson
Dominador Manongdong
Domingo Colon
Don Fiore
Don Morton
Donald E Belsito Sr
Donald Rubbo
Donna Minshew
Doria Cook-Nelson
Dorothy Naipo
Dorothy Ramien
Doug Brown
Douglas Zhu
E Paul Campbell

Earl Mussett
Ed Sevilla
Edivaldo Ximenes
Edward Niam
Dr Effie Chow
Elaine Yap
Elder Friend
Elizabete Vieira
Elizabeth Keith
Els Eijssens
Ellen Reitsma
Emma Livia Mangual
Eng Chor Khor
Enzo Bordi
Dr Eric Jarman
Eric Reiss
Erik Myrland
Estin Kiger
Faeeza Keshavjee
Fiorella Trentini
Fran Schultz-Starr, RN
Francine Hershkowitz
Frank Hediger
Franziska Rüscher
Frederic Lecut
Wang Fu-lai
Gad Levy-Golan
Master Gao Fu
Gary Dolan
Gary Huff
Gary Paruszkiewicz, CSME
Gary Shaw
Gary Tong
Gen Vallenari
George Hoffman
Gerrie Sporken
Gerri Gurman
Gert Clerckx
Gianna Sabatelli
Gigi Minet
Giuseppe Paterniti
Glenda Hesseltine
Gloria Dean
Gloria Untermann
Grace Wu
Graham Pritchard
Greg Woodson
Master Guangzhi Xing
Han Hoong Wang
Hans Strock
Harm Leerling
Harriett Grady
Harvey Kurland
Hazel Thompson

Hector Cruz
Hector Pozo
Hector Santiago
Helena Fukuta
Heloise Gold
Henry Look
Hilary Smith
Hilda Cardinaels
Hildo Honório
Homer Nottingham
Howard Fraracci
Hung Man Fei
Igors Kudrjavcevs, MD,
Ilona Garrett
Irene R Chia
Irene Huisman
Iqbal Ishani
Isabel Cepeda Link
Isabella Rennie
Isidoro Li Pira
Ismael Santiago
Ivan Pinheiro
Ivo Melotte
JC Carter
JC Cox
J R Roy
Jacek Kozlowski
Jack Fu
Jackie Halbin
Jackie Watt
Jacqui Shumway
James Garrett
Jan Graves
Jan Gyomber
Dr Janet Garrett
Janet Shoeman
Janice Langham
Janice Rinehart
Jason Richards
Dr Jay Dunbar
Jean Anderson
Jeanna Daykin
Jeanne Sippy
Jeannie Koran
Jeff Herda
Jeff Hughes
Dr Jeff Lan
Jeff McCann
Dr Jeff Miller
Jeff Zauderer
Jeffery L "JT" Vogt
Jenni Balis
Jeremy Bennett
Jeremy Ladd Cross

Jerry Gardner
Jerry Levine
Jerry Steffenhagen
Jess F Craig
Ninjuwusu
Jesse A Arenas II
Jessica Myers
Jill Heath
Jill Reed
Jim Bush
Jim Hoople
Jim Mellot
Jim Starshak
Jingyu Gu
JoAnna Gee Schoon
Joanne Zeitler
Jocelyn Simpson
Joe Brady
John Bartlett MA,
CHt
Dr John Garrett
John Stover
Jonathan Walker,
PhD
Joop Brouwer
Jorge Melendez
Melchor
Jose Luis Munoz
Jose Torres
Joseline Spirig
Joseph Esteves
Joseph Lopez
Joseph Petrosi
Joseph Quinn
Josephine Perez
Joshua A Jackson
Juan Alvarez
Juan Ignacio
Vilanova
Judith Budd-Walsh
Judith Schwartz
Julio Caraballo
Justin Meehan
Jutima Levine
Kaal Nath
Kalila King
Karen Schreiber
Karen Taxada
Karen Jeffers Tracy
Karen Kohlhaas
Karim-Ben
Saunders
Kate Pearson
Kathy Falzone

Kathy Varga
Kay Thoren
Keith Roost
Ken Ryan
Kenneth Marx
Kevin Chen
Khadi Madama
Kitty Frey
Krystal Young
Krystle Pass
Laddie Sacharko
Lama Tantrapa
Lamont Thomas
Larry Gordon
Dr Larry Trott
Laura Gonzalez
Lauri J Rowe
Laurince D McElroy
Lee Fairweather
Leigh-Ann Cris
LeRoy Alsup
Lester Fong
Lillian Pennington
Lillian Thompson
Linda Cosma
Linzi Martin
Lisa Topping
Loril Harley Garner
Lotte Cherin
Louisa Wever
LuAnn Cibik
Luce Condamine, MD,
PhD
Luciano Oliveira
Lung Kai Ming
Lyn McMahon
Lynda Wells, PhD
Lynn Thomas, PhD
Lynne Donnelly
Lynn Ellen Ruwet
M A Greenstein, PhD, RY
Mae Lovell, RN
Magno Bueno
Maku Cuizon
Mal Stainkey
Manuel Marquez
Marc Gerson
Marcelino Salvador
Marcello Giffoni
Marcia Kerwitt
Marcus Evandro
Marek Wajsman
Maria Maia
Maria Padro

Marie Lew
Marilyn Cooper
Marilyn Miller
Mark Melchiorre, LAc
Mark Lee Pringle
Mark Reinhart
Marleen Colangelo, RN, AP
Martha Fiddes
Marty Burrow
Mary Cuchna
Mary Ronge
Mary C Ryan
Mary Sturtevant, MEd
Massimo Mori, MD
Maurice Crenshaw
Max H Anderson
Dr Mfundishi Baba Serikali
Michael Clark
Michael DeMolina
Michael Hernandez
Michael Howie
Dr Michael Lan
Michael Neiman
Michael Rhoades
Michael Rinaldini
Michael Stephens
Michael Steward, Sr
Michael Ward
Mikal Keenan, PhD
Mike Howell
Milton Oliveira
Mindy Panunzio
Mingtong Gu
Mitzi Orr
Monica Han
Moo-Shong Woo
Nan Doty
Nancy Compton
Nancy Fiano
Nate Mohler
Neil Chernichaw
Nico Snyman
Nicole Dickenson
Nikki Mandel Desch
Nikolas Maricic-Wolf
Nir Malhi-Zaltzman
Ofélia Rabelo
Olga M Guzman Marrero
Olive Yin-Foon Hui
Orlando Garcia Morales
Upper Ottawa Valley
Tai Chi Club
Pat Gorman
Patrice Wooldridge

Patricia Corrigan
Culotti
Patricia Coulthurst
Patrick Harries
Patrick Stahl
Patrick Watson
Paul Brewer
Dr Paul Lam
Paul Ramos
Paulette Silber
Pedro Rentas
Peggy Wheeler
Penny Harrison
Peter Asco
Peter Chin Kean
Choy
Petesy Burns
Philip Lai, CMA
Phyllis Lefohn
Ralph Dehner
Randy Stevens
Raul Ayala
Raul Pujol
Rebecca Kali
Rena B Borenstein
Renee Ryan
Rhea Bu'ao
Rhonda Donahoo
Richard Chu, PhD
Richard Jesaitis
Richard Laoshi
Dinsmore, OMD
Richard Ellis
Richard Kosch
Rick Ekum
Rikk Mayr
Rita Mikalauskas
Robbie Miles
Robert Chung
Robert P Goodman
Robert A Gott
Robert W McNulty
Robert Roscosz
Robert J Woodbine,
ND, LAc
Robin Malby
Rod Ferguson
Rod Madigan
Rodrigo Lemos
Roger Jahnke OMD

Roger Thompson (Taoger)
Rolland Miner
Ronald C Pfeiffer, Jr
Ron Sewell
Ron Williamson
Roque Severino
Rose Peterson
Rudi Beverley
Rudolph Petalver
Russell F Smiley, PhD
Russell Therrien
Ruth Saha
Sal Casano, PhD RN
Sally Gordon
Samuel Krucek
Sandra Diamond, MA, CtH,
RMT
Sandra Eckstein
Sandy McBride
Sara Howard
Scott Cole
Scott Richie
Sergio Raimondo
Sergio Villasboas
Dr Shaka Zulu
Shelia Baker
Shelia Rae
Shelley Leong
Sher Dano
Sherry Fideler
Shin Lin, PhD
Shirley Hildreth
Shizue Naka
Wang Shu-chin
Shu Chou Wang
Siegfried Elsner
Stan Rossi
Stancho Stanev
Stephanie Thompson
Stephen Salkof
Steve Geibel
Steve Perry
Steve Shulman
Steven Haidinger
Steven Shomo, DOM, AP,
CSCS, E-RYT
Stuart Innes
Sue Glick
Sue Michaelsen
Suman Barkhas

Sunny Ainley
Susan Scheuer
Suzanne Lum
Suzanne McLauchlan
Suzanne Schinkel
T Rita Beth
Talita Kumi
Tania Carmo
Tat Lui
Ted Cibik
Terence Barnes BSc
Teresinha Pereira
Thilo Krienke
Thomas Taj Johnson
Tina Webb
Toby Plourde
Tom Goeltz
Tom Hynd
Tom Lesniewski
Tom Mount ND PhD
Tom Rogers
Tony Everts
Tony Hardiman
Trevor Reynaert
Tricia Yu
Troy Bennett
Master TT Tchoung
Ty Wheeler
Tzyann Hsu
Uruguay (all organizers)
Vicki Dello Joio
Vicki Neiman
Vicky Ahern
Vicky McGhee
Victor Perez
Vince Cobalis
Vince Lasorso
Vladimir Pankov
Wang H Po
Wendy DeGraffenried, RN
William Ferrel
William Larmour
William W Wojasinski
Dr Yancy Orchard
Hong Yijiao
Yoni Kiggen
Master Yun
Master Su ZiFang
Zulma Clavell

Many other World Tai Chi & Qigong Day organizers not mentioned above can be found in the "Find Local Events/Classes" directory at www.WorldTaiChiDay.org, a website that has connected over one million visitors to local teachers in their areas.

Thank you to Pat Kahn and Dr. Richard Yennie who have been a great healing force in the world. Dr. Yennie, thank you for playing a large role in saving my life. Thank you to Chris Powell of Missouri Acupuncture for your wonderful herbal and seeing skills, and to Reiki master Susan Warner.

I'd also like to thank my old friend Tim Carpenter, the founder of the Progressive Democrats of America, for teaching me that we do have power in this world to express what our heart tells us is just and right.

A great thank you to Art Occole of the Anishnawbe Nation, Executive Director of the 2-Spirited People of the First Nations in Canada, and also to Crisosto Apache of the Mescalero Apache Nation, Director of the Two Spirit Society of Denver.

Thanks to my friend Mitsu Sato for his insights into Buddhist mantra meditation. It was a big part of my healing.

Deep gratitude to the thousands of organizers from Brasilia to Tehran, from Caracas to Cairo, from Kansas City to Montevideo, working in hundreds of cities in over 70 nations, to organize *World Healing Day* events in their myriad forms of WorldYogaDay.org; WorldTaiChiDay.org; WorldPrayerDay.org; WorldReikiDay.org; WorldSufiDanceDay.org; WorldArtDay.org; WorldQigongDay.org; WorldNativeAboriginalSacredDanceDay.org; WorldThespianDay.org; WorldMusicHealingDay.org; and WorldHealingMeditationDay.org for your unprecedented vision of focusing world consciousness on *world healing* for a 24-hour period on the last Saturday of April each year to strike the global tuning fork of human consciousness. Readers can learn more at www.WorldHealingDay.org.

*With a slight turning of the human consciousness, everything becomes possible.*
– Ravi Shyamalan

*What people are saying about Bill Douglas's coming environmental-spiritual thriller,* **A Conspiracy of Spirits:**

*Before we reach a tipping point, we must change the ways we use energy. But before this, we must change the way we think about our place on Earth.*

A Conspiracy of Spirits *describes the journey toward spiritual maturity necessary to face this looming dilemma. With a newfound spiritual maturity, we may be able to face the current crisis with wisdom.*

**— David M. Caditz, Ph.D., former Director, Stanford University Solar Vehicle Project**

A Conspiracy of Spirits *is an exciting and refreshing new take on the potential of the human spirit to connect to the mystery of life in ways which often go unnoticed. Bill Douglas has, in an almost poetic way, woven together timeless spiritual insight with a timely crisis affecting us all, to create a narrative tapestry with as much wisdom as suspense.*

*This is a story the world needs to hear!*

**— Reverend Nathaniel G. Haaland**

*With the advent of Bill Douglas's extraordinary tales, we may well be witnessing the establishment of a wholly new genre of fiction . . .* the transcendental novel.

**— Jais Booth, Founder of San Francisco's Liminal Arts Movement**

---

Learn more about Bill Douglas's upcoming novel, *A Conspiracy of Spirits,* and his other acclaimed works, including inspirational and instructional books, CDs, and DVDs, at www.IlluminationCorporation.com.

Illumination Corporation Publishing creates entertainment designed not to *fill your time,* but to *nourish your heart and mind.*

# Keep In Touch with the Author of *2012 The Awakening*

Bill Douglas

Join the author's free *2012 The Awakening* Newsletter email list for updates on his work, as well as global healing info, events, and efforts.

Also find fascinating videos on human consciousness, humane economics, and sustainable living, and take a fun quiz to test your knowledge of *2012 The Awakening*, its vision, and its characters.

Learn more and discover a wealth of informative and fascinating and soul-stirring videos at:

www.2012TheAwakening-TheNovel.com

or at

www.IlluminationCorporation.com

7751933R0

Made in the USA
Lexington, KY
12 December 2010